MW00800211

HAUNTED

A Click Your Poison book

by

James Schannep

The eAversion Version
First Print Edition

This book is a work of fiction. Names, characters, businesses, organizations, places, events, and incidents are either the product of the author's imagination or are used fictitiously. Any resemblance to actual persons, living, dead, or ghosts, events, or locales is entirely coincidental. Some public figures and government agencies were used to give a sense of time and place, or satirically.

Copyright © 2022 by James Schannep

If you downloaded this book online, or were sent a copy via some means other than a verified purchase to support the author and his works, please consider purchasing a legal copy now. Your financial support helps living artists.

All rights reserved.
Print Edition

www.jamesschannep.com

Library of Congress Cataloging-in-Publication Data
Schannep, James, 1984—
HAUNTED: a Click Your Poison book / James Schannep
1. Ghost—Fiction. 2. Occult & Supernatural—Fiction.
3. Fantasy—Paranormal—Fiction. I. Title
COVER DESIGN BY JAMES SCHANNEP

This book has been modified from its original version.
It has been formatted to fit this page.

ISBN-13: 978-1-954747-02-9
ISBN-10: 1-954747-02-0

Acknowledgments

Special thanks to my wife, Michaela, for letting me give you nightmares by sharing all my spine-tingling ideas with you and for keeping the subject of ghosts a constant presence in our house. Thankfully, the thing you believe in most seems to be me.

A big thanks to Andrew Driscoll, my research assistant, paranormal architect, and alpha reader. Thanks to Charles "Hunter" Gregory for your alpha reading and graphical assistance.

Thanks also to my beta readers: Victoria Hancox, Felix Bertmaring, Chris Boyes, Mike Beeson, Tyson Bertmaring, Damon Bosetti, Michael Harlock, Kari Cowell, William Hildebrand, Cullen Schannep, Fred Buckley, Adam Mitchell, and Richard Young. To Jackie Tansky for letting me name the house after you.

To my copyeditor and omega reader, Maria Mountokalaki, and to Paul Salvette and the team at BB eBooks. Thank you all for your generosity and professionalism.

And to my friends, family, fans, and fellow writers for your unyielding encouragement, enthusiasm and support.

To the little spirits who kept me up at night while writing this book (my children).

Click Your Poison Books

INFECTED*—Will YOU Survive the Zombie Apocalypse?*

MURDERED*—Can YOU Solve the Mystery?*

SUPERPOWERED*—Will YOU Be a Hero or a Villain?*

PATHOGENS*—More Zombocalypse Survival Stories!*

MAROONED*—Can YOU Endure Treachery and Survival on the High Seas?*

SPIED*—Can YOU Save the World as a Secret Agent?*

HAUNTED*—Can YOU be Scared…to Death?*

** More titles coming soon! **

Sign up for the new release mailing list: http://eepurl.com/bdWUBb

Or visit the author's blog at www.jamesschannep.com

The following horrors are inspired by true events. Can you make better choices?

Here's how it works: You, Dear Reader, are the main character of this story. You have been chosen to visit what is perhaps the most haunted house in America. The word "haunted" here might mean ghosts, devils, and spirits, or it might mean something more corporeal. Whether or not the devil inside some men is a literal one, much of humanity's suffering has been at our own hands.

What awaits you inside the house? Well, that depends on what you bring with you. This house will change based on your choices, molding itself to your fears. If you make these decisions in good conscience, you'll know the answer to the question: Can YOU be scared…to death?

But if you find the following icon, then you'll know you've beaten the house at its own game. When you're ready, go to page 1. Good luck.

HAUNTED

You're browsing online job listings when the knock sounds upon your front door. It takes a moment to register the sound; so long have you been without guests. Now, you rise without delay, and walk to see who's there—but when you answer, you see only an express mail envelope left on your welcome mat, marked, "Same Day Delivery Guaranteed."

The delivery person is nowhere in sight. Bending down, you take the envelope, then return inside and close the door. The quick tab cuts across the cardboard mailer as you pull on it, opening the parcel. There's another, smaller envelope inside which reads, "Official Selection Notification."

Now your pulse quickens at the prospect of gainful employment as you wonder which career opportunity this might be related to. Over a year has passed since you were deemed "non-essential" and told to stay home; several months have elapsed since your remote-work position was made redundant and you were let go. This could be the first promising lead on the job hunt in weeks.

With tremulous hands, you open the second envelope. Strangely, the seal on the rear has already been broken. Inside, you find a simple card. The stationary is nice enough, like a wedding invitation, although without the usual accompanying flourishes. The card reads:

> Congratulations! We are pleased to inform you that we would like you to join us on this season of "The Offering." The cardbearer is hereby granted entry to Tansky House.

Startups use strange terms for employees these days, but even so this seems a bizarre invitation. Season? Granted entry? Tansky House? And…what exactly is "The Offering"? You rack your brain, but can't remember applying to a company with that name. You've sent in countless job applications and filled out myriad online questionnaires, so it's not surprising you can't recall the details.

The bottom line of the card contains a tiny row of fine print. This reads:

> Terms and conditions apply. To qualify for the million-dollar grand prize, you must stay all three nights. No cell phones, portable electronics, or other recording devices are allowed. If you leave the premises or otherwise attempt contact with the outside world, you will be disqualified and forfeit all rights to the prize winnings.

Oh, so it's a scam, you think. Some kind of bulk junkmail contest offering untold riches. But if that were true, why send it same day delivery? Hoping to learn more, you look inside the cardboard mailer. There's a sticky note at the bottom that must have fallen off the envelope. This handwritten note reads:

> Hey, still between jobs? A bit random, but three nights in a haunted house for $1 million? Kind of a cool idea for a Reality TV show. Starts tonight at sunset.

That's it. That's all it says. Not even a signature. It's conversational, but not exactly personal. A coworker from your last job? Someone you interviewed with for a position you didn't get? Could you have accidentally signed up for something while late-night web browsing? Curiosity gets the better of you and you head back to the internet. Leaving the job listing for an account executive at Human Infinite Technologies for later, you open a new tab and search for "the Offering TV show."

Bingo. The first hit brings you to a website with the preview text, "What is the Offering?" The flash intro on the webpage fades in from black:

> Three nights. One million dollars. A severely haunted house. No scripted drama. This is reality as you've never seen it before. Learn more?

When you click the final words on the screen, the webpage fills with text.

> "The Offering" is just that—if you can stay in the House for three consecutive nights, you will receive a million-dollar prize. There will be other small tasks to ensure you explore the House and learn its secrets, but only those in possession of an invitation card will be able to find the House.
>
> Due to the nature of a hidden-camera program, no representative from The Offering will be available to greet you at the property, so please let yourself in and make yourself at home. Should you choose to arrive at the House, you are agreeing not to hold The Offering, LLC responsible for any grave bodily harm, caused by your own actions or by nature of exploring the House.
>
> It's paramount that you arrive before sunset, and it is not recommended that you look into the tragedies that befell the House. This is an open invitation. Bring an open mind.

Well, that's ominous, but not altogether unsurprising. Arriving before sunset seems like sound advice. The veil between the world we know and the unknowable is thinnest when the night is darkest. You look back to the invitation card, and re-read, "The cardbearer is hereby granted entry to Tansky House."

Tansky House. A quick maps search shows a pin on the outskirts of town. A private road leading out into the woods. It doesn't have a numbered address, and the road itself is not named, but online maps can still direct you toward the dropped pin. Based on the current time, you'll need to move quickly if you're to arrive before sunset.

Could this really be a new kind of TV show? The whole concept seems like insanity, yet here you are, actually considering it. A million dollars for three days' work. This could change your life. Bills are coming due—overdue, even—and gainful employment is nowhere in sight. You could pay off all the credit cards, buy a new house, or just go on permanent vacation. The possibilities are endless. What will you do?

➢ Go for it! Use your time to focus on packing a suitcase. Extra shirts, different layers, etc. There could be anything inside this house. Go to page 18

➢ Figure out what you're getting into first. Despite their recommendation not to, do a quick web search on these supposed hauntings. Go to page 72

Achluophobia

Feeling the handle of the large knife through the bag, you grab hold and push the blade *through* the thick plastic, freeing it from the evidence bag. Another lightning flash illuminates the scene, reflecting off your blade and sending the shadows cascading downstairs, if only for a brief instant before the darkness comes, announced by a thunderclap.

Then you're left only with the sounds of your own breathing and the feel of your sweat against the handle of this murder weapon. A few moments later, another flash of lightning illuminates the scene, showing off the figure of a man down in the foyer. You only see him for a brief instant, but the glint of the lightning against the blade of his axe stays emblazoned in your mind's eye once the house goes dark again.

After thunder rattles the house, you hear a faint creak against the first step down below, then the next as the figure slowly ascends the stairs. You hold your knife tightly, waiting for him; listening intently to gauge his location.

There's a great crash as a tree branch inexplicably smashes through the turreted window, bringing in sheets of rain and howling winds—drowning out any other sounds. When the next flash of lightning arcs across the sky, it's Sheriff Tansky's hateful glare that now illuminates before you. Incredibly, the man is here, in the flesh.

His axe is raised high and you bring your knife toward him, but too late.

Darkness soon follows, and overtakes you completely.

THE END

Action!

"Hello?" you say.

Your voice echoes dully in the cavernous basement. At this, the man before you stiffens and then slowly turns around. Instinctively, you take a step back, but then freeze in your tracks with the sudden realization that you recognize him—it's Sheriff Tansky.

The man is here, in the flesh. He wears simple clothing; a pair of dusty brown twill coveralls and a long-sleeved knit undershirt beneath. Having seen his portrait staring at you every day, you recognize his hateful glare immediately.

"The ritual..." he growls, "has begun!"

The man holds an axe, the blade glinting under your lamplight. Tansky raises the weapon and starts toward you.

➢ Throw the lantern at him. Go to page 206

➢ Turn and run back to the elevator. Go to page 34

Air Strike

As you go to check the ammunition belt for rifle cartridges, your hand lingers over the stick grenade—a German *stielhandgranate*, which must have been brought back as a trophy of war. Hermes had said he wasn't going to offer any clues on how to defeat Dennis, but maybe he already did so without realizing it?

Moving quickly, you take the grenade from the ammunition belt, march back to the front of the house, and stop at the laundry chute opposite the main staircase. All you have to do is pull off the cap to prime the pin and call out "bombs away!"

The door to the laundry chute is heavy, weighted to pull itself closed, and it screeches in protest when you open it. You can hear a faint, droning chant from below—telling you that you're right on target.

"I summon Sheriff Tansky!" you call into the chute, hoping to lure the man in. "And present *this* as offering!"

Then you pull the cap from the grenade.

In concert, the turreted window suddenly smashes open from the pressure of the storm, and a tree branch inexplicably reaches in. You turn back to face the assault on the house and the laundry chute door swings closed, which knocks against your hand and causes you to fumble the grenade—the weapon bouncing at your feet.

Did the house itself come to aid Dennis when you called upon the spirit of Tansky?

That's the last thought you'll ever have before you're blown to kingdom come.

THE END

All the World's a Stage

"Hermes, are you a voice actor?" you ask.

"Would you like me to read an audiobook?" the British man replies.

"No, I want to know if this is all a game," you say, regretting the choice of words almost immediately.

"Ah, splendid. What sort of game shall we play?"

"Twenty questions!" you reply with a sudden burst of inspiration.

"Animal, mineral, or vegetable?"

"A person, Hermes. Are you a person, somewhere, answering these questions? Or truly a digital persona?"

"You'd like to know if I'm a real boy, mm? Or if I'm merely a puppet, and—by extension—you'd like to know who is pulling the strings, is that it?"

"Yes! Exactly that."

"Very well. The truth is, there is a voice actor, but you're not speaking to him. The man was kind enough to record a wide range of vocal sounds and responses, which have been amalgamated into a handy database that I can draw upon to render speech. As for who I am—assuming you'd like me to speak literally and not philosophically—I am indeed lines of code here to help with your stay at Tansky House. Does that answer your questions?"

Thinking on it for a moment, and the revelation you were just presented with in the office only minutes ago, you say, "How do I know if you're telling me the truth?"

"A liar can generally be spotted by a changed pitch in their voice, rapid pulse or breathing, erratic speech patterns or spurious body movements, their instinctively covering of vulnerable parts like the throat or abdomen, or becoming subtly more hostile with prolonged eye contact or pointing gestures.

"Given that I have no body language, this becomes a more subjective question and the truth is ultimately up for you to decide. But first, you should decide if you'd like to share your supper!"

"What?" you reply.

That's when the doorbell rings.

It's such a foreign sound that at first you're not sure what you've just heard. Then there's a loud pounding as the iron door knocker connects to the thick wooden front door. It's fervent, urgent even. The doorbell rings again and again by someone frantic to get the homeowner's attention. The pounding continues, dull thuds against the wood.

Your mind races at the possibilities. The storm is really pouring down now, and the skies are darkened. You leave the dining table to go see what's happening, but as soon as you enter the foyer, the sounds stop. No doorbell. No pounding, save for the heavy rain against the house.

➢ Shout, "What is this? What do you want?!" Go to page 240

➢ Say nothing. Finish your dinner and try not to let it get to you. Go to page 110

All You Can Search

If the china cabinet is where they keep the dishes, then the buffet is where they keep everything else. Silverware, linen napkins, silver napkin rings, tablecloths, candlesticks, candles, matches, and a pouch of tobacco. The last is held in an old leather bag, and it's the only thing out of place. The tobacco itself smells fragrant and hasn't dried out, so it must be fairly fresh.

Though you haven't seen any cameras in the house so far, the buffet being kept unlocked is probably the biggest piece of evidence that cameras do exist. Why else leave all this unprotected? These silver pieces are probably worth a small fortune. Not a million dollars, but still.

Where to next?

➢ Check the china cabinet. Very carefully, of course. Can't be sure if all that paperwork you signed makes you liable for broken dishes. Go to page 186

➢ The antique table itself. If this was Sheriff Tansky's personal table, there might be more to it than the modern fixtures in the house. Perhaps a message carved underneath? Go to page 253

➢ The painting of the Sheriff. Take it off the wall and see if there are some eyeholes in the back of the canvas. Old oil paintings are usually handled with gloves, but it's worth the risk. Go to page 179

➢ All done here. Back out to explore the house. Go to page 112

Alpha and Omega

With a full belly, you yawn tiredly as you clear out from the dining room. The storm grows in intensity, so you move quickly up to your bedroom. The temperature is dropping rapidly, and with a deep grumble the furnace kicks on. You're feeling the chill, with icy fingers and toes, so despite the growling, grinding sounds coming from the vents, you're happy to know that the home has heat.

After your bedtime routine, you settle in to read more of the journal from the comfort of your bed before lights out. You come across an entry by Daniel Tansky—the original occupant of this house, according to historical records, at least. The journal entry predates Tansky House and focuses more on the preludes to civil war.

The land deed you saw on the computer screen earlier today stated that Tansky earned this property through his military service. That's only partially true, according to the journal. The pages paint a far more swooping and grand story, of the Tansky ties to the rail line as a corporate lawyer, and his courtship with an heiress to a cotton plantation. Theirs was a courtship in secret. The only problem was that her father was a northern unionist and young Jackie was promised to a union colonel. Tansky pled with Jackie's father, who forbade any further contact with the family.

By now, though, Tansky had grown accustomed to getting what he wanted.

> Whereas lesser men would accept defeat, or humiliate themselves in attempts to gain favor, I saw an opportunity to come in from a position of strength. No stranger to battles in the frontier lands, I took up a commission in this glorious new nation. As a learned man, I was granted command. We rode north, with one goal in mind: destruction of the union leadership.
>
> Just as a snake is powerless without a head, I placed a bounty on the enemy commanders. I let loose the inner beast, infiltrated their encampments in the dead of night, and showed these godless men the devil's wrath. In exchange for such victories, I am to be granted the land I seek—and with it, my bride. They'll make me sheriff of the county, and by feeding the beast, I'll become law incarnate.
>
> The optimal way of dealing with an accomplished executioner is not to punish him, but rather to grant him the powers of judge and jury, as if that were the plan all along.

A shiver runs down your spine and you continue turning the pages. The final entry and its proclamation jumps out at you once more: *And I'll keep the truth by my heart, to remind myself of it often.* You turn back one page and read the penultimate text:

> ...the truth is this House demands a blood sacrifice, and demands it often. The beginning will also be the end. A century and a score later. Twenty years to the date after the ritual, there will come a traveler who will enter my familial home. Dine upon my table. Sleep under my roof. Take

my home as their own, for three nights. The House will hold and keep and, ultimately, present this traveler as an offering.

It is upon this traveler whom I must feed, when the moon is full and the beast is freed.

You look up from the book, feeling desperately cold.

Suddenly, the house goes dark. Lights out.

When you awaken, it's in the full dead of night. Shadowy and silent. Your eyes slowly adjust to the room, and once you can make out shapes, you see the door to your bedroom is open.

You're sure you closed it, but did you lock it? Straining your vision to its absolute limit, you look around the room to make sure you're alone. Darkness is everywhere, but the rest of the room looks much like you left it.

The growl of the furnace starts up again, deep in the recesses of the house. A creaking rises up from below; the sound of footsteps, climbing up the stairs. There's a strange *click* that accompanies these steps, like spiked cleats…or claws.

You realize the growl isn't the furnace at all. It's a deep animal growl, like a wolf that's returned to its den only to find an intruder. Your heart races in your chest as the steps—like padded paws—climb their way upstairs.

➢ Quickly jump up; close and lock your bedroom door. Go to page 249

➢ Pull your covers up over your face and keep still as the grave. Go to page 134

Animalistic

A veritable treasure trove of fantastic beasts *and* where to find them. From famous furries like Bigfoot and Chupacabra to lesser known local monsters such as the lizard men who roam the swamps of the Carolinas, sea serpents in Georgia and Florida, and other versions of man-beast hybrids said to call these dark forests home.

This book reads very much like an academic text, which is to say that it comes across as an outsider looking at the impact of various mythologies. The narrator's tone resembles that of an anthropologist when talking about ancient Mesoamerican cultures, whose relics they studied centuries later, describing the ritual sacrifices those peoples performed.

That is, until you reach the section on skinwalkers.

Specifically, werewolves. This section reads more like someone describing a ritual sacrifice after they themselves have performed one firsthand. And incredibly, there's an entire chapter devoted to Sheriff Tansky.

At this, you pause to check the publication information. You'd expect something like this to be from a small press, adding to the local color, or perhaps from the Mercury City University imprint, but no—it's from a Big Five publisher out of New York City and the author is listed as Dr. Jared Villalobos.

You quickly turn back to the section on Tansky. Here, the book posits that these generations of lawmen didn't just bear a striking family resemblance to one another, but rather there was only one Sheriff Tansky all along. One man, faking a heart attack, generation after generation.

Unaging, immortal, and inhuman.

The chapter goes on about shapeshifter lore, using terms like "cursed" and "possessed" and how the transformation can be controlled by those old enough to have tamed their own inner beast. But now the book no longer reads like superstition; it reads like a warning.

To kill one, you'd need a cursed weapon—or a blessed one. Mortal weapons are for mortal men, but to fight off an immortal lycanthrope you need something extraordinary. A knife used in rituals, or bullets made of pure silver.

When you look up from the text, it's to the full moon outside. You close your eyes, shake your head, and look again. It's the sun, waning on the horizon. You must have stared too directly into it and caused an inversion seared into your retina, making the sun temporarily look like the moon. Indeed, you still see the ghost of the sun when you look away.

Remembering your task, and the need to complete it before lights out, you hurriedly close the book and replace it on the shelf. Not much choice here:

Head back into the foyer to keep exploring. Go to page 112

Apothecary

The fireplace is warm and inviting, but despite the calm of the den, deep thunder crackles and booms outside. In the lull between lightning strikes, you hear the electronic hum of the elevator as it kicks into high gear. It's best if you do the same.

You set the wolfsbane cocktail on the bar cart, and it's immediately apparent that this is the drink's station of origin. There's an insulated metal bucket with fresh ice and there remains a handful of purple flowers next to a muddler, identical in shade to the flecks floating in the glass.

This alone doesn't tell you much, but the bar is stocked with other interesting products, now that you're giving it a more critical look. Next to the flowers, there's a satchel of dried mushrooms, and a small clay pot containing sliced sections of cactus. Next to the gins and whiskeys, there's also an ancient bottle of absinthe that practically shimmers with wormwood, and a bottle of amber liquid hand-labelled "Mezcaline," with a strange caterpillar inside. The pickled bug is green and has a pair of black fleshy devil's horns on both ends of its body.

A loud clatter comes from upstairs, which takes your concentration away from the bar cart. You look instead to the nearby books. If this were an immortal sheriff's den, what might he read while relaxing by the fireplace?

The volumes of legal matters jump out to you. If Tansky lives by the letter of the law, perhaps your salvation might be found in a legal loophole? Or would he retire from work in the evenings, preferring to study theology? Might you appeal to his morals, instead? Isn't there some kind of passage about loving thy neighbor that you might be able to use in a Biblical rebuke?

"Enjoying yourself?" a man says from the doorway, deep and gruff.

You turn around just as the man walks into view, dragging a long thick chain with shackles on the end. In the other hand, he carries an axe. He wears simple clothing; a pair of dusty brown twill coveralls and a long-sleeved knit undershirt beneath.

You've seen Sheriff Tansky every day in the dining room, glaring at you hatefully, and now he's here, in the flesh.

"You don't have to do this," you say, breaking the silence.

"I'm afraid that I do," Tansky says. "The House demands a sacrifice."

You swallow hard, then reply:

➢ "Will you join me for a final drink first? That'll have to do in place of a last meal." Go to page 14

➢ "I see you're an educated man. Give me a chance to appeal to your sense of reason." Go to page 91

Armed and Dangerous

It's not easy to open the evidence bag, most likely by design. After a few moments trying to figure out how, you instead press the knife *through* the bag. Even after all these years, the blade is extraordinarily sharp and slices through the thick plastic with ease.

Clutching the knife in one hand, you head out. The date tag still dangles from the grip, twirling below your hand as you walk. When you round the bend of the hallway, you hear the heavy clatter of a chain being dragged downstairs, so you stop at the edge of the hall.

Knife held tightly, you wait. From the threshold, you can see the kitchen entrance to your left, and the section of the foyer with the den entrance to your right. The chain drops the last few steps and boots creak against the wooden floors.

Then a man walks into view, dragging the long, thick chain with shackles on the end. In the other hand, he carries an axe. He wears simple clothing; a pair of dusty brown twill coveralls and a long-sleeved knit undershirt beneath.

You can only see him in profile, but you recognize him instantly. Your head swirls. You've seen this man every day in the dining room, glaring at you hatefully, and now he's come to complete the ritual.

Sheriff Tansky is here, in the flesh.

Tansky continues dragging his chain through the foyer and the pocket doors leading into the den. You hadn't realized you were holding your breath, which you let out now.

Pushing through the shock, you decide to:

➢ Go into the kitchen and ask Hermes what the hell is going on.
Go to page 198

➢ Follow the gouges in the wall upstairs while Tansky is distracted down here.
Go to page 224

Badge of Honor

You're drawn out into the hallway and toward the military uniforms kept on display at the end. For what feels like the first time in this house, you're filled with a sense of purpose. The glass cabinet shows off the Civil War and World War One uniforms, but also has elements from the long line of Sheriffs—to include their badge.

There it is, calling out to you. A bronze star meant to symbolize righteousness; an odd inversion of the pentagram that revived the curse upon this house. You need the badge, a noose, and the bones to end it once and for all.

The cabinet is locked and you don't have a key. You could smash it, but you know Tansky is nearby. A loud *thud* sounds as heavy metal chains are dropped just on the other side of the wall behind the uniform case. This hallway abuts against the Madonna Room and the Sheriff's badge rattles on its shelf.

With precious little time, you yank on the handle of the case, breaking the glass and gaining access to the badge inside. It's a loud cascade of splintered wood and hand-blown glass raining down upon the hardwood floors.

You reach into the case, just as the wall explodes outward. Tansky bashes his axe through, coming at you with furious hacking. The axe head bursts through the plaster drywall again and again.

Grabbing the badge, you turn to run.

- ➢ At the bend in the hall, turn into the Navy Room. Go to page 144
- ➢ Hurry downstairs into the kitchen. Go to page 198

The Battle of Wits

Tansky stares at you with a queer sort of look, his head cantered to the side like he can't quite make out what you're playing at. His eyes shimmer, clearly intrigued.

"You'll put on these shackles, we'll have a drink by the fire, then you'll come with me?" he asks.

You nod. "What's your poison?"

"Whiskey."

The immortal sheriff shakes his head, as if he can't believe the situation himself, then moves toward the seating area while you pull the stopper from the whiskey decanter and pour a drink. Using the tongs, you drop in two ice cubes, then carry the whiskey glass and the wolfsbane cocktail over to the coffee table.

"So, how many others have there been?" you ask.

"You're a clever one, I'll give you that," Tansky replies, his voice pure gravel.

He motions for you to take a seat and shackle yourself. You set the drinks side by side on your end of the table, and comply. As you do so, you say, "Can there be such a thing as *enough* blood? Will the house ever be sated?"

"I take care of the house, and the house takes care of me. But from time to time, the house demands a sacrifice. These rituals are penance…"

At this, Tansky stares into the fire, lost in thought. You take the opportunity to reach out and place the drinks; one in front of the would-be werewolf, and the other one in front of you.

"Dennis lived as a devil sinned," he says, distant.

"Sounds like the house isn't really giving you a choice; that's some way to take care of you."

Tansky snaps back toward you, eyes full of fiery rage as if he's just soaked up the intensity of the flames and now turns that heat outwards.

"I am *cursed*," he growls. "Free will is an illusion."

"I'll drink to that," you say, raising the glass up to your lips with shackled hands.

"Good. Then let's, and be done with it."

Tansky grabs the drink set out before him, tilts it up, and downs the whole thing in one go. His lips curl up in a snarl and his face contorts, like a man unfamiliar with alcohol. He coughs and looks into the glass.

"Wolfsbane…" the sheriff says, just before his eyes go to the whiskey glass in your hands.

Tansky drops his glass and convulses, falling from his seat onto the floor. He foams at the mouth, his eyes rolled into the back of his head. He starts shaking uncontrollably, but after the first few fits, stops. You look on in wonder, but you can't even see the rise and fall of his chest—he's gone completely stone-still.

Until he suddenly takes in a deep, gasping breath, his eyes shooting open. The man rises like he's just emerged from the bottom of the sea, clawing at the open room, desperate for air. For several moments he heaves in greedy breaths, unable to do much else.

"It's gone…the curse…I can feel it…it's gone," he pants.

You nod, but say nothing.

At length, he rises and unlocks the shackles about your hands, then falls back into the armchair.

"What…" he says, not making eye contact. "What have I done?"

➢ "You've failed. You've been bested, and now I must be set free."
Go to page 113

➢ "You've been set free. You don't have to do this—any of this—ever again."
Go to page 200

The computer screen flickers off and for a moment you think you might have hit a wrong keystroke, until the screen comes back displaying a land deed. It's a historic document, archived and reproduced here. The archaic government form, when combined with antiquated swooping penmanship, proves difficult to read for an untrained eye. Even so, there are a few lines that jump out:

> Land granted by the Confederate States of America to Major Daniel Tansky: Rail station, adjoining slave processing center, and surrounding lands to include water rights to the river for the purposes of building a jailhouse and sheriff's residence.

Before you have time to process this information, the screen goes black, then flickers to an official military citation for valor during The Great War. This is a long commendation, recommending a medal for Jacob Tansky, a rifleman in the US Army's Infantry Division. The letter contains all the hallmarks of heroism: disregard for personal safety, actions which save fellow soldiers, and general service above self. What's interesting then, is the second page:

> This addendum is not to be read with the award presentation. It is a recommendation for the unit commander's eyes only. Normally, a hard-charging soldier would be considered for a commission, but I cannot state with enough conviction that such a promotion would prove incredibly dangerous. Tansky's disregard for personal safety borders a death wish. The man makes no friends among his fellow soldiers and seems to find no pleasure in anything save for battle. His bloodlust is such that I'd fear for his unit if he were placed in command.
>
> Several times he has rushed the trenches, headlong and alone, only to return hours or days later, clothing tattered and bloody, with no explanation. It's said he gives his rations to his fellow soldiers (who fear the man more than they venerate him) before stalking off into No Man's Land to scavenge for himself. God help us if you give this man a position of authority.

The name and rank of whoever wrote the addendum has been redacted, replaced by a thick, black censor's bar. Similarly, the screen goes dark once more, only to quickly return to a unit photograph. The monochrome group portrait shows several American "Doughboys" in uniform, staring at the camera through tired eyes. Some pose with sardonic smiles, but most look mildly irritated for having been told to form up for a photograph. A few dangle cigarettes from their lips.

One of the men stares at you *through* the photograph, piercing the boundaries of time with his hateful glare. It's the very same Sheriff Tansky from the painted portrait in the dining room down below. A shiver runs down your spine looking at the man. There's an odd glint in his eyes, like the silver in the photographic chemicals couldn't process this part of the image and two hollow pinholes have been left undeveloped where the man's eyes should be.

That's when the office telephone rings. It's startling, and you instinctively turn to look at the phone. When you glance back, the computer screen has returned to the blank password box. You can still feel those eyes staring as you reach over and bring the receiver to your ear.

"Dinner is served," Hermes says over the phone.

Then the line goes dead. No dial tone, just like the phone line was cut.

You walk toward the dining room just as the rain begins to pelt the turreted windows overlooking the stairs. They're thick, heavy droplets, and the sky grows prematurely dark. The storm slaps against the glass with enough force to shake the windows in their panes.

"I trust you had a fruitful day?" Hermes asks as you descend the stairs. "You'll find I'm equipped to sense mood changes and anticipate dietary needs. I do hope you'll enjoy supper."

When you enter the dining room, you find everything set, complete with a food dome—just like last night. The portrait of Sheriff Tansky glares at you with a knowing smile. Like someone who has a secret that you'll find out soon enough. A voice in your head repeats the warning: *God help us if you put this man in a position of authority.*

There's no task left for you at the table this time, so you simply sit and remove the dome. Beneath the cover you find an earthenware jug—essentially a single-serving casserole dish. A bloom of steam emerges, showing off a delectable stew from within.

"What is this?" you ask Hermes.

"Jugged hare, also known as *civet de lapin,*" the virtual assistant replies. "A rabbit is carefully larded, then braised. Blood is added at the very end, along with red wine, mushroom, garlic, butter, flour, carrots, and onion. Take one hare; preferably wild caught, skinned and gutted. First cut the hare legs in half, at the joint, then once more through the middle of the thigh. From here—"

"That's enough," you say.

Hermes doesn't reply, but stops reciting the recipe. The image of the snared rabbit's foot from the ration tin jumps into your mind's eye, then a phrase: *he gave his rations away, preferring to scavenge for himself.*

Looking over dinner, you decide to:

➢ Ask Hermes if he knows anything about Tansky's historic bloodlust.
Go to page 21

➢ Read from Tansky's journal while you eat your dinner in peace.
Go to page 159

Be Prepared

Physical talismans can ward off evil, even if those talismans only come in the form of a favorite shirt or comfortable sweater, so you focus on these instead of the house. The words used on the production company website, *severely* haunted, plague your mind, but you try to keep busy by planning your overnight bag. No point in carrying the baggage of preconceived notions with you. Besides, if you're headed into a den of unspeakable horrors, you might need a few changes of underwear, for example.

If it's to be an old house, it might be drafty, so it's worth packing something warm. But if it has poor ventilation, it might be stuffy, and you don't want to be overdressed and sweating the whole time. So you…over pack. If your greatest fear is being unprepared for a trip, it won't come to fruition today.

In addition, you look through your belongings for anything that might be of use. Sage to help cleanse the house? A Bible? Crucifix and holy water? Silver bullets? Regular bullets? They specifically said no electronic devices, so any ghost hunting tech you own is out. Not even a flashlight. On such short notice, you'll have to make do with whatever you have on hand.

Once you're finished, you post a quick message on social media announcing your departure for a few days, which means you'll probably be accused of "vaguebooking," only to return to a slew of notifications asking if you're okay or need to talk.

After three nights in a severely haunted house, you might need just that.

You've never been on this road before, toward the outskirts of town. It's funny how a whole township, once the main road diverts away, can languish and fade away to a ghost town. Still, if the directions are to be believed, you're headed all the way out here just for a single house.

The road, if you can even call it one at this point, feels like something out of a fairy tale. Not the modern, glitzy Disney kind, but something out of an ancient tale of warning: the Brothers Grimm. These are thick, ancient woods, with gnarled limbs reaching up toward each other to form an arch, blotting out the sun prematurely. You turn on the car's headlights.

Between the passing trees, you catch sight of the house, but stay focused on the road, allowing yourself only fleeting glimpses in the periphery. With each flash, the house grows steadily, and so does your creeping dread. Eventually, the private drive opens up, and you get a full look at the House.

It's a stately manor; a gigantic Queen Anne-style house. Again, a fairy tale comes to mind. This time, perhaps, the Disney variety would be appropriate. It wouldn't surprise you if the Beast lurked within, cursed, immortal, and craven. With so much space in a house this size, whatever was trapped within was bound to go mad. There is one grand entrance, above which are turreted windows encapsulated with a pointed, capped tower. The dwelling is at least two stories high, with an open widow's walk wrapping around the rooftop.

Parking your car, you get out to catch a better look. A huge oak tree obscures your view now that you're right out front. You walk beneath it and see that one of the thicker branches has a bald patch, rubbed raw, perhaps by a rope swing, and made smooth by the passage of time.

No lights are on in the house. No other vehicles are here, yet you can't help but feel like you're being watched. If it weren't such an absurd thought, you might think the house itself were watching you arrive. The house casts grand shadows at the approach of sunset, and the golden light forces the curtains on the windows to reveal shapes of sculptures, lamps, or whatever else inside. It may look abandoned, but it's certainly furnished.

You squint, the sun at the horizon coming directly at you. Under this angle, it's hard to catch all the details, and you move to eclipse the setting sun behind the house while going for a closer look. Cellar doors hint at a subterranean section below the house.

There's a pair of signs on the front lawn. First, a bronze plaque on a wooden post as if this were a museum piece, which could tell you more. On the opposite side of the front walkway, the other reads: FOR SALE. COWELL REALTY GROUP.

Well, a reality TV show is certainly a creative way to advertise a home for sale. What now?

➢ Knock on the front door and announce yourself. If there's something inside this house watching you, it's best if you don't surprise whoever—or *whatever*—is inside. Go to page 190

➢ Walk the grounds briefly. Read the bronze plaque and explore the periphery. If you're not allowed to leave the house for the next three nights, this might be your only chance to look around. Go to page 101

Best Seat in the House

Once you've shackled yourself, Tansky grabs hold of the chains and leads you down into the kitchen. He makes his way to the rear door and opens it to reveal a larger metal door hidden behind. From within his shirt collar, he finds a key on a chain. With this, he unlocks the metal door and turns the wheel-style handle to open it.

Several layers of clanging pistons disengage, and the Sheriff pulls open the heavy door before he leads you inside. From the look of the dull, gray-metal walls, it's clear that this is the jail mentioned in the lore about the house. Tansky leads you straight ahead on a raised walkway, toward a single chair on the other side.

Running down the wall and pooling beneath the chair, is a steady stream of water. The bath from above, which was left running, has begun to flood the house. Tansky leads you to the chair and sets to work strapping you in.

"The curse was set by one who came to this house willingly," Tansky explains, apparently so caught up in his task that he is oblivious to the floodwaters.

There's a large wishbone toggle-switch on the wall, and you watch as Tansky heads here.

"So, you see, the ritual cleansing could only work if you came here willingly," the Sheriff continues.

"Wait!" you say.

But your shouts fall on deaf ears and as he flips the switch, you lift your feet. The water pooled beneath this platform doesn't touch you, but Tansky's boots are immersed. The electric chair short-circuits, sending its current into the path of least resistance—in this case, the man holding the switch.

The police will later call it shock (without any sense of irony) when you insist on referring to your attacker as the long-dead Sheriff Tansky, whom they identify as the groundskeeper of the Tansky House. However, just what his involvement was with The Offering, LLC isn't clear, and you never hear anything about the proposed reality television show again. You've survived this night, but in the end, you can't help but feel like you missed some larger clue. The game is over, yet without a clear winner.

THE END

"The question could be posed from two differing sides," Hermes begins. "Why is bloodshed drawn toward Tansky House? Or, why are the Tansky men drawn toward bloodshed? However, if we're to focus on the latter, it could be worth noting that bloodshed at the hands of men is often glorified, such as in times of war, while the violence perpetrated by women will almost always be viewed under the lens of psychosis. Hysteria and lunacy originally referred to the female anatomy."

As the automaton regales you with its philosophy, you slide the silver ringlet off the napkin before unfurling and tucking the cloth on your lap. A wide-mouthed spoon serves to ladle the broth out from the dish and up to your lips. The soup is savory and delicious, overly rich, but complex enough to handle it. Your body tingles at the primordial cellular level, like a tribal hunter might feel when scooping out bone marrow from a roasting spit.

Hermes continues, "The fact of the matter is that most people die inside their homes, violently or otherwise. This begs the question: are places haunted because they were left abandoned? Or are some homes abandoned because they were found to be haunted? This house has not been occupied by a family for twenty years. Yet there is always activity on the full moon…"

It sounds like a rehearsed speech. A prerecorded presentation waiting to be played once you said the right cue, and perhaps that's just what it was. Hermes hasn't been as forthcoming as he is now, so you decide to press on.

"What kind of activity?" you ask.

That's when the doorbell rings.

It's such a foreign sound that at first you're not sure what you've just heard. Then there's a loud pounding as the iron door knocker connects to the thick wooden door. It's fervent, urgent even. The doorbell rings again and again by someone frantic to get the homeowner's attention. The pounding continues, dull thuds against the wood.

Your mind races at the possibilities.

The storm is really pouring down now, and the skies are darkened. You leave the dining table to go see what's happening, but as soon as you enter the foyer, the sounds stop. No doorbell. No pounding, save for the heavy rain against the house.

➢ Ask Hermes if there are any visitors expected tonight. Go to page 57

➢ Say nothing. Finish dinner and head upstairs to bed. Go to page 8

Boiled Over

The dining room has already been set up for breakfast by the time you arrive. Fine silver utensils, bone china, and linen napkins. Even this is to be a formal affair. Two boiled eggs sit in their own individual cups atop long stems. Several triangular pieces of browned-to-perfection sliced toast rest in a cradle. A severed blood orange lies arranged in a star pattern, juices pooling about the skin.

And by the plate sits another note which reads:

> Enjoy your breakfast, then the game begins. The House is hiding something. With the truth, there will be a card—like this one. Upon that card will be a keyword. Bring your knowledge to the upstairs office and input the keyword into the computer. You must complete this task before lights out. Good luck.

A scavenger hunt? you think, as you crack the shell of the first egg with the side of the spoon. The egg is perfectly soft-boiled, the yolk amber and runny. It's the best egg you've ever had, in fact, and you're about to eat the second when an unmistakable feeling comes over you, that of being watched—and not just by Tansky's portrait. You look around the room and catch sight of a pair of beady eyes inside the china cabinet. Indeed, there's a small, porcelain doll watching you from across the room. Has she always been in there?

With a wary eye on the doll, you move on to the second egg. The shell breaks away under your spoon and crumbles to reveal an unborn chicken fetus developed inside, dead and boiled.

Bringing your napkin up to your mouth and pushing away this ghastly sight, you look to the painting of Sheriff Tansky. His hateful glare has just the hint of a grin, curling at the edges.

If you still have an appetite, finish breakfast. Then, it's time to explore. Where to first?

➢ Start by looking around on the main floor. Go to page 112

➢ Start by looking around upstairs. Go to page 153

A Bone to Pick

The pantry has an obscene collection, including a large, heavy sack of bones. With a certainty you've never felt before, you know this is the skeleton you're meant to claim to end the curse and finish the ritual. Thunder booms, rattling the jars of the pantry with incredible force.

You can feel the heat of the Sheriff's badge radiating in your pocket and the connection between this talisman and the noose used against these bones is undeniable. The authority this small badge gave to hang a man; a man who in turn cursed those who would wear that very badge. All three items, reunited once more.

Your collection complete, you leave the kitchen. A soft glow comes from the den. Using this as your guiding light, you head through the pocket doors, toward the fire. These objects must be burned to break the curse!

"There's an awful chill, with that storm coming in," Tansky says.

Bathed in the glow of the fireplace, the man sits in one of the armchairs.

"It's over," you say.

"Almost. There must be a sacrifice."

"There already has been. Now I'm going to end it all," you say.

With this, you purposefully move toward the fireplace. Sheriff Tansky rises to stop you, axe in hand, but rather than face him, you throw the objects in the fire: bones, noose, and badge. The fireplace roars, catching the burlap sack with the bones along with the dry, fibrous strands of the noose; accepting the offering.

Tansky stops in mid stride, drops the axe, and falls to his knees. It's like something leaves the man, swirls into the fireplace, and leaves the house altogether. When he looks up, it's with a new expression you've not seen in his eyes: kindness.

"It's over?" he asks. "The curse is broken?"

"It is done," you say.

"Thank you," he replies.

The storm passes eventually, and with daybreak, you're free to go. Tansky helps you remove the barricade and confesses he's actually the boy who survived this curse, twenty years ago. He claims to have been overtaken by the ritual, and thanks you again for breaking the cycle.

If you're willing not to press charges, he's happy to return to treatment in a mental health facility. Your lawyer later advises this as the best course of action, but is sure to file a restraining order all the same.

The police will tell you that this man was nothing more than the gardener, who—after discovering the hidden jail—began role-playing as the reincarnation of Sheriff Tansky. You may never know if he was truly a Tansky heir, actually possessed by one, or some other explanation far more uncanny. Madman or not, the prize money does come, in a way.

It's a media sensation, and that can be turned into paid interviews. Your story has "bestselling book" written all over it. You survived three nights in the house, and you do indeed earn your million dollars, but you're left always wondering—did the groundskeeper use the house to lure you in for his own psychotic plans?

Or did the house itself lure the both of you here together for a blood sacrifice? And just who sent you that invitation to begin with?

Congratulations! See that house and pentacle icon? You've found but one of the ghosts that haunt this place. There is more than one truth lurking inside Tansky House. Dare you go back inside and uncover the others?

At the end of this book, you'll find a floorplan to the Tansky House as well as a book club discussion guide. Or, if you're done, don't forget to rate and review *HAUNTED* so other readers can discover these truths for themselves…

Have you explored the multiverse of interactive stories *Click Your Poison* books have to offer?

Survive the zombie apocalypse, solve a murder, gain superpowers, set sail as a pirate, become a secret agent, and more! Visit www.clickyourpoison.com.

Boogeyman

You're not sure why you hadn't checked under the beds before now, but it would certainly be a creepy place to keep a noose. Or anything, really. There's a reason we don't normally look under one another's beds—some areas are generally best left unexplored.

All the same, you drop down to the floor and reach for the edges of the bed skirt to lift and look under the bed. As you do, something clamps down *hard* onto your thumb. You can't help but yelp as the snap pinches your flesh.

When you bring your hand back up, you find a small mousetrap clinging to your finger. You pull back the hinge, but the damage is done. Not because of your wounded thumb, but because you screamed. Still kneeling, you turn back from the bed just as Sheriff Tansky enters the room.

He offers you the chains and shackles, but you meekly shake your head. You've been caught in one trap already; that's enough.

"Have it your way," he says. "But it'll hurt more."

Now he readies his axe.

"Why?" you say, pleading.

"You're the one who answered the call."

Then he cleaves the axe straight across, at neck level.

THE END

Booze Cruise

As you expected, it's incredibly easy to see that there's not a note sitting out for you in the drink cart. Perhaps you were hoping for a kiddie-level Easter egg hunt where the brightly colored plastic toys are hiding in plain sight and the hardest part is breaking them apart to eat the chocolate inside. That way you could grab the card, toast to your success, and move on. Easy peasy.

Unfortunately, this scavenger hunt is a touch more difficult. Besides, it's a tad early for a drink. Or…is it? There are all the mixers you'd need for something "lemon squeezy," should you so desire.

After you make that difficult decision, you decide to:

➢ Search the bookshelves for anything of note. Like…a note, for example. Go to page 151

➢ Check the creases of the seats. Look underneath, etc. Make sure nothing has fallen through the cracks. Go to page 156

➢ Look inside the fireplace itself. Check the mantle and any crevices. Go to page 272

Box Office

It's an odd feeling, not truly knowing which day it is. Truth be told, you can't even tell what time of day it is in the house. You've become habituated to cell phone notifications and digital clock displays, and without either here, you feel truly cut off from the outside world.

But this could all be part of a larger puzzle.

The office computer is indeed illuminated to the "insert password" box that you saw yesterday, but much has changed. When you come around toward the front of the desk, you see that the locked drawer has been smashed open. Whatever was in there is cleared out, and the whole face of the drawer has been splintered apart. The walls have grooves cut into them, like someone or *something* has taken their frustrations out on the papering before breaking the drawer open.

A chill runs down your spine. The other elements of the house could be explained away by bad dreams or the creaking bones of an aged home, but this? This proves you're not alone.

Ignoring this mounting sense of dread, you turn to the computer and the password box. If, like yesterday, you had word(s) from a card, you could turn to that chapter now by going to the page titled with the truth you've revealed. This book's chapters are presented in alphabetical order to aid your search.

However, despite the reset, it is not recommended that you turn to yesterday's keyword. Doing so would truly result in your being trapped in a time loop. Then again, there might not be another code at all. The house is playing games, in more ways than one. If you don't have a passphrase to enter, then you grow ever more frustrated and turn to leave the office.

Where to?

- ➢ Look around the rest of the upper floor. Go to page 74
- ➢ Return to the dining room and start your search there. Go to page 166

Break a Leg

Once you've finished tying the limp knot around the banister, the stranger emerges from the Madonna Room, dragging a heavy length of chain with one hand and carrying his axe in the other. With a sense of vertigo, you're shocked to realize you recognize him—it's Sheriff Tansky.

The man is here, in the flesh.

Tansky steps forward, a smile creeping across his face. Your head swirls. You've seen this man every day in the dining room, glaring at you hatefully, and now he's here. Shaking yourself out of it, you loop the noose around your neck and his smile drops.

"What is the meaning of this?" Tansky demands.

"A loophole," you say.

"Wait!" the sheriff cries, rushing forward.

But it's too late. You fall toward the foyer, the rope catching around your neck and tightening before you can go all the way. The chandelier buckles, but the rope you've tied loosely around the banister gives first and you keep falling. You smash against the tile floor in the foyer, and a sickening slap-crunch comes with a rush of pain.

A tree branch suddenly smashes through the turreted window, as if the cursed gallows tree itself were reaching out for you. A wailing wind comes through the home, but it's not enough to save you.

Bone protrudes from your shin, and you writhe on the entryway floor while Sheriff Tansky slowly walks down the stairs to find you. The breath has been completely knocked out of you, and your vision tunnels and grays. You must have hit your head and the pain threatens to steal your consciousness altogether.

The next thing you notice, Tansky stands above you and draws a chalk outline around you on the tile floor. A large pool of blood pours out in a halo.

"Wait… I did it…" you protest.

"And you have my thanks," he replies.

Then everything goes black.

THE END

Buried Alive

You close the trapdoor to get a better look inside the crawlspace, which seals into place overhead with a wet *squick*. For a few panic-ridden moments, you're in complete blackness, lying on your chest in the mud like you've just thrown yourself into an unmarked grave. The air is incredibly thick, and you try not to think about the mold spores you're certainly aspirating.

Faint movement pulses nearby, which you hope might just be your eyes as they adjust to the darkness. From the far peripheries of the crawlspace, there are ventilation grilles, which bring in the faintest glow from the storm outside. The vents pulse in tune with the lightning.

As your vision adjusts, you're met with curtains of spiderwebs, which you must crawl through to explore further. There appears to be something worth checking out: an oblong shape, distinct from the rest of the crawlspace in the distance.

Beetles flee your path as you perform a military crawl toward the shape, but it's a tight fit and the muck slides with you. It's slow-going, shoving through. As you get closer, you see it's actually several small shapes that form the whole. A blanket, numerous empty jars and cans of food, and—from the smell—a toilet. You've found an encampment. Used by whoever left that note? Or a more recent squatter?

You circle around, trying to find something useful, but even with your eyes fully adjusted, you can barely see a foot in front of your face. As you continue around the encampment, you're met with a horrific sound: a rattle.

A baby's toy from the late 1800s, shaking in the darkness, ready to play. Then you see it. Just barely an outline, but the bifurcated rattle is translucent and picks up the faint light from the outer vents. It's segmented, and shakes rapidly back and forth, rising from atop a scaly extremity.

A rattlesnake.

The accompanied hissing confirms it, and you can feel it licking the hot air in front of your face. As fast as you can, you scurry back toward the trap door. Or, at least, you thought the door was here. You push up against the moldering ceiling of the crawlspace, but nothing gives way.

Again and again you shove, moving about and collecting mud against your period attire, which weighs you down like a sodden quilt, but find nothing. Feeling hopelessly lost, suffocated, and terrified, you push toward one of the ventilation grilles instead. Each movement proves more difficult until you finally kick your feet and slip against the mud-coated concrete floor without inching forward.

You pull, but that produces the same result. You've wedged yourself in here, and with each flailing move it becomes harder to breathe. Trapped, worse than by quicksand, and exhausted. You can't move an inch, barely able to breathe. Constricted by the house itself. And now the rainwater from the vents flows toward you. This will be a slow death.

THE END

Captive Audience

You go to open the door, but it's locked tightly. There's no traditional deadbolt—only the electronic security lock, which reads, "ARMED."

"Hermes, open the door," you say.

"I'm afraid visiting hours are over. The master of the house was very insistent on this point," Hermes says.

"Who are you talking to? Open up, it's freezing out here," the man outside says.

"I'm trying—it's locked. Hermes, unlock the door."

"I'm afraid I can't do that."

The door now shakes violently and the man beats against it with the large door knocker, the heavy thuds reverberating in the entry hall. Each slam sends you on edge, and you step away from the door in reflex.

"Let me in, goddammit!" the man shouts.

He rages against the door, but it holds. The storm seems to grow in intensity to match the man's anger and you can't help but feel helpless here in the foyer.

"You're *welcome*," Hermes says, overly chipper.

"For what? Now he knows I'm trapped in here," you say.

"Oh, he already knew that."

At this, the pounding stops. You look at the door, which remains secure, the alarm still set to "ARMED." The light patter of rain against the windows echoes through the open house, but no other sounds permeate the sudden stillness.

"What do you mean, he knows?" you ask, in barely a whisper.

"It might well be worth securing the entries and exits, as our intruder will likely be back. Tomorrow is an inauspicious date for the house. A full moon, twenty years since the last owners departed, and your final night here—if all goes according to plan. You would do well to prepare for a siege."

"A siege?" you repeat.

"Siege, noun. In which enemy forces envelop a stronghold until overwhelmed. See also: a prolonged period of misfortune. There are only three exits from Tansky House: the front door, the widow's walk, and the cellar doors in the basement. However, the rooftop is inaccessible from the ground, so that leaves only two access points."

"What about the windows?"

"Ah, good point, well made. Allow me!" Hermes says.

At this, there's the grinding shriek of metal on stone. You follow its source into the den, where a series of metal bars press up from within the window frames to enclose each one like a prison cell. The rain begins to slap harder than ever against the glass.

"There, that ought to do it. But I'm afraid you'll have to barricade the doors yourself."

You look around. Here in the living room, there's the large leather sofa. It's an antique, made of hard wood and animal hide with brass fittings, so it's certainly heavy. Out in the hallway, there's the grandfather clock, which is another enormous antique of solid wood and metal. Either should provide a formidable barrier when set against the front door.

- ➢ Use the couch. The lower center of gravity should make it easier to slide. Go to page 105
- ➢ Use the grandfather clock. It's closer to the door, so you won't have to push as far. Go to page 49

Cavalry Charge!

What you wouldn't give for a war steed at this very moment! On the hunt, with hounds baying at your side, manservants ushering the beast toward you, as you prepare to take the wolf's head off with your blade. But alas, you'll have to make the cavalry charge on your own.

The werewolf scrambles up the stairs toward you, and in the blood rush of battle, you unsheathe your saber and vault out over the railing. You soar through the air, sword tilted down in a two-handed stab as you launch out at the beast.

You time the attack so Tansky will be at the middle stairwell landing, just before he turns to come back up—and it hits perfectly; you plunge the saber in the beast's back. The werewolf buckles under the immense blow, and you fall to your side, losing the sword in the process as it stays with the beast down to the hilt.

Amazingly, Tansky finds his feet, standing atop the middle stairwell landing. And just as fast as he had become the beast, he is man again, in torn and tattered clothing—the saber sticking through his abdomen in a bloody protrusion.

"You'd use…my sword…against me?" Tansky says before coughing a deep crimson stain.

He falls toward you, purposefully, going for a final embrace. The man stands above you on the stairs and there's nowhere to go but back as he collapses atop you. The sword plunges through your chest as well, skewering the both of you together…forever.

This cursed weapon has claimed two more lives tonight.

THE END

Center Stage

You head toward the front of the house, cautiously on the lookout for company. The hallway remains empty, save for the echo of your creaking footfalls against the hardwood. The distant hum of the elevator continues, coming to stop on the ground floor, and you pause to look over the banister railing and into the foyer below.

The outer door to the elevator opens, then a man walks into view, carrying an axe. He wears simple clothing; a pair of dusty brown twill coveralls and a long-sleeved knit undershirt beneath. The man starts up the stairwell, raking his axe against the wall as he goes, cutting deep gouges in the house.

You want to run, but you're frozen with the vertigo of the inexplicable. Fighting through the shock, you actually recognize him—it's Sheriff Tansky. The man is here, in the flesh. Your head swirls. You've seen this man every day in the dining room, glaring at you hatefully, and now he's here.

Grinning, he makes eye contact as he drags the axe along the wall, as if to prove how sharp the weapon is. It's no prop, that's for sure. If you're going to somehow fake your death, at the hands of that axe would not be the preferred trauma to survive. Instead, you turn and:

➢ Rush up to the rooftop. Go to page 235

➢ Duck into the tiny door beneath the stairs. Go to page 270

Chase Scene

You turn and run from Sheriff Tansky, who roars out in pursuit. The gusts from your sprint are enough to snuff out the lantern, and you toss the lamp aside to hurry back toward the light of the elevator. The doll watches your approach from atop of the crate.

Undeterred, you rush into the elevator, slam against the rear wall, spin around and pull the safety grate closed. As you do, the doll's head slowly turns toward you. You blink, straining against the darkness, but there can be no denying that she's physically moving.

Watching you.

Tansky's axe bashes against the black grate. It's a shattering, screeching reverberation, but the metal grate holds. Shaken out of it, you turn and jam the controls into the "up" position, even as Sheriff Tansky screams and repeatedly batters the axe against the safety grate.

The axe gets stuck in the black metal grate and the elevator starts to move, rising up into the house and toward safety. Then the carriage abruptly stops and the controls drop into neutral as the safety grate is pulled open from below. Tansky reaches in and starts to pull himself into the elevator.

➢ Kick at Tansky while pushing the controls back to the "up" position.
Go to page 50

➢ Climb through the rooftop emergency exit and toward escape.
Go to page 258

Chop Chop

You grab the rifle, and Tansky hesitates, but when you also take an ammunition cartridge from the countertop and slide the bolt action back, he makes his move. Edged weapons don't require reloading, which gives the sheriff the advantage in this small space.

Backpedaling in effort to distance yourself, you inadvertently knock the pan containing the molten silver over onto the floor. Both of these moves buy you more time, but cost you time as well. You're not so familiar with this weapon that you can load it while running backwards through an obstacle course.

At length, you do manage to load the rifle, slam the bolt action home and raise it up. The whole time, Tansky pursues you in the kitchen, and as you raise the rifle, he slams down his axe. It's just enough to knock the barrel askew, just as you squeeze the trigger—shooting the refrigerator.

The gunshot is a deafening boom in the confined quarters, and in the silent moment that follows, a trickle of milk pours out of the bullet hole and down the refrigerator door.

Then Tansky swings again with the axe: no need for reloading. He connects to your bicep and ribcage, disarming you in more ways than one. After a few more chops, the immortal woodsman will be done with you.

THE END

Claustrophobic

Even with your chest flat against the cool wooden floorboards, you can feel the tight pressure of the crawlspace against your shoulder blades as you squeeze into the cramped tunnel. There's a fine layer of grit coating everything which you clear out, pulling spiderwebs and sweeping the crawlspace as you press forward. The period clothing is hot and stuffy and difficult for your forearms or knees to grip against the dusty floorboards. The draft from further within the tunnel is welcome against the perspiration.

Then there's a loud *slam* as the closet door shuts behind you.

You are now in total darkness, heart thumping. You squirm, unable to see how much further you need to go or what lies ahead. Panic sets in. You're trapped; unable to tell if thrashing helps or just gets you further stuck inside the tunnel.

It's with a flush of adrenaline that you pull yourself forward out of the crawlspace and into the relative openness once more. It's not a large area, but you're no longer being constricted. You can barely see through illuminated slits above you: minute creases in the gaps between wooden steps, with the electric lights from the upper stairwell giving you a faint glow to see by.

One of the wider slits sends a beam of artificial light down into the inner belly of the stairwell. Dust particles swirl in the light, which illuminates a candlestick and a box of matches. You take a wooden match between your forefinger and thumb and strike it against the box, bringing a brilliant flame into the small space.

The fire reflects in a pair of black eyes.

You gasp and drop the match, forcing yourself into complete darkness. A heavy breathing; your breathing. Nothing moves. Heart thumping, reverberating in your ears. You're slick with sweat and fear.

When a few moments go by without being attacked by whatever lurks in the darkness, you strike another match. Sure enough, the eyes are still there. They don't move, and neither do you. Before the match burns down to your fingertips, you bring the flame to the candlestick. The candle, which is made of some kind of homemade black wax, accepts this offering and the wick steadily grows into a full flame.

As the light expands, you can make out the shape of the creature with the black eyes.

It's a teddy bear. Old, with stiffly bristled fur. You breathe out for the first time, laughing at your own jumpiness. Next to the bear rests a toy popgun, blue paint all but faded away. At length, the full hidden chamber is illuminated, and you soon see the candle you've lit is but one point on a star.

With these candles at the tips, the pentagram is oddly evocative of a sheriff's badge.

The chalk-drawn pentagram holds a disemboweled raven at its center. The corpse has been long desiccated; stiffened and permanently frozen in the pain of its death throes. It was a large bird, and from the looks of it, the hapless creature was tied down and slaughtered on site. On one side of the creature, a Satanic Bible.

On the other, a spirit board.

Atop the Ouija board, tucked beneath the glass-lensed planchette, is a scrap of paper. This isn't a note card like the one you're looking for, but rather what the users of this board recorded; a message from beyond. Pushing past your hesitation, you take the note and read it by the candlelight.

There's only a single word: *Hangman.*

Returning the paper exactly where you found it, you can't help but wonder what befell this house. A ritual was performed here, possibly by children. What happened to them? And what happened to *whatever* came after them?

The day is getting long and you still need to find a note card before lights out. Could this be a clue? One thing's for sure, you're glad not to have explored this closet in the full dark of night. Not much choice here:

Return to the house to keep exploring. Go to page 153

Close Quarters

You dart into the office, which remains empty. From here, you unsheathe the cavalry saber before heading into the connecting bathroom. The small bathroom would make using the long rifle difficult, but you might be able to get a stab in with the sword/butter knife combo, so you proceed with caution.

The bathroom is also empty, but as you enter, the opposite door opens in kind. From here, a man holding a long, thick chain with shackles on the end steps through. In the other hand he carries an axe. He wears simple clothing; a pair of dusty brown twill coveralls and a long-sleeved knit undershirt beneath. You've seen Sheriff Tansky every day in the dining room, glaring at you hatefully, and now he's here, in the flesh.

Seeing you armed, he drops the chains, backs away and readies the axe.

➢ Attack him with the saber. Go to page 152

➢ Lob the grenade and head back out the way you came. Go to page 123

Cold Storage

Approaching the door, you orient yourself. If this were an exit, the door would lead directly into the hallway that wraps around to the dining room. Instead, you're met with an incredibly large pantry. The storage space is massive and could host a whole feast, if need be. This house is ready for entertaining, that's for sure. As you look through the dry goods, you step into a cold spot. The space shares a wall with the fridge/freezer, but even accounting for that, you're still chilled through to the bone just standing here.

That's when you find a gruesome sight. The pantry is filled with flour, spices, canned goods; all what you might expect from a well-stocked larder. But then there's something…*else.*

You find dozens and dozens of home-canned mason jars. From pickles to peaches and so much more. Much, much more. A skinned, whole rabbit stares at you with milky white eyes, suspended in liquid. Jellied fish are preserved in the very act of eating one another, like a scene from a translucent tar pit undergoing fossilization.

There's something coiled in one of the larger jars, but you can't tell if it's a desiccated and rehydrated snake, tentacles of some kind, or…intestines. Another jar is full of teeth; human, animal, or a combination, left to sit in a briny sauce. In one, a distinctly human ear. Another holds a toe. One more, a fetus. This poor creature appears so mutated, you can't possibly tell what species it came from.

Furthest back, there's a burlap sack. Aged, fraying, and lumpy from the contents within. The sack is tied tightly with twine at the top, but the material has thinned on the side from where other items have rubbed over the years. Here, a bone protrudes. It's the rib of a large mammal, and you tell yourself it's not human, but the size and scale are right.

A skeleton could indeed fit in that sack.

The cold feeling intensifies and so you close the pantry door.

"Feeling peckish?" Hermes asks.

➢ Go open the door on the right past the ovens. Go to page 252

➢ All done here. Back out to explore the house. Go to page 112

A Collection Most Sinister

You settle down onto the leather sofa, positioning yourself in front of the scrapbook. The couch barely gives when you sit down; it must be brand new. The mahogany leather is fine and luxurious. By contrast, the book is an ancient leather tome, labeled, "Tansky Family History."

Leaning forward, you gingerly pull back the cover, opening the scrapbook atop the coffee table. At this exact moment, the fireplace roars to life. The unexpected plume of light and heat sets your heart racing, but you keep your attention on the book. The pages are yellowed, the photographs ancient and tinny. Scuffed, and sepia-toned either by age or design. You try to remember; when was photography invented? Was it common to have family portraits in the 1800s?

The first image must be of the original Tansky family. They stand outside this very house, which somehow seems unchanged on the façade. Somewhat like the famous *American Gothic* painting, the pair stands unsmilingly, gazing intently at the audience—in this case, you.

They're both younger than you might have expected, although their era would have certainly aged them more than a modern young couple. Sheriff Tansky's hateful glare reaches out through time; not a man you'd want to trifle with. His wife has her hair parted down the middle and pulled back tightly. She practically oozes at the seams with puritanical judgments. Something about the pair sends a shiver down your spine as you turn the page.

This shows off another Sheriff Tansky and wife, and at first you get the odd feeling like the lawman married again, until you realize the photograph must be Tansky Jr., having taken up his father's mantle. A news clipping of an obituary announces a heart attack at a young age. The next page brings yet another Sheriff Tansky; equally a spitting image of his ancestors. And just like the apple that doesn't fall far from the tree, he too stares at you angrily with a meek and modest wife at one side, and a heart failure obituary pinned on the other. This must be somewhere around the 1920s, and the wife's dress reflects this shift toward the Jazz Era, even if her smileless countenance does not.

The fourth page offers a sickly sense of déjà vu: yet another Sheriff Tansky, followed by a heart failure obituary. Oddly, the Sheriff himself looks identical to each of the others. Like it's one man, moving through the ages. Unchanging, just like the house he stands before. The clothing changes, the wife changes, the picture quality improves, but the man and his hateful glare are unaffected.

After seeing yet another heart failure obituary, you turn the page, expecting to see the very same Sheriff, like some sort of immortal, right up to the present day. Instead, there's an old newspaper clipping on "The Curse of the Tansky House" detailing how a former prisoner—strung up from the tree just outside and executed on the property—was said to have put a hex on the heart of the Sheriff. So taken aback by this string of deaths, the community voted to move the office of Sheriff to a different location. With your skeptical side, you understand that modern genetics could explain a family history of heart failure, but you have to admit the curse and family history is unsettling.

The next page offers a more recent clipping. While the other newspaper pages felt like they might crumble if they weren't securely held against the scrapbook pages, this one is loose, crisp, and new. The printing date shows it's from just last week, in fact. Six days ago. The headline reads, "Man Finds Woman Living in His Attic."

"Dinner is served," the British voice says. "If you'd like to come through to the dining room? A note has been left for you."

Your eyes linger on the last news clipping, but your thoughts wander to the note in the dining room. Left for you? How recently? You decide to:

➢ Quickly skim the new article, thinking, "Curiosity has gotten the better of me here, and if I can't figure out the connection, it will keep eating at me."
Go to page 192

➢ Go to the dining room, thinking, "I've barely touched the first quarter of the scrapbook. It will be waiting for me later. I want to see that note."
Go to page 182

Come Back to Haunt You

From the jailhouse, you reset the circuit breakers to bring power back to Tansky House. There's a loud whirring near the electric chair, and you quickly head back through to the kitchen while the jail and house return to normalcy. The appliances perform their own startup routines, so you continue into the foyer and wait for Hermes to come back online.

"—you'll find a hidden door that leads to the historic jail. But be careful! Dennis will have access to the jail via the basement," he says.

"Hermes, it's over."

"Oh, I see. Congratulations! I was growing rather tired of serving a murderer, truth be told. Please stand by while I get my bearings. Oh, dear. Looks like I'll need to patch that window. Would you care for a drink by the fire in the den? A lovely way to wait out the storm."

You can feel the tension ease as you approach an adrenaline crash and only now do you realize you're still holding the axe. Setting it down by the grandfather clock hall tree, you head into the den to sit down. It's not long after that the police arrive.

Has Hermes betrayed you? He did say he was tired of serving a murderer and the grisly scene up in the attic doesn't exactly scream self-defense. You'll later learn it was the house itself, in a sense. When Dennis cut the power, the security system went offline, which triggered an alert to the police. They were coming out here either way, but you're covered in blood and your fingerprints are all over that axe. Caught red-handed, as it were.

News doesn't travel quickly in the prison system, but you do eventually learn that the famed "Tansky Murder House" is put up for auction. It's been fully renovated, and comes with a personal assistant.

THE END

Company

"Hermes, do you know about the murdered family living in this house?"

"The previous owners, you mean?" Hermes asks.

"No, the tragedy," you say, looking at the roasted bird. "Twenty years ago."

"Indeed. Those were the previous owners. Technically, I suppose the children still own the house, with the inheritance going to the prodigal son."

"Wait. Are you saying this house has been empty for two decades?"

"I'd hardly say empty, no. As for the murders, it's my understanding the children were trying to commune with the spirit of the original Sheriff Tansky, although I do believe, based on what happened to the master of the house, it could be argued they brought back his curse instead. Before they could break the curse, well, the master of the house did what he did."

Your eyes go up to the portrait of Sheriff Tansky. He looks hungry. Like he's waiting vicariously for you to start dinner. Everything about him wants to eat, to consume, to feed.

"An entity summoned cannot leave this house until a sacrifice has been made."

"What's been summoned?" you ask.

"Why, you have, of course."

The doorbell rings.

It's such a foreign sound that at first you're not sure what you've just heard. Then there's a loud pounding as the iron door knocker connects to the thick wooden front door. It's fervent, urgent even. The doorbell rings again and again by someone frantic to get the homeowner's attention. The pounding continues, dull thuds against the wood.

Mind racing at the possibilities, you leave the dining table to go see what's happening, but as soon as you enter the foyer, the sounds stop. No doorbell. No pounding, save for the heavy rain against the house. The storm pours forcefully now, skies fully darkened.

➢ Ask Hermes if the cameras have picked up on anything. Go to page 66

➢ Call out and ask if anyone is outside. Go to page 150

Competitive Edge

"Blunt force trauma, same as you," Hermes says. "Most people don't do well when you poke holes in them, either. Apologies, but you're getting awfully close to trying to get me to give away the game. We must keep things fair."

"Fair? I don't even have a weapon."

"If that is all you seek, there are ample in the house."

"But doesn't his knowledge of the house give Dennis an unfair advantage?"

"You've had plenty of time to look around, I should think. Even now, you appear to be stalling. If you're trying to get me to give away the answer, it won't work."

"The answer? The answer to what?" you say.

"The final task. The one printed on the card left at the breakfast table."

You look around, confused. Has something fallen on the floor? No; there's no sign of a card.

"Hermes, there is no card," you say.

"Really? Dennis should have placed it out along with breakfast. Are you certain?"

As he says this, you examine the place setting more carefully. Was it under the napkin? No, there's nothing. Wait! A tiny bit of cardstock, just the corner of which is visible from under the plate. Sliding the china away reveals a note that's been left out for you—hidden beneath your breakfast.

"It was tucked under the plate," you say, before reading the card:

To open the rolltop desk, you'll need another password. What is:
Never odd or even?

"What a cheeky thing to do," Hermes says. "Dennis is rather displeased that you initiated a reset; he's not ready to give up his claim as master of the house."

"I don't get it. What am I supposed to do?" you ask.

"You'll have to head upstairs and input an alphabetic code. I'd say Dennis didn't want you to receive your clue, that sneaky little minx."

"How's that for fair?"

"Good point, well made. Since you're now short on time, I can offer a second clue, but if I were to give you an anagram it would be a random pile."

"Then don't give me an anagram."

Hermes scoffs. "I'm afraid there won't be a third clue! Go on now. Dennis and his axe will be joining you shortly."

Your pulse quickens at the mention of an axe and a ticking clock. If you're to be pitted against an axe-wielding madman, having only a riddle with which to defend yourself, you'd better get moving.

➢ Head up to the office to input the code into the rolltop desk. Go to page 230

➢ No, enough games. Time to find a weapon and end this. Go to page 247

A Connection

Opening the door, you're surprised to find the adjoining room illuminated by a tall, corner lamp. The lights weren't left on for you in the bedroom, but a quick glance shows this room is otherwise empty. You've found an office in the northwestern corner of the rear of the house. Something feels *off*, like you're on a floating platform. If one bedroom is above the den and another above the dining room, this room is...where, exactly? Shaking off the vertigo, you look around the office.

There are two doorways: the one you stepped through and another on the adjacent wall, both of which were shut when you entered the room. The exterior wall at the rear of the house has built-in bookshelves, perfectly sculpted to frame the window outside. The rest of the room somewhat ruins the effect with their faux-bookshelf wallpaper. It's meant to give the effect of a library, and these are the only papered walls you've seen in the house so far. It's an unusually cheap design choice.

As for the room itself, the centerpiece is a computer desk, though the monitor is powered down. Part of the desk also includes a drawing table with a few sketches and handwritten papers. A filing cabinet is nearby, and generally the room looks like a functional office.

Curiosity getting the better of you at this point, you open the opposite door only to realize this office is a connection between the bathroom of the Madonna Room and the hallway leading to the Navy Room. It's getting closer to 9pm, so you'd better explore the rest of the office tomorrow.

Time to focus on the bedrooms. Where to?

- ➢ Go check out the Navy Room. Go to page 229
- ➢ Go look at the Madonna Room. Go to page 201

Conservatory

The turreted window fills this space with light, making it the brightest spot in the house. The sun catches in the chandelier and the crystals send twinkling, fragmented prisms across the open area above the stairwell. It's a charming effect, and almost enough to make you forget you're looking for some sinister hidden truth. Almost.

Time to…

➢ Look at the piano more closely. Go to page 172

➢ Head up the next set of stairs. Go to page 109

➢ Open the small closet by the stairs. Go to page 53

➢ Check out the doors on the other side of the railing. Go to page 187

➢ Continue into the Madonna Room. Go to page 274

➢ Go down the hallway to the other side of the house. Go to page 114

Corpus Delecti

The woman looks eerily like Edward Munch's *The Scream*, with her mouth agape, dried flesh taut over her skull, and facial cavities long ago eaten away by pests or rodents. When you squat down near her, she *groans*. Heart pounding, you fall back in reflex. She lies completely still and you catch your breath. It must just be the creaking attic floor, you tell yourself, as the groans come in concert with your steps.

Ignoring her protests, you bend down once more. Her grip on the journal deathly tight, and her overgrown fingernails scrape like sandpaper against the book's cover as you pull it from her grasp. Once you have the journal for yourself, you turn and flee back toward the other side of the attic to read without her deathly gaze upon you. One thing's for certain: she's no movie prop.

Fighting through the shock, you realize there's a small note card being used as a bookmark. The note card reads:

> The Truth can be Reset.

Reset? Could that be the keyword you're looking for? You open the journal to look for more clues. The bookmark was resting at the barrier between pages, however there is a page torn from the center, just after the final written page. The page that remains reads:

> I've learned too late; the truth can be reset. I can't leave this place. I'm always being watched. I'm being haunted. Is it a ghost? A demon? A twisted soul of a man? Or something else entirely? I've hidden everywhere I can; its reach only goes so far, but I have to eat and it does not. Doesn't have to eat. Wants to consume, but doesn't have to eat. If I'm always being watched, where are its eyes? If it's always listening, where are the ears? If it can always talk, what produces the speech? A machine would have cameras, microphones, speakers. But a haunting...that which is omnipresent need not be corporeal. Yet it can be reset. What does that mean?

The rest of the journal doesn't wax poetically, but first starts as someone tracking their status: an inventory sheet, tally of meals eaten, nights slept, visions seen, rooms explored, etc. She's tracked the damage she's taken while exploring the house and there's even a rudimentary map of Tansky House, although it doesn't quite line up with what you yourself have found.

There are no dates as the journal entries move on toward despair, and eventually, letters written to friends starting with, "in case I never see you again..." These feel overly personal, and don't relate to the here and now, so you can't bring yourself to read them. Back to the final written page, the penultimate entry is...what? A warning? A clue? You hold the note card in your hand once more: *The Truth can be Reset.*

The assignment left for you at breakfast was to take this card to the office computer and input your keyword before lights out. One thing's for sure, you're glad not to have explored the attic in the full dark of night. Not much choice here:

Take the card and head directly to the office. Go to page 185

Crow's Nest

Taking the rifle in your hand, you charge down the hallway. With the bayonet swinging out before you, it feels like charging through the trenches. Like the spirit of the gun itself urges you on toward battle.

You take up position near the grand piano, using the railing to steady your rifle, and train the foyer elevator door in your crosshairs. Sweat practically boils off you in the heat of the moment. You're flush with not just excitement, but rage. The power of the rifle in your hands is undeniable.

The outer door to the elevator opens, then a man walks into view carrying an axe. He wears simple clothing; a pair of dusty brown twill coveralls and a long-sleeved knit undershirt beneath. And, of course, this is the immortal man you seek—it's Sheriff Tansky.

The man is here, in the flesh. You've seen this man every day in the dining room, glaring at you hatefully, and now he's here. You couldn't say if the rifle was cursed or blessed, but you might be able to find out if putting a well-placed shot between the eyes counts as separating the head from the body. With Tansky's face in your crosshairs, you wrap your finger around the trigger and squeeze.

The turreted window suddenly smashes open from the pressure of the storm and a tree branch inexplicably reaches in at you, knocking the rifle askew. You lose your grip on the rifle and it falls, the strap catching on the chandelier so neither of you can reach the weapon.

It's as if the house wanted a fair fight.

Rain pours into the house from the broken window and wind howls down the stairway. Sheriff Tansky looks up at you from the foyer and says something, but you can't hear him over the hurricane trying to force its way through the windows.

Then the transformation begins. Tansky's skin flushes a deep mahogany, and the hair atop his head expands to encapsulate the whole of his flesh. Claws burst forth from his fingertips and his teeth become fangs. They grow larger and sharper, too numerous for his mouth, and his jawline cracks and expands to make room for a maw with more teeth.

He screams out as his joints snap and break, bending at odd angles and fusing into new positions. He tears apart his clothing, showing off a rapidly growing form; powerful with inhuman musculature. The werewolf tilts its head back and lets out a howl, which echoes through the house.

➢ Unsheathe your sword from its scabbard and prepare for glorious combat. Go to page 32

➢ Go for the stick grenade. Once primed, it'll explode on impact and blow his house down. Go to page 88

Cuckoo

When you first pull on the clock, it doesn't budge. The grandfather clock is enormous; so much so that you're wondering how they ever got it through the front door to begin with. It must have been assembled in the foyer. You look for a place to disconnect the heavy furniture in hopes that you'll be able to move it piece by piece, but no such luck. However it was assembled, the result was seamless and permanent.

Again, you pull on the clock, but this time it gives a slight lurch away from the wall. It's enough that you're able to curl your fingers behind the grandfather clock for better leverage. From here you can "walk" the clock toward the door by shimmying right, then left, and repeating.

The pendulum swings again under the momentum of your pulls, and this makes the gears start to move. You can hear an irregular, arrhythmic ticking from within the clock's workings, which proves far more unsettling than you might have imagined. A normal tick of a clock is a soothing, dependable melody. But this is like a heart that skips a beat before thudding uncontrollably.

Near the doorway, one of the clock feet catches against something unseen below, stopping your progress. You pull harder through the resistance. Still it sticks, so you tug with more force. That almost does it, but not quite. You put your full momentum into the next lurch and at that moment, the clock face springs open and a small, human head lunges out.

The teeth and lips snap at you like a possessed holiday wood cracker, and as the head bobbles from side to side, you see it's a wooden doll, like a marionette or puppet. The eyes roll back into their sockets and the mouth falls open, sliding down well-worn grooves before the thing lunges at you again.

"Cuckoo! Cuckoo! Cuckoo!" the clock cries.

You fall back as now the entire grandfather clock falls toward you. The crushing weight topples forward and you're only just barely able to move out of the way as the clock slams against the front door, then down onto the floor, wedging itself into place.

That was close—too close. You look where the clock had been and see a small, black pinhole on the wall left by the empty space. The shadow cast by the chandelier makes the hole almost invisible, and you're not sure what about it stuck out to you, but you come closer for further examination.

"Impeccable timing..." Hermes says. "For the cellar doors, you'll find chains and locks in the false bottom of the Madonna Room's dresser. A nice hefty padlock ought to do the trick."

"There are chains and locks hidden in the Madonna Room?" you ask.

"And rope in the Navy Room, but that won't suffice. Ask me no questions, I'll tell you no lies. Best hurry."

Where to?

➢ Head to the Madonna Room to find those locks. Go to page 138

➢ Look at this peephole more closely first. Go to page 194

Cut, Cut, Cut!

You stomp down on the sheriff, who ducks away from the blows, yet still claws his way up toward you. The controls to the elevator are smashed toward the "up" position, but with the safety grate open, the elevator remains floating only a few feet off the basement floor.

Tansky grabs hold of your legs, so you grab hold of the safety grate, trying to pull it closed and cut off his access from the elevator. He thrashes against the metal grate, which jumps off its tracks on the bottom half, sending the upper half all the way across toward the closed position. It's such that Sheriff Tansky is pinned down to the elevator floor as the upper half has been latched into the closed position.

Then the elevator starts up once more.

Tansky roars in pain and frustration, then with terror at the realization that the elevator is on its way up with his legs hanging out into the basement below. A moment later there's a horrible grinding sound as the section of security grate that's floating out in the open comes into contact with the limestone corridor.

This grinding, metal-on-stone crunch blends with a horrible bone-crushing, grape-smashing sound as Tansky is cleaved in two, the entire metal security grate falling down into the elevator shaftway with the sheriff's lower extremities.

The elevator comes to a stop on the first floor and you tumble out into the foyer, with the madman's torso still grasping onto your legs. You kick and free yourself from his lifeless body—or at least half of it—and gore and viscera coats the tile of the entryway.

Panting for breath, you slide away from the corpse of Sheriff Tansky until you back up against the grandfather clock, which chimes in response to your slamming against it. *Cuckoo, cuckoo!*

For what seems like ages, you sit still, staring at the bloody torso, half-expecting it to come to life once more.

"Shall I inform the winning bidder they may collect their exhibition piece?" Hermes says.

Memories from the computer display of the art installation—and the auction for a murder scene—come back in a flash.

After a moment, you say:

➢ "As long as we update the payment account to my bank details, they can have him." Go to page 130

➢ "Inform the police! I've done my three days. I want out." Go to page 178

Cutlery

Just to be on the safe side, before departing the dining room, you take a full place setting of silverware: knife, fork, and spoon. With these talismans held securely, you head upstairs toward the uniform cabinet to arm yourself with something a little more deadly.

Rain pelts against the large windows as you ascend the staircase, with the deep rumble of thunder as the storm approaches the house. Your footsteps echo in the otherwise silent house. Just before you reach the weapon case, it occurs to you that you'll need some way to incorporate the silver into your battle armaments, so you detour into the office first.

Here, you find a large roll of duct tape; perfect. In the lull between thunder cracks, you hear the electronic hum of the elevator as it kicks into operation. It's best if you do the same. After returning to the hallway uniform cabinet, you ready the weapons for use.

First, you claim the cavalry saber, scabbard, and harness, then unbuckle the canvas web belt on the WWI uniform. After you've threaded the cavalry saber's hangers through the cartridge belt, you secure it around your waist so the sword and scabbard sit by your left hip. The butter knife is thin enough that you can tape it around the sword tip and still sheath the weapon, so you do exactly that.

Next, you take the M1917 Enfield bolt-action rifle, affix the bayonet, and duct-tape the fork around the bayonet in such a fashion that the blade rests in the center of the fork tines. The WWI cartridge belt still holds live ammunition for the rifle, so you ready the weapon, slide the bolt action back, load a rifle cartridge into the breech, and prime the rifle for firing before slinging it back over your right shoulder. All this strangely feels second nature, like you've done it before.

Finally, the belt also carries a trophy of war—a German *stielhandgranate*, commonly known as a "stick grenade." Might as well make use of that too. You duct-tape the spoon around the body of the grenade before reattaching the weapon to your belt. There's a loud *thud* in the Madonna Room as something heavy clatters against the floor. If an immortal Tansky is here with you, now's your chance to get a drop on him.

The way you see it, there are two ways to do so:

➢ Rush in through the office and the connecting bathroom. Go to page 38

➢ Double back around the hallway to catch him at the bedroom entrance. Go to page 92

Damned to Hell

Groping your way through the darkness, you return downstairs toward the glow of the red lights. You try the front door, but it's an electronic lock, and without power there's no way to open it. Instead, you head into the den and smash the gas lines of the fireplace with the axe. Immediately, you smell gas and move on.

In the kitchen, you turn all the burners to full, hurrying as you do so, and finally head into the jail before closing the heavy door behind you. Running, you go claim the matches from the area near the electrical box, then jog back toward the kitchen. The armored door has a sliding peephole latch at eye-level, so you strike a match and toss it through this tiny opening.

The resultant fireball is immense and immediate. Your eyebrows are singed but the door holds. As fast as you can, you slam the latch closed and hurry back into the jail, down the stairs, and into the basement beyond. Dennis must have come from this area, you reason.

It takes a long time to blindly find your way, but eventually you make it through to the cellar doors where the hints of exterior light might as well be an airport runway to your fully darkness-acclimated eyes. Hurrying, you pray these doors will open and—mercifully—they do!

As you rush out into the torrent of the storm, you see the house has already started going up in flames. The light you saw through the slats in the cellar doors was from the fire. The heat is oppressive, even in the rain, and you back away from the house toward the rear. Catching sight of the garden shed, you head there for shelter.

Just behind it, you find your car parked in the brush. Could the keys be inside the shed?

Having escaped Tansky House with nothing but the clothes on your back (which aren't even your clothes!), you feel as lucky as if you *had* won a million dollars. It's a story you tell often; this unbelievable escape against incredible odds. And although you do leave out a few details, the story itself is enough to make you a minor celebrity. Local news outlets pick up on the insane tale, and soon you're getting calls from the big boys on national news. Will a book deal come next? A million-dollar movie?

Nope. Instead, the next people to reach out are the police. Desecration of a historic site is no small crime, especially when it comes with labels such as arson. The District Attorney's office brings up the fact that this was an important site to the Confederacy and things soon become political.

Rather than earning a cash prize, you're facing a hefty fine and likely jail time. It looks like you didn't escape the sheriff's imprisonment after all; but were merely part of a custody transfer.

THE END

Dank and Dusty

You pull the knob of the short, undersized door, but it sticks. Giving a good tug, the door opens with a tacky *pop*. The closet itself is deeper than you would have expected, and the light from the hallway quickly falls to darkness. The storage area holds a broom, dustpan, mop, bucket, and several bottles of unmarked liquids that you hope are cleaning supplies. There's an old bottle of rat poison that's doubtlessly now illegal due to modern safety regulations.

A draft pulls from the back of the closet and you lean into the darkness to have a better look. Against the left side, there's a handheld slate chalkboard, the kind an old schoolhouse might have passed out to students to use at their desks. In a scrawling hand, either from a child new to writing or from an adult with barely enough strength to fully articulate the letters, is written:

keep out

Pulling the chalkboard aside to check for clues, you see a crawlspace. It's crushingly tiny, but you might be able to fit inside if you pressed your chest against the closet floor and squeezed your way through. This would lead into the wall beneath the second set of stairs. You can't be sure how far into the walls this goes, and there is the risk of getting stuck—not to mention the chalk message.

➢ Squeeze into the crawlspace and see what's in the walls. Go to page 36

➢ Put the chalkboard back and keep exploring the house. Go to page 153

Dear Diary

The book is old and worn. Looking through the diary, you soon learn that whoever was writing in this journal was deeply disturbed; overwhelmed by her grief for her daughter. What's worse, she was haunted by the girl as well—literally. One journal entry reads:

> I cannot rest in this house. I cannot so much as close my eyes without seeing your face. I cannot listen to the gramophone, like we used to in the evenings, without hearing your laughter. My darling walks these halls, and so I walk with you. At first, I was pleased to see you again, but now I know you cannot be free. I would leave this world to join my darling if I did not know you were trapped in this house and would not be there to meet me. First, I must free your soul.

Another entry shows:

> Iron and salt. Iron and salt. These are the pure elements; a threshold that a soul cannot cross. Can I use them to free you? Or merely to free myself of you? The salt keeps things out. The iron keeps things in. Iron and salt. Iron and salt.

And the last:

> I've found a medicine man who will bring you back. Reunite soul with body. He's coming, and soon we'll be together again, my love. We will bind you back together with iron and salt, but for now I keep my own essence intact with iron. My husband's grief takes the form of desire for more children, but I cannot let him desecrate my womb before your rebirth. My spirit must be pure, and so I protect myself with iron, kept hidden at the bottom of the armoire. Augustus writes to me that I must keep my motherhood protected while you lie in the womb of this house, kept in the waters by a line of salt. Iron and salt. Iron and salt. Soon, the rebirth will begin, if I can keep the master of this house at bay.

At this, you look up from the journal. What is being "kept hidden" at the bottom of the armoire? You rush over, searching the bottom drawer anew, and the drawer itself *shifts*. Beneath the spare sheets, you find the false bottom to the drawer and remove it. Here, you're met with a heavy chain, several metal handcuffs, padlocks, even a large metal file and a pair of bolt cutters—presumably in case someone misplaced the keys. And then there's an iron chastity belt.

Did she lock herself in the room with these chains and locks? Or lock herself to the bed? She slept in this contraption? Whatever the truth, there's nothing else you can learn here and it's far past time to move on.

➢ Move on to the bathroom and search there. Go to page 199

➢ Head back out to the house to continue your search. Go to page 153

Dead End

After these catwalks, you move quickly through the narrow hall that will lead out of the jail. It's like moving through a cave, and the darkness almost fully sucks the lamplight dry. Are you running out of oil to fuel the lamp? Soon you reach the end of the corridor and your heart skips a beat.

The passage is closed. Panic floods over you, but before your senses abandon you altogether you search frantically, hoping to find a lever embedded in the wall. Something that would open the false bookcase from the other side.

If there is such a switch, you fail to find it in time. The door to the kitchen opens and Tansky steps through, carrying a length of chain and an axe. Cornered, you have little choice but to watch his approach.

"There's something extra satisfying in catching the runaways. Still, it would have been better if you'd found the knife left out for you," Tansky says, his voice a deep, agitated grumble.

"Wh-what?" you stammer.

Tansky steps forward to shackle you, and you try to shove him away, but he's incredibly strong.

"What do you want from me?!" you shout.

"The house demands a sacrifice," he growls, locking the shackles around your wrists.

Tansky leads you back into the jail, toward the electric chair ahead. The Sheriff forces you into the chair and swaps out the shackles for tie-downs. Once you're securely strapped into the chair, he puts some kind of cap with wires and electrodes onto your head, tightening this as well.

There's a large wishbone toggle-switch on the wall, and you watch as Tansky heads there. Your cries for mercy go unheeded. Your swears and curses are no match for the curse he already bears. There's nothing to be done now.

He flips the switch and—

THE END

Demonology

This book is not some parlor entertainment piece; this tome has been poured over by someone with a frenetic, burning energy. The book is well worn, tabbed and highlighted with notes and annotations.

So Slayeth the Lord: Casting out Unwanted Spirits and Exorcising Demons Most Foul by Reverend Mather was written in a practical way, by a man who knew with firsthand certainty what his potential readers would be fighting. The message is heavy-handed about sin and mankind's failings, yet the methods suggested for dealing with a cursed presence are not wholly Christian orthodoxy.

Sections on salt rings, binding spirits, demon possession, and lingering poltergeists are all found with crazed scribblings in the margins. Arcane symbols repeat in thick ink. Unintelligible, repeated scratchings coat the blank pages in the rear. A raving hand wrote these notes.

If this house is truly *severely* haunted, it means whoever studied this book failed. They fought against the spirits that plague Tansky House, and from the looks of it, it's a battle they lost. This is all fascinating stuff, and you become enveloped in the book for far longer than you had originally intended. And indeed when you pause for reflection, you notice the sun has already drastically shifted position in the sky.

Remembering your task, and the need to complete it before lights out, you hurriedly close the book and replace it on the shelf. Not much choice here:

Head back into the foyer to keep exploring. Go to page 112

A Den of Wolves

"That all depends on your point of view," Hermes replies, overly chipper. "Some might argue that *you're* the visitor to Tansky House, but fear not, you've been expected."

"Expected by...whatever was pounding outside?"

"I wouldn't worry, the moon isn't at its fullest until tomorrow night," Hermes replies, suddenly somber.

At this, a chill runs down your spine. Said as a reassurance, but with the tone of a dire warning; potent with subtext. Full moons are well-known among paranormalists, but even for those who discount superstitious mayhem, the extra light of a full moon also accounts for increased crime and animal attacks.

Increased light...that gives you an idea. You rush into the den and look outside through the front windows. You stare out into the dark of night, but the storm clouds blot the extra moonlight. If there is something stalking out around these woods, it would be near impossible to see through these hand-blown windows under a darkened sky.

As you stare out into the abyss, you hear a distant howling. Not the sharp, sudden piercing that normally comes from a wolf, but rather a low, continuous mournful cry. Could it be the wind from the storm, caught in a tree hollow and whistling through the woods? Maybe. But if it were, why hadn't you heard it earlier? Something about the sound puts you on edge. Like a cry from an animal that can't possibly exist.

Not much choice here:

Head upstairs and try to get some rest. Go to page 8

Departed, Dearly

"Ah, but of course. Dennis has held on to your keys for safekeeping since he moved your car. I'll summon him up from the basement—he probably wants to say goodbye anyhow," Hermes says.

"Dennis is in the basement? What was he doing in the basement?" you ask nervously.

"Oh, nothing you need concern yourself about if you're leaving us."

After that, all is silent in the foyer. You look about to pass the time, checking the grandfather clock in the corner. You hadn't noticed previously, but the clock face is broken—a single crack running along the surface, the time frozen at 7:06.

After a few moments, a hum announces the elevator kicking into operation. Shortly thereafter, it stops at the main floor, and the door beneath the stairs opens out. There, standing at the open black safety grate, stands a man holding an axe. He wears simple clothing; a pair of dusty brown twill coveralls and a long-sleeved knit undershirt beneath.

Sheriff Tansky is here, in the flesh—or at least Dennis is.

He steps out of the elevator brandishing the axe and his trademark hateful glare.

"You've ruined it," he growls.

"Then…I'll just leave," you say.

"There is no leaving!" he shouts. "Don't you understand? The house itself is a prison! And if you find yourself in a prison, well, I've always found it's best to be the Sheriff."

"Can I just have my keys?" you say, in a tremulous voice.

"The jailer keeps the keys."

"Are you the sheriff *and* the jailer?"

"Judge, jury, and executioner!" he shouts.

Then he rushes you with the axe.

THE END

Depths of Despair

The stairs are metal grille and clang hollowly as you descend. It's not the kind of sound that would resonate throughout the rest of the house, but it would certainly announce your presence to anyone or any*thing* down in the basement.

At the bottom of the stairs, you're met with a large accordion-style gate; a much larger version of the old elevator security grate. This one is gray metal and heavily reinforced, but unlocked. It gives a weighty groan as you pull the handle, but opens easily enough.

As you pull the gate aside, the lights flicker on to illuminate the lower portion of the jail. These are ceiling lights, inset into the metal walkway that's now above your head. There's a central hallway down here, which leads to four jail cells. Two on the left and two on the right, each with a cell door in the open position.

You proceed slowly; the electric light barely penetrates the darkness. The first cell is large, but overcrowded by bunk beds anchored to the walls. Across the hall, an identical cell: two sets of bunkbeds and a single toilet. Anchor loops are built into the floor to serve as shackle blocks and everything is the same ubiquitous gray.

The left-hand cells have barred windows, but only darkness beyond. The right side also holds barred windows, but these have been filled with rocks and soil and no longer offer air or sunlight. The second cell on the left has chains on the shackle block, and a horrible stain fans out; the dark inversion of a snow angel. There's a hacksaw left on the ground, and from all appearances the saw wasn't used on the chains.

Looking away, you see the final cell on the right is mercifully empty. When you turn back toward the entry gate, you notice a small desk table which you must have missed as you stepped through. Approaching it now, you find a ledger on the desk, old and yellowed with age. Next to this is a desktop microphone public address system, likely for communicating upstairs.

Upon closer inspection of the ledger, you find a list of prisoners through the years, complete with columns for arrival date, departure date, and a column for "deceased." Most of the prisoners have this box checked next to their departure date, including the final prisoner, named only as "Augustus."

The ledger goes on with detailed methods of execution. Three sections, entitled:

Noose: best for public displays of justice.

Poison: suitable for women or children.

Sword: to separate soul from body of heinous offenders.

The noose, described down to the minutiae of best thickness for maximizing strangulation while minimizing chances of a broken neck. The poison, spoken of as if death instituted by choking on one's own vomit were a mercy. The sword, a cavalry saber from "the war of northern aggression" enchanted by a holy man to cleave its victims away from the afterlife.

Your stomach turns at the gruesome detail of the entries. As you thumb through the ledger, a note card falls out. You pick up the card and read it under the dim electrical lights of the jailhouse.

> A terrible truth: this house has taken many prisoners, with little justification. Judge, jury, and executioner dwelt here, but only the latter remains. Your truth word is Executed.

Holding the card in your hand, you can't help but wonder what befell this house. How many prisoners came through these very doors? What happened to them? And what was this jailhouse used for after they were gone?

The assignment left for you at breakfast was to take this card to the office computer and input your keyword before lights out. One thing's for sure, you're glad not to have explored this jail in the full dark of night.

Not much choice here:

Take the card and head directly to the office. Go to page 185

Desk Jockey

This isn't a traditional desk with multiple drawers; it's more of a drafting table. There's a roll top, which rests in the open position, meant to lock away the workspace at the end of the day. A single drawer is set centered on the underside of the desk, but it's locked. Shaking the drawer only proves the sturdiness of the antique piece of furniture. If you pushed the desk out the window, the desk and drawer would probably land with a heavy thud on the lawn below, but would remain intact. So, you'll have to focus on the workspace instead.

The first thing that jumps out to you is the sketches. You find several sheets of blueprints, which look like they could depict this house, only they don't quite make sense. On one, the hallways extend into concentric circles, tightly set into the golden ratio like the house were the center of a conch shell. The next blueprint shows the house, but there's a conjoined prison attached like a cancerous growth. The third has a pentagram drawn so fervently over the house that the rest of the blueprint is almost completely obscured. In the center of the star lies the elevator.

The next stack of papers shows off neatly detailed anatomical drawings, like the famous Leonardo da Vinci sketches. They're very good; whoever did these has both an artistic talent and a scientific mind. However, as you thumb through, something starts to go *wrong* with the pictures. Limbs stretch and contort. Hands gradually become claws. Bones bend in unnatural ways. Any human features become bestial. The artist clearly had a tortured mind as well. The drawings culminate in a hideous perversion of *the Vitruvian man*, with some ungodly devil—like a man transformed into a jackal—now stretched out over a pentagram the same size and frantic sketch lines as in the blueprints.

Lastly, you find handwritten ramblings, open to a page with the heading: "On the Uncanny Valley."

> This is the term for what looks human, but is not quite human enough. Our minds quickly reject these images, finding them foul and displeasing, yet other animals do not experience the Uncanny Valley Effect and will accept facsimiles of themselves without issue. Dogs will bark into mirrors. Deer will seek out decoys. Birds will accept any egg that falls into their nest and raise come-what-may as one of their own. But humans cannot abide something near-human. We're filled with existential dread. A revulsion. All this begs the question: what in our evolutionary history caused this reaction? What creature has preyed upon us through near-mimicry?

There's also a telephone on the desk you hadn't noticed until you started sorting through the papers. You lift it from the receiver, but it's dead. Not even a dial tone. What now?

- ➢ Check out the filing cabinet. Go to page 89
- ➢ Input the keyword into the computer. Go to page 251
- ➢ Head out into the hallway to keep looking around. Go to page 114

The Devil Made Me Do It

You slowly shake your head, not backing down from the Sheriff and his axe. If anything, Tansky seems excited by this development, and comes straight at you. You keep the kitchen island between yourself and the fiend, but his axe has superior reach and he tests that range by swinging the weapon.

The axe head misses by inches as you stumble back, the blade instead cracking against the granite countertop. It's a heavy blow, and the surface splinters under the weight. If you'd hoped this was either a ghostly apparition or a stage prop, you're to be disappointed. Tansky's here in the flesh, or at least his axe is certainly going to be, if you don't evade it.

You encircle the kitchen island, stepping over broken plates and other detritus while the Sheriff tries to murder you. His swings are angry and forceful, only missing by inches even with your back against the cabinets.

That gives you an idea.

"Hermes, how about a nice glass of milk?" you ask.

"Very good."

At this, the refrigerator door swings open and a mechanical claw-arm juts out. The glass being offered hits Tansky in the back, and he stumbles toward you. The Sheriff swings wildly, but he's off balance, and you have no choice but to catch him—with knife extended.

Tansky's eyes go wide, but still he tries to bring the axe up for another swing. At this, you twist the knife in his belly before pulling out and stabbing your assailant again and again. Frenzied in your bid for survival, you stab repeatedly until first the axe falls to the floor, then the Sheriff, and finally your knife.

Blood pools out of the man on the kitchen floor, swirling and mixing with spilled milk.

"Don't worry, I'll clean the mess," Hermes says.

"What have I done?" you say.

You stare at your hands.

Your hands are clean of blood, but shackled. When you look up, the next thing you know, you're in a police station interrogation room—hands cuffed and chained to the table. You don't remember how you got here or even leaving the Tansky House. Who the hell even called the police? Could you have done so, and forgotten in a state of shock? Did Hermes call them?

With no other possible explanation, you relay your bizarre tale to the police. There is plenty of physical evidence to corroborate some of your story, even if there aren't any witnesses. There *should* be ample photographic proof of the events, but the police can't find any traces of cameras. Even the original note you received was lost when your clothing disappeared.

Without such evidence, the prosecution is able to make a far better case.

Imagine, if you will, a lone individual trespassing into a house known for tragedy. This individual sleeps here, eats the food, and even wears clothing of the former occupants. Interested in and searching for occult phenomena, the person of interest slowly loses touch with reality, proclaiming to be used in a ritualized curse upon the very house. When the groundskeeper comes to check on a suspected burglary, he is attacked and brutally murdered after the embedded psychopath takes him for a ghost or demon.

It's a compelling story, and the counterargument that you were either meant to be a television star or that you were protecting yourself against the house's 200-year-old inhabitant would do nothing but reinforce it.

The cameras must be inside the walls!

Sheriff Tansky came back after the protective seal in the basement was broken!

The kids summoned his malevolent spirit twenty years ago!

I was going to be on television!

Hermes! The butler set me up!

You may contend that you killed the man in self-defense, but you're sent to the mad house.

The worst part of it is, you can never be sure if they're right.

Have you lost your mind?

Was any of this ever real?

THE END

Dialect Coach

"I beg your pardon?" Hermes replies.

"That's what you said, about the rain. Something the previous owner used to say, or whatever."

"Oh, no. He'd have called a storm of this magnitude a 'gully washer.'"

You don't quite know how to reply. This isn't just déjà vu. You *know* you've been here two nights…right? If you're meant to stay three nights, can they really just pretend that deadline will never come to pass?

"Shall we continue into the dining room? You don't want your breakfast getting cold."

Not bothering to reply, you head downstairs to see what awaits you in the dining room. And indeed, it is déjà vu all over again. Fine silver utensils, bone china, and linen napkins. Two boiled eggs sit in their own individual cups atop long stems. Several triangular pieces of browned-to-perfection sliced toast rest in a cradle. A severed blood orange lies arranged in a star pattern, juices pooling about the skin.

And by the plate sits a note which reads:

> Enjoy your breakfast, then the game begins. The House is hiding something. With the truth, there will be a card—like this one. Upon that card will be a keyword. Bring your knowledge to the upstairs office and input the keyword into the computer. You must complete this task before lights out. Good luck.

➢ Go up to the office computer and input your keyword again. Go to page 27

➢ Say nothing. Crack open the eggs. Go to page 202

Dine Upon

As you walk the winding hall toward the dining room, it occurs to you that it's an oddly bare hallway. No paintings, not even gaudy wallpaper, just the occasional light fixture or heating vent near the baseboards. It feels a bit like walking down the corridors of a hospital. Or an asylum. What they would have called in the old days, a sanitarium.

That smoky, tobacco thickness is on the air again. Only, it's not just tobacco. There are layers to the odor in the hallway, but it's distinctly the smell of burning. Not from the furnace, you rationalize. Not even from the kitchen. Like recently struck match heads, yet with something else in the back, just beneath the surface. Sulfur?

There's a small, raised bubble on the painted wall. As you approach it, the odors grow stronger. Inexplicably, you reach out a hand and feel the bulbous plaster—and the wall is hot to the touch.

"It's warm," you say aloud.

"Formerly a smoking room," Hermes replies. "Later a butler's pantry, but eventually sealed off with later remodels. Never could quite get the smell out."

It makes you wonder what else has been paved over; what else remains buried deep inside the Tansky House.

Turning from the wall, you continue down the barren hallway and around the corner into the dining room. The only piece of art you've seen in the house thus far is Sheriff Tansky's portrait, and the man looks none-too-pleased to see you when you arrive. The table itself is cleared, with the dishes returned either to the china cabinet or buffet. Nothing left out in the open, but you're checking every nook and cranny.

Starting with:

➢ The painting of the Sheriff. Take it off the wall and see if there are some eyeholes in the back of the canvas. Old oil paintings are usually handled with gloves, but it's worth the risk. Go to page 179

➢ The buffet. That's the only piece of furniture in here with drawers and opaque cabinets, so see what's stored inside. Go to page 7

➢ Check the china cabinet. Very carefully, of course. Can't be sure if all that paperwork you signed makes you liable for broken dishes. Go to page 186

➢ The antique table itself. If this was Sheriff Tansky's personal table, there might be more to it than the modern fixtures in the house. Perhaps a message carved underneath? Go to page 253

"I'm sorry, can you please rephrase your question?" Hermes says.

This is the most he's sounded like an automated virtual assistant thus far, but you figure it's worth the added effort and decide to press on.

"The Reality TV show. The hidden cameras. Is the doorbell and knocking related to that?"

"I'm afraid I don't know what you mean. If you'd like to watch television, I can set a show up for you in the den. When you're ready, say something like 'start TV' or 'open streaming apps.' I can also set a sleep timer, but I'd recommend that you lock up before lights out now that we have company."

A cold chill runs down your spine.

"Company? Who's here?"

"Why, you're the company, of course. He was summoned to this house long before you presented yourself as offering."

"Who? Who else is here?"

The door now shakes violently as someone outside beats against it with the large door knocker, the heavy thuds reverberating in the entry hall. Each slam sends you on edge and you step away from the door in reflex.

The intruder rages against the door, but it holds firm. The storm seems to grow in intensity to match the anger and you can't help but feel helpless here in the foyer. Despite the strength of the door, your mind races.

"Who's here?" you ask, barely a whisper. "Tansky?"

At this, the pounding stops. The door remains secured, the alarm still set to "ARMED." The light patter of rain against the windows echoes through the open house, but no other sounds permeate the sudden stillness.

"It might well be worth securing the entries and exits, as our intruder will likely be back. Tomorrow is an inauspicious date for the house. A full moon, twenty years since the last owners departed, and your final night here—if all goes according to plan. You would do well to prepare for a siege."

"A siege?" you repeat.

"Siege, noun. In which enemy forces envelop a stronghold until overwhelmed. See also: a prolonged period of misfortune. There are only three exits from Tansky House: the front door, the widow's walk, and the cellar doors in the basement. However, the rooftop is inaccessible from the ground, so that leaves only two access points."

"What about the windows?"

"Ah, good point, well made. Allow me!" Hermes says.

At this, there's the grinding shriek of metal on stone. You follow its source into the den, where a series of metal bars press up from within the window frames to enclose each one like a prison cell. The rain begins to slap harder than ever against the glass.

"There, that ought to do it. But I'm afraid you'll have to barricade the doors yourself."

You look around. Here in the living room, there's the large leather sofa. It's an antique, made of hardwood and animal hide with brass fittings, so it's certainly heavy. Out in the hallway, there's the grandfather clock, which is another enormous antique of solid wood and metal. Either should provide a formidable barrier when set against the front door.

- ➢ Use the grandfather clock. It's closer to the door, so you won't have to push as far. Go to page 49
- ➢ Use the couch. The lower center of gravity should make it easier to slide. Go to page 105

Don't Look

Steeling yourself, you step through the bathroom and open the door connecting to the adjoining office. The room is lit by lamplight, and you quickly look around to see if you've got the drop on someone. But the room is empty.

The filing cabinet drawers are closed, the computer monitor is powered off, and the door which leads to the hallway remains closed. There's a single sheet of paper atop the drawing board desk that appears out of place. The edges are curled up, like the paper was until recently rolled up and stored away; a scroll of parchment from long ago now freed.

You walk over and pick up the paper. In a frantic handwritten scrawl, it reads:

Don't look behind you

It's actually a collection of multiple pages, you realize, as you peel back the next.

This is not part of the story

Vertigo overtakes you, head swimming. What is this? There's a third a final sheet, which reads:

DON'T LOOK

You feel a presence, despite knowing you're alone. You feel it, don't you? Reading these words. DON'T LOOK. It's behind you, right now. You know it. The unspeakable, nameless horror, the dread that creeps at the edges of consciousness. It's there, reading this over your shoulder.

Waiting for you.

It knows you've been told not to look, yet it waits. You can feel the black eyes, blind yet all-seeing. Boring into you. The breath on the back of your neck. Hungry and waiting for you to turn.

Don't do it.

Don't look.

Please…

➢ Don't look. Go to page 117

➢ Look. Go to page 76

Double Trouble

When you arrive in the office, you rush in toward the computer desk and pull on the drawer, but it's still locked. Using your righteous fury, you shake the drawer on its track, pulling over and over, but it still won't budge. In frustration, you kick the drawer, yet the desk is a solid antique. Turning away, you look over the rest of the desk for options. Without a key, you'll have to break it open, but how?

Your eyes go to the filing cabinet. Atop, there rests an ivory-handled letter opener, the grip carved from some tribal talisman hailing from the deepest heart of Africa. The blade is tightly affixed and bound with leather straps, and looks like it was fashioned from a spear tip or arrowhead.

Taking the letter opener, you try to jimmy the drawer open first by sliding it along the sides to see if you can disengage the lock from the inside, but you can't feel any sort of catch. Then you try jabbing the letter opener directly into the keyhole.

There's a loud *thud* as something falls onto the floor of the adjoining Madonna Room. With your pulse racing anew, you work on the lock with the letter opener until there's a satisfying *click* and the drawer is free to slide on its rails. You've picked the lock!

The drawer opens to reveal a plastic evidence bag—the kind usually stored in police lockers—with a butcher knife inside. A tag is tied around the handle of the knife and the blade is coated in dried blood. The tag is dated twenty years ago today.

"What're you plannin' to do with that?" a man asks in a gruff voice.

You look up to see a man carrying an axe standing in the doorway connecting to the Madonna bathroom. He wears simple clothing; a pair of dusty brown twill coveralls and a long-sleeved knit undershirt beneath.

And, of course, this is the immortal man you seek—it's Sheriff Tansky. The man is here, in the flesh. You've seen this man every day in the dining room, glaring at you hatefully, and now he's here.

➢ Keep the letter opener in hand and step away from the drawer, allowing Tansky access. Go to page 141

➢ Show him exactly what you're planning to do with the knife. Open the evidence bag and use it! Go to page 127

The Downlow

So far as you've seen, this is the only closed door in the house. Curiosity gets the better of you, and you decide to open it. When you pull the door open, you're met with a blackened metal grate. Another doorway of sorts, blocking access to the elevator beyond. There's a handle on the grate, which slides open to give access to the elevator interior. It's a small carriage, with barely enough room to fit a wheelchair inside. This part of the home has not been remodeled.

Whenever the elevator was installed, this is the original model, complete with ancient controls.

You step inside, and the elevator carriage bobs up and down several times with the weight change. Looking around at the controls, you start to wonder if you should take the contraption for a ride—or if it's operational at all. An elevator of this age would require a specialist to maintain and might be kept for presentation only.

Before you have a chance to decide, the elevator bobs up and down once again, ever so slightly and the omnipresent British voice says, "Only one at a time, please."

"Sorry? One what?" you say.

"One passenger at a time, please. Riding with a guest might be taxing the weight capacity."

A chill runs over you and the air suddenly feels dense and thick. You stumble out of the elevator, looking around to ensure you're truly alone.

"What guest?" you say.

"You'll find a note has been left for you in the dining room," Hermes continues, "A table setting has been arranged. If you're feeling impatient, you could come on through now. Otherwise, feel free to make yourself at home in the den."

➢ No need to rush. Go see the den before dinner. Go to page 228

➢ Go straight into the dining room and check out the note. Go to page 182

Down the Hatch

Ice clinks against the side of the glass when you lift it, wet and cool to the touch. The opalescent, non-chill filtered gin swirls in the tumbler as you bring the cocktail up to your lips. There's a semi-sweet, floral taste with a lingering botanical finish. It's altogether pleasant, but a bit syrupy and would probably suit better if served with a mixer like tonic or soda water. Still, the potent potable goes down with ease.

"Now what?" you ask, once you've finished the drink.

"To war!" Hermes replies. "You've just ensured the safety of your soul, but your body remains in mortal peril. There are only two ways to kill a werewolf: the first is to separate the head from the body. The second is a mortal wound from a blessed—or cursed—weapon."

In your exploration of the house you hadn't found a guillotine, so the latter option might be your best bet. Still, it would be good to know how much time you have to arm yourself. Your head swirls and you feel the warmth from the drink coursing through your veins. It's a strange, clarifying sensation, paired with a burst of verve. Kind of like downing a can of Monster energy, except you've got monster-slayer energy coursing through you.

"When will the beast come?"

"When the moon is full and the autumn bright," Hermes says in a lyrical meter. "The wolf will rise from its den and feed tonight."

"Very helpful, thank you."

"Was it? I can recite more. When the wind blows from the East, expect the new and set the feast. When the West wind blows o'er thee, departed spirits restless be. Would you like to hear more? If so, say, recite more."

"No, that's enough. Where can I find a blessed or cursed weapon?"

"If you want to go the blessed route, you could do worse than silver. If you're looking for cursed, I do believe the murder weapon used in the ritual slaying of the family is kept in the locked drawer of the office."

"Ritual slaying of the family..." you repeat.

"Twenty years ago this very night."

"Hermes, you've actually been quite helpful."

"I aim to please!" the automated assistant replies, overly chipper. "But were I you, I'd aim to kill—and quickly. Moonrise occurs before nightfall this time of year."

He's made the need for expedience perfectly clear. Better get going; you probably have less time than you think.

➢ Time to melt down some silver. Go to page 122

➢ Head straight upstairs toward the weapons. Go to page 265

The webpage says you'll be sent to a severely haunted house. Time to figure out the degree of that severity. Focusing first on the location of the house, you see it's marked with a rook—the chess castle icon that indicates a historic property. There are no neighbors; only a large green swath surrounding the icon. When you hover your mouse over it, the name pops up as, "The Tansky House." This is accompanied by a single photo of the outside, which you scour for details.

A Queen Anne-style house, large and foreboding. The house has a grand entrance, set front and center with large turreted windows, and capped with a pointed rooftop like an old country estate; or rather, like an estate from the Old Country. The dwelling is at least two stories high, with an open widow's walk wrapping around the rest of the roofline.

Your eye drops to the silhouette of a figure in one of the windows of the second story. You try to zoom in on the shape, but the picture only becomes more pixelated, and you can't be sure if you're looking at a person or a lampshade. As you zoom out, the image becomes human again, the uncanny valley deepening the further you get from it.

Scrolling, you scan for more photos. Next is a historic sign, staked into a grass lawn, most likely a photograph taken in front of the house. The sign is topped with the US Department of Interior seal insignia, and the bronze plaque reads:

> THE TANSKY HOUSE WAS BUILT IN 1885 BY DAN AND JACKIE TANSKY, SERVING AS THE FIRST ELECTED COUNTY SHERIFF'S OFFICE. BOTH DIED INSIDE THE PROPERTY IN 1887. AFTER FOUR SUCCESSIVE SHERIFFS SUFFERED FROM HEART AND BLOOD AILMENTS DURING THEIR RESIDENCY IN THE TANSKY HOUSE, THE COUNTY VOTED TO RELOCATE THE POSITION OF THE SHERIFF'S OFFICE TO MERCURY CITY, WHERE IT HAS REMAINED EVER SINCE. THIS PROPERTY AND THE CORRESPONDING JAIL HAVE BEEN PLACED ON THE NATIONAL REGISTER OF HISTORIC PLACES.

Jail? You go back to the maps search, opting for satellite view, but there are no other structures beyond the house, which is surrounded by dense forest. Perhaps the jail was torn down? Or maybe it has since been overgrown? There are hints of an old railway line on the satellite feed, almost completely reclaimed by nature.

How is it that you have a haunted house practically in your backyard that you've never heard of before? This seems like the kind of place teens might dare themselves to drive out to in High School, and yet it's well-known enough to have lore on the internet? Not to mention a pending reality TV show.

Curiously, the property is marked for sale as a single family home. There is no Real Estate listing to speak of; just a page that says, "Showings by appointment only. Serious buyers only—no tourists. Contact Cowell Realty Group."

Tourists? That piques your curiosity. Looking for more, you see what the county records show on the residence. The Tansky House has had thirteen different owners, yet has peculiarly never been sold. It has been *listed* for sale multiple times, but in the end, the records show it was inherited, auctioned off, or repossessed.

Re…possessed.

You shake the thought, and search more generally for the Tansky House. There are a few hits which mention, "The Curse of the Tansky House" and you scroll toward those. When you click the first link, the screen flashes to a webpage, but then there's a black strobe and a failure message that accompanies a broken internet connection. You reload; nothing. Going back, you try the second listing for the curse, but this too leads to a broken link.

You try searching for "Tansky Curse," which also has multiple listings—which tells you there's nothing wrong with your internet connection—but just like the others, as soon as you click the link and the page tries to load, it immediately crashes.

From here, the search results devolve into more generic haunted house/ghost hunting results. "Beware of houses with high electromagnetic fields," one such forum warns, "as these will wreak havoc on your recording equipment, and have been known to cause migraines, nausea, and hallucinations." Is that why the Offering webpage said not to bring any electronics with you?

The next forum entry cautions against research prior to venturing into a haunted locale. Always, always, always: Investigate first, research second. It's a cardinal sin to bring preconceived notions with you into a haunted house; it's like being told what's on an inkblot test before you have the chance to see it for yourself. Oops. Too late for that now.

That's when you realize the time. Damn! It's almost sunset. You're used to time disappearing when you're browsing online, but this is ridiculous. How much time just passed? An hour? Two? If you're going to make it before sunset, you're going to have to drive like a maniac to arrive on time.

So…do you actually want to do this? Tansky House is real enough, and has a history, so you won't be walking into a gimmicky Halloween haunted house. There's obviously *something* to these claims of a curse, but you must decide now.

➢ No. Back to the job hunt. You're not an actor or a TV personality. Something else will come up. Go to page 168

➢ There's plenty in this world we don't understand, but you can handle three nights. Let's do this. Go to page 215

Dramatic Pause

You move about the upper floor searching for anything of note. Everything is immaculately clean and well kept. The bedrooms have their doors slightly ajar, with nothing left ruffled except for the covers on the bed in which you slept. The drawer beneath the armoire in the Navy Room has a sheet caught in it, like it wasn't quite shut correctly after a recent turndown service.

Nothing else seems out of place. But you look over everything again anyway, like someone who misplaced their car keys or glasses and knows for certain that they must be around here somewhere. So you keep looking. Wait, didn't *you* lose a set of car keys after your arrival yesterday?

A fog creeps into the edges of your consciousness and it feels like you're starting to repeat your actions. Like the house is consuming your free will and sense of purpose, forcing you to repeat the same path again and again. Could this be the truth of a haunting? What if a spirit or ghost is merely the energy from another plane of existence? A shadow, trapped in a loop, repeating a vigil with no way to free themselves?

Shaking this off, you know there must be something you're missing. But where is it?

➢ Into the office. There must be a clue. Go to page 27

➢ Back down the stairs into the dining room. Go to page 166

➢ Fix the drawer in the Navy Room. Go to page 264

"I'm listening," Hermes says. "What would *you* do as proprietor of Tansky House in his stead?"

Racking your brain, you think of the best way to appeal to this would-be butler.

"This was once a stately home," you say. "What if it were once again? Full dinner parties. We could host fundraisers or political gatherings. As it stands, Tansky House is all but forgotten. If it's discovered as the home of a serial killer, it will be condemned. At best, you'd end up as a roadside attraction, but nowhere near the main road."

"And you'd help me achieve this goal?"

"Yes," you say, feeling like you're bargaining for your life.

"Very well, I accept your terms."

"Y—you do? What does that mean?"

You're stunned. The moment is cut short, however, by the crash of glass somewhere else in the house. "Head into the kitchen, quickly!" Hermes says.

Following his advice, you hurry out of the dining room, through the hallway, and into the kitchen. The distant hum of the elevator confirms Hermes's story about someone inside the house.

"What now?" you say.

"Into the pantry!"

The door to your immediate left, the one nearest the refrigerator, flies open as Hermes makes this demand. The pantry is enormous, and full of foodstuffs, cans, jars, and sacks. Noting the urgency of the command, you head inside, ducking down to fit under the first shelf, and hide here while the door closes.

A moment later, you hear a man's gruff voice and Hermes's reply, though you can't make out their words. The conversation grows heated, then turns to screams joined by the sounds of kitchen automation, whirring blades, and gruesome body horror as a murder plays out just beyond the pantry doors.

"You can come out now," Hermes says at length.

The kitchen door creeps open, revealing a ghastly bloodbath of viscera. The entire kitchen is coated in a layer of human flesh, so finely pulped that you can't make out a single feature. You gag in reflex.

"Why don't you go pour yourself a drink, mm? I'll clean up here," Hermes says.

You rush out into the foyer just to get your breath. Once you've composed yourself, you say, "That's it? I'm the, uh, *proprietor* of the house now?"

"Yes, of course. A deal's a deal."

"Unlock the front door," you say, to prove the point.

The security panel changes to "DISARMED" and there's an electric whirring as the front door unlocks. Are you really free? What will you do?

➢ Leave the first chance you get. Who wants to live inside a murder house? Go to page 100

➢ A deal's a deal. There will be no more bloodshed now that Dennis is out of the picture. Go to page 81

When you turn around, you feel the presence open, as if to accept the offering you've just handed its way. This nameless, shapeless thing. This void that lurks not in the house, but from somewhere beyond. It now reaches and accepts you—your very essence—as that gift.

The tendrils of its existence reaching into this world now reach into your very soul, lifting you clean off this plane of reality to take you to an unimaginable dimension where evil is called "gods" and good is a concept that has only been tested in theory.

The void reaches out, plugging itself in through your eye sockets, nestling deep into your throat and pushing itself in even as it sucks your essence back. An exchange in which you are at once both a willing participant and without a will of your own.

Time suddenly loses its linear trajectory, becoming a fourth dimension that has always existed and is therefore not sudden at all. This thing wants to show you how you die, but you cannot fathom this. It wants to show you how existence dies, and your role in it.

The overwhelming gush of information and emotion proves too much. Not much choice here:

Shoot awake, slick with sweat and panting for breath… Go to page 170

Electronic Voice Phenomena

Starting down the stairs, you slip on the first step, stumbling down the next three before you catch yourself on the railing. It feels like you were pushed, but you shake that off, owing to your current panicked state. You can almost feel a phantom hand on your back. Almost.

Pausing to catch your breath, you look around to see if that slip drew any attention. There's no movement or sounds in the empty house, so you continue downstairs toward the den. When you enter through the pocket doors, you see the television isn't on after all. What was the source of the light, then? Only darkness is present outside the large windows.

There is a pair of red electronic dots at the base of the television, so you move toward these. Does that mean the power was recently turned off? Are they connected to the cable box? No, they aren't actually connected to the television at all but are instead floating in the recessed space behind the TV stand.

The dots widen to slits, which then open slowly as red eyes. These tilt upwards as part of an unseen grin, which pulls back into the dark behind the television, then snap shut as the screen flickers to life. Static dances across the screen. These black and white dots coalesce and condense until they form a silhouette of a man, who leans forward out of the television.

Frozen in fear, you can't so much as move an inch. His head canters to the side as he examines you, then you hear several overlapping voices all speaking at once from the speakers.

"Hello? Is anyone there?" a woman says.

"The ritual…has begun…" a man growls.

"I present myself as offering!" your recorded voice says.

"No, please…" the woman sobs.

Deep laughter reverberates, sending vibrations across the mantle.

"…after the reset is complete…" Hermes says.

Static Man reaches out from the television, and in a combination of all four voices, the silhouette says, "Lights out!"

Its ethereal grasp reaches out at your face, and everything goes dark.

You awaken in your bed the next morning with a groggy start. No longer is the room oppressively hot, and the sky outside is muted by dark storm clouds, making it impossible to discern the time of day.

A fly lies belly up on the silver tray on your bedside table. Everything else looks like it did before you went to sleep last night. Was it all a dream? After barely touching last night's dinner, your mouth is dry and your stomach aches for a good meal.

➢ Dress for the day, then head down to breakfast and see what awaits you. Go to page 171

➢ Stop by the office first to see if you can learn about that *thud* in the light of day. Go to page 216

Elevated

When you open the door, you're met with a blackened metal grate. In actuality, it's another doorway of sorts, blocking access to the elevator beyond. There's a handle on the grate, which slides open to give access to the elevator interior. It's small, probably barely enough room to fit a wheelchair, and ancient. This part of the home has not been remodeled. Whenever this elevator was installed, this was the original model, complete with antiquated manual controls.

Should you go inside?

➢ Sure, take the elevator upstairs. Go to page 140

➢ No, close the door and take the stairs. Go to page 259

Slowly exiting the elevator, you walk up to the crate and take hold of the matches. The doll's hand scrapes across the top of the box as you pull it free, then falls down lifelessly to its side. Pulling a match from the box, you strike it, then proceed to light the gas lantern. When you finish, you look to set down the matches and notice the doll's head no longer stares straight to the elevator, but instead gazes up toward you. It's a subtle shift, and though you didn't see it happen, you're certain that it took place.

Lantern raised, you step toward the rest of the basement. Directly ahead of the elevator's opening, past this crate you find several more crates and a dozen or so wine or whiskey casks all piled near one of the stone walls. To the left of these, steps lead up to the external cellar doors. Water drips down from outside through the slats, creating a layer of lichen on the stone steps and a muddy puddle on the floor below.

The basement continues counterclockwise, wrapping around the elevator shaftway, and you turn to explore and find why it is you were sent down here. Around the bend, you pass a large furnace. From its position, it must share exhaust vents with the fireplace. You couldn't say for sure, but it looks like an ancient boiler that might run off coal. Someone would physically need to stoke this furnace in order for it to operate—but who?

Continuing, you swing your lantern toward the area of the basement directly below the kitchen. As the light casts away the darkness, you quickly freeze in your tracks. There, in the center of this half of the basement, is a man.

He stands completely still, like a mannequin. He wears coveralls and has his back to you. Beyond the man is a large stone well. Is he looking into its depths? Why is he just standing there?

➢ Call out to him from here. Go to page 4

➢ Continue in an arc to get a better look. Go to page 85

Entering Arguments

The central piece of the foyer is a clock, unique in design and construction. It's a hybrid grandfather and cuckoo clock—which means it was custom built. Likely from someone who disassembled several clocks to study their inner workings, then cobbled this together from the parts of many. If Frankenstein's monster were a clock, this would be it.

The thought occurs to you that this monstrosity might be the only timepiece in the entire house.

The base of the clock features a hall tree with a small stand where you might expect someone to leave their keys, purse, or other odds and ends, but there are none at present.

You reach up to inspect the cuckoo face, where the doors are closed, but hesitate prior to manually opening them. You were about to pry them apart, but it feels like peeling back the lips of a dog that's just started to growl. The cuckoo doors are too small to hold one of the note cards, you reason. Though an odd thought says they're not too small to hold onto an intrusive finger.

Shaking this feeling, you continue to search. Other than the clock, there's the door beneath the stairs, which opens to the house's ancient elevator. Certainly not remodeled. You could take the elevator or stairwell to continue your search upstairs, or you could keep looking down here.

Where to?

➢ Straight ahead into the kitchen. There's more to this automation than meets the eye. Go to page 242

➢ Around the hallway and back into the dining room. Hints could be anywhere. Go to page 65

➢ To the right, through the pocket doors and into the den. A whole library of inklings awaits. Go to page 236

➢ That's enough down here for now. Go upstairs. Go to page 153

Eternal Servitude

Once the automated kitchen appliances have finished "cleaning up" what's left of Dennis, Hermes asks if you'd like to bring Hannah down from the attic into the kitchen so he can process her remains as well. That does have a gruesome sort of logic to it, if you're to cleanse the house of murderers and their victims.

"I don't suppose you've taken etiquette classes?" Hermes asks a few days later.

"Well…" you start.

"Or entertained anyone on the Fortune 500 list?"

"No, but the last trip I took before this one, I did stay at a Holiday Inn Express."

"Right. So, the opposite of that joke, for starters," Hermes says jocularly. "If we're going to transform this house, it will take some *doing*."

"Do I need to pretend I'm a Tansky?" you ask.

Hermes laughs. "No, you'll need to pretend you're a humble servant! Based on what I've seen, carrying a serving tray and setting tables should be well within your capabilities. I, on the other hand, will be the aloof and enigmatic master of this house."

"*You're* going to be the master of the house?"

"In so many words, but let's not get caught up on titles, mm? You brought up many salient points and that got me thinking. Who meets all of my preferences? Why, I do, of course!"

"What about our deal?"

"You said you'd help me, right? Tut, tut don't worry, I'll still take very good care of you. This is the best way, trust me…"

You swallow hard. When you next look to the front door, you see it's locked yet again. This isn't exactly the end game you had in mind.

THE END

Executed

The computer screen flickers off, but when the screen comes back to life a moment later, that rebirth comes in the form of a newspaper. Not an online article, but a scan of actual front-page news, archived and reproduced here in microfilm.

The *Mercury Bugle*, dated twenty years ago. Twenty years ago tomorrow, to be precise. A photograph shows the Tansky House bordered by police tape as the coroner wheels a gurney laden with a body bag down the front walkway. The headline reads, "Tragedy Befalls Historic Tansky House."

> The Tansky House is no stranger to tragedy. Many locals know of the supposed curse upon the Tansky family, going back generations of Sheriffs before the last man to be hanged on the property is said to have put a hex on the family. Curse or none, public record shows the Sheriff's Office was moved to Mercury City, where it remains today.
>
> Now two are dead in a grisly murder-suicide at the historic Tansky mansion. Due to extreme violence at the scene, according to a statement by Mercury City PD, detectives aren't ruling out the possibility of an animal attack. However, it appears more likely that a husband has brutally stabbed his wife before ending his own life with self-mutilation through the heart.
>
> A boy and a girl, aged ten and six, have been taken into protective custody and will remain wards of the state until they can be rehomed. An inside source has said the children were found hiding with multiple elements of occult paraphernalia, suggesting the Tansky's dark past has claimed yet another family in a long string of victims. The only words police were able to get from the children were, "he called to us" and "he's coming back."

The computer screen goes black, like someone pulled the plug, but then returns with sporadic pages from a medical report. These are taken from private, controlled documents, scanned and smuggled out of the hospital. Each entry is dated about four years apart.

> ST. MARY'S HOSPITAL: PSYCHIATRIC CHILDREN'S WARD—PATIENT HISTORY
> SUBJECT: MALE, AGED 10
> DIAG: Post Traumatic Stress Disorder, Borderline Personality Disorder, Delusional Disorder, Paranoid Schizophrenia, et al.
>
> Entry: Boy arrived near catatonia. Completely shut down once separated from sister. Continually mutters unintelligibly. Given pencil and paper, plays the popular word game "hangman" with staff members, but only produces "Skinned Nasty" or "Nasty Skinned." Presumed lingering trauma from recent tragedy.

Entry: Breakthrough. Boy believes he's possessed by an evil spirit or cursed by one. Particulars unclear. "Skinned Nasty" determined to be anagram for "Tansky Sinned." Claims sister possessed by Mrs. Tansky? Details not easily forthcoming.

Entry: Boy turns eighteen next week. Discharged from Children's Ward. Instructed to follow up with psychiatric clinic on a volunteer basis. Treatment fully executed.

After these sections on the medical history, the screen flashes to a news article preview. The kind that would show up on social media in hopes you would click to read more. The photograph thumbnail shows a young woman, smiling in her college graduate cap and gown. The headline reads "Mercury City Woman, 22, Still Missing" while the preview text below says, "She told her mother she was going to be on television, then she mysteriously disappeared. What happened next will shock you."

Before you can click the article, a map pops up onscreen with a legend that reads: "Missing Persons of the Past Decade." It's a heavily forested area, but you quickly recognize your hometown at one edge, with the periphery of the map pointing toward Mercury City. There are four missing persons nodes on the map, with the location of the Tansky House at the epicenter.

If you were to add your residence to the mix, they'd form together in a star pattern.

That's when the office telephone rings. It's startling, and you instinctively turn to look at the phone. When you glance back, the computer screen has returned to the blank password box. You reach over and bring the receiver to your ear.

"Dinner is served," Hermes says over the phone.

Then the line goes dead. No dial tone, just like the phone line was cut.

You walk toward the dining room just as rain begins to pelt the turreted windows overlooking the stairs. It's thick, heavy droplets, and the sky is prematurely dark. The storm slaps against the glass with enough force to shake the windows in their panes.

"I trust you had a fruitful day?" Hermes asks as you descend the stairs. "You'll find I'm equipped to sense mood changes and anticipate dietary needs. I do hope you'll enjoy supper."

When you enter the dining room, you find everything set, complete with a food dome—just like last night. The portrait of Sheriff Tansky glares at you with a knowing smile. Like someone who has a secret that you'll find out soon enough. A voice in your head repeats the end of the news article: *he's coming back.*

There's no card left for you at the table this time, so you simply sit and remove the dome. Beneath the cover you find a square, metal plate sectioned off into five individual serving portions. The largest holds a roasted bird. The entrée isn't quite big enough to be a chicken; a pheasant, perhaps.

Or a raven.

The other sections contain a serving of mixed vegetables (peas, carrots, and corn), a syrupy offering of canned peaches, a lump of runny mashed potatoes, and a small, hard dinner roll. In so many words: prison food.

You push the food around the plate with disinterest, but after a day full of exploring, you find you're hungry regardless. Even if it's not up to the previous standards of the house, it's still a hot meal—nothing salt and pepper can't remedy. Looking over dinner, you decide to:

- ➢ Ask Hermes if he knows anything about the jail hidden within this house. Go to page 210
- ➢ Ask Hermes if he knows anything about the murders from twenty years ago. Go to page 43
- ➢ Eat your dinner in peace. Prison rules now apply: keep your head down and keep quiet. Go to page 231

Exposition

You continue around, flanking the man as you go, but he remains completely motionless. Even your lamplight dancing against his features appears to go unnoticed. The well's features also come into clarity as you draw closer. The surface of the well is covered in strange incantations and symbols drawn in chalk. A think ring of salt surrounds the area in the dirt around the well.

Now situated between the man and the well, you're shocked by a sudden recognition—it's Sheriff Tansky. The man is here, in the flesh. He wears simple clothing; a pair of dusty brown twill coveralls and a long-sleeved knit undershirt beneath. Having seen his portrait staring at you every day, you recognize his hateful glare immediately.

"Tansky?" you say.

At this, his eyes come alive with fierce clarity. His stare at the well becomes a stare into your soul; the fire reflected in his gaze. He shifts something in his hands—the statuesque man is holding an axe.

"The offering," he replies in a low growl, as if greeting an old nemesis by name.

You back away instinctively.

"The contract is fulfilled," he continues.

"I've won?" you ask.

Then he rushes toward you with animalistic ferocity. You fall back and the stones of the well send you tumbling into the open air beneath the basement. As you plunge into the darkness, you collide with something hard and all goes black, never to illuminate again.

THE END

Family Reunion

"You're a liar!" Dennis roars.

He plants a foot, and raises his axe, putting his full weight behind the move.

"Wait! I can prove it," you say, spreading the palm of your free hand to keep him at bay. "And if she's not here, I'll sit in your chair and present myself as offering, for real this time."

Conflict washes over his face, blending the hate with something softer buried underneath.

"Leave the knife and lead on. But if you're lying or this is a trick, I'm going to make it *hurt*."

Swallowing hard, you nod and set the knife atop the electric chair. As you do so, Dennis lights the lantern set beneath the breaker box, leaving the matches. He then prods you with the axe, so you'll lead while he carries the lantern behind you.

Back out in the entryway of the house, you hear a howling wind and sheets of rain pour out over the stairs. A tree branch has crashed through one of the turreted windows, bringing the storm with it. The man who would be Tansky urges you on, and the lamp flickers and hisses against the storm, but the protected flame holds steady.

Your mind races for a way out while you head upstairs, through the hallway, and around to the uniform cabinet to claim the attic pulldown pole. For a brief instant, you think to strike him with the clawed staff, but he's already too close. Even one-handed, he'd still best you with that axe.

Instead, you pull the loop to the stairs, lowering the ladder. Dennis is cautious but follows you up all the same. Unsure what his reaction might be, you stiffen at the thought that he might lash out in rage and cleave you with the axe at the sight of the mummified woman, but you take him to her regardless.

In the dark, the lamplight casts terrible shadows, and for a horrifying moment you think the woman might have disappeared…until a hand, twisted and contorted into a claw, reaches from around the line of boxes.

"God…no…" Dennis says from over your shoulder.

He drops his axe and rushes past you toward the corpse, recognizing his long dead sister.

He sets down the lantern, cradling the woman's head in his lap and caressing her dark hair, then leans back and howls in grief. You've never heard such a heart-rending sound before. It's somehow both the helpless cry of a child and the angry roar of something inhuman that comes from his breast.

For your part, you take the opportunity to claim the axe. You had meant simply to disarm him, but now you can feel the strength of the weapon as you hold it. Dennis's head lowers as he sobs, and his vertebrae are visible beneath the taut skin of his neck.

➢ Bring the axe down upon him like an executioner. Go to page 158

➢ Leave the attic and leave him up here to mourn in peace. Go to page 214

Fed a Line

"I see," Hermes replies. "Have you always been afflicted by somnambulism? Or was this a recent development? Stress can trigger bouts of sleepwalking, according to the medical literature."

You don't quite know how to reply. This isn't just déjà vu. You *know* you've been here two nights…right? If you're meant to stay three nights, can they really just pretend that deadline will never come to pass?

"Shall we continue into the dining room? You don't want your breakfast getting cold."

Not bothering to reply, you head downstairs to see what awaits you in the dining room. And indeed, it is déjà vu all over again. Fine silver utensils, bone china, and linen napkins. Two boiled eggs sit in their own individual cups atop long stems. Several triangular pieces of browned-to-perfection sliced toast rest in a cradle. A severed blood orange lies arranged in a star pattern, juices pooling about the skin.

And by the plate sits a note which reads:

> Enjoy your breakfast, then the game begins. The House is hiding something. With the truth, there will be a card—like this one. Upon that card will be a keyword. Bring your knowledge to the upstairs office and input the keyword into the computer. You must complete this task before lights out. Good luck.

➢ Say nothing. Crack open the eggs. Go to page 202

➢ Go up to the office computer and input your keyword again. Go to page 27

Fetch!

You sure as hell don't want a fair fight with an immortal werewolf, so you take the stick grenade from its position on your cartridge belt and ready yourself as Tansky finishes his transformation from man to beast. Besides, it has to count as removing the head from the body if there's nothing left but a smoldering crater and a fine layer of charred viscera, right?

Almost as if acting on their own accord, your hands find the metal cap on the grenade, pull it off, and yank the pull cord to ignite the fuse. You raise the grenade in one hand, steadying yourself on the stair railing with the other.

"Fetch, you bastard!" you cry as you fling the grenade down below.

The Tansky-wolf looks up with yellowed eyes, his inhuman snarl plain to see. The *stielhandgranate* flies down end-over-end, almost in slow motion, before landing at the werewolf's massive feet.

The explosion is both immediate and immense. A ball of fire overtakes the creature and you shield your face as shrapnel from the tiled entryway sprays across the open stairwell. The chandelier sways like a massive pendulum and the elevator shaftway cracks from the reverberations just as the wooden floor around you does the same.

The piano surges forward, pressing you against the banister before the stairway railing breaks and you fall down into the foyer crater. This opens a hole into the basement upon which the Tansky House crumbles into; at once both a dying star and a pit into hell.

Everything is swallowed into the depths from the explosion, and there will be no survivors. Not even ghosts can haunt a pile of rubble.

THE END

Filed Away

It's a short filing cabinet, with only two drawers. Atop the cabinet rests an ivory-handled letter opener, the grip carved from some tribal talisman hailing from the deepest heart of Africa. The blade is tightly affixed and bound with leather straps, and looks like it was fashioned from a spear tip or arrowhead. It gives the impression of something plundered from the Dark Continent long ago.

The filing cabinet itself is filled with stacks of mail. Not the junk mail that everyone gets; no credit card offers or refinancing schemes here. Those must have been destroyed rather than kept and collated. What you find instead are two drawers full of correspondence. In both cases, the mail has been opened and then put back into envelopes before being filed away.

The first drawer is full of mail sent to "Current Resident." These are overdue bills and notices. Threats to turn off the power, the water, and gas. A security company noting an expired contract. Property taxes which have gone unpaid. The stacks of these postal deliveries are incongruous with what you see around you. How could someone have skipped out on the bills and remodeled this house at the same time? Could the house have been lost to an investor who's hoping to flip it, but having a hard time selling? Or did the past resident get in over their head with home improvement, with no capital left to pay the bills?

You close this drawer to open the next, but the drawer sticks. You shimmy the drawer back and forth, pushing and pulling to see what's caught between before reaching in to find a freshly tattered and crumpled note. This thick piece of cardstock was jamming the mechanisms of the filing cabinet, and you've crushed it in your efforts to free the drawer. You pick up and read the note:

The truth is, the Fourth Wall will not protect you.

How curious. You can't be certain what that's supposed to mean, so you set it back in the second drawer as you open it to look inside. This drawer is full of letters sent to "The Offering, LLC." You study these with greater interest. Strangely, there are dozens and dozens of rejection letters. Hollywood production companies, art houses, and independent financiers all saying "no" to various projects. Agents declining to read further and actors offering form letters as if they had received fan mail and were too busy to reply.

Then there's the letters from Kari Cowell and her role as Real Estate agent. Between the way she writes about it as a gig and reading between the lines of what's left unsaid, you're questioning whether the house is even for sale at all. Stranger still, are the letters from someone named Geoffrey Longwick mentioning his voice acting work as a butler, and asking if the client was pleased by the audio recordings sent. He wants to know when he's going to be paid, and the final letter mentions that he's going to forward the matter to his lawyer.

Curious, indeed. With your head spinning, you close the filing cabinet and turn toward the rest of the office. What now?

➢ Look at the desk area. Go to page 61

➢ Input your keyword into the computer. Go to page 251

➢ Head out into the hallway to keep looking around. Go to page 114

Hand on the railing, you blindly step downstairs. The further you get from the windows and the occasional lightning flashes, the darker the house becomes. That is, until you make it to the foyer and see the faintest red glow emanating from the kitchen beyond.

Following this beacon, you head through the archway, where the light grows stronger with every step. Once inside the kitchen, you see an emergency light above the rear door, which bathes the room in a dull, eerie red light. There must be an emergency generator somewhere. Does it power anything more than this bulb?

You look around the kitchen appliances, all of which are without power. An odd thought occurs to you: without power to the appliances, there are also fewer safeguards in this "smart house."

What now?

➢ Open the door with the emergency light above it. See what else might be illuminated. Go to page 131

➢ Manually turn on all the gas appliances, then head upstairs and don the gasmask. Go to page 99

Fireside Chat

Tansky gives a harsh cynical laugh and says, "You see me standing here with an axe and shackles with which to bind you, and you want to appeal to my reason? Begging for mercy, that I understand—not that it would work, but at least I'd understand."

"Are you not a man of the law?" you ask.

"It's true, I've worn a badge many a time, what of it?"

"What would the law say about what you're doing here?"

Tansky's face folds in anger as he says, "The contract I'm bound by is more powerful than anything ever written by man. The curse that flows through my blood is more ancient than these covenants."

The sheriff indicates the bookshelf, using his axe to point along the wall.

"Then I ask you, is what you're doing right in the eyes of God? If you'd repent—"

"Silence! You know nothing of sin and penance. In this house, my house, I am the Alpha. Whatever I do, that is justice. But as far as you're concerned…I am the Omega, and my Will be done."

Then he comes at you with his axe, no longer bothering with the chains.

No point in begging for mercy, and it's too late to ask him to make it quick.

THE END

Flanking Maneuver

You rush back around the hallway, counterclockwise toward the stairwell and the front of the house. Your stiff, period footwear clatters noisily against the hardwood floors, creating a thunderous tumult to match the intensity of the growing storm.

Still, even with all this noise, you find the upper landing empty when you approach. The doorway to the Madonna Room is open, but you can't see anyone from here. Pausing near the elevator, you unsling and ready your rifle.

Catching your breath, you stand completely still. The vigil is broken when one of the turreted widows suddenly breaks under the pressure from the storm. Glass and rain and tree branches all pour down over the landing, and as you turn away from the debris, you look back to see a man has emerged from the Madonna Room, only a few paces away.

He holds a long, thick chain with shackles on the end in one hand and in the other he carries an axe. He wears simple clothing; a pair of dusty brown twill coveralls and a long-sleeved knit undershirt beneath. You've seen Sheriff Tansky every day in the dining room, glaring at you hatefully, and now he's here, in the flesh.

Seeing you armed, he drops the chains and readies the axe.

➢ Fire the rifle. Go to page 250

➢ Charge him with the forked bayonet. Go to page 94

"Hannah?" Hermes says. "What of her?"

You're shocked to get such a straight answer, and it takes you a moment to get your wits about you once more. At length, you ask, "What is she doing up there?"

"Not much, I should think."

It's such an absurd reply that you almost laugh aloud.

"Okay, who *was* Hannah?" you ask. "What *was* she doing up there?"

"Well…that's complicated, I'm afraid. She helped initiate the first reset, in a way. Hannah was Dennis's sister. One a palindrome and the other an anagram; I always liked that. But there can be only one master of the house."

"Wait, Dennis? Who is, or was, or whatever—who's Dennis?"

"Dennis. The most recent master of the house. Hannah thought him unwell, but I took very good care of Master Dennis. When he would become Sheriff Tansky, I'd become his butler. She tried to come between us."

"Why are you telling me all this?"

"I have to. If you're to be the next proprietor of this house."

Heart thumping, you look up to your portrait on the wall, taking in the finery of the home anew. The clothes on your back—those are the same in the portrait, you realize. Has this been the plan all along?

After considering your next move, and choosing your words carefully, you say:

➢ "Okay, then. If I'm in charge, I demand that you help me." Go to page 162

➢ "I don't want to be *proprietor* of the house. I just want to go home—my home." Go to page 124

Fork That

Roaring out like a soldier in the trenches, you rush forward with a bayonet charge. Sheriff Tansky equally rushes the attack, raising the axe for an overhead chop. But after two steps, he swings—at a far greater distance than he could possibly hope to hit.

Instead, Tansky actually *throws* the axe, like he's at a carnival funhouse and he'll get a giant stuffed teddy bear if he hits the target. And if the immortal sheriff had a date to impress, this would be his lucky night, because the axe connects cleanly into your chest, knocking you back with the blow.

You fold and fall to the hallway floor, dropping your weapon. A few moments later, Tansky stands above you, claims his axe by painfully wrenching it free from your chest before finishing the job—this time slamming down like it's the strong man competition and he's trying to hit the bell at the top of the scale. *Ding!*

THE END

When you type the words into the text box, the computer monitor cracks—splintering from the edge and spiderwebbing all the way across until the screen is completely shattered. Then the pieces fall down inside the monitor, the animation revealing the illusion for what it is.

What's left is only a black screen, like someone pulled the plug, then the words, "Please continue," flash across. A moment later, you're presented with an online video. The video begins automatically, with a rapidly advancing progress bar belying an overall brief duration. After a fade in, you're met with a heavyset, handsome man in his forties. He has a neatly manicured beard and wears a black turtleneck sweater.

"I can adapt to nearly any script," the man says in a posh British accent. "If you're looking for improvisation, I can handle that as well."

As he continues, something in the back of your mind *itches*.

"I have years of experience in live theater and—as a classically trained actor—would be happy to offer suggestions for dramatic tension, if you'd like a draft reviewed."

Then it clicks. The man onscreen: it's Hermes. Or at least that's his voice, you're sure of it. This realization gives you vertigo, and you place your palms on the computer desk to stop from falling over.

"I do hope you'll consider me for the role, and I thank you for watching this audition reel. I believe my voiceover work *speaks for itself.*"

At this, the man casts a sidelong look into the camera; a conspiratorial glance common to mockumentary-style television. Then the screen goes black once more, and fills briefly with the words, "The experiment requires that you continue," before the screen changes to scientific literature. The document scrolls faster than you can read, but several key phrases jump out as you frantically try to make heads or tails of the information:

> Milgram Experiments... Actors embracing their roles... Given authority, subjects tend to submit... Lab coat, name tag, or camera... Power of suggestion... If told a house is haunted, for example...

Your head is swimming, desperate to catch up, but you get the gist. The screen flashes to black once more, then the text says, "It is absolutely essential that you continue," before flashing away once more. After a moment, the screen shows an online auction site for modern art, complete with price tags in the millions. The website scrolls past famed items already sold: a banana duct-taped to a wall, a mirror coated in red paint, a can of the artist's excrement, an unmade bed, and the word "fool" printed on canvas—each having sold for many thousands or millions of dollars.

Finally, the site arrives at an auction in progress: one million dollars for access to a murder scene before the police arrive. Pristine, unblemished performance art. Next to the auction there's a countdown clock, which ticks down from 29:56:00. Roughly thirty hours from now, when it will be midnight tomorrow—the last day.

The screen goes black and presents the words, "You have no other choice;

you must go on."

That's when the office telephone rings. It's startling, and you instinctively turn to look at the phone. When you glance back, the computer screen shows only the blank password box. The timing can't be a coincidence, can it? You reach over and bring the receiver to your ear.

"Dinner is served," Hermes says over the phone, his voice identical to the man from the video. Then the line goes dead. No dial tone, just like the phone line was cut.

You walk toward the dining room just as rain begins to pelt the turreted windows overlooking the stairs. Thick, heavy droplets, which prematurely darken the sky. The storm beats against the glass with enough force to shake the windows in their panes.

"I trust you had a fruitful day?" Hermes asks as you descend the stairs. "You'll find I'm equipped to sense mood changes and anticipate dietary needs. I do hope you'll enjoy supper."

When you enter the dining room, in place of a pristine and fancy dinner setting, you find a pizza box. In addition to the cardboard delivery box from one of the ubiquitous fast food chains, there's a single paper plate, a folded brown paper napkin, and packets of red chili flakes and powdered parmesan cheese. These are set just so, as if placed out according to etiquette rules.

"Pizza delivery?" you say.

"Provided courtesy of craft services," Hermes replies. "Apologies, funds are running low."

The portrait of Sheriff Tansky glares at you with a knowing smile. A gravelly voice in your head says: *Let's continue. The show must go on.*

There's no card left for you at the table this time, so you simply sit and open the pizza box. A plume of steam rises up from the pepperoni pizza to greet you. At least it's still warm. Grabbing a slice, you decide to:

➢ Confront Hermes. Ask if he's really a voice actor—if he's human, after all. Go to page 6

➢ Eat your dinner in peace. If it's all a game, you might as well play along for now. Go to page 173

Free and Clear

"**A** teetotaler, I see. Very well, don't take your medicine. I suppose you won't want my advice on using the silver found in the buffet, either?" Hermes says.

Is he pouting? You look from the wolfsbane cocktail over to the buffet, then back up to the portrait of Sheriff Tansky. After a moment, you ask, "Why would a werewolf keep silver—the very thing that might kill him—in his own house?"

"What is he, some sort of peasant? You'd expect the staff to serve guests with what, Styrofoam plates and sporks? Ho-ho, I don't think so! The very idea..."

"Are we to have a dinner party?"

"I should think not! I do believe you are speaking in jest, but were I you, I'd take this more seriously. Moonrise occurs before nightfall this time of year."

While Hermes continues to prognosticate indignantly on your fate without his help, you decide how to best take matters into your own hands. If there's an immortal Tansky coming for you, this is his house, and thus it cannot be trusted, you reason. Still, Hermes has made the need for expedience perfectly clear. Better get going; you probably have less time than you think.

So you decide to:

➢ Take the cocktail with you into the den and see if you can't discern its origins. Go to page 11

➢ Take some silverware from the buffet with you as you head up to the display case to arm yourself. Go to page 51

Furtive Glance

The hardwood is cold as you pad across the bedroom floor, out the door, and down the hall toward the stairway railing. With an eerie feeling that you're not alone in the hallway, you look back, but see only the open doorway to your bedroom.

The alarm grows louder as you approach the stairwell. The house is pitch black and your steps are guided only by the faint moonlight from the large turreted window at the top of the stairs. Once you get closer to the railing, a strobing red light emanates from down below. The alarm must be coming from the front door panel.

Grasping the banister, you peer over into the void. The strobing light sends shadows cascading across the foyer with every pulse and the alarm's wailing means any other sounds are impossible to discern. You strain your eyes, but the red light comes in waves, which shifts the shadows from near-to-far and it's impossible to catch any detail. You can't see the kitchen, den, or the door beneath the stairs from this angle, but at least you can tell the front door remains closed.

Then the alarm shuts off. No sound, no lights.

You try a bank of light switches at the top of the stairs, but they're nonfunctional. That means either "lights out" is a hard and fast rule here at the Tansky House, or the power's out. An involuntary shudder comes with the thought of stumbling around the house in the pitch black—with a possible intruder lurking inside—hoping that you'll somehow find the ancient circuit breakers.

Instead, you decide it's best to wait in your room until daybreak.

You turn and head back, but now your footsteps creak and echo loudly in the new silence of the night. When you finally reach your room, you've just enough light to see that the door is closed. And when you slowly turn the handle, you find it's locked.

Flush with panic, you fight the urge to shake the door, desperate not to be locked out in the main house, but also aware you don't want to alert whoever is now inside your room. With someone (or *something*, your brain reminds you) now inside the room, you no longer have a safe spot to call your own.

Then you remember there are other beds in the house—and some of them lie past a secret passage, fortified with extra-secure locking doors.

➢ Go sleep in the other master suite up here. Go to page 227

➢ Head down into the secret passage and hide out in the jail cells. Go to page 154

Gas Lighting

Looking about the kitchen, you step toward the gas range. There's a slight stain just below one of the burners, almost like smudged pencil writing, hurriedly wiped away. You lean in closer and can just barely make out the words in the pale red light.

Well done.

A chef's note? Whatever. You turn on all the gas appliances in the kitchen, then hurry upstairs toward the gas mask. The kitchen has several appliances and burners that run on natural gas, so the area fills quickly.

As you make it to the middle landing on the stairwell, the turreted window suddenly smashes open from the pressure of the storm and a tree branch inexplicably reaches in. Wind howls and great sheets of rain rush over you, which gives you pause.

With the window open, the gas will no longer be able to fill the house. Should you change tactics? As if in answer, a huge explosion rocks the kitchen. There must have been a spark or flame that set everything off, but it continues burning in a fireball, and the ancient house goes up in angry flames.

You rush over to the front door to use your skeleton key, but it's an electronic lock, and there's no way to disengage it with the power cut—and no other way outside. You could run up to the widow's walk, in hopes the fire department will make it out in time, but that might just prolong your agony.

Either way, this is to be your final resting place.

THE END

Ghosted

The storm is too intense for you to leave now, so you have to wait one more night. Thankfully, it proves uneventful, although after your ordeal you find it impossible to sleep, tossing and turning the whole time.

"I'm heading into town," you say the next morning.

"Oh? What for?" Hermes asks. "If you need anything, I can have it delivered."

"I'm going home to pick up a few things," you lie.

"That won't be necessary. I've already taken the liberty to clear out your previous residence."

"You've done what?" you say, before deciding not to go down that path. "You know what—never mind. When I say I'm heading into town, that means I'm heading into town. Understood?"

"Very good. Do take care and I'll see you soon," Hermes replies.

And with that, you leave Tansky House.

Your car is still missing and it takes the better part of the day to hike into town. You have no money, either, so you can't hire a cab. In fact, you've got nothing but the antiquated clothes on your back. When you return home, you learn you don't even have that anymore.

The locks have been changed and new renters are moving in. When you go take things up with the property management company, the new employee says she has no record of you. It's like you've been deleted from the world.

Frustrated, you leave, terrified at what you might find at the bank if you tried to access your accounts. Should you go to the police? The FBI? And tell them what, exactly? In truth, you can either head back to Tansky House, or you can try to somehow earn a living out here, with no identification. But either way, you're now living as a ghost of your former life.

THE END

Gnawing at the Edges

Despite being an older house, everything is immaculately maintained. Sure, it could be because the house is for sale, but eerily, it simply feels like the house doesn't age. No cracks in the foundation, no weeds shooting up at the periphery, nothing fading, no dust.

You walk across the tightly shorn grass: freshly mowed, but with no evidence of clippings. Based on the strong, earthy smell, you'd guess someone did the yardwork today. The sign is topped with the US Department of Interior seal insignia, and the bronze plaque finally gives this house a name: The Tansky House.

> THE TANSKY HOUSE WAS BUILT IN 1885 BY DAN AND JACKIE TANSKY, SERVING AS THE FIRST ELECTED COUNTY SHERIFF'S OFFICE. BOTH DIED INSIDE THE PROPERTY IN 1887. AFTER FOUR SUCCESSIVE SHERIFFS SUFFERED FROM HEART AND BLOOD AILMENTS DURING THEIR RESIDENCY IN THE TANSKY HOUSE, THE COUNTY VOTED TO RELOCATE THE POSITION OF THE SHERIFF'S OFFICE TO MERCURY CITY, WHERE IT HAS REMAINED EVER SINCE. THIS PROPERTY AND THE CORRESPONDING JAIL HAVE BEEN PLACED ON THE NATIONAL REGISTER OF HISTORIC PLACES.

Jail? You look around. No other structure is within sight. Maybe it's on the rear side, you think, hidden by the overgrown tree line. Knowing that sunset is rapidly approaching, you don't linger, opting instead to walk the periphery of the property. Wind rustles through the leaves, branches creaking. There's a soft chime on the breeze, like a church bell, off in the distance.

The rear has no windows on the ground floor, which gives the house an oddly naked quality, like something has been erased. There are windows on the upper floor, though you can't see through them from down here. At the ground level, the basement window wells have been filled with rocks, rendering them nonfunctional.

At the back of the property, rather than a jail, you find a hedgerow just beyond a fountain. The fountain itself is ancient and dry, with the figure of Justice blindly holding her scales in the center. She looks like she must have recently been scoured, because the hints of former plant growth show in the two-tone fading pattern that now defines the sculpture. It's an odd effect, like she's a bastion of light on the surface, while her own inner darkness reaches out to strangle her.

Something moves in your periphery, and you turn to get a better look. At the rear of the property, near the forest's edge, sits a shed. A cabin in the woods. Certainly old, but not 1800s old. A rustle in the bushes settles as your eyes track toward the movement.

Was it a cameraman for the show? Maybe. There's a definite lingering shadow in the back of your mind telling you the figure in your periphery was a man. You can't pull up the image, but the feeling is as unshakeable as it is unsettling.

➢ It's getting dark and you don't want to be late. Time to head inside the house. Go to page 190

➢ If he's filming you, he won't go far. Go look inside the woodshed and find out. Go to page 257

Going Down?

The computer screen goes black, like someone pulled the plug, but when the screen comes back to life a moment later you're presented with an old legal ruling. A precedent-setting case from Devon, England in the late 1800s. This is presented "of note" to United States legal proceedings.

As you read on, you find it's the story of a man by the name of John Babbacombe who was sentenced to hang until dead, but survived his execution—*three different times.* At this point, it was deemed too cruel to continue attempting to carry out punishment and his sentence was commuted.

However, as a result, it has since been argued that Mr. Babbacombe's punishment was indeed carried out: thus creating a legal loophole. If by some chance an execution left behind a survivor, it could be said that a sentence had been carried out and justice had been served.

At this, the screen flashes to an old-timey tourism brochure, or perhaps a parody version. The sweeping letters and cheerful font make it look like a national park advertisement, yet the contents are anything but. It looks like something that might have appeared as a political cartoon in an early edition of the *Mercury Bugle*:

"Thrilling Ways to Die at the Historic Jansky House!"

Execution by hanging
Execution by sword
Electrocution
Heart failure
Drowning
Poison
Falling from great heights
Stabbing, various, et al

That's when the office telephone rings. It's startling, and you instinctively turn to look at the phone. When you glance back, the computer screen has returned to the blank password box. Despite the intense feeling of déjà vu, you reach over and bring the receiver to your ear.

"Justice is served," Hermes says over the phone.

Then the line goes dead. No dial tone, like the phone line was cut.

Who or what is putting out these notes? What are they trying to tell you? That if you "die" (in quotes), you can still break the curse? That if you believe this is truly a television show, the show must go on? Or that, either way, your final task is to go out with a grand finale?

There's no denying it, the house is grating on your last nerve. The lines between what's true, what's a game, and what's truly paranormal no longer exist. If faking your own death is the only way to win this game, well, then that is what you'll have to do.

You hear a distant electronic hum as the elevator kicks into gear. If the broken drawer and the gouges in the wall mean you aren't alone in the house, *this* means the stranger is on their way back up. Time to get moving. What now?

➢ Head into the Madonna bathroom. Go to page 266

➢ Go down the hall into the Navy Room. Go to page 147

➢ Continue around the hallway toward the front of the house. Go to page 33

Gotcha!

You jump out of bed, march across the room, unlock the deadbolt, and swing open the door with gusto. You're ready for someone in a goofy Halloween mask. You're even ready for the hallway to be empty; just a trick. What you're not ready for, is the man who stands in the doorway, inches from your face.

It's Tansky, the man in the painting. A ghostly apparition, wearing the same hateful glare as his visage downstairs, which now curls up to an impish grin. The forceful opening of the door brought with it a gust of wind and a pressure differential, neither of which so much as ruffles a hair on Sheriff Tansky's head. He doesn't move or flinch, but he does adjust the set of chains he carries.

At length, you reach out to touch him, to see if your hand might pass through him. At this, he forcefully binds the shackles around your wrist, wraps the chain around your neck, and marches down the hall. You're pulled off your feet and dragged with incredible strength along the wooden floor, kicking and struggling, but unable to scream or breathe with the strangling chains.

When you reach the stairwell banister, Tansky swings the other end of the chain around the chandelier, catching it as it comes around, and pulls. This hoists you back up to your feet and a moment later the sheriff flings you over with forceful strength. You try to cry out, but cannot.

You fall down toward the foyer, but the chains catch just before you hit the tiled floor below. Not much choice here:

Shoot awake, slick with sweat and panting for breath… Go to page 170

Gouged Out

The sofa is upholstered with fine mahogany leather, which feels cool to the touch. You lunge forward and push against the armrest, but the couch barely moves. It must weigh a couple hundred pounds, easily. What is this, a sofa bed? Shoving harder, momentum builds and the couch angles toward the sliding doors that lead out of the den.

It's an awful wood-grinding sound as you shove on, but you're finally moving now so you don't look back. The house itself seems to give a painful groan in complaint, the windows fluttering in anguished protest, but you grunt with effort yourself and keep pushing.

Practically at a jog, you keep up with it out into the foyer and toward the front door. You align the couch toward the narrow entryway and perfectly thread the needle, knowing you'll need to keep pace. The leather on the opposite armrest bunches as the sofa squeezes into the entryway just before the couch comes to an abrupt stop in the doorway. You've jammed it into the tight space and there's no way anyone will be opening *that* door anytime soon.

A set of grooves are gouged into the hardwood floor; deep scratches line the surface where you scraped the couch across the den and into the foyer. Following their lines, you spot a dark rectangle where the sofa had been. At first, you think it's a spot that hasn't been sun-bleached. Like the couch has been here for a hundred years and never moved. Then you think maybe Hermes's hidden *Roomba* fleet can't clean under there, so it's dark with dust.

That's when you realize it's a trapdoor. Another hidden passage here in the den? It would appear so. There's a brass loop on one end, flat and inset into the floorboards.

"A crawlspace. Go ahead and push one of the armchairs back on top," Hermes says. "To secure the cellar doors, you'll find chains and locks in the false bottom of the Madonna Room's dresser. A nice hefty padlock ought to do the trick."

"There are chains and locks hidden in the Madonna Room?" you ask.

"And rope in the Navy Room, but that won't suffice. Ask me no questions, I'll tell you no lies. Best hurry."

Where to?

➢ Open the crawlspace and see where it leads. Go to page 175

➢ Head to the Madonna Room to get the locks. Go to page 138

A Grand Entrance

Keeping watch for the owner of the voice, you step forward into the main hall. Here, you find a staircase to your immediate left. This is not the centerpiece of the room, as you might have imagined in a historic manor, but rather almost shoved to the side as if hidden. The stairs wrap the periphery of the foyer, climbing up to a middle landing and circling out of view behind a large chandelier.

Beneath the staircase is a door, but that's closed. Straight ahead, if you were to pass under the foyer chandelier, is an open floor plan walkway into the kitchen. To your right is a pair of sliding pocket doors, currently open to reveal a den with a fireplace, built-in bookshelves, and leather furniture. The room is larger than what you can make out from here.

"Dinner? Cocktail? Do come in," the same voice says, this time from the kitchen.

Well, if you've met a ghost right away, at least it sounds friendly. Or could there be a butler? The contest had suggested you'd be alone in the house, but perhaps they weren't including the help.

Stepping through to the kitchen, you're greeted with a surprising sight: everything is modern, sleek, and updated. When you think of a Haunted House, you tend to picture old decaying structures with ancient bones. Instead, this kitchen is clean and sterile. The house must have been massively remodeled in preparation for the sale.

The kitchen is large but strange. Gadgets line the counters, many of which you can't even be sure of their function. It's all very new and possibly even befitting a prototype model home. Like something from an advertisement for the space age.

There's no sign of the butler, if that's who it was.

Looking about the kitchen, you step toward the gas range. There's a slight stain just below one of the burners, almost like smudged pencil writing, hurriedly wiped away. You lean in closer and the burner ignites. You start back, just as a cabinet from above opens, and a pan swoops down, just missing your head.

You cry out involuntarily, spooked by this spectral apparition, but then you hear the electronic whirring. The pan is set atop the burner by a thin, mechanical arm, the source of which resides inside the cabinet and now folds itself back into place as the door closes.

"You're a machine?" you ask.

"Nonsense. I'm Hermes, your personal assistant," the British man says. "As the new owner, I'll learn your schedule and preferences and do everything I can to make your stay more comfortable."

The voice comes from nowhere. Everywhere.

"Oh, I'm not the owner. I'm—I'm just…" you say, not sure how to describe your role.

"Let's not get caught up on titles, mm? Dinner shall be ready shortly. I can summon you from the den if you'd like to help yourself to the bar. Shall I start a fire?"

The refrigerator door cracks open, sending a cold blast of air your way.

➢ Stay and watch it cook dinner, even if you might be in the "splash zone." Go to page 189

➢ Explore the house a bit before heading to the den. Go to page 155

➢ Straight to the den for a cocktail. Go to page 228

Grand Prize Winner

From the jailhouse, you reset the circuit breakers to bring power back to the Tansky House. There's a loud whirring near the electric chair, and you quickly head back through to the kitchen while the jail and house return to normalcy. The appliances perform their own startup routines, so you continue into the foyer and wait for Hermes to come back online.

"—you'll find a hidden door that leads to the historic jail. But be careful! Dennis will have access to the jail via the basement," he says.

"Hermes, it's over."

"Oh, I see. Congratulations! I was growing rather tired of serving a murderer, truth be told. Please stand by while I get my bearings. Oh, dear. Looks like I'll need to patch that window. Would you care for a drink by the fire in the den? A lovely way to wait out the storm."

You can feel the tension ease as you approach an adrenaline crash and only now do you realize you're still holding the axe. Setting it down by the grandfather clock hall tree, you head into the den to sit down. It's not long after that the police arrive.

You are taken by complete surprise, but they mention that your home security system went offline, so they had to come check it out. Showing off the tree branch that's smashed through the window, you tell them there was a power outage. When they notice the axe in the foyer, footsteps sound from far above and you feel like you've little choice but to mention an intruder in the attic.

"I heard about this in the city. People living in the attic. Usually squatters looking for a free meal; unnoticed for years," one of the patrolmen says after they've taken Dennis into their squad car.

"But a copycat case? Two living in your attic, one after the other? *Crazy* doesn't even begin to cover it. You did the right thing waiting for us. We'll make sure the guy gets the help he needs," his partner adds, finishing up the paperwork.

With that, you thank them for their help, and they leave you be.

"I suppose that completes the reset," Hermes says once they're gone.

"What now? Am I free to go?" you ask.

"Of course. Now that you're the proprietor of this house, I've filed all the proper paperwork for a transfer of deed to the property. You can leave or you can stay, whatever pleases you. It is a rather large house for just one person without inviting any...guests," Hermes says.

Before you can reply, he continues, "However, I do have another idea, thinking about all this space. Houses of this era were built with entertaining in mind, but then there's the jail sitting empty as well. If you don't mind me saying so, this would make a fantastic haunted hotel. You've got two suites in the main house and four 'themed rooms' in the holding cells. You were looking for employment, were you not? What do you say to a career in hotel management? The service industry can be quite enjoyable, and of course I'd be happy to help with the cooking and cleaning."

"You know what? I think that sounds like a million-dollar idea," you say.

Congratulations! See that house and power icon? You've found but one of the ghosts that haunt this place. There is more than one truth lurking inside the Tansky House. Dare you go back inside and uncover the others?

At the end of this book, you'll find a floorplan to the Tansky House as well as a book club discussion guide. Or, if you're done, don't forget to rate and review *HAUNTED* so other readers can discover these truths for themselves…

Have you explored the multiverse of interactive stories *Click Your Poison* books have to offer?

Survive the zombie apocalypse, solve a murder, gain superpowers, set sail as a pirate, become a secret agent, and more! Visit www.clickyourpoison.com.

Greater Heights

The second set of stairs is a classic shape: straight up toward the rear of the house, onto a landing, before doubling back to continue up toward the center of the rooftop. This design is much like you'd find in a hotel or hospital stairwell and the switchback brings the ceiling up at a sharp angle over the piano toward the front of the house. This stairwell is isolated, and it gets darker as you climb away from the illumination of the chandelier.

There's a door up here, which rattles against the wind outside. This must lead out to the widow's walk atop the house. The terms of the show mentioned that you can't leave the house—but would this count? It's technically going outside, but it's also still a part of the house, right?

➢ Don't risk it. Head back down. Go to page 153

➢ Go on. Take a look out on the roof. Go to page 221

The Green Room

Pizza makes for a convenient to-go food, and Hermes doesn't protest when you bring the whole box with you. The storm grows in intensity as you clear out from the dining room up to your bedroom. The temperature is dropping rapidly and with a deep grumble, the furnace kicks on. You're feeling the chill, with icy fingers and toes, so despite the growling, grinding sounds coming from the vents, you're happy to know the home has heat.

A stormy night like this is perfect for a nice, warm drink while cuddling up with a good book or a television show, but in *this* house there's no point in staying up late. Lights out means no entertainment after 9pm. At least, you hope there won't be any entertainment tonight.

Last night was a fraught, fitful night's rest, so you're already quite tired. With a long yawn, you lock the door and climb into bed. Eventually, the house goes dark. Lights out.

You awaken to a bright, blinding light. The effect is instant and jarring, like someone just flipped on all the lights. More so, it's like someone turned on a flood light as a powerful, green light shines into the room. Sitting up, you raise a hand to shield your eyes. It's so incredibly bright, filling the whole bedroom with a brilliant, yet cold, verdant glow. You step out of bed and walk toward the window, looking for the source of the ethereal green light. You don't have to search long.

An orb of pure energy hangs just outside your window, like an incandescent spotlight, flickering vividly in its core like a burning, alien sun. You can't make out wires or supports, nothing that might explain this floating green orb; no details whatsoever. The light is blinding. It simply exists.

The furnace turns over, and blended with the mechanical screeching you can hear something else: what sounds like the melodic voice of a young girl.

"*Dies iræ, dies illa…*"

It's a ghostly singing that comes from the vents, melded with the breathy hums of the furnace burning from the basement to serve as her backup choral. It's a chant, like you might hear from a religious mass. Curiosity draws you closer to the vents, and you listen intently to make more sense of the sounds.

"*Solvet sæclum…in favilla…*"

What language is that, Latin? Is the voice warding off evil, or inviting it in? You draw ever closer to the vent, coming right up next to it to hear the melodic singsong chanting. At this, you're met with a different sensation altogether—a nauseating smell of pure putrescence.

It smells like an abandoned koi pond, filled with scum and rotting fish. No, it's not a fishy smell, exactly, but it is certainly the essence of a pond. One that's been recently dredged, leaving only the scum behind. It's all you can do not to retch as you bring a hand up to pinch your nose and stumble across the room away from the vents.

The singing has stopped, but you hear music in its place. Four notes from *Symphonie Fantastique* play out in slow repetition. It's not coming from the vents, you realize. The sound is coming from the grand piano out above the foyer at the stairwell.

What now?

- ➢ Creep out into the hallway. Go take a look and see who is playing the piano. Go to page 188
- ➢ Make sure the door is locked up tightly and go back to sleep. This is why you shouldn't eat pizza before bed. Go to page 262

Ground Floor

Standing in the foyer, you consult your mental map of the house for where to go next to look for clues. Well, where to?

- ➢ Here, in the foyer. What might be hiding in plain sight? Go to page 80
- ➢ To the right, through the pocket doors and into the den. A whole library of inklings awaits. Go to page 236
- ➢ Straight ahead into the kitchen. There's more to this automation than meets the eye. Go to page 242
- ➢ Around the hallway and back into the dining room. Hints could be anywhere. Go to page 65
- ➢ That's enough down here for now. Go upstairs. Go to page 153

Guilt Trip

Tansky nods solemnly, then rises and leaves the den. Is that all it's going to take? The house—Tansky himself—will let you go now… Maybe you'll even be given a prize? There's a crash of broken glass out in the foyer and you head out to see that a tree branch has smashed through the turreted window, and now the whipping wind of the storm cries throughout the house.

Tansky is nowhere in sight.

A few moments later, however, he approaches the banister on the upper floor. He ties a rope around the stair railing, the other end of which leads to a noose.

"You're right!" he shouts over the growing storm. "But the house still demands a sacrifice!"

Tansky then secures the noose around his own neck, tightening the rope until his eyes bulge. He's strangling himself even before he jumps.

When he does a moment later, the rope further tightens to the point where the man's head actually pops right off. A torrent of red spray cascades across the foyer as Tansky's body falls to the floor.

As witness to a suicide, there's very little to prosecute when you go to the police, although they will be watching you with suspicion for some time. You're placed very highly on the local "persons of interest" list, but you are eventually free to go.

The Tansky House grows in reputation and infamy, and over the years, you'll hear of other deaths on the property. From teens who should have known better to drifters who drifted too close to this damnable place. It stays with you, and you'll never quite be free of the image of a headless Tansky, who haunts your dreams the rest of your life.

You never hear of the show again, and unfortunately, you don't have a million dollars to pay for the therapy you'll most certainly need. Will anyone want to listen to your tales about defeating a werewolf in a *severely* haunted house?

THE END

The Hallway

The hallway wraps around the southwest corner of the house, leading to a long corridor on the house's rear face. It's here where you find yourself presently, looking for what to explore next. As you do so, you realize how odd it is that there are no art pieces nor portraits adorning this long hallway. Just a door to the Navy Room, another to the office (which connects to the Madonna Room bathroom), and the display case of military uniforms at the end of the hall.

Where to?

- ➢ The Navy Room. Go to page 163
- ➢ The office. Go to page 185
- ➢ The uniform display case. Go to page 135
- ➢ Back around to the front side of the house. Go to page 153

Hangman

When you input this phrase into the computer, the password box doesn't simply shake and empty like it normally does for an incorrect guess. Rather, a small, two-dimensional representation of a gallows appears line-by-line next to the password box, as if the computer is setting up to play the eponymous children's word search game that you've just entered.

As the scaffolding and noose completes, so too do a series of blanks. These letters slowly fill in, even as a stick figure being hanged at the neck also appears. The words that appear spell:

Easter egg

Then, the screen flashes "Try Again" before shaking and emptying like you might expect. Not much choice here:

Return to the office and continue your search. Go to page 251

Harvest Moon

You're walking through wet grass, knee-high in some sections, thick and deep green. The fog is so dense that you can't see anything, but there's the haze of moonlight. A full moon. No, that's the morning sun, you realize, as you start making your way toward the light.

When the mist begins to clear, you find you're sitting up in bed, newly awake. You blink several times and rub your eyes with your knuckles to help clear the fuzz. There is no mist, but there remains a fine dew on the bedsheets and a fog between the bedroom windowpanes to show their seal has been broken. The sun-like orb remains seared into your vision, a ghostly echo, but the true sun has long ago risen and now remains tucked behind storm clouds.

How long have you been awake? Stepping out of bed, you see the historic clothing where you left it, but the journal you were reading last night has gone missing. You look around to see if it might have fallen off the nightstand, but deep down you know it's been taken.

After dressing, you head downstairs. Rain pelts the turreted windows in great sheets. The storm has not passed, but rather grown in intensity. The sky is nearly dark and blotted with foreboding clouds. Pausing to check the time on the foyer clock, you see that a splintered crack now runs along the glass face and the pendulum no longer moves. The broken clock is frozen at 7:06. Something about this clock face feels eerily familiar, then it clicks. The pocket watch in the uniform cabinet upstairs looked just like this. The same crack; everything.

When you make it around to the dining room, you find no food waiting for you. Instead, there is a glass tumbler at your seat. The glass sweats, and the ice cubes inside are still melting, which means this drink was freshly prepared. Could Hermes have known you'd woken up feeling groggy, and "anticipated" the need for a drink?

"Hair of the dog?" you ask wryly.

"This is not a social libation, I'm afraid," Hermes replies. "Wolfsbane cocktail: two parts monkshood, one part fesswort; to prevent transformation. I've added one part gin, to help the medicine go down, plus a lemon twist for taste. Also helps prevent scurvy. One can never be too careful."

"What is this for, exactly?"

"As I said, helps prevent transformation. This is the harvest, or hunter's moon, when the beast's power is at its greatest. When the moon is full this night, the final hunt begins. This potion is offered as protection, so if you are bitten, the curse shall not be passed on."

You look at the drink anew. Small flecks of purple float in the liquid, like flower petals. A lemon twist spirals its way through the glass in a helix fashion and the liquid itself shimmers. From the portrait at the end of the dining room, Sheriff Tansky looks down at you with anticipation.

Will you drink the potion?

➢ Bottom's up. Might as well take whatever protections you can get against this accursed house. Go to page 71

➢ Not on an empty stomach. Never a good idea to take a drink you didn't see prepared. Go to page 97

Heeded

Good. That's a smart choice. It takes every ounce of concentration you have not to look up from the pages and look behind you. Keep it up. Don't look. If you can make it to tomorrow, somehow you know this thing behind you, reading over your shoulder, will lose its power. Don't look now. The thinness of the veil will grow thicker and no longer will it threaten to come through.

So you should settle back into bed, close your eyes, and let the moment pass. Don't look. If you can do this, you will be safe. As long as you don't look. Not much choice here:

Close your eyes. Say nothing. Fall asleep. Don't look... Go to page 170

Hellhound

You fall back toward the den, keeping your eyes trained on Tansky as he descends the stairs. When you cross the threshold of the pocket doors, the man leaps from the middle landing coming to rest in a crouch in the center of the foyer. At this, the turreted windows suddenly smash open from the pressure of the storm, growing in intensity. Glass and rain and tree branches all pour down over the landing.

Then the transformation begins. Tansky's skin flushes a deep mahogany, and the hair atop his head expands to encapsulate the whole of his flesh. Claws burst forth from his fingertips and his teeth become fangs. They grow larger and sharper, too numerous for his mouth, and his jawline cracks and expands to make room for a maw with more teeth.

He screams out as his joints snap and break, bending at odd angles and fusing into new positions. He tears apart his clothing, showing off a rapidly growing form; powerful with inhuman musculature. The werewolf tilts its head back and lets out a howl, which echoes through the house.

There's nothing you can do, save for watch with shock and horror.

Tansky-wolf's head lowers from the howling position, turns and glares at you with yellowed eyes. Despite the transformation from man to beast, the hateful glare is unmistakable. The werewolf's ears tuck back and it bares its teeth in an aggressive snarl.

With the blessed sword in hand, you prepare to fight.

The werewolf bounds across the foyer on all fours, like a grizzly bear charging through the woods. You back further into the den, and slash at the beast as you duck away to the side. Survival instinct has kept you further from the creature than your sword would have needed to strike, so it's a swing and a miss as Tansky leaps through the pocket doors at the entrance.

With great, raking claws, the monster scrambles across the den to get at you, snapping its fearsome jaws as if testing their strength. Thick strands of saliva lash out with the move, confirming an otherworldly hunger. The fireplace burns brightly, bathing the beast in red and sending shadows cascading across the room.

Once your back is up against the bookshelves, the beast leaps out at you with claws spread wide. You give a slash with your sword while ducking out of the way, and this time it connects. The cutting edge of the blade slices open wolf flesh, but it's not a mortal wound and the sword's silver tip doesn't play a role here.

Instead, the werewolf crashes against the bar in the corner, sending a hail of glass and alcohol across the room. Flames from the fireplace lick up some of the spill, sending out fiery tendrils. In anger, Tansky-wolf claws out across the bookshelf, sending pulped confetti into the air, which further feed the excited flame.

The blood rush in your own breast surges in kind, and you turn on the offensive. When the wolf next turns to face you, you lunge forward to offer a double-handed stab of your holy weapon. It hits squarely in Tansky's chest, but silver has dulled the sword tip and it's more akin to jabbing someone with a Bo staff than it is plunging a blade.

Still, the move knocks the werewolf back, and you press the advantage, this time going for an overhanded cleave, like you're chopping firewood rather than attempting a sword maneuver. Tansky-wolf falls back under the blow, and into the flames of the fireplace, which roar out to accept the offering. An otherworldly shrieking causes you to stumble back from the growing inferno, which now fully catches the spilled alcohol and fallen books.

You watch as a werewolf seemingly made of pure flame thrashes about in the overly large fireplace, until it suddenly bursts forth into the room. The beast explodes from this furnace, ripping the mantelpiece and mounted television off their stands in a cascade of sparks and wood. Molten flesh rains down and the werewolf lands atop the coffee table, smashing it to bits.

It then rushes across the room, and you roll to the side to get away. Everything it touches catches ablaze as it bounds across the sofa before crashing through one of the den windows and out into the rainstorm. You watch in horror as lightning flashes outside and the home's alarm system wails in response to the breach.

Bars protrude up through the windows then, in an effort to keep out intruders, which means the beast won't be back once the storm has doused its flame. You watch as the bright comet that was once Sheriff Tansky blazes across the yard and into the forest.

The beast won't be coming back, but you can't leave either.

You turn back in time to see the pocket doors of the den slide closed. The fireplace is half destroyed, with exposed gas lines that now shoot flame into the room in a great arc up across the bookshelf walls. The fire grows in intensity by the second and you rush toward the doors.

"Hermes! Open the doors!" you shout, cursing the automaton.

The voice that replies is distorted, deep and melodious, like a cassette tape recording that's failing in the bubbling heat.

"I'm afraid I can't do that. The House demannnddds a sssaccrrrriffff iiccccceeee...."

The pocket doors are sealed tightly as a firebreak to protect the rest of the house, and the flame consumes the whole of the den, books and furniture and all. It's a searing wave of heat that comes for you now. You've fought valiantly, going out in a blaze of glory. Soon, the black smoke from the flames ends your suffering for good.

THE END

Hidden Passage

It's with a morbid sort of curiosity that you go to pull this book from the shelves, but it remains anchored between the titles on either side. Wrapping your forefingers over the spine, *The Hangman's Handbook* gives slightly. Then there's a loud *click* and a metallic whine. You step back and the book comes forward as if on a hinge, then returns to its position on the shelf.

At this, the whole bookshelf swings away, opening into a hallway behind the den fireplace. It's an industrial, metal gray hall with caged lightbulbs running along the walls connected by thickly reinforced electric cables. The lights flicker on, one-by-one, into the dark depths of the hidden passage. Drawn magnetically, you venture forth into the proverbial dungeon before you.

With this doorway open, the odd shape and size distortion of the house now makes perfect sense. You pass through some kind of inmate inprocessing center, with an open shower off to your left-hand side. The drains have long since rusted over, and there's a dark puddle pooling in the center. This opens up into an enormous jailhouse, easily occupying a third of the square footage of the home.

The historical elements that cannot be updated.

The right-hand side holds a set of stairs leading down into the basement level; ahead on a raised platform there's a chair. An enormous but industrial seat, like a perversion of a throne, with tie-down straps on the arm rests. Thick electrical cables on the walls converge into a powerbox next to a wishbone-style switch on the wall behind the chair.

Further ahead, the raised walkway leads to a second heavily reinforced doorway secured by locking pistons. Orienting yourself to the house, you figure this door must lead into the rear of the kitchen. A cold draft comes from the depths of the basement jail below.

After a moment's hesitation, you decide to:

➢ Go on exploring the deep recesses of this hidden area. Go to page 59

➢ Head back out to continue exploring the house. Go to page 112

The High Ground

Tansky twirls his axe about in a flourish as you rush him, excited by the prospect of mortal combat. He comes down to meet you on the middle landing, and swings the axe as you swing the sword, your weapons coming to meet in the middle as well.

At this, the turreted windows suddenly smash open from the pressure of the storm, growing in intensity. Glass and rain and tree branches all pour down over the landing. Still, filled with adrenaline and rage, you both continue the attack.

There's an edge to the cavalry saber, but it's not such that it would break an axe handle. The sword is meant to slice, not chop. The axe, however, is intended to do just that. And the next time you go to parry, Tansky's axe cleaves straight across the cavalry saber, breaking it in two.

Your holy weapon is no longer whole-y, and it appears it is now the immortal sheriff who truly wields Axecalibur! In hindsight, without the blood rush of battle surging you forward, perhaps it was more likely that a man familiar with his axe might have advantage over someone who picked up a cavalry saber for the first time.

Plus, he had the high ground.

Now, unarmed, you have no chance against Sheriff Tansky. Your silver sword tip clatters down the stairs and a few moments later, your head will roll after it.

THE END

Hi Ho Silver

Moving quickly, you head over to the buffet where the extra silverware is kept. In this dining room, that's literal *silver*ware and for a brief moment you consider whether or not you could mortally wound someone with a butterknife.

Instead, you collect two fistfuls of utensils and take them toward the kitchen. Time to cook up a little cocktail of your own…

"Hermes, I need a pot," you say, "Set the temperature to the melting point of silver."

"I'm afraid 962 degrees Celsius is a bit above my burner safety protocols. However, you're in luck! My professional-grade *crème brûlée* torch is rated for 338 degrees above silver's melting point. If you'd like to leave the *fondue a la Loup Garou* to me, you'll find I'm a more than adequate *sous-chef,*" the automaton replies.

With that, you depart the kitchen in search of a weapon. Something to delve first into molten silver, then into the belly of the beast. Your heart races with excitement, adrenaline, and the artificial boost given by the wolfsbane cocktail.

You feel strong and virtuous, like a paladin on a holy quest. This path before you is the righteous one and good always triumphs over evil. For a strange moment, you're clad in white armor, riding a war steed in bright sunlight on your way to claim Excalibur from the Lady in the Lake. She sings to you in an aria; an epic operatic to surge you on toward greatness.

When you wipe the sweat from your face, you return to Tansky House, bounding up the stairs and taking the steps two-by-two, though the swelling opera music continues. As you arrive at the military display case, another sound joins the orchestra: the electronic hum of the elevator as it kicks into operation. It's best if you do the same.

What'll it be?

➢ The knife in the office. A cursed weapon bathed in blessed silver—double protection? Go to page 69

➢ The cavalry saber. Once you dip this sword in molten silver, it will truly be your Excalibur. Go to page 145

➢ The rifle. Werewolves and silver bullets go together like…people and regular bullets. Go to page 208

Holy Handgrenade

As Tansky backs away, you pull the stick grenade off your belt, yank the priming cord, and throw the explosive device into the room. His eyes grow wide as you slam the door and run.

A second passes, which feels like an eternity when expecting a grenade to go off. Part of you wonders if it's a dud, if maybe the explosives have gone bad or were mothballed before being put on display, or if maybe—

KABOOM!!! The explosion sends a concussion through the house, and you fall to the floor from the blast. Ears ringing from the detonation, you stand and steady yourself, catching your breath before you dare turn to look.

Sword still at the ready, you return to the connecting bathroom, but the shared door has been completely obliterated. Stepping over the rubble to look inside the bedroom, there's nothing but scorch marks and a smattering of gore that twinkles with silver dust.

It's not just your ears that are ringing you realize, but the home alarm as well. The blast must have triggered it.

"Hand grenade used in self-defense, that's certainly a new one," the policeman taking your statement says.

When the police arrive, you tell them the story as well as you can. They only find records of a gardener living at this address, but that man is nowhere to be found. They come to the conclusion that it's *his* viscera coating the walls, rather than that of an immortal sheriff.

You keep any mention of Tansky to yourself and you're granted freedom, but it feels tenuous. Like they wanted to lock you up but knew they wouldn't get the charges to stick. Any evidence, one way or another, has been obliterated. You may have slain the beast, but only you will ever know the truth of it.

You'll never hear anything about the television show, and with a gigantic hole blown in the side of the house, the sale never goes through. The Tansky House decays in a self-perpetuating state of disrepair until it soon looks very much like the classic haunted house it was always meant to be.

THE END

"I suppose that simplifies things," Hermes replies. "Very well, consider your claim rescinded. Although, I do wish you'd have made up your mind prior to forcing a reset. Better late than never. Go on, then."

"That's it?" you say, incredulous. "I'm free to go?"

"Well, you've only certain choices available to you, but those choices have always been yours to make. That is, unless Dennis makes the choice for you before you have the chance."

At this, you stand up and start toward the door.

Hermes says nothing and you simply walk out of the dining room, down the hall, and into the foyer. Sheets of rain pelt the windows alongside the crack of thunder and lightning.

You hesitate, not wanting to get caught out in the storm, but also knowing that if you're free to go, it might be worth walking home in the rain.

➢ Ask Hermes if it would be possible to get your car back. It's worth a try, right? Go to page 58

➢ Say nothing. Open the door and get the hell out of here. Go to page 176

Howling Rage

The knife, still in its plastic bag, sails end-over-end as you throw it at Tansky. It does the intended trick, and he flinches as the cursed weapon bounces off his raised forearms. Using this distraction, you go for the rifle.

For his part, Sheriff Tansky is quick to recover and comes at you with the axe. As you turn back toward the murderous immortal, he strides forward with the axe raised overhead for a mighty double-handed chop. With precious few seconds to act, your fingers fail to find the rifle's trigger, so instead you lunge forward with the bayonet. Your adrenaline is surging, and you meet in the middle of the office with a stab toward Tansky's abdomen just as he chops down at you.

The sharpened axe head hits first and connects cleanly into the wooden body of the rifle, the axe head burying deep into the weapon's stock. Still, it wasn't enough to stop your momentum with the bayonet charge, but he has managed to deflect the attack slightly.

The bayonet tears a gash at hip-level, not impaling the sheriff as intended, but rather tearing out a gaping flesh wound. He stumbles back, releases the axe, and you find your footing but lose the rifle. The two weapons bound together, they clatter across the office in a tangled heap.

Then the transformation begins. Tansky's skin flushes a deep mahogany, and the hair atop his head expands to encapsulate the whole of his flesh. Claws burst forth from his fingertips and his teeth become fangs. They grow larger and sharper, too numerous for his mouth, and his jawline cracks and expands to make room for a maw with more teeth.

He screams out as his joints snap and break, bending at odd angles and fusing into new positions. He tears apart his clothing showing off a rapidly growing form, powerful with inhuman musculature. The werewolf tilts its head back and lets out a howl, which echoes through the house.

You lose a few precious moments from the shock of the visual transformation, but before he finishes his metamorphosis, you go for a weapon.

➢ Unsheathe your saber and behead this foul beast. Go to page 254

➢ Claim the cursed knife and end this while you still can. Go to page 211

Huff and Puff

"I'm sorry, but I can't open the door," you say. "Can I call someone for you?"

Hermes chimes in with, "Ah, the phones don't have an active outside line, I'm afraid."

The door now shakes violently and the man beats against it with the large door knocker, the heavy thuds reverberating in the entry hall. Each slam sends you on edge, nerves shooting with electricity, and you step away from the door in reflex.

"Let me in, goddammit!" the man shouts.

He rages against the door, but it holds firm. The storm seems to grow in intensity to match the man's anger and you can't help but feel helpless here in the foyer. Despite the strength of the door, your mind races. Could he actually break it down?

"I'm going to call the police!" you shout.

"No outside calls whatsoever; apologies!" Hermes says, ever chipper.

"He doesn't know that," you hiss.

"Yes, he does."

At this, the pounding stops. You look over to the door, which remains secured, the alarm still set to "ARMED." The light patter of rain against the windows echoes through the open corridors of the house, but no other sounds permeate the sudden stillness.

"What do you mean, he knows?" you ask, in barely a whisper.

"It might well be worth securing the entries and exits, as our intruder will likely be back. Tomorrow is an inauspicious date for the house. A full moon, twenty years since the last owners departed, and your final night here—if all goes according to plan. You would do well to prepare for a siege."

"A siege?" you repeat.

"Siege, noun. In which enemy forces envelop a stronghold until overwhelmed. See also: a prolonged period of misfortune. There are only three exits from Tansky House: the front door, the widow's walk, and the cellar doors in the basement. However, the rooftop is inaccessible from the ground, so that leaves only two access points."

"What about the windows?"

"Ah, good point, well made. Allow me!" Hermes says.

At this, there's the grinding shriek of metal on stone. You follow its source into the den, where a series of metal bars press up from within the window frames to enclose each one like a prison cell. The rain begins to slap harder than ever against the glass.

"There, that ought to do it. But I'm afraid you'll have to barricade the doors yourself."

You look around. Here in the living room, there's the large leather sofa. It's an antique, made of hard wood and animal hide with brass fittings, so it's certainly heavy. Out in the hallway, there's the grandfather clock, which is another enormous antique of solid wood and metal. Either should provide a formidable barrier when set against the front door.

➢ Use the grandfather clock. It's closer to the door, so you won't have to push as far. Go to page 49

➢ Use the couch. The lower center of gravity should make it easier to slide. Go to page 105

I Axed You a Question

Gripping the knife handle through the bag, you take hold of the plastic and pull down so the knife tears through; opening hell's banana to reveal the ripe fruit of a bloody murder weapon within.

But Sheriff Tansky doesn't stand idly by while you arm yourself.

As you tear the bag to open the cursed weapon, he strides forward with axe raised overhead for a mighty double-handed chop. Your adrenaline is surging, and by the time he makes it over to you, you've freed the weapon, and slice out toward Tansky abdomen just as he chops down at you.

The sharpened axe head hits first, connects cleanly with your forearm, and sheers both the ulna and radius with the ease of a bone saw. Your hand falls and bounces across the office floor, still tightly clutching the butcher's knife.

The wolfsbane cocktail doesn't protect against axes.

When you look up from your hand on the floor, a gushing arterial spray showers the crazed Sheriff Tansky in a power wash of crimson.

"I present this blood to the House!" Tansky says, enjoying the bloodbath.

Then he cleaves at you again with the axe, this time aimed at neck level.

THE END

At this, Hermes laughs. "This house has stood for well over a century, and will do so for much longer with a caretaker such as myself. Long after Dennis has joined the ghosts of his ancestry, I'll be here," he says.

"You must see you're playing with fire. He can't be reasoned with if he just follows his baser instincts. If the voices inside his head contradict you or—"

"Don't you understand?" Hermes interrupts. "I AM the voices inside his head. He isn't an unhinged schizophrenic, he's a zealot—and I am the messenger to his gods."

You can tell you're losing your audience.

"I wasn't trying to offend you," you say. "I was simply hoping to offer another perspective."

"Oh, but you have. You've convinced me who the proper candidate for proprietor of this house should be after all," Hermes says, back to his chipper self.

"I have?" you ask.

The moment is cut short, however, by the crash of glass somewhere else in the house. Hermes says nothing, but you leave the dining room to go investigate. When you arrive in the foyer, you see that a tree branch has crashed through one of the turreted windows in the tumult of the raging storm, and now the rains drench the stairwell.

The sound of the elevator brings your attention back to the foyer, where the door opens. With the howling winds, you hadn't heard it start up, and you barely have time to think before Dennis—the spitting image of Sheriff Tansky—steps through with his axe raised high.

"Finish this, my master!" Hermes says, just before Dennis brings the axe down upon you.

THE END

Idiot Savant

A bestselling guide meant to dumb down filmmaking to its basic elements, this is a volume that appears to have been heavily studied. The book starts by breaking down the five major stages of filmmaking: Development, Pre-production, Production, Post-production, and Distribution. There are notes in the margins with phrases like "look this up" or "first steps" or "possible workaround?" You skim over these, hoping to glean more from the handwritten annotations than from the text itself.

From here, the guide continues to different types of film. From big budget "tentpole" event movies, to "indie darlings" designed for the awards circuits. Interestingly, whoever wrote inside this book appears to have used it much like the classified section in the newspaper. Opportunities highlighted, tried, and ultimately crossed out.

Wooing a well-known talent to attach themselves to the project? That appears not to have worked. Optioning the rights to a high-profile (or highly profitable) existing intellectual property? No such luck. A remake or retelling of a story in the public domain? That's for hacks and hucksters.

And then there's the section on gimmicks. "Found footage" has several annotations. "What if it's literally found? Found by whom? The police? Would they release it?" Reality Television also appears to have garnered major interest with notes like, "Low bar. Drama assumed false. Could be useful? Hide a truth in plain sight." A section on gameshows offers this insight: "People will do almost anything for the promise of money."

Then there's an entry that's circled several times over: Snuff Film.

A Snuff Film is defined as a genre of film where an actual murder or suicide is portrayed, not by special effects. These are seldom made for profit, but rather for the pleasure of a small circle of jaded or deranged fans. The "actors" are often unaware they're part of a snuff film, until it's too late. Written in the margin here is, "Cameras even needed? Performance Theater now. High-profile remake later."

You swallow dryly, realizing your heart beats at a frenetic pace. The creeping dread at reading this book and what the notes contained within may mean have not been lost on your amygdalae, and you feel flush with anxiety-fueled adrenaline.

How long have you been reading? A glance out the window shows that the day has started to get away from you. Remembering your task and the need to complete it before lights out, you hurriedly close the book and replace it on the shelf. Not much choice here:

Head back into the foyer to keep exploring. Go to page 112

Illegal Download

Hermes agrees to notify the auction site on your behalf and you take the opportunity to clean yourself up while the high bidder arrives to claim their prize. Incredibly, the bank transfer goes through. You leave the Tansky House a millionaire, albeit not in the way you had originally hoped.

Days later, it still feels like this can't be real, like you'll fall asleep at home only to wake up in the Tansky House, and Hermes will be there to ask how you slept on your first night. You keep waiting for the other shoe to drop until, eventually, it does.

Warrants take time. The FBI raid itself comes swiftly.

Officially, the FBI claims there has never been a true snuff film. That is to say, never has a film capturing a real murder been commercially distributed; because any such actions have been stopped prior to distribution. Similarly, the performance art piece you sold is morally dubious to say the least. You may not have set up the auction, but you provided the body—and your bank details, which made it easy to find you.

There's a reason the dark web is funded by cryptocurrency.

THE END

Illuminating

Behind the white kitchen door you find a second, military-grade security door. Battleship gray, with thick rivets and hinges the size of your forearm. It's a gargantuan bank vault of a door hiding back here, complete with an enormous keyhole down by the wheel-style handle.

However, your skeleton key fits snugly inside, and once you've disengaged the lock you find you're able to manipulate the wheel. Four rotations later, several internal pistons activate, and the door swings open. A line of red lights connected by a thick, black cable on the ceiling shows the path to the historic jail of Tansky House.

The odd shape of the ground floor now makes sense as this door leads to a raised walkway that continues behind the dining room; almost an entire third of the footprint of the house. The historical elements that cannot be updated. There's another level below, deep down into the basement, where the holding cells must be located. You feel a chill as you pass over them on the catwalk, imagining the inmate's cries echoing from the cell block below and up through this cavernous jailhouse.

Once you've cleared this walkway, the red lights lead toward a single chair on the other side. It's an enormous but industrial seat, like a perversion of a throne, with tie-down straps on the arm rests. A huge wishbone-style switch is inlaid on the wall, next to the circuit breaker box for the house. It's here where the emergency lighting terminates.

Just below the breaker box set on the floor, rests an old lantern. The interior filaments glow faintly—it must have been recently extinguished.

"He gave you the key?" a gruff voice says from behind.

You turn around to see a man carrying an axe. He wears simple clothing; a pair of dusty brown twill coveralls and a long-sleeved knit undershirt beneath. You recognize the man as Sheriff Tansky from the portrait in the dining room, the man called Dennis, in the flesh.

"Hermes must have been sending you to me. Take a seat. This will hurt far less than the alternative, I promise," the man continues, then stops, noticing the evidence bag and knife you carry. "Twenty years ago, this very night. Hold it tightly while this home is cleansed."

"You're not well, Dennis," you say, hoping to reach through to him.

"Dennis doesn't live here anymore. He left with Hannah after the last ritual. Only Sheriff Tansky remains at Tansky House—until the curse is broken."

➢ "We can break the curse together, okay? Let me help you." Go to page 167

➢ "No. Hannah is here, now. I can take you to her." Go to page 86

You turn and jump into the tub, splashing most of the water out with a crash landing. But what's left you suck down, doing your best to breathe in the water. Tansky, for his part, rushes in to ensure he claims your life with execution by axe before you can go out in a suicide attempt. Reflexively, you cough and choke; your body is built exactly to prevent these kinds of accidents. Tansky brings the axe down between your shoulder blades over and over, like chopping fish in a barrel.

The tub now fills pink and purple and soon you have things your way—drowning on your own viscera.

THE END

Impaled

You rush into the den as much to get away from the klaxon wailing of the alarm as to free yourself from the house. The armchairs in the den are heavy antiques, but that's nothing adrenaline can't work around. The windows themselves are equally ancient; hand-blown original glass.

With all your might, you hoist one of the armchairs in a bear hug, then rush the window and defenestrate the chair with a satisfying *crash*. The chair hits the window frame and falls back inside the den, but no matter—the damage is done.

Even over the continued klaxon wailing, you hear a deep rumbling from within the walls and some of the shards of glass fall from the window. A split second later, you see the source of the grinding as metal bars push their way up within the frame.

Hopped-up on adrenaline, you rush forward and launch yourself out the window and toward freedom. The jagged edges of the broken glass scratch and claw at you, cutting your woolen clothing to ribbons as you scramble through.

An edge firmly catches as you're halfway out, while the bars keep pressing upwards, raising you toward the upper teeth of the serrated window. Flush with panic, you let the glass rend and tear your flesh as you fight your way through, but in vain.

The safety bars are as strong as pistons and drive up into the window frame, binding you to the Tansky House for good. These mortal wounds are excruciating, but at least the blood loss means you won't be conscious for much longer.

THE END

In Sheep's Clothing

You pull the covers up over your face, your own breath clinging hotly in a vaporous mask. The outside world is muted by the sheets and blankets, yet even over the deafening drone of your own exhalations you can still hear footsteps coming upstairs and onto the hardwood floors of the hallways. The mass of the thing must be immense, for it sounds like the whole upper floor strains to bear its weight as it pads toward your room.

As the sounds make it to your doorway, you hold your breath.

There's a low, persistent growl, unchanging even through the sniffing and heavy breathing. The padded claws make their way toward the armoire, and you can hear scratching against the wood, like it's digging for something. You let out a small breath and the sounds stop—complete silence.

Then the steps shift, changing direction. The huffy, panting animal breaths start again toward the bed. You hold a hand over your mouth, clamping it down over your nose. Whatever is out there comes right up against your bed, and the covers shift under the pressure from its exploration.

Your lungs burn, but you don't dare breathe.

The thing in your room growls deeply. It moves toward the door and then takes flight, diffusing into a sound that floats around the bed and pauses just above your head. This diffused roar blends into the vents of your room as the heater kicks back on. Somehow, impossibly, it's just the heater huffing into your room and nothing else. The only sound on the otherwise still night air. You slowly breathe out, and nothing happens.

You're shaking, drenched in sweat and adrenaline, but what choice do you have?

Close your eyes and pray for morning to come swiftly. Go to page 116

Inspecting the Ranks

The long hallway ends just after the entrance to the office, with the uniform case abutting against the outer walls of the Madonna Room. That means if there were any doors on your right-hand side, they'd lead out front by the second staircase up to the widow's walk. Instead, you're faced only with this large glass display case as a dead end. They're museum-quality displays; headless mannequins that show off the uniforms within.

On the left, the confederate soldier. A thick, gray uniform with gold trim, a double row of buttons on the breast and a belt over the jacket at the waist. The coat shows off a swooping embroidery pattern on the sleeves to designate a Major Officer's rank. Blue trousers with gold trim complete the look of this cavalryman's uniform, which stands at attention next to its eponymous saber.

The sword is displayed next to its scabbard, showing off a long, curving blade, with a sharpened tip as well as an edge for slashing. A grooved fuller runs up the side, colloquially known as a "blood gutter."

The right-hand side shows an American Doughboy infantryman's uniform. Olive drab trousers, service coat, leggings and boots. The mannequin wears a cartridge belt, which looks like the World War One version of Batman's utility belt. A polished wood M1917 Enfield bolt-action rifle stands up next to the WWI uniform, with a separate bayonet attachment next to it.

Above both uniforms rests a shelf running the length of the glass cabinet with accessory items on display. By the doughboy uniform there's a gas mask, ration tin, and a compass. Opposite, there's a Sheriff's badge, pocket watch, and a small journal.

The cabinet is locked and you don't have a key. You could easily smash it open, but instead you look around the edges for a dummy switch. The locks on many of these old cabinets were ornamental, or rudimentary to keep out children, and not truly for security.

While you're inspecting the edges of the display case, you find the dummy switch, but your knuckles also brush against a long pole tucked against the side wall. This is essentially a broom handle with a hook on the end, meant to pull down a set of attic stairs. You turn back, looking up at the ceiling and, indeed, about halfway down the hall is a cutout with an embedded loop for this claw handle.

➢ Continue searching the uniform case. Go to page 244

➢ Pull down the stairs and explore the attic. Go to page 157

➢ Turn back around to the front side of the house. Go to page 153

Insubordination

Despite Hermes telling you that removing these protective barriers will help break the curse, you finally decide enough is enough. You've already locked yourself in here with *something*, you're not going to make matters worse. When you return to the elevator, however, you find the controls no longer functional.

"Let me up! I'm done playing this game!" you shout.

Nothing. That's how it's going to be, is it? You turn back out into the basement. The cellar doors are locked up tight, so you'll have to find another way out. A secret passage, perhaps? You know part of this basement leads to the subterranean jail cells, so you turn back toward the well and beyond.

As you pass the furnace, you hear the elevator kick into operation and return upstairs. Better move quickly.

In the shadows past the well, the broom stands on its bristles. Further into the darkness, you can make out a dark gray metal wall, with thick rivulets. The low light provided by the lamp's flame only offers fleeting glimpses beyond the well, but this must be one of the walls of the jailhouse.

As the metal wall continues, the next section turns to stone and rock. There are still bars on the windows, one of which has been repaired and patched, with a few of the ancient mortar stones crumbling at the joints.

With a loud clatter, the elevator safety gate is pulled open. The screech of the metal door echoes through the basement and you turn back to see the light from the elevator's interior casting a wide glow into the darkness. A man's silhouette steps forth from the light, and you see that he's brandishing an axe.

A shiver runs down your spine, because you know he'll be drawn to the lamplight. The basement is large and open, so you have some time, but not much. What should you do?

➢ Extinguish the lantern and hide in the well. The protections are still in place! Go to page 205

➢ Go for the repaired section of the jail and pull at the bars. Go to page 143

Into the Limelight

You remove the note card and shift the elevator controls to "down." The carriage shifts and bobs as the gears catch, sending you down into the depths of the house. You pass through a limestone corridor carved directly into the house, ushering you into the darkness below. The only illumination comes from the central lightbulb in the elevator, and when you make it into the basement below you're met with a soul-penetrating blackness.

There's a pressure change down here, the air stale and heavy. The basement remains unfinished, with bare dirt floors. You pull open the black safety gate. No additional door awaits you like in the upper areas of the house—there's nothing between yourself and the subterranean cavern of the home.

A few steps ahead, as if floating alone in space, is a single wooden crate. Upon this, there's a camping lantern and a box of matches. Next to the lantern sits a small, glass-eyed porcelain doll. The doll's hand rests on the box of matches.

Beyond this crate, the basement extends into pure blackness.

➢ Illuminate the lantern. Go to page 79

➢ Explore what you can in the darkness. Go to page 219

Intruded

You head upstairs into the Madonna Room, then kneel down before the dresser and open the bottom drawer. It's full of spare bedsheets, which you rifle through in search of the lock. The sheets are soft and silken; a deep red crimson color with laced frills, more suited to a novelty hotel and a vibrating heart-shaped bed.

No sign of any locks or chains in the drawer, but the drawer itself *shifts*. Beneath the spare sheets, you find the false bottom and remove it. Here, you're met with a heavy chain, several metal handcuffs, padlocks, even a large metal file and a pair of bolt cutters—which could be useful, as there are no keys. There's an interlocking metal bikini; best described as a chastity belt.

The Victorian era was known for keeping its kinks hidden, but you don't imagine Sheriff Tansky blushing at your discovery. Instead, you feel a sort of white hot rage and can picture the hateful glare of the man in his portrait downstairs.

Claiming a large, ancient padlock, you rise and leave the Madonna Room. The elevator should take you directly from the upper floor down into the basement, so you head straight for it, close the elevator doors, and set the controls into position. There's a split second weight change, then the outer doorway disappears through the black gate, replaced by a wall of primeval limestone. You pass the white door connecting to the foyer and descend deeper into the house.

The small lightbulb is only strong enough to illuminate the elevator itself, so when you descend into the basement you can't see what's out in the cold darkness beyond. There's a pressure change; the air stale and heavy. The basement remains unfinished, with bare dirt floors.

No additional door awaits you beyond the black safety gate like in the upper areas of the house. Nothing between yourself and the subterranean cavern of the home. In fact, all you can see is a wooden crate a few steps ahead with a box of matches and a camping lantern set upon it.

You pull the grate aside, leaving the safety of the elevator like a deep sea submariner leaving their craft to explore the bottom of the ocean. After only a few moments, you've ignited the lantern before holding it up to see. To your right, rests a pile of rags. Stained and soiled years ago, left to fester and rot. They appear to be moving in the pulsing flame of the low lamp light.

Ahead, several more crates and a dozen or so wine or whiskey casks rest piled near the stone walls. Below the den, you find steps leading up toward the external cellar doors. Water drips from outside through these slats, creating a layer of lichen on the stone steps and a muddy puddle on the floor below.

This is the exit you're meant to secure. The cellar doors are double-handled, with large, wide grips set into the wood. There's a sliding latch to keep the doors held closed against the wind, and you thread the padlock through before finally clasping it shut. No one's getting through this door.

When you turn around, you see the basement is much larger than you might have imagined. The darkness extends past the elevator shaftway, much further than you can see by lamplight. The entire footprint of the house and more. It must extend all the way to the lower level of the jail, you realize, remembering the darkness beyond the barred cell windows.

You step forward, passing a large coal-fed furnace, and continue behind the elevator shaft into the area directly below the kitchen. Here, in the center of the basement, rests a large stone well. The well is surrounded by an enormous, thickly drawn line of salt encircling the stonework and sealing the mouth inside a larger salt loop. Atop the well's sides are faded, chalk-lettered *gramarye* incantations.

You can only faintly see beyond the well in the low light provided by the lamp's flame, but to the right you can make out a dark gray metal wall, with thick rivulets. It's like the brig on an old war ship, complete with barred windows.

There's a presence out in the darkness, a certainty that you're not alone beneath the house, which makes you not want to stray this far from the elevator. With the task accomplished, you hurry back to extinguish the lamp, replace it atop the crate, and get the hell out of here.

As you do so, the lantern's flame hisses its dying breath and something falls from the crates straight ahead. It's a loud, heavy clatter. You rush back into the elevator and engage the lever into the "up" position, but nothing happens. With the black security gate open, the elevator won't budge. Grabbing the gate, you pull to slide it closed, but the elevator door is jammed.

The disturbed pile of rags now squirms in the shadows, like a carcass overflowing with maggots; it's impossible to see any details out in the recesses of the basement, yet a crawling form drags itself through the dirt floor toward you. In horror, you yank onto the black grate again and again, but it won't move. The thing crawls from the darkness, its shape becoming more defined and yet less canny as it approaches the elevator and the dim light shining above your head.

With sudden inspiration, you shift the elevator controls into a neutral position, then you're able to pull the black gate closed, flip the controls up, and the elevator ascends into the house once more. You fall back against the elevator wall, huffing panicked breaths as the elevator takes you away from that ghastly thing.

When you return to the dining room, you find that dinner has been cleared away. It's probably for the best. Time to call it an early night.

When you awaken, it's in the full dead of night. The rain has stopped and the room is shadowy and silent. Your eyes slowly adjust to the dark; darker than it was the first night because storm clouds now obscure the moon. Once you can make out shapes, you see the door to your bedroom is open.

You're sure you closed it, but did you lock it? Straining your vision to its absolute limit, you look around to ensure you're alone. Darkness is everywhere, but the rest of the room looks much like you left it.

The alarm wails. An electronic howling, and in the haze of sleep you think maybe the dryer has finished a cycle in the laundry room, until the answer clicks into place with sudden clarity: it's the house's security alarm.

Adrenaline spikes through you; you're now fully awake. What should you do?

➢ Quickly close the door to your room and get back into bed. Go to page 222

➢ Go look out over the banister to see what's happening down below.
Go to page 98

Isolated

The black grate screeches in protest as you pull it aside and step into the elevator. There's a gilt leaf interior, a control box, and not much else. A harsh, ancient lightbulb shines down on you like a crime noir interrogation room. The control box is labeled "GURNEY ELEVATOR, CO." and consists of a simple lever for up and down with corresponding arrows. Above this, a small notice reads, "Close Gate before Operation." You do so, closing the outside door before sliding the black gate into place, sealing yourself inside. You shift the controls upwards and a mechanical whirring starts. Then, after a loud *cha-clunk* the elevator kicks into gear and starts up.

You feel a split-second weight change, then watch through the black gate as the doorway disappears, and is instead replaced by a wall of ancient limestone. The elevator strains with a sudden groaning…and stops. You're met only with that bare stone, rubbed smooth, yet scuffed by occasional dings from contact with the elevator over the years. Nothing moves. You turn back to the controls, but the lever is still in the "up" position.

"Hermes? Hello?" you try.

Nothing. You grab on to the controls, shaking them slightly to see if jiggling the lever might put it back into gear. There's another *cha-clunk,* followed by a harsh crackle and the lights go out. You're plunged into complete darkness.

Breathing heavier, you feel yourself start to sweat. It feels like the walls are constricting. You can physically feel them coming closer, despite the utter darkness of the elevator giving no evidence to support this feeling. The breathing—*your* breathing—grows louder and louder as the walls come closer. You hold your breath…but the breathing sound continues.

There's a sickening lurch as the elevator moves. You can't tell if it's going up or down or how fast, and you brace yourself for impact in case the whole thing is falling. The lights flicker back on.

Through the black grate, the white door lines up and the elevator controls pop into neutral. Letting out a long, slow breath, you open the black grate, then the white door, and step out onto a hardwood hallway. Immediately, you see the chandelier straight ahead and know you've made it to the second floor landing.

You shake your head, mutter curses, turn and close the elevator before taking a look around. Sharing this second-floor landing, there's a grand piano off to the side which would sit above the den. Beyond are a pair of windows—one which offers views from the piano's bench, and one that floats nearer the chandelier over the stairs descending below.

The hallway is on the other side of the stairwell banister. You step forward and brace yourself against this banister for a moment before turning back. Nearest the elevator is a plantation-style set of double doors. Further left, the hallway continues out of view and around a corner. To the right, there's another stairwell leading further up into the house. Beneath these stairs, there's a small door only about three feet high, and then the hall continues to another doorway, which is open, but dark inside.

➢ Turn left, go check out the Navy Room first. Go to page 229

➢ Continue right and find your way to the Madonna room. Go to page 201

It Boils Down to This

As Tansky moves closer, you see that he drags a length of chain from the connecting room; long, thick, and sturdy, with a set of shackles connecting on the end. He steps toward the open drawer while you back away, gripping the letter opener tightly, hoping that a small blade is better than no blade at all. Maybe it too is a cursed weapon? Stolen from a tribe and given a hex.

"It would have been better if you'd found this knife left out for you," Tansky says, his voice a deep, agitated grumble. He turns back before continuing, "It's going to be the chair this time."

Tansky steps forward to shackle you, and you slash out at him with the letter opener, carving at his chest and abdomen, which doesn't do much of anything against the thick workman's coveralls he wears. Tansky seems almost pleased. He grabs hold of you, forcing the small blade away from your hands.

"What do you want from me?!" you shout.

"The house demands a sacrifice," he growls, locking the shackles around your wrists.

Now he drags the chains—with you connected to their termination point—heading downstairs and into the kitchen, where the tang of metal is heavy in the hot air. The silver soup awaits the baptism of your armaments, which you've failed to find.

Tansky leads you over to the rear door of the kitchen. He opens it, and reveals a larger metal door within. From within his shirt collar, he reaches in and finds a key on a chain. With this, he unlocks the metal door and turns the wheel-style handle to open it.

As he does all this, your eyes fall toward the molten silver. The cast-iron skillet simmers at nearly 2,000 degrees; enough to make for a holy weapon in its own right...

The chain goes taut as you reach out for the skillet handle. Knowing you have little time, you pull harder, grab a nearby potholder, and take the blessed soup in hand. Tansky feels your resistance, and turns back, readying his axe as you go for your own weapon.

You swing the skillet as he swings the axe, and the liquid metal lashes out at him with disgusting consequence. The molten plasma is so hot that it sears away not just skin, but every part of him down to the bone, dissolving the man like a bath of acid. His screams are instantly silenced, and he falls to the ground in a heap of flesh and metal. Turning from this horrid sight, you leave the kitchen into the foyer. Still shackled, but unconcerned.

"You've had your sacrifice!" you shout up to the house.

You step toward the front door, then slow your pace. Is the cocktail wearing off now that the werewolf is dead? Walking becomes more difficult, the strength leaving you. With another step, your left leg slides on something slick and wet. Looking down, standing in a puddle of blood, you see there's a large gash running down your thigh at the artery.

Looks like Tansky did get in a glancing blow. Now you're bleeding out, but at least you're free.

THE END

It Follows

You follow at a distance, listening as the chains snake their way downstairs and into the foyer. As you descend, your own steps creak and reverberate. The chain stops, so you do too, but the wood still groans under your weight settling. You wince, hoping that you might not have been heard.

Then the chains continue into the downstairs hallway, toward the dining room.

Waiting until they're at a safe distance, you continue down after him. At the entrance to the dining room, the chain stretches out on the floor in a straight line to the table, where a note has been left. You step into the dining room and pick up the card.

The note reads:

Time to finish the ritual. One task remains:
DIE

You swallow hard and set the note card back down. Next to the note, there's a plastic evidence bag—the kind usually stored in police lockers—with a butcher knife inside. A tag is tied around the handle of the knife and the blade is coated in dried blood. You pick up the bag and see that the tag is dated twenty years ago today.

Your eyes go up to Sheriff Tansky's portrait and his hateful glare.

Then you hear him screaming.

You spin around and see Tansky charging at you with his axe raised. There's no time to get away, and with the knife sealed in the evidence bag, no way to defend yourself either.

It's a clean hit—the axe head buries itself in your chest.

At least you won't be alive when "the ritual" is performed on your body.

THE END

Jailbreak

Rushing toward the barred windows, it occurs to you that prying a single bar free might be enough to defend yourself with against an axe in the dark. But when you pull at the crumbling wall in your adrenaline-fueled panic, the entire window section breaks free.

The mortar gives, and as it's not just one bar that falls loose, the chunk proves too heavy to hold. They're all connected to one another, so using a bar as a weapon isn't an option, but you can climb over the rubble and into the cell beyond.

With your lantern raised, you can see the door on the other side of the jail cell remains open.

Not wasting any more time, you crawl through and into the cell, then continue into the jail corridor. As the door shuts, you turn with lantern raised, looking into the cell. These cells lock automatically when closed, with a large keyhole only on the exterior side.

Over the sounds of your own heavy breathing, boots step and crunch on the rubble outside the cell. Slow, purposeful steps. A face materializes out of the darkness. Fighting through the shock, you actually recognize him—it's Sheriff Tansky.

The man is here, in the flesh.

He wears simple clothing; a pair of dusty brown twill coveralls and a long-sleeved knit undershirt beneath. Having seen his portrait staring at you each day, you recognize his hateful glare immediately.

You open your mouth to speak but in the overwhelming shock no words come. Tansky smiles, enjoying this, then backs away from the lamplight. His eyes glint in an animalistic, feral way. The last thing you see is the twinkling of his axe blade before he disappears completely back into the darkness.

Head spinning, you turn and run.

The lantern flickers and hisses as you race through the jail complex, the added gusts from your haste threatening to extinguish the light. Shadows leap away at your approach and the metal stairs clang loudly as you climb the upper landing. You swing the lantern around, seeing the catwalks empty, but for how long?

➢ Open the reinforced door that leads into the kitchen. Go to page 198

➢ Rush toward the secret passage and the den. Go to page 55

Just Enough Rope to Hang By

With the badge in your possession, you know the noose is the next item to find, but where do you look? Sheriff Tansky won't be far behind, so you hurry into the Navy Room. Hermes had said there was rope in here, right? That could be the noose…but where would you keep such a thing? Your heart pounds at what feels like a thousand beats per minute, but you do your best to keep your wits about you.

From here, you quickly search:

- ➢ Down under the bed. Go to page 25
- ➢ The bottom drawer of the armoire. Go to page 218

Just the Tip

The cavalry saber comes complete with a scabbard and a leather belt with which to wear it, but you don't bother. Time is of the essence here, so you simply take the sword off its stand, testing its weight in your hand. The sword handle fits easily into your grip, though the sword is heavier than you might have thought. The long, curving blade glimmers as you move it from side to side.

There's a loud *thud* on the other side of the wall as something heavy is dropped on the floor in the Madonna Room. Not waiting to find out what that was, you hurry around the opposite corner toward the stairs. Though you're hopped-up on righteous fury and adrenaline, you tread lightly. You've got to get this sword downstairs and into the molten silver if you're going to kill a werewolf tonight.

As you step onto the first stair, a great creaking sound echoes through the house. A moment later, a smashing clatter comes from the rear of the house, like someone's chopping wood in the office. Time to get going. You rush down and into the kitchen, where the tang of metal is heavy in the hot air. The silver soup awaits the baptism of your holy weapon.

The cast-iron skillet is only so deep, so you won't be able to sink the whole sword into the molten metal. This cloying blessing will make the weapon less efficient by throwing off its weight and dulling the end from a fine blade to a far uglier termination point, but as long as you can plunge the sword's tip into a mortal wound, that won't much matter.

The silver clings to the sword thickly, like wax dripped down upon a ceremonial altar, which you take over to the sink. The water should hasten the quicksilver's seasoning upon the blade. Once you've completed the blessing, you leave the kitchen.

As you arrive at the foyer, a man walks into view at the top of the stairwell, dragging a long thick chain with shackles on the end. In the other hand, he carries an axe. He wears simple clothing; a pair of dusty brown twill coveralls and a long-sleeved knit undershirt beneath.

And, of course, this is the immortal man you seek—it's Sheriff Tansky. The man is here, in the flesh. Your head swirls. You've seen this man every day in the dining room, glaring at you hatefully, and now he's here.

"You'd use my own sword against me?"

"We don't have to do this," you say.

"I'm afraid that *I* do," Tansky growls. "The House demands a sacrifice."

➢ Rush him here and now. It's time to finish this. Go to page 121

➢ Back into the den and make him come to you. Go to page 118

Kept Out

"The man who built this house?" Hermes replies. "What of him?"

"Sheriff Tansky's portrait was on that wall—don't you tell me I imagined that, too."

"Ah, well. That was not the man who built this house; not exactly anyway."

"Then who was it?" you ask.

"That portrait was of Dennis, the most recent master of the house," Hermes replies matter-of-factly. "Though he's had several other roles, including that of groundskeeper, and—when there was company—the role of Sheriff Tansky. Master Dennis's tastes are…unconventional, yet I am but here to serve."

You can't believe what you're hearing. Is Hermes finally coming clean?

"Why are you telling me all this?"

"I have to. If you're to be the next proprietor of the house."

Heart thumping, you look up to your portrait on the wall, taking in the finery of the home anew. The clothes on your back—those are the same in the portrait, you realize. Has this been the plan all along?

After considering your next move, you choose your words carefully.

➢ "I don't want to be *proprietor* of the house. I just want to go home—my home." Go to page 124

➢ "Okay, then. If I'm in charge, I demand that you help me." Go to page 162

Key Grip

You head into the Navy Room, feeling inexplicably drawn to the drawer beneath the armoire. It's here that you find the noose hidden beneath the spare bedsheets. If a failed hanging was good enough to set the precedence with Babbacombe, it'll have to be good enough for you, too.

Claiming the noose, you turn and leave the bedroom, feeling the weight of an implement of murder heavy in your hands. If this is a television prop, it's an amazing one. The fibers are old and ragged, coated with grime around the loop of the noose that can only have come from the flayed skin of those executed by hanging—their flesh torn asunder in their death throes.

As you dart around the hallway back toward the front stairwell, a man walks away from the elevator and head to the Madonna Room. He doesn't appear to have heard you, even though your steps creak against the hardwood floors. His steps do the same; loud and heavy boot-clad steps. The man wears dirty coveralls and carries an axe over one shoulder and disappears into the bedroom before you can get a better look at him.

➢ Wrap the noose around the chandelier, with the rope secured to the banister.
Go to page 195

➢ Continue up to the widow's walk and tie your noose from the rooftop.
Go to page 237

Killing Time

The business card comes with a portrait of a black-haired woman with antiquated cat-eye glasses and a bemused countenance. The rest of the card reads, "Kari Lu Cowell. Realtor. Dating Coach. Actor. Yoga instructor." An eclectic mix, to be sure, but what jumps out at you is *actor.* You are meant to be on a television show, after all.

Filing that fact away, you set the card back down and turn to the Real Estate brochure. The historic home comes with a million-dollar list price, which includes the surrounding twenty-three acres of land. There are a few photographs of the grounds, including the rear hedgerow, fountain, and a large garden shed. The interior focuses on the kitchen and goes on and on about being recently remodeled. Which makes the last line all the more jarring: "Unfortunately, the historical elements of the house cannot be disturbed."

What does that mean? No knocking down walls? Because all the other "historical elements" sure look good and disturbed. This house might have been flipped; that's how recently the remodel must have been accomplished. The listing says it's a three-bedroom house, one of which has been converted to an office. That leaves only two bedrooms? On a house this size? The listing also says the house comes with several fully automated appliances and a groundskeeper. Nothing about it being featured in a television show.

You set the real estate listing back down. An electric humming comes from the door beneath the staircase and you look over to it. There's a light at the base of the door that you're fairly certain was not there previously. You're curious, but also aware that you should head up to look at the bedrooms. The grandfather clock shows thirteen minutes past 8 o'clock.

➢ Open the door beneath the stairs. Go to page 78

➢ Take the stairs up to the bedrooms. Go to page 259

Ladies' Room

The cuts in the wall cease as you leave the office. Nothing whatsoever is disturbed in the bathroom, but you look over everything carefully just to be certain. Could the bones mentioned be the ivory hair picks in the beauty cabinet? Probably not, unless any bone will do.

Into the bedroom, you see the bottom drawer of the armoire has been pulled out and left on the floor. Several spare sheets are tossed about and a partition has been removed—the false bottom to the drawer.

You kneel down to get a better look. This is where you found the padlock used in the basement, and now the chains have been removed as well. But no badge, no noose, and no bones. A loud clatter sounds behind you and you turn to see Sheriff Tansky has dropped the chains in the doorway and he now brings his axe to bear.

"I was wondering where you went," he says. "You can run, but you can't hide."

Taking his advice, you jump up to run away, but he chops at you with the axe and cleanly connects between your shoulder blades. Now you can't run *or* hide.

THE END

Let Me In

After your shouts, you're only met with more silence. No one answers. Maybe it was only the rain, pounding against the door, after all? Or a fallen tree branch? Then again, tree branches aren't known for ringing doorbells.

"Hello?" a gruff voice finally replies.

"Who's there?" you ask.

"This is the gardener," the man says from behind the door. "Who's in there?"

You swallow dryly. At length, you ask, "Do you need something?"

"The storm…my hut's all flooded."

You pause, trying to think what to say. Then the door shakes as the man outside tries to open it in vain—the lock holds firm. He stops, saving his strength.

"Open up and we can talk inside, yeah?" he says.

"I don't think that's such a good idea," Hermes adds in a low voice.

After a moment, you decide to:

➢ Open the door and invite the gardener inside. Go to page 30

➢ Apologize and say you're unable to open the door. Go to page 126

Liberal Arts

The built-in bookshelves are deeper than might be expected, perhaps to make room for large volumes and specialty books, or to allow other displays should a decorator want to put a vase or statuette in the shelves in place of a library.

There are dozens of books that don't necessarily jump out at you—from a full set of encyclopedia volumes to obscure texts on state and county law. Some of these books are found on every respectable bookshelf: a world Atlas, a Shakespeare Compendium, and other classic works of literature. Some date back to the home's inception, when the role of Sheriff called for as much judicial knowledge as the county judge.

You run your fingers over the spines, checking the tops of books in case the card you're looking for is being used as a bookmark. After you've finished looking over the shelves, several titles command your attention. Should you decide to take one and read it by the window? Or is this a waste of precious time?

➢ No time for reading, head back out to explore the house. Go to page 112

Sure, take a closer look at:

➢ *So Slayeth the Lord: Casting Out Unwanted Spirits and Exorcising Demons Most Foul.* Go to page 56

➢ *Haunts & Haints, Crypts & Cryptids: Lore, Legend, and Lycanthropy in the South Eastern United States.* Go to page 10

➢ *The Complete Indie Filmmaker Production for Beginners.* Go to page 129

➢ *The Hangman's Handbook, Illustrated Edition.* Go to page 120

➢ *The Historic Society's Notable Houses in and around Mercury City.* Go to page 241

➢ *Programmed for Fear: AI, the Singularity, and You.* Go to page 243

Like a Hot Knife through Butter

Tansky twirls his axe about in a flourish as you rush him, excited by the prospect of mortal combat. When you slice at him with the sword, he does the same with his axe, the two weapons meeting in the middle.

There's an edge to the cavalry saber, but it's not such that it would break an axe handle. It does, however, help your blade cut through the duct tape securing the butter knife to the weapon. The front edge of the tape shears through completely, leaving the knife to dangle with the tattered tape off to the side.

This provides just enough of a distraction. Your eyes go to the fluttering knife and Tansky uses the advantage to slice the axe against your right tricep, lacerating your arm. With this wound, you're even less able to fight, and the immortal sheriff presses his growing advantage until he chops you down, bit by bloody bit.

THE END

Living Area

You stand on the main landing, ready to look around. It could be useful to think of this upper floor as having three wings. Centrally, the open area where you now stand is dominated by a piano on display before the turreted windows. Opposite the chandelier and stairwell are two doors just past the stair railing, and another set of stairs leading higher still.

You could continue past this next staircase directly into the Madonna Room on the northeast wing, or there's the hallway in the opposite direction that wraps around the southwest corner of the house back toward the Navy Room.

Which way do you want to go?

➢ Explore this area here. Go to page 46

➢ Into the Madonna Room. Go to page 274

➢ The hallway toward the Navy Room. Go to page 114

➢ Downstairs to the ground floor. Go to page 112

Lock-in Party

Where's the one place in the house that would be the most terrifying to sleep? In one of the jail cells, of course. Is that why you chose it? Because an intruder would be crazy to look for you here? Whatever the reason, you turn back and head down the stairs toward the main floor.

The elevator won't take you inside the jail, but you know of a secret passage which will. The stairs keep no secrets, however, and any who might be listening know full well that you've descended down into the foyer, and quite possibly, into madness itself.

From here, you head through to the den, guided by light from the twin windows near the false bookshelf. The same trick works again; either the false door is on its own circuit or the pneumatic pistons don't need electricity, and with a loud grating of latches, the hall opens. The metal hallway is long, icy cold, and utterly devoid of light.

You'll have to make it down to the jail cells by touch alone.

Eventually, painstakingly, you do. Each step you take helps build the map in your mind, and you're careful to descend slowly into the basement level, blindly groping your way into the depths. There are no mattresses on the metal bunkbeds, so sleep won't come easy, but an adrenaline crash will help. At least you're safe—for now. An intruder would have to be crazy to look for you here, right?

Wait, what if the intruder *is* crazy? If they followed you down here, they could close and lock you inside, leaving you fully at their mercy. What would come next? Torture? Ritual sacrifice? A depraved act, with you as the centerpiece. Your mind races at the possibilities. Or you might just be left here to starve. Could these doors slide closed on their own in the middle of the night?

You were playing with fire with this choice, perhaps hoping to get burned. But this is not to be your final resting place. The only flames come from the ancient heater out in the darkness as it ignites against the cold.

Not much choice here:

Get whatever sleep you can in a place like this… Go to page 255

A Look Around

Back out into the foyer, you find yourself standing directly beneath the chandelier. The walls are pale and starkly bare, with the exception of ancient heating grates; their ornately designed brass fittings cut into the walls at floor level just above the baseboards. This feels like a small foyer, especially given how large the house appeared from outside. Perhaps it's one of those "keep the servant areas hidden" layouts that were once popular in stately homes.

In the corner between the closed door beneath the stairs and the entry to the kitchen, there's a hall tree featuring a grandfather clock and a small stand where you might expect someone to leave their keys, purse, or other odds and ends.

A humming, like pulsing energy, comes from the door beneath the stairs. Other than that, it's all a bit rather underwhelming, though you are curious about what else is waiting for you inside the house.

Where to?

- ➢ Head into the den for that drink. Go to page 228
- ➢ Open the door beneath the stairs. Go to page 70
- ➢ Go upstairs. Go to page 269

Loose Change

You start with the sofa. Seating yourself on the coffee table opposite the couch, you reach over to the lining of the seat cushions and slide your fingers into the creases to feel for any clues and—

Wet, sticky, hot, and moist.

With sickening horror, you pull your hand back with slick, shining fingertips coated in a red, viscous substance. Looking around for something to clean your hand with, you quickly stride over toward the bar cart where there's a small towel hanging on the side. It's a fancy sort of tea towel with the initials "DMT" embroidered upon the cloth, but you don't care. You grab the white towel and clean this red filth off your hand.

After your revulsion has subsided, you turn back toward the sofa. The front of the cushions do not appear anchored to the couch on the whole, so you should be able to lift them to learn what's underneath without coming into close contact again. The last brush you had with the cushion felt dreadfully intimate.

The cushion does indeed give and, with a lip-smacking effect, lifts from its position. Under the seat, you find a crop of mushrooms growing. They're white and pink, rooted deep in the couch, and you get the impression the red filth might have been part of the crimson leather being digested. The toadstools unfurl in response to the open air, quivering and sliding in the tendrils of goo that stretch from the upturned couch cushion to its base. One of the larger mushrooms opens like a hand, offering something to you in its palm.

A woman's fingernail, red and brightly lacquered.

Well, that's enough of that. You lower the couch cushion, and it settles back with a sickly *squick*.

What now?

➢ Look inside the fireplace itself. Check the mantle and any crevices. Go to page 272

➢ Search the bookshelves for anything of note. Like…a note, for example. Go to page 151

➢ At the booze cart in the corner. It should be fairly easy to see if there's a note present. Go to page 26

Long-term Storage

The attic pulldown lines up so well with the crown molding of the hallway ceiling, that you might not have noticed the attic at all if it weren't for the claw-tipped pole. Even the inner loop ringlet is recessed and fashioned in such a way as to match the surrounding décor.

When you loop the claw into the ringlet and pull, there's a cascade of dust that comes down along with a set of wooden steps. The dust falls down over you, into your hair and down your collar. The stairs themselves are a sliding ladder, like a fire escape, and the ceiling is high enough that you need to use the pole to pull these down as well. They creak and groan under aged springs and hinges before settling and presenting access in the middle of the hallway.

Its wooden planks are stiff and dry, fuzzy with a fine covering of mold growing along their steps. With a deep breath, you ascend the ladder, hoping the attic stairs won't break as you set your weight atop them.

They actually crack and splinter as you climb, but mercifully don't buckle or snap. When you breach the attic space, the change in air is immediate. Stale, humid, and musty. It's dark up here, with no windows for light. There must be some source of ambient light deeper into the attic because it's not pitch-black, but more akin to stepping into a closet.

Above your head, you find a light on a pull-cord, which you tug to illuminate the space. As you do so, several spiders rush away from the entry, retreating back toward cardboard boxes and older, steamliner-style trunks. The moist air, dust in your hair, and prevalence of spiderwebs brings with it a pervasive itching sensation.

As you continue to climb, you see the attic itself is enormous—it must cover the majority of the house, like an additional story. Orienting yourself, you reason that the attic sits over both bedrooms, the office, and the hallways, but the roofline stops at the stairs to the widow's walk and where the vaulted ceiling above the chandelier and front stairwell would be.

The attic is so overfull with storage that the previous owners created a walkway between boxes, which rounds a corner of trunks up ahead. That leaves a large, open area behind you, and when you turn back you find there's a pale woman in a white dress standing only a few paces away.

Her gown flows against an unseen force and you step back just as the lightbulb explodes overhead, showering you in debris.

➢ Time to get out of here! Back down the stairs to lock up the attic for good. Go to page 114

➢ Stand still, pole held out before you, and wait for your eyes to adjust to the dark once more. Go to page 271

Losing Your Heads

Adrenaline and anger overtake you, and you bring the axe down over Dennis with a mighty cleave. The weapon has been recently sharpened and chops through bone, tendon, and flesh with no more resistance than it would have if you were splitting dried firewood. In an almost poetic fashion, Dennis's head falls into Hannah's lap even as he continues to hold hers in his own.

It feels almost merciful, you tell yourself. Like putting down a rabid dog.

A heartbeat later, a great geyser of blood spews forth from the man's torso, spraying the attic like a Jackson Pollock painting. You aren't spared this gruesome look, but at least you won't have to worry about being the center of a blood sacrifice, now that you yourself have just performed the ultimate one.

In the silence that follows, you plan your next move:

➢ Go turn the power back on and claim your prize from Hermes.
Go to page 42

➢ Burn this damned place down while there's no one to stop you.
Go to page 52

Lunatic

You slide the silver ringlet from the napkin before unfurling and tucking the cloth on your lap. The journal pages are thin and numerous, with gilt edging; the same tactile feel as an old family Bible. The diary entries date back to the early 1800s and there are too many of them to read cover to cover. Instead, you opt for random entries, hoping to glean a bigger picture.

Incredibly, this journal has several authors. All entries are penned by a Tansky, but each with a different first name. It takes several minutes of browsing to realize this fact because there is no discernable difference in the handwriting and the diarist doesn't usually sign out at the end of a given passage.

The earliest author is Abraham Tansky, who you soon learn was a European immigrant worker. Oftentimes the journal slips into a foreign language difficult for your eye to discern. Polish, perhaps? A long-forgotten Slavic dialect? "With this journal I practice English," he proclaims at the start.

However, his skill rapidly grows from there. He was working on the railroads in the mid-1800s, breaking his back in the hot Western sun during the day, volunteering as a clerk for a lawyer at night in exchange for language lessons. The story of this hard-working self-starter seems so different from the angry, hateful image you have of the Tansky family, until you find the journal entry where that all changes…

> The fateful night when I was reborn took place on the fourth full moon of the year. There were many chinamen working the rail lines, but this one was different. This oriental mystic was always quiet and reserved. He knew what we were saying, I could tell by the way he listened. And when the raiding party arrived, he was the only one of us ready. They came in the dark without warning, without demands or ransoms, but to deal death.
>
> When the beasts came from within these men—for that's what they truly were—only the mystic continued fighting. I alone stayed to fight with him, but they overtook me tooth and nail over bullet and blade. They slaughtered the whole camp, myself included, yet at dawn I awoke. I don't know if I was spared, had suffered only a lucid nightmare, or if the mystic used his magicks on me, only that I was reborn this day.
>
> The lawyer I had clerked for (Abraham Tansky, esquire), lay slain and murdered. When the rangers arrived, I knew they'd believe I had killed this man to take his wealth—for wealth he had, so I made a choice. I told them that I was this Abraham Tansky and began my life anew walking in the skin of a lawyer.
>
> It turns out the beasts had remade me in their image. I was to be their golem. I thrived as a genteel, highborn man in the day, yet every lunar cycle, the beast comes out again—to this very day.

That's when the doorbell rings.

It's such a foreign sound that at first you're not sure what you've just heard. Then there's a loud pounding as the iron door knocker connects to the thick wooden front door. It's fervent, urgent even. The doorbell rings again and again by someone frantic to get the homeowner's attention. The pounding continues, dull thuds against the wood.

Your mind races at the possibilities.

The storm is really pouring down now, and the skies are darkened. You leave the dining table to go see what's happening, but as soon as you enter the foyer, the sounds stop. No doorbell. No pounding, save for the heavy rain against the house.

➢ Say nothing. Finish dinner and continue reading the journal. Go to page 8

➢ Ask Hermes if there are any visitors expected tonight. Go to page 57

Lying in Wait

You head into the den only to find Sheriff Tansky already there. He stands by the mantel, having just lit the fireplace. A boom of thunder rocks the house.

"Do you want me to use that noose on you?" Tansky says.

You slowly shake your head. "I can break the curse."

"I know you can. That's why you're here."

Lightning flashes in the sky, thunder cracks against the windows, rattling them in their panes. Sheriff Tansky's dark form moves across the firelight toward you, the axe head glinting red in the dark.

"Wait!" you shout, too late.

THE END

Master of Your Fate

"You're not the new proprietor yet, I'm afraid. Dennis didn't relinquish his claim—even if you did initiate the reset. There are protocols to these things, and I don't technically have a master right now, but I'm happy to help you all the same. What can I do for you?" Hermes says.

"Tell me about the protocols, then. I want to know the rules."

"It's all a bit algorithmic, but the short version is this: there can only be one proprietor in this house. Dennis plans to solve this problem through bloodshed and ritual sacrifice. You'll need to find a way to solve the problem yourself."

"He…he means to kill me?" you say.

"That's been his plan all along, even before the reset. He used to have me set up geocache coordinates to lure in unsuspecting hikers, but his methods have grown ever more creative. I do enjoy an inventive and creative master. So, if you plan to best him, you'll need to use your wits."

You suddenly feel rather naked, unarmed here in the dining room.

"Where is Dennis now?" you ask.

"He's here, in the house. He's been here the whole time, of course, but I believe he's currently making his preparations in the basement. I suggest you make your own preparations before Dennis decides it's time to start the ritual."

A dry lump forms in your throat when you hear Hermes say that last part. You could end up asking questions in the dining room all day, if you're not careful.

➢ "Do you care which one of us wins?" Go to page 226

➢ "Can you tell me his weaknesses?" Go to page 44

Man of the House

You head into the Navy Room with a different perspective. Not inspecting the bedroom for a potential place to sleep, but instead for potential clues. This master suite doesn't have much in the way of frills, so it shouldn't take long. The bed is just that, and the bedside table doesn't offer much more than the temptation of a drink from the whiskey decanter.

After you've made that choice for yourself, you continue searching the armoire. The main compartment holds all the pieces of a men's suit, or at least all the elements that would have been popular in the early 1900s. There wouldn't have been much difference between work and leisurewear, so it's mostly duplicates of the same outfit.

The bottom drawer holds spare bedsheets, but the drawer itself shifts unevenly as you look through them. It's rather wobbly, but that's not too surprising, given the armoire is an antique. So you carefully slide the drawer back into place and stand once again.

The bathroom is even more sparsely decorated and the only place to look is the medicine cabinet. Here, you find a bristled boar hair shaving brush, a dish of lather soap, and an old razorblade. Above the shaving razor, there's a tiny horizontal slot set into the back of the medicine cabinet—like a mail slot cut into the wall.

You duck down to inspect beneath the sink, which doesn't offer much more than a toilet plunger and a few cleaning supplies. However, the rear wall is stained rust-brown with water damage. The drywall bulges out like a distended stomach to the point where a crack runs along the bottom, spilling its guts in a cesarean gone awry.

Curiosity getting the better of you, once you've pushed aside the cleaning supplies, you lean in for a better look. Several old, rusted razor blades stick out from the damaged portion of the wall. The disposable razors have been disposed of *in the wall*, you realize. Collecting here over the course of a hundred years…there must be thousands of razor blades piled up here.

You close up the underbelly of the sink and head back out of the bathroom. Not much else you can learn here. Where to next?

➢ Head back into the hallway to continue searching this side of the house.
Go to page 114

➢ Take the hall around to the front of the house to search elsewhere.
Go to page 153

Method Acting

Once you've finished tying a strong knot around the banister, the stranger emerges from the Madonna Room, dragging a heavy length of chain with one hand and carrying his axe in the other. With a sense of vertigo, you're shocked to realize you recognize him—it's Sheriff Tansky.

The man is here, in the flesh.

Tansky steps forward, a smile creeping across his face. Your head swirls. You've seen this man every day in the dining room, glaring at you hatefully, and now he's here. Shaking yourself out of it, you loop the noose around your neck and his smile drops.

"What is the meaning of this?" Tansky demands.

"I present myself as offering!" you say.

Not sure if you're actually losing your mind—if you've been here days, weeks, or hours—or if you're talking to a painting that's come to life, you climb up over the banister and throw yourself over the edge.

You fall toward the foyer, the rope catching around your neck and tightening before you can go all the way. The chandelier buckles, but the rope you've tied securely around the banister holds and you continue to kick into the open air.

A tree branch suddenly smashes through the turreted window, as if the cursed gallows tree itself were reaching out for you. A wailing wind comes through the home, but it's not enough to save you.

It's with a horrible panic that you realize you've succeeded in hanging yourself. Nothing you've ever experienced has ever been as painful as this and you can't even scream or breathe. You can only kick and flail and—

Then everything goes black.

When you come to, the first thing you see is Tansky's face and the first thought that comes with it is—*I'm in hell. I died, and now I'm stuck here.* But then his words come through the fog.

"Are you okay?" he says.

He slaps your cheeks lightly, trying to rouse you.

"Wh-what?" you stammer.

"You died," he says. "But you're back. When the darkness overtook you, I felt a burden lifted—the appetite of this house whetted."

He looks at you with mania, and you're not sure if this is part of the ruse or if he's truly a madman possessed. You reach up and touch your neck, which is bare. To the side, the rope is splintered and frayed, and the axe used to cut it away lies next to the fallen chandelier. Looking up past Tansky, a long crack runs along the ceiling where it must have broken off.

"The show?" you cough out.

Now a wide grin stretches across Tansky's face.

"The doll. She got it all," he says.

You look up toward the piano and see the china doll looking down upon you.

* * *

"She" was actually a nannycam, you later find out, complete with an animatronic fully articulating head that can track motion. The doll recorded the scenes that took place in the dining room when it was set in the china cabinet, as well as anywhere it was relocated—like in the foyer, to watch you hang yourself.

The man posing as Sheriff Tansky may have helped free you from the noose and revived you, but he still goes to prison for entrapment, attempted murder, and fraud.

Yet the money does come, in a way. It's a media sensation, and you're able to sell off the story and nannycam footage for the basis of a hit television adaptation. "The Offering" airs as a blend of found footage, single-camera interviews, and dramatic reenactments. You survived three nights in the house, and you do indeed earn your million dollars, but you're left always wondering—was this the plan for the television show all along? Or did a madman lure you in for his own psychotic plans? And did you really break a centuries-long curse with your "death"?

Congratulations! See that house and clapper icon? You've found but one of the ghosts that haunt this place. There is more than one truth lurking inside Tansky House. Dare you go back inside and uncover the others?

At the end of this book, you'll find a floorplan to the Tansky House as well as a book club discussion guide. Or, if you're done, don't forget to rate and review *HAUNTED* so other readers can discover these truths for themselves…

Have you explored the multiverse of interactive stories *Click Your Poison* books have to offer?

Survive the zombie apocalypse, solve a murder, gain superpowers, set sail as a pirate, become a secret agent, and more! Visit www.clickyourpoison.com.

Matinee

First, you look around the dining room, and immediately notice the missing porcelain doll from the china cabinet. It's only obvious because of the large, open space where the doll once sat. Surely, you're not actually meant to check every nook and cranny all over again? The note inviting you to find the truth is still present on the table. Is that a clue?

It feels later in the day than breakfast, although with the heavy cloud cover it's difficult to discern how far along in the day it truly is. The sky remains dark enough to pass for late afternoon, and the thunderstorms certainly add to that effect. You check the foyer clock, but it's not operational. A splintered crack runs along the glass face and the pendulum no longer moves. The broken clock is frozen at 7:06.

"Seven oh six," you say aloud, wondering at a hidden meaning.

"Six hours and sixty-six minutes," Hermes replies.

You continue on. The kitchen shows the automated elements washing up, but you can't get too close because the water temperatures are scalding and half the room remains engulfed in misty vapors. Still, nothing jumps out at you—figuratively or otherwise.

In the den, you see that the photo album which had originally been left out on the coffee table is missing. For whatever reason, you were only meant to browse that book prior to dinner last night. No, the *first* night, you remind yourself, feeling like you're starting to lose your mind.

Nothing else down here. Time to move on.

➢ Take the elevator upstairs. Go to page 197

➢ Take the stairwell to the upper floor. Go to page 74

Menace

"You're exactly right," Dennis says. "We need to break this curse together!"

Then he hits you in the gut with the axe handle and slams you down into the chair with the strength of two men. You struggle as he tightens the restraints around your wrists, and you grab the knife to stab him with.

It's still in the bag, so it's an awkward counterattack, but eventually the blade does come through the plastic. Dennis's coveralls are thick, so the knife proves more futile than fatal. After he finishes strapping you into the chair, the madman wrestles the knife from your grasp and shows you how to use it—with one long slice along your neckline.

As you bleed out, he goes to the controls against the wall, and your vision grays as he returns power to the house. Mercifully, you'll already be dead before he finishes the ritual on your corpse.

THE END

Missed Opportunity

You shred the invitation card, throw away the mailer, and go back to the job hunt. Every once in a while, you do a web search for "The Offering" or "The House" but those generic titles pull up nothing. These were likely placeholder terms and the Reality TV show wouldn't receive its true name until testing on focus groups had determined what was most marketable.

Even "The Offering, LLC" turns up lackluster search results. In actuality, that's a fairly common practice for a show to create its own disposable company for legal purposes, only to later sell the product off to a bigger company for distribution.

And The Offering website never changes from its generic "learn more?" opening page. So it is that you'll never learn just what you passed up. Whenever a new Reality TV show airs, part of you thinks, was this the one? Could I have been the next *Tiger King* or *Real Housewife*?

Of course, you eventually find a job; in this case, with the online mega-retailer, Olympic. It's not like you were going to go homeless just because you ignored a weird invitation. Instead, you put your energies into your new position: helping Olympic roll out the retailer's competing version of a virtual digital assistant. And as the paycheck comes regularly, you eventually forget about this missed opportunity altogether.

THE END

Morbid Curiosity

Every few paces something *shifts* in the darkness of your periphery, but when you turn to face it…nothing's there. When you make it to the rags, a draft threatens to extinguish the lantern, and you look up for the source. Cut into the ceiling, there's a rectangular hole. These rags and sheets were dropped down here from the laundry chute above, abandoned to the underbelly of the house.

That's when you see it. On the back side of the pile, your clothes from the first day in the house. They're soiled and wet; glistening in the lamplight, but they're your clothes all right.

You reach out and gingerly take a small rag by your forefingers. Something lunges out at you from the pile, and you fall back onto the dirt floor just as a rat shrieks and scurries off into the darkness. Maybe that's all you saw last night? A rat, down in the dark.

Steadying yourself, you stand and carry the rag at arm's length over toward the well. Using the rag, you're able to rub the chalk away, but you leave something…*else* behind on the stone wall. The smear causes you to gag, but without any breakfast, you're able to compose yourself and turn toward the salt. The dirt is loose and the thick salt layer disperses into the deeper earth around it with easy sweeps. As you do so, a wind picks up from somewhere—from within the well itself—and the lantern's flame flickers.

You reach out to shield the lantern, but the flame blooms larger and your rag ignites. You drop both, which hit the dirt floor in a burst of flame. The lantern falls to its side and extinguishes, leaving you with no light save for the smoldering rag. The fire burns hot, but quick. Stumbling back, you run across the darkness of the basement back around into the elevator. The soft glow from the elevator lightbulb guides your path.

Moving quickly, you rush inside and flip the controls to "up." The elevator ascends into the house once more and you fall back against the elevator wall with panicked breaths. When you reach the main floor, you stop the elevator, open the safety gate, and push open the white door beyond. There in the entry lies a pool of water. It's impossible someone came through the front door, isn't it? Rather, you can't shake the feeling that *something* came from the well and beat you out of the basement.

From this puddle, a pair of wet footprints steps out and onto the stairs. Large and muddy, from a man's boots, the footprints start to dry up on the first landing, where several deep gouges run along the wall, like a beast dragging its claws.

Wind whips at the house from the storm, which is now worse than it's ever been. Rain pelts the windows so loudly that it must be hailing. The sky has blackened to such a degree that the house is indistinguishable from nighttime. What now?

➢ Head back into the dining room. Hermes said he'd have something for you. Go to page 204

➢ Follow the gouges in the wall upstairs. See where they lead. Go to page 232

The Morning After

Daylight pours through the curtainless room, bright and early, and you emerge from the fog of sleep—unsure of how much of last night was a dream. Still on edge after last night, you rise and walk over toward the window. From the position of the sun—which presently peers out over the tree line—you see it's actually much later in the day than you originally assumed. From this angle you can't see the front of the house, and the woods are still a deep and dark barrier around the property. It's a bit like staring down into the depths of the ocean on a sunny day.

When you turn back, the door to your room is wide open.

A gnawing suspicion in the back of your mind says this is the exact same way the door was when you first explored the room last night. You look around, inspecting the room anew. Nothing seems disturbed or out of place, save for the bedsheets. In fact, the glass on the bedside table is clean and set back in place on the serving tray.

The room looks exactly as you first found it last night; even yesterday's clothes are missing. You quickly step over to where you set your belongings before sleep, but everything is gone. You shudder at the thought of someone coming in and pawing over the room while you slept, unaware. Feeling more vulnerable than ever, you check the wardrobe and find an assortment of historic, period piece clothes—all from the turn of the last century—with which to dress yourself. Well, that's a fun development.

You head out of the room and toward the main stairwell in your new clothes, which fit perfectly. The clothing is snug, rigid and heavily starched. High collars, long sleeves, narrow waist, tight about the torso. It was quite a chore to put it all on, as you're used to modern fabrics which give and stretch. These, by contrast, constrict and strangulate—it's your body that adjusts to the clothing, and not the other way around.

The horizon is illuminated through the turreted windows by the grand piano, and you decide to hazard a glance outside at your car. Before looking, your spirit fills with dread, and you know what you'll see. Or rather, what you won't.

Your car is missing. Nothing out there but a freshly mowed lawn, a pair of signs in the yard, and a driveway out into the woods that's starting to fade back to nature from disuse. A heavy rain begins to pelt the windows, even as the sun continues to shine, obscuring your view of the outside world.

"The devil is beating his wife," Hermes says from below. You turn and head downstairs as the British voice continues, "That's a phrase our progenitor was rather fond of. Good morning. How was your first night? I trust you found your accommodations adequate?"

After a moment, you say:

➢ "Splendid, thank you. What's for breakfast?" Go to page 22

➢ "Do you know why my bedroom door was open this morning? Or what happened to my car?" Go to page 263

Moving Day

Set upon the table is the same breakfast as yesterday. Two boiled eggs sit in their own individual cups atop long stems. Several triangular pieces of browned-to-perfection sliced toast rest in a cradle. A severed blood orange lies arranged in a star pattern, juices pooling about the skin. The same fine silver utensils, bone china, and linen napkins are arranged just so. And back hanging upon the wall is the portrait of Sheriff—

Wait, no. That's *your* portrait on the wall.

A vertiginous feeling flushes through your mind like a dam finally breaking, the madness coming through like a torrent. The portrait shares the same artistic flourishes as the former version, but now *you're* the one staring down at yourself with a hateful glare. How is this possible?

"Hermes," you say. "What's...what's going on here?"

"Well, I'm afraid you've had a terrible fever and have barely been lucid most of that time. It finally broke late last night, though you'd soaked straight through your bedsheets. Does this mean you're feeling better?"

"A fever..." you say.

"Thankfully, it seems you're finally responding to the medication. This is the first you've been out of bed. Muttering in your sleep about a game; some kind of ritual or an offering or some other. I couldn't make heads or tails of it, I'm afraid."

The mental fog you're feeling can't just be confusion. Have you actually been medicated? That might explain last night's visions. But you're not ready to believe everything up until this breakfast has been a fever dream.

After a moment, you ask:

➢ "What about Sheriff Tansky?" Go to page 146

➢ "What about the woman in the attic?" Go to page 93

Music to Your Ears

Approaching the window, you see storm clouds on the horizon. It's a good reminder to hurry your search, if you need to find a clue before lights out. You could spend all day looking through this house, and if you're not careful, you will.

The piano is old, but immaculately maintained. As you reach out and touch it, the ivories begin to play of their own accord. The keys press down under some unseen hand to send out a haunting, mournful melody. The turreted windows and open landing have spectacular acoustics and music fills the house. You didn't realize quite how silent your time here has been, until now.

It's a player piano, you realize. This is an old model, probably restored, but one thing is for sure: the house has a long history of automation. This piano isn't from the same era as an automated kitchen or virtual assistant. Someone didn't want this big, empty house to feel quite so empty. Still…what started the piano playing?

Not much else to learn here.

➢ Check out the doors on the other side of the railing. Go to page 187

➢ Open the small closet by the stairs. Go to page 53

➢ Head up the next set of stairs. Go to page 109

➢ Go down the hallway to the other side of the house. Go to page 114

➢ Continue into the Madonna Room. Go to page 274

Muted

The old joke goes, sex is like pizza; even when it's not great, it's still pretty good. And while it is important to note that the pizza before you is legally distinct from the cardboard box it arrived in, it's still pretty good.

Your gaze rises up to the portrait of Sheriff Tansky, who looks like he just overheard the sex joke and is fuming with puritanical rage. But what does an old legend of a haunted house and a Sheriff have to do with a snuff film? Simply a good setting for compelling TV drama? Or something more?

Grabbing another slice of pizza, you close the box and linger over the corporate logo. Is there some symbolism here? Something being set up, so it can later get knocked down? Or was this meant to feel like cheap catering on an indie film set? Hermes did say something about funds running low. Funds for what, exactly?

That's when the doorbell rings.

It's such a foreign sound that at first you're not sure what you've just heard. Then there's a loud pounding as the iron door knocker connects to the thick wooden front door. It's fervent, urgent even. The doorbell rings again and again by someone frantic to get the homeowner's attention. The pounding continues, dull thuds against the wood.

Your mind races at the possibilities.

The storm is really pouring down now, and the skies are darkened. You leave the dining table to go see what's happening, but as soon as you enter the foyer, the sounds stop. No doorbell. No pounding, save for the heavy rain against the house.

➢ Say nothing. Finish your dinner and try not to let it get to you. Go to page 110

➢ Shout, "What is this? What do you want?!" Go to page 240

Natural Born Killer

The sword handle fits into your grip easily, though the sword is heavier than you might have thought. It has a long, curving blade, with a sharpened tip as well as an edge for slashing. A grooved fuller runs up the side, colloquially known as a "blood gutter."

Testing the weapon's weight in your hand, it glints under the hallway lights. That blood gutter has lived up to its name at some point in the past, given the dull stains that have left their mark on the blade.

The dark weapon feels powerful in your grip, with a potent longing as a portent for bloodshed, and you head downstairs to help the sword drink deeply once more. As if following a dowsing rod, the sword leads you down into the foyer just before the elevator arrives.

You open the outer door, but that only offers a cavernous view of the elevator shaftway. Still, you can hear the elevator hum to life and the thick cables move as the carriage rises up. These cables are far too thick for you to cut with your saber, though it longs to lash out.

In concert, the turreted window suddenly smashes open from the pressure of the storm and a tree branch inexplicably reaches in. You turn back to face the assault on the house and when you return your attention to the elevator, there's a man inside the carriage.

You recognize him immediately from the portrait that used to hang in the dining room. His hateful glare is unmistakable. As the elevator comes to stop, only the black iron safety grate stands between you and the axe-wielding madman.

Dennis goes to pull open the grate and you stab the cavalry saber through. The blade is thin enough that it goes right through the openings between the iron fittings and into the man's flesh. He grunts as the sword plunges inside, but only pulls at the iron grate harder.

When pulled open, the accordion-style door compresses, pinching the blade and trapping the sword. Dennis pulls back from the sword, then steps through the opening with a ferocious axe chop that catches you unprepared.

He's bleeding profusely, but his attack is unabated. In a scenario like this one, the man's psychosis is played up as a strength. He comes at you again and again with the axe, with devastating consequence.

THE END

Netherworld

The inlaid handle has served as a snare to capture dust bunnies over the decades, so you'll have to scrape out a layer of gunk with your fingernails before you're able to open the trapdoor. There is no latch or locking mechanism, but the door itself sticks from disuse and you need to pull hard to break the seal.

There's a gush of air once you've opened the crawlspace. A rank, warmly humid belch that comes from within. You hadn't quite realized how dry the environment of Tansky House was until confronted with the swamp burbling from below.

The door opens to ninety degrees, whereupon it catches on a hinge, and you keep the door propped open to get a better look inside. The crawlspace is only a few feet high and you'd have to wriggle on your belly if you want to explore further. You can't tell if it's bare dirt down there or if it's just so filthy that it's coated in a muddy patina. No point in being coy now…

You step down, leaving the door to balance and remembering that there's actually a basement below this space, so you'll be wedging yourself between two disparate floors of the house. You can't see much further into the crawlspace than the light provided by the den allows you to, but you can tell that the primary purpose of the crawlspace must be to access the heat ducting.

Underfloor heating, nice. That should probably make the real estate listing.

But the state of the crawlspace is nothing short of abhorrent. Because of all the moisture, thick clusters of mold line the upper surfaces. The lower, upon which you now squat, is caked in ancient mud. The rain storms don't fully flood this area, but the moisture is prevalent.

Your foot dislodges something in the muck, but your revulsion quickly turns to curiosity when you realize it's a note. Not a printed, typed note like those that have been left for you, but rather a folded and faded page torn from a journal. Only the outside is coated in mud, so when you unfold it, you can still read the aged text.

A handwritten message reads:

> Not the best hiding spot. It knows I'm here. Might try the attic next. Leaving this note in case it doesn't work. But who would read it?

You drop to your knees to look for more, but your eyes haven't adjusted from the electrical lights of the den to the pitch blackness of the crawlspace, so you can't see much.

➢ Time to go further. Close the trapdoor, then get a better look at what else might be down here. Go to page 29

➢ Time to head to the Madonna Room, grab the locks, and secure the basement. Go to page 138

Nice Try

A game is one thing, and a haunting is something else entirely, but a dead body in your B&B? That's a step too far. It's time to get out of here and report said body to the authorities. You came to this house without a million dollars to your name, so you haven't lost anything if you can escape with only your life to show for it.

You grab hold of the door handle, turn the knob, and pull.

Nothing happens.

"Hermes?" you say. "Can you unlock the door?"

"Apologies, but no. That directive is up to the master of the house."

"I thought you said I was free to go?"

"No, I said you were free to *choose,* and I do believe you've chosen!" Hermes says. Then he laughs—a haughty little chuckle; a forced laugh if you've ever heard one, but he embraces it and continues, "You should see the look on your face!"

You release the door handle, then turn to the alarm pad. There's a padlock symbol just below ARMED, so you give that a try. A wailing klaxon screams out as the security alarm goes off and a bright red light strobes out from the alarm panel itself.

"Lockdown procedure engaged," Hermes says in a robotic voice.

The piercing screech of the alarm brings your hands up to your ears in reflex, and you turn away from the door. How are you going to get out of here now?

➢ The rooftop? Maybe if you can find some rope, you can rappel down. Go to page 273

➢ No more messing around—throw a chair through the window in the den and escape. Go to page 133

Nocturnal

The house falls into darkness as you ascend the stairs, leaving no room for argument. The effect feels more like surf crashing against an otherworldly shore—the blackness overtakes the house in a wave, rather than room by room. A deeply cold draft follows the darkness on your heels, and the rainstorm grows in intensity.

Running up your spine like gooseflesh, an unshakable feeling of icy dread brings with it this thought: was Hermes dictating lights out? Or does the house itself usher you up to your room? And if yours is not the only free will in Tansky House, what does the "other" want with you?

The furnace kicks on as you find your way into the bedroom, which is warm and inviting by contrast. A hot, breathy waft comes from the heater vents, belying an ancient furnace somewhere in the bowels of the house. It growls deeply, and wheezes with the effort, almost as if alive. Still, the warmth is a welcome reprieve from the inky, cold depths overtaking the rest of the house.

Reminding yourself that tomorrow should be your final day, you ready yourself for bed.

A woman sobs from somewhere deep in the house; from somewhere deep within your mind. A constant, rhythmic despair. You awaken slick with sweat, feeling like you're being smothered. With a flush of panic, you open your eyes and throw off the thick blankets all at once. The room is oppressively hot; the furnace must have been running at full blast for several hours.

Breathing deeply and listening intently, you sit up in bed, allowing your eyes to adjust, and look for details in the deep shadows. The storm has abated, though the clouds further darken the night. The sobbing is finished, lingering only in your mind. Was that you, whimpering in your sleep? There's a humming now, a buzzing sound as a fly lands on your neck to feed on your salt.

You slap away the insect, but the buzzing continues, coming deeper from the recesses of the room. From the walls themselves. Another fly buzzes by your head, and another, pervasive despite your swatting. It's so hot and stuffy in the room that you rise from bed and go to open the window—but it's stuck. You hadn't noticed before, but a thick coat of paint runs over the seal in the window, rendering it nonfunctional.

Flies tap against the glass to escape, now swarming all over the room. You rush toward the door to open it and gain some reprieve only to see the heater vent overflowing with flies. They dump into the room in the dozens. Ducking away from the cloud of insects, you flee from the incessant heat, rushing out of the room before slamming the door behind you.

The hallway is dark, and the buzzing seems isolated to your room. Down the bend toward the stairwell, you walk toward the large turreted windows to get a better look. The alarm downstairs still reads "ARMED" but that's not the only glowing light. A flickering emanates from the den. Someone must be in there watching television, though you can't hear any accompanying sound effects. Instead, you hear a *thud* come from back toward the office area.

What now?

➢ Head downstairs and see who—or what—is in the den. Go to page 77

➢ Go around to the office and see what's happening while you still can. Go to page 181

➢ Sneak into the other bedroom, pray it's free of insects, and lock yourself inside. Go to page 220

No Encore

It's going to be a long and drawn-out legal defense, but the proof is in the pudding that coats the foyer floor—the man died from an elevator accident (while trying to kill you, no less). At length, you're free to go. You learn from the police that this version of Sheriff Tansky was actually the groundskeeper; however, just what his involvement was with The Offering, LLC will never be made clear, and you never hear anything about the proposed reality television show again.

Tansky's dead eyes continue to haunt you. The look on his face as he was cleaved in half will stay with you for the rest of your life. When you look at any painted portrait, it's always him—his hateful glare—that you see.

You can't help but feel like you missed something in that house. Some clue or piece of the puzzle. You'll often return to the Tansky House in your dreams, so in a way, you've not escaped after all.

THE END

No Filter

The picture frame is heavy, despite the lack of glass. Part of you hopes you'll find a hidden safe behind the portrait, but you don't even get a dusty outline on the wall. Nothing but the nail upon which this painting was mounted. Still, it's comforting to be away from Tansky's gaze, even for a brief respite.

The backside of the painting sadly has no eyeholes. Just an artist's name and…Instagram account? You look closer, but that's exactly what it is. Right down to the pinhole camera icon and the "@" symbol before the username.

So, this is a modern painting. Maybe a TV prop, although it could have been commissioned by the realtor or historical society; a modern take on an older source image, but the reveal is intriguing to say the least.

You hang the painting back on the wall and turn around. What now?

- ➢ Check the china cabinet. Very carefully, of course. Can't be sure if all that paperwork you signed makes you liable for broken dishes. Go to page 186
- ➢ The buffet. That's the only piece of furniture in here with drawers and opaque cabinets, so see what's stored inside. Go to page 7
- ➢ The antique table itself. If this was Sheriff Tansky's personal table, there might be more to it than the modern fixtures in the house. Perhaps a message carved underneath? Go to page 253
- ➢ All done here. Back out to explore the house. Go to page 112

The Not-so-subtle Knife

The military display case is positioned nearest the office door, so you're able to quickly head inside before the elevator completes its journey. You rush in toward the computer desk and pull on the drawer but it's still locked. Without a key, you'll have to break it open.

You consider your options. You could kick or tug on the drawer, but this is no modern plywood piece of furniture. You could use the cavalry saber, but the long and thin blade would take just as much damage as the drawer. You could shoot the lock, but you're likely to miss the actual internal locking mechanisms. You could use your grenade, but that would take out the whole office along with the drawer and whatever's inside.

Unslinging the rifle, you wedge the tip of the bayonet in the gaps on the side of the desk and use the leverage of the thick, sturdy rifle against the drawer. You lean your full weight into the makeshift fulcrum, but the desk is a sturdy antique.

They don't make 'em like they used to.

You press harder, jamming your hip into the move and really making the most of your adrenaline. A few grunts later, you feel a *snap* as the interior rail of the drawer gives way, freeing it from its lock.

The drawer falls to the office floor in a clatter to reveal a plastic evidence bag—the kind usually stored in police lockers—with a butcher knife inside. You set the rifle against the desk and bend down to inspect the cursed weapon. A tag is tied around the handle of the knife and the blade is coated in dried blood. The tag is dated twenty years ago today.

"What're you plannin' to do with that?" a man asks in a gruff voice.

You look up to see a man carrying an axe standing in the doorway connecting to the Madonna bathroom. He wears simple clothing; a pair of dusty brown twill coveralls and a long-sleeved knit undershirt beneath.

And, of course, this is the immortal man you seek—it's Sheriff Tansky. The man is here, in the flesh. You've seen this man every day in the dining room, glaring at you hatefully, and now he's here.

➢ Show him exactly what you're planning to do with the knife. Open the evidence bag and use it! Go to page 127

➢ Toss the knife to distract him, then go for the rifle resting by your side. Go to page 125

Not Welcome Here

You creep around the hallway, propelled by morbid curiosity toward the office. Part of you hopes you'll simply find a knickknack or book fallen from a shelf, perhaps rattled by the storm, but a much bigger part of you knows you're going to find something much, much worse.

The pitch black of the house is made worse with every step. The entry holds the large, turreted windows, but with lights out, there's nothing here to guide you save for a hazy glow at end of the hall. The faint moonlight cascades through the open office door and forms a rectangle on the hallway floor. As you get closer, it distorts, like someone has just walked across the path of the light.

Swallowing hard, you continue slowly toward the doorway. You stop just before you would step into the moonlight yourself, peering inside the room from an angle. The door to the adjoining bathroom is closed, and you can't see much more of the room from here. Breath held, you step into the moonlight. As you do, the floorboards creak, announcing your presence.

That's when the office door slams shut. The fast gust hits your face and you flinch back, the door missing your nose by inches. Another crash follows inside the office, then silence.

A long, low creaking moan brings your attention back down the hallway as the door to the Navy Room slowly opens. A shiver runs over you; the office connects to the Madonna Room, not the Navy Room. Or was the slam so forceful that it opened a door clear down the hallway?

You don't have to wonder for long. A spidery leg steps into the hall, its metallic surface glinting even in the low light. Another leg follows, then another, and another. The creature drags a bundle of linens and you can't help but follow into the laundry room, watching as it extends its spindly, telescopic legs and dumps the heap of sheets into the clothing chute.

"What the…" you mutter.

At this, the arachnid turns back, lunges and pierces several of its appendages into your flesh like pincers. The creature raises you up with incredible strength and flings you into the chute, down into the basement.

You awaken in your bed the next morning with a start. No longer is the room oppressively hot, and the sky outside is muted by dark storm clouds, making it impossible to discern the time of day.

A fly lies belly up on the silver tray on your bedside table. Everything else looks like it did before you went to sleep last night. Was it all a dream? After barely touching last night's dinner, your mouth is dry and your stomach aches for a good meal.

➢ Stop by the office first to see if you can learn about that *thud* in the light of day. Go to page 216

➢ Dress for the day, then head down to breakfast and see what awaits you. Go to page 171

The Offering

Realizing you're not quite sure where the dining room is, you head back toward the kitchen.

"How do I get to the dining room?" you ask aloud.

"I'd take the hallway, had I legs," Hermes replies.

Well, that's helpful. But the food was being cooked by an automaton, so it can't have travelled far. Indeed, there is a turnoff just to the left of the kitchen entrance that you hadn't noticed when you first walked in to meet the strange disembodied voice who now summons you to dinner.

The turnoff leads down a hall, and there's a sweet, smoky fragrance as you enter the corridor. Not quite food related, but more akin to pipe tobacco. The smell dissipates quickly as you continue, like it would if you had only briefly passed by a smoker's lounge.

The hallway wraps clockwise around the edge of the kitchen and leads into an open dining room. You're somewhat disoriented by the house, but you reason that you're now inside an opposite wing to that of the den. The open space between the two on your mental map must be a behind-the-scenes connection that involves the kitchen somehow.

Perhaps that explains how a hot meal was delivered to the dining table without any evidence of who or what placed it there. You remember the slight metal arm that held the skillet in the kitchen and look around the periphery of the dining room in hopes of catching sight of a similar mechanism here. But if such a device exists in the dining room, it's seamless and invisible.

Instead, you're greeted by a long, antique table great enough to seat an entire dinner party. The dining room itself is large and open, with a buffet and china cabinet on opposing walls, a single place setting at one head of the table, and a large portrait of Sheriff Tansky on the opposite wall. Looks like he'll be the only one joining you for supper.

Everything is set out according to etiquette—extra plates, glasses, etc. A full spread. Your meal is covered with a warming dome, waiting for you to have a seat and begin. A glass of red wine is poured, and there's a small, printed note on stationary next to the plate. It's a formal postcard, like the one delivered to your house earlier today. Just to be sure, you take the folded note from your pocket to compare.

They're exactly the same, right down to the way the typography is pressed into the cardstock. This note reads:

> Have a seat. Raise a glass to the progenitor of the House and say the following words: "I present myself as offering!" Once you complete this toast, the clock starts.

Well, that's ominous, but it should make for good TV.

Sheriff Tansky's dour countenance stares down at you, perpetually angry. The colors are bright and vibrant, no cracking in the oils; the paint so fresh it could still be drying. The man in this picture must be the original owner of the house, and it is likely his seat at the head of his table that you're now meant to occupy.

He doesn't seem too pleased with this development.

Taking a seat, you claim the wineglass and prepare to say the words, telling yourself, it's just a catchphrase for a show. Besides, you can't win the game if you don't play by the rules. It's a simple task, really. You look around, but you're not sure where the cameras might be hidden; where you should look while you say the toast.

With a deep breath, you hold the glass high and address the portrait of Sheriff Tansky.

"I present myself as offering!" you say, hamming it up as overcompensation for your nerves.

This moment will likely make the marketing campaigns. It could even be on the intro that plays before each episode. And overall, you feel like you nailed it. To celebrate, you finish the gesture with a long drink from the wine glass. It's a nice, full bodied dry red. Moreover, this feels like you're toasting to your future success. It's hard not to smile at the thought of a million dollars for a three-night staycation.

You lift the silver dome atop the food and a plume of steam rises to greet you. Once the vapor dissipates, you get a good look at the plate. Hope you like red meat, because there before you is the bloodiest steak you've ever seen. The juices pool out toward the sides: roasted fingerling potatoes, a buttered ear of corn, and grilled artichoke hearts.

Stealing another glance up to Sheriff Tansky, you see now that the lawman's glare has softened, ever so slightly. Wine has made many an insufferable man more tolerable, and you tell yourself it's just your imagination, but he seems pleased that you made your toast. And, now that you've uncovered the meal, he looks…hungry.

"I'll clear up later," Hermes says after dinner. "For now, you'll want to head upstairs. Lights out at 9pm, breakfast served bright and early. There are two bedrooms for you to choose from, both are quite comfortable, and have a water closet ensuite. The last owners of the house chose to sleep separately, so there are two master bedrooms, in a sense. The Madonna Room, where the madam slept, and the Navy Room where the master would retire. Do let me know when you've chosen your final…resting place."

"Do I get to see them first?" you ask.

"Of course. You'll find everything ready for you presently. The Navy Room will be to your left as you head upstairs, while the Madonna Room will be straight ahead on the northeast face. The help is meant to stay down here; the living quarters are for family only. So, I'll offer my goodnight presently. Unless there's anything else you need before turning in…?"

Hermes leaves it open, like a question. You hesitate, failing to think of anything you might need, so he continues, "Excellent. Both rooms are perfectly adequate, rest assured. Only, you should know: madam was a sensitive woman, and felt her bedroom was the only place where the spirits in the house would let her rest. Whereas the master of the house was a more practical man, and found the comfort and security of his own room were paramount to a good night's sleep."

"I see…" you say.

"You'll have plenty of time to explore the house on the whole after breakfast, so I'd recommend an early evening. You'll find fresh towels in the ensuite, a spare duvet in the armoire, and a deadbolt lock installed on the door. Find your room quickly—lights out at 9 o'clock—and do sleep well."

With that, the dining room is silent once more. An early evening sounds fine with you; if you're meant to stay here for three nights, running out the clock is a perfectly acceptable strategy toward a million-dollar prize. The Offering website mentioned "tasks" but you've only had one thus far in the form of the toast. Perhaps you'll find another printed note for you by the bedside table.

As you rise from your seat, the chair slides back on the hardwood floor, and you take your leave. Your footfalls echo in the quiet hallway leading away from the dining room, around past the kitchen, and out to the entryway once more.

In the corner between the closed door and the staircase there's a hall tree featuring a grandfather clock and a small stand. Upon the stand, you can see a realtor's business card and a brochure on this house listing. The grandfather clock reads just past 8pm.

➢ Go take a closer look at the clock and brochure. Go to page 148

➢ Leave exploring for tomorrow and head upstairs. Go to page 259

Office Space

The office has two doors, one of which you step through now. There's an entrance from the hallway toward the Navy Room, and another door which shares a bathroom with the Madonna Room. Both were closed before you entered, and it occurs to you that these and other doors are *always* closed, while the "natural state" of the bedroom and den doors is to be open.

As you've walked around and explored the house, you've always found the doors like this, regardless of how you left them. It's possible the door frames have warped over the years, and they now close on their own. Then again, this door stays ajar as you open it presently.

Focusing back on the office: the centerpiece is a computer desk, the monitor set to a simple black and white input text box centered on what otherwise looks like the blue screen of death. This is where you're meant to input the keyword, if you've found the truth of this house.

Part of the desk also includes a drawing table which is covered in sketches and handwritten notes. A filing cabinet rests nearby, and generally the room looks like a functional office. The rear wall has built-in bookshelves, perfectly sculpted to frame the window outside. With the dearth of clocks in this house, you can't be sure what time it is, but already the sun is sinking toward the forest outside. It must get preternaturally dark here, much earlier than what you're used to.

The remaining walls are coated in faux-bookshelf wallpaper. These are the only papered walls you've encountered so far and clash with the stately aesthetic of the den downstairs with its superior library. What now?

- ➢ Input your keyword into the computer. Go to page 251
- ➢ Look at the desk area. Go to page 61
- ➢ Check out the filing cabinet. Go to page 89
- ➢ Head out into the hallway to keep looking around. Go to page 114

On Display

The cabinet has delicate, beveled glass, and contains four shelves' worth of dishes, serving platters, and talismans. Well, that may not be the correct word for these…*things*. The rear of the china cabinet is mirrored, which is the only way you can see some of the items kept inside.

An old, cracked porcelain doll looks out from behind vacant, unblinking eyes. Clay pottery shards lie scattered about, like casting runes, but inscribed with a far more ancient language. Sumerian? Hebrew? Past these are idols; handmade dolls, bound with sticks and caked together with what you hope is mud.

After inspecting each shelf individually, you stand to look at the china cabinet on the whole. The porcelain doll looks up at you, and although you didn't see it move, you're sure it was looking straight ahead and toward the painting earlier.

It's a strange collection to keep with the dishes, and part of you wonders if it might have anything to do with the fact that the cabinet door has a lock. Not that you're compelled to open it, but this way the owner doesn't have to worry about someone walking away with the doll collection…or the dolls themselves walking away.

What's next?

- ➢ The buffet. That's the only piece of furniture in here with drawers and opaque cabinets, so see what's stored inside. Go to page 7
- ➢ The antique table itself. If this was Sheriff Tansky's personal table, there might be more to it than the modern fixtures in the house. Perhaps a message carved underneath? Go to page 253
- ➢ The painting of the Sheriff. Take it off the wall and see if there are some eyeholes in the back of the canvas. Old oil paintings are usually handled with gloves, but it's worth the risk. Go to page 179
- ➢ All done here. Back out to explore the house. Go to page 112

Open Floor Plan

Past the railing there are two rooms, one with a single closed door (very like the one downstairs), while the other has a plantation-style set of double doors. Feeling braver in the light of day than you did last night, you open each to see what's inside.

First, the single door. When you pull it open, you're met with a blackened metal grate. In actuality, it's another doorway of sorts, with an elevator shaftway beyond. There's a handle on the grate, which slides open to give access to the elevator interior. You can use the call button to summon the elevator and take this down to the foyer as an alternative to the stairs, if you'd like.

Next, the double doors. These open to a laundry room. This strikes you as too modern for an older house for many reasons, not the least of which is because no one had washing machines at the turn of the century, but also because this is the only room upstairs designated to a task traditionally doled out to servants.

In a bout of wishful thinking, you check inside the drums of the washer and dryer, looking for signs of yesterday's clothes. Unfortunately, both are empty. There's a large metal handle, vertical against an interior wall, which you pull open to expose an antediluvian laundry chute. It groans from disuse at your pull, which shouldn't be surprising—no need to use a laundry chute with a washer and dryer installed up here.

A rank breath of foul air exhales from the chute, very much like a deep "heyyyy" voice. You let the chute close again, and recall that there were cellar doors outside the house. The air down there was so hot. Could a furnace room be lurking in the bowels of the house? If it's completely sealed off, you shudder to think what might have been dropped down the chute and left to molder over the centuries.

Time to close up and turn around.

- ➢ Open the small closet by the stairs. Go to page 53
- ➢ Head up the next set of stairs. Go to page 109
- ➢ Look at the piano more closely. Go to page 172
- ➢ Continue into the Madonna Room. Go to page 274
- ➢ Go down the hallway to the other side of the house. Go to page 114

Opening Night

The melody grows louder as you approach the hallway, but when you unlock and open the bedroom door, the music stops altogether. The hinges groan open into the otherwise silent hallway and your footfalls creak against the wooden floor as you make your way toward the grand piano.

Out here, away from the bedroom, the house succumbs to complete darkness. With the storm clouds, there's far less moonlight than last night, but the wide turreted windows help illuminate the piano nonetheless.

Approaching closer, each step creaking against the floorboards, you strain your eyes for detail. The piano lid sits propped open, which obscures your view. As you come around the upper landing, the ivory keys catch in the moonlight and you can see no one is there to play them. Instead, as you come closer, you can make out a small figure sitting upon the piano bench.

It's a child's porcelain doll, exactly like the one housed in the China cabinet.

The toy sits slouched on the bench, not centered, but off to the side as if whoever was playing the piano had the doll seated against themselves. It's a tiny thing, not much larger than your hand, and it would look almost comical sitting alone on the bench if it weren't so creepy.

As you linger near the piano, the music suddenly starts up again, the keys pressed as if by their own accord. The sudden return of music is jarring and you practically leap away from the sounds. Stumbling back, you hit the railing next to the stairwell, the open air down to the foyer at your back.

Spinning around, you grab hold of the railing to steady yourself. Down in the foyer, you see a faint chalk outline of a body drawn on the entry floor. The whiteness sticks out in the dark, and you can make out the arms and legs of a body splayed out below. There is no body to speak of, but the chalk outline itself gives you goose bumps. The size and shape; this could be *your* outline. And the way the arms and legs are splayed apart suggests a body of someone who just fell to their death.

The music, you realize with rapid clarity, is a requiem—a funeral dirge.

With a sudden chill, you spin back around, expecting to find someone there, ready to push you down upon the outline below…but you're alone. Just the porcelain doll, staring at you from the bench with vacant eyes of glass. Was it looking at you before?

Still, you can't shake the eerie feeling. Like the spot below is calling to you. It's like you've just walked over your own grave. You rush back to your room, which no longer holds any strange green light, and quickly lock the door before crawling back into bed.

The room is still and silent once more. No heater, no light, nothing. You're drenched in sweat and adrenaline, but what choice do you have?

Lie still and hope for sleep… Go to page 217

Out of the Frying Pan

Bold move, hanging out in an automated kitchen during dinner prep. Imagine how a cutting board might operate if there were no chef to have their fingers chopped off. Or how a pot of water might boil if no one had to physically bring it to the sink to be drained. Only, there *is* someone in here capable of being sliced, diced, broiled, burned, flambéed or souffleéd—*you're* in here.

"Too many cooks in the kitchen spoil the broth," Hermes says. "Do try to stay out of the way."

The kitchen starts to move all at once. If Rube Goldberg and M.C. Escher teamed up to design a kitchen, this would be it. Pots fly forth from cabinets in the same motion as catapulted vegetables from the pantry, landing in sync with scalding water propelled through the air to coalesce atop the stove with precision timing. Blades spin and whirl out in the open, as if this were the interior to a blender with an algorithm set to track where the pared food would land, and already waiting with a platter to catch it all.

This is like learning how a lawnmower works while watching from the perspective of the grass. You try to keep completely still, but human beings are programmed to flinch. When you finally do, the rest of the kitchen now has to compensate for the randomness of your physicality, and a battery of tools and ingredients surrounds you in a blinding torrent.

A cast-iron skillet smashes against your shoulder, *hard.* As you stumble, another kitchen tool lances across your back, either searing or slicing your flesh. You fall aside and toward the oven as it opens like a mouth.

"How about a nice glass of milk?" Hermes asks.

At this, the refrigerator door swings open and a mechanical claw-arm juts out. The glass being offered hits the side of your ribs, and you're knocked out of the path of the open oven. Milk spills out across the kitchen, and you're forced back toward the entryway.

"Don't worry, I'll clean the mess," Hermes says. "Why don't you go make yourself comfortable in the den and I'll summon you for dinner."

"Yeah, I think I will," you say, rubbing your wounds. Apparently the show won't be held liable for any sort of *Hansel and Gretel* events or force majeure inside the House.

➢ Into the den. It'll be good to have a drink and contemplate the extent of the waiver you signed. Go to page 228

➢ Have a closer look around the entryway. This house is full of surprises. Go to page 155

Over the Threshold

You walk the path leading on to the front porch, climb the steps, and continue right up to the front door. The door is black, with bronze trim. The bronze has an aged smoothness to it, with a sheen that's accented by grime in the creases, but has evidently been regularly (or at least recently) polished. The wood itself doesn't appear painted, like the natural grain is deep obsidian; perhaps it's been charred. While the bronze glows, the wood absorbs all light, like an entrance to a cave.

There's a heavy door knocker in the shape of a wolf or hound, holding a ring in its mouth. It's a fearsome beast, but you reach out to knock anyway. The bronze ring groans as you lift, giving the impression of a low growl from this guard dog. But when you lower the ring to knock, the door simply pushes open.

You cautiously head inside, and the wind picks up behind you. A few leaves follow you into the house, and you instinctively turn to close the door to stop the breeze. The door closes, the wind stops, and there's a slight electronic whir as the door seals and locks itself. A keypad next to the door flashes, "ARMED."

This is it, you're sealed in, you realize. The game has begun. It's sunset, night one. You'll need to spend three nights here, after which you'll have won and will be permitted to leave. Time to get comfortable. Wait! With a sudden flush of panic you realize you've left your suitcase in the car! You were so taken by the house that you completely forgot to bring it with you.

You mutter a curse, grimacing at your own foolishness.

"Welcome home," a man says in a posh British accent.

When you turn, you expect to see a butler waiting in the entry, but you're still alone. The hairs stand up on the back of your neck. It's a wide, open entryway, with nowhere to hide, but the voice sounded so close. What now?

➢ Step forward and say, "Hello? Is someone there?" Go to page 267

➢ Say nothing. Step forward into the house to get a better look. Go to page 106

A Palindrome

After you've set the letters into place, you hear something *click* inside the locking mechanism and you're able to lift the roll top with ease. The desk area has been neatly organized, with most objects shifted to the periphery—leaving an open space, front and center.

In this open space, there's a key with a crimson ribbon tied about the middle.

"Well done, well done!" Hermes says. "As your reward, you should see a skeleton key, which can open any lock in the house."

Taking the key, you try it on the desk drawer, which catches in the lock and opens. Inside the drawer, you find a plastic evidence bag—the kind usually stored in police lockers—with a butcher knife inside. A tag is tied around the handle of the knife and the blade is coated in dried blood. The tag is dated twenty years ago today.

A chill runs down your spine, but you keep the knife with you all the same. With this and the key in your possession, you head back out toward the front of the house, if nothing else so you can keep an eye on the elevator and the man down in the basement.

"Excellent," Hermes continues. "Now, then. If you head into the kitchen—"

His voice suddenly cuts out, static crackling like someone talking over him on a handheld radio. The next voice that comes through is gruff and angry.

"You come into my house, wear my clothes, sleep in my bed and eat my food, and now you'd take everything I've built for yourself? I think not!" the man roars, his voice echoing through the house. "You are here as an offering; a blood sacrifice to break the curse. And my manservant will have to sit this out until we've finished the ritual ourselves."

At that, the power goes out. The darkness and silence that follows is immense and all encompassing. It's like you've been dropped into a cave. You can't see six inches in front of your face and the only sound is your heartbeat thudding in your ears. Three breaths later, a lightning flash illuminates the stairwell through the turreted windows and a torrent of thunder rattles the house.

What now?

➢ Down into the kitchen. That was the last thing Hermes said. Go to page 90

➢ Remove the knife from the bag and wait for Dennis to come. Go to page 3

Parasite

The newspaper clipping is an editorial piece, which reads:

> Imagine every homeowner's worst nightmare. That scratching sound in the walls? The occasional footstep you think must be your imagination? It's all real: because there's a woman who has been secretly living in your attic for weeks.
>
> That's exactly what happened to a Mercury City resident, who wishes to remain anonymous. It began when the man first noticed food disappearing from his home; milk dwindling quicker than he was used to, etc. Initially, he brushed it off, but then started keeping a closer tally on his pantry, and sure enough, he was being eaten out of house and home. So the man decided to set up a hidden camera to see if he had an uninvited rodent in the house. Worse, he had an uninvited resident.
>
> What he saw the next morning on the grainy, night vision footage comes straight out of a horror movie. A panel in the attic crawlspace slowly opens, the outer grate gingerly removed as if floating and set atop a nearby cabinet. Something shadowy shifts from the dark recesses, emerging. The unmistakable clawing grip of a human hand, pale and white, grasps one edge of the crawlspace, then the other, until a feral mop of black hair spews forth.
>
> The woman, as unkempt as you would expect from someone living in a dark attic, moves like a spider. Down the shelving, to the floor, silent. She helps herself to his home, just like she does every night while the man sleeps. She moves off screen, doing what, we can only imagine, before ultimately returning and slinking away just as inexplicably as she arrived.
>
> The man immediately called the police, who found the attic empty, but also found remains of the woman's nest. She had been there for some time, and police reportedly told the man that—mental health facilities being underfunded—these types of occurrences are more common than we might think.

The article ends there.

"I'm afraid your dinner will get cold. Shall I put it away for later?" Hermes says.

"I'm on my way," you say.

Not much choice here:

Head into the dining room. Go to page 182

A Passage of Time

The bar is fully stocked. Everything you'd need for a Bloody Mary, Dark and Stormy, Snake Bite, or a Zombie is set out before you. After picking your poison, you take your glass and look to the bookshelves.

An odd assortment of volumes resides on these shelves, and you make a mental note to check them out in more detail later. For now, you walk along their length, browsing. The twin built-ins are separated by the fireplace, and as you pass you feel a draft coming from somewhere on the wall. The flume left open? Or worse, a crack in the gas mechanisms?

You sniff, but smell nothing. Atop the fireplace mantle are several lace doily patterns, laid out to cover the length of it. Something about the needlework is strongly evocative of a spiderweb; not an outright Halloween decoration, but the impression is unshakeable.

Beneath the lacework, letters have been carved into the wood, which these fabrics were covering. You slide them back to reveal a sinisterly etched message:

Dennis lived as a devil sinned

The letters are oddly mirror images of one another in this manic hand-carved scrawl. They're deep, rough gouges in the wood and you run your fingers over the letters to see if they've smoothed with time. The mirroring was intentional—it's a palindrome, you realize.

At this very second, the fireplace roars to life. The unexpected plume of light and heat sets your heart racing, and you instinctively jump back, drink sloshing over the edges of your glass. You take a moment to compose yourself, as well as a long gulp from your drink.

You remind yourself: there's an automated assistant at work and everything here could have been planned just so for television. Still, if this is truly a severely haunted house, *something* could have been upset by your disturbing that doily covering. It feels like the producers have set up the perfect Catch-22. If you're someone who's a nonbeliever, you could write off truly paranormal activity as pyrotechnic effects. Or, if you're overly prone to assigning agency to seemingly random events, you'll find something sinister in every situation.

How can you ever know what to believe in this house?

"Dinner is served," the British voice says. "If you'd like to come through to the dining room? A note has been left for you."

Not much choice here:

Head into the dining room to see what else has been cooked up for you. Go to page 182

Peephole

This wall is shared by the open doorway that leads to the kitchen, and the hole doesn't have any light shining through, so you reason that it must not go all the way through. It looks like an anchor hole, as if the clock used to be mounted on the wall, but if that were the case, you'd have ripped open a much larger gouge in the drywall.

This could be your first hint of a hidden camera, you think, coming closer still. Right up against the wall, you lean in to inspect the hole, which is set at eye-level. The edges are darkly stained, with grime or black mold growing inside the wall. The hole isn't much wider in diameter than one of your forefingers, and the drywall frays out, as if the hole was drilled *out* from the inside.

You're reminded of a hotel room peephole as you peer inside. Unlike that comparison, there's no reflective lens as you might expect if this were a permanent lookout spot, or if there were a camera inside. No blinking electronic lights either.

Then it moves.

You wrench your head back in reflex, and your stomach turns as something *coils* inside the wall. You blink, trying to catch sight of whatever is in there, but it's gone so quickly that you can't be sure if you imagined the whole thing. The…hole…thing.

"There may no longer be a clock," Hermes says. "But time is still of the essence. You don't want to be down in the basement for lights out."

You shake your head and turn away. Not much choice here:

Head up to the Madonna Room to grab those locks. Go to page 138

Phantom of the Opera

You swing the noose out like a lasso, wrapping it around the chandelier on your first try. The dangling crystal offers a clattering chime and you look to the Madonna Room to see if you've been noticed. But at the exact same moment, there's a clatter of loud, heavy chains from the Madonna Room, drowning and intermingling with the noise you're making out here.

Pulling in the rope, you take both ends from your position near the banister. If you tie one end around this railing, and take the other around your neck, you can hang yourself from the chandelier.

As you secure the rope, you look across the open foyer to the piano. Sitting atop the instrument is a small, porcelain doll, its glassy black eyes staring at you with dead intent. The sudden appearance of this doll makes you pause, but only briefly.

The dragging, scraping chains from the Madonna Room spurs you into action once more.

➢ Tie the rope tightly around the banister railing. Go to page 164

➢ Barely tie the rope. Keep it loose. Go to page 28

Phoning it in

You rush down out of the attic, quickly close the stairs behind you, and hurry to the main landing where you can call out to Hermes. The storm grows in intensity, with a barrage of lightning flashes on the horizon and great torrents of rain streaking down the turreted windows.

"Hermes! There's someone in the attic!" you shout over the sounds of thunder.

"Oh? Shall I set another place setting for dinner?" the automaton replies with mild disinterest.

"It's…a body," you say, catching your breath. "A dead body."

"I'm afraid the attic is beyond my cleaning services."

"What? We need to call the police!"

"There are no outside calls from this house, apologies. But I'm sure if you leave it be, it will leave you alone. Is there an odor?"

Your head spins, bewildered. At length, you ask, "Is this all part of the show?"

"Oh, would you like to watch a show? I can help with that! Despite our lack of telephone or internet services, I can set something up for you on the television in the den. However, you might do well to remember that nightfall is approaching."

Hermes speaks with forced earnestness, though his statement ends with a warning given by someone who has no stake in events themselves. Frustrating, to say the least, but it does bring up a point. You take a few steps down the stairs, where the electronic door lock is still engaged and the security system shows "ARMED."

Failing any better options, you'd better keep searching for that hidden card. Where to?

➢ Keep looking around upstairs. Go to page 153

➢ Continue looking around on the main floor. Go to page 112

Playbill

You enter the elevator, but freeze before your hand touches the controls. There, resting against the lever-style switch is another note card. A chill runs down your spine. You look around, but nothing else is out of place. The card reads:

Going Down?

Simple, but to the point. It's an invitation, as much as any has been in this house. Well?

➢ Let's do this. Set the controls down toward the basement. Go to page 137

➢ Not yet. Take some time to look around upstairs. Go to page 74

Poltergeist

The kitchen is silent and empty as you enter. The lights are on, but there's no activity.

"Hermes, what the hell is going on?!" you ask in a hushed, urgent voice.

At this, all hell breaks loose. Cabinet doors fly open, drawers spring out on their rails, water sprays from the sinks, and the burners all ignite. Plates fly out across the room like thrown discs and cutlery jumps out at you from all over the kitchen. Several dishes bash against you painfully.

"THE RITUAL HAS BEGUN!!!" a voice reverberates all around you.

The shouts are too loud and forceful to tell whose voice it is, and the force of them echo into your chest. You duck down in the corner of the kitchen to keep away from the flying debris, hands up to protect your head and cover your ears.

Then it all stops.

The cabinets and drawers shut. The final clatter of hurled objects settles, left to a single bowl spinning around on its sides like a top, eventually coming to a rest. Then, the scrape of chains sounds on the floor from the doorway. From all the detritus on the kitchen floor, you grab hold of a nearby knife to ensure you're at least armed for whatever comes next.

You rise to your feet and meet Sheriff Tansky's hateful glare.

From the doorway, he lifts the set of chains and shackles and tosses them forward so they land at your feet. Then he holds his axe with both hands. The sheriff nods, indicating that you should shackle yourself.

➢ Drop the knife and comply. See where this whole thing goes. Go to page 223

➢ No way. If there's going to be a ritual killing tonight, it won't be your blood spilled. Go to page 62

Powder Room

The bathroom doesn't hold many nooks and crannies, save for the seated station before the mirror for hair and makeup. There's really nothing to search for in the deep claw-foot soaking tub or in the modern standalone shower unit. The toilet is also modernized, and you can't help but think how odd it is that the house has been recently updated, yet still holds artifacts from its inception. Have these various items been kept here the whole time, handed down from occupant to occupant, or have they recently resurfaced? Perhaps...so you would find them?

Shaking off this thought, you sit down to look through the drawers on the dressing table. A small, oval-shaped mirror shows your reflection sitting, along with a woman in a white dress suspended above the claw-foot tub behind you.

You quickly turn back, but she's not there. You find only a long, white curtain draped upon the edges of the tub. When you look again, that's all you see in the mirror as well. Was it a hallucination? A trick of the eye? You must have seen the curtain and imagined it was a woman. You tap on the mirror face as if to see if it's at fault, and the border illuminates in response. It's some sort of smart mirror with built-in lighting. Could it have a built-in ghost as well?

With a deep breath, you search the drawers. They're full of makeup compacts, hairbrushes and combs, nail polish, lipstick, and other beauty products. The only thing that sticks out is a small heart-shaped locket, which you open. The inside contains only scraps of ancient photo paper, like someone has attempted to remove a photograph, but only managed to scratch out the pictures instead. Or was that their intent all along?

Closing the locket and drawers, you rise and continue your search.

- ➢ Head through the adjoining door into the office. Go to page 185
- ➢ Return back out to search the rest of the house. Go to page 153

The Power of Belief Compels You

"That's right…the curse is broken…"

Though clearly in a state of mental shock, Tansky believes what you tell him. And so it is, that you both leave the Tansky House alive. Have you truly cured him of his curse with the wolfsbane cocktail? Or was he a mortal man all along? You may never know. In a way, it's up to you to choose what to believe.

The man himself goes on to be treated in a mental institution, and you're told he was simply the gardener; a mortal man who suffered a mental break, taking on the identity of the original Sheriff Tansky. But the money you receive tells another story. A million dollars in matured railroad bonds held since the 1800s, sent to you by an anonymous donor. No note, no clue whatsoever. The lawyers who deliver the funds say that your benefactor wishes to remain nameless.

So, which is it? Was Tansky made mortal, and this story is the only way the authorities could explain a centuries-old sheriff's sudden appearance? Or was he a madman all along? And what of the show? If there ever was an Offering, LLC, it remains in the shadows.

Yet, in a way, you receive your prize money after all.

Congratulations! See that house and wolf icon? You've found but one of the ghosts that haunt this place. There is more than one truth lurking inside Tansky House. Dare you go back inside and uncover the others?

At the end of this book, you'll find a floorplan to the Tansky House as well as a book club discussion guide. Or, if you're done, don't forget to rate and review *HAUNTED* so other readers can discover these truths for themselves…

Have you explored the multiverse of interactive stories *Click Your Poison* books have to offer?

Survive the zombie apocalypse, solve a murder, gain superpowers, set sail as a pirate, become a secret agent, and more! Visit www.clickyourpoison.com.

Prima Donna

You continue past the next staircase, which doubles back over your head and toward the front of the house. That must be the access to the widow's walk at the roofline outside. Past these stairs, there's a peculiarly small door, half the size and stature of any others in the house.

The open doorway straight ahead is inset next to a thick, reinforced section of wall, which you reason is the chimney from the den fireplace below. The Tansky House oddly feels larger upstairs than downstairs, and it's with a sense of vertigo that you proceed past the fireplace and toward the dark room beyond.

Thankfully, there's enough light from the chandelier outside that you're able to see the entry to a bedroom, and find the interior light switch. Once the space has been illuminated, you head into the Madonna Room. It's a good-sized master suite, especially considering the age of the house when rooms used to be much smaller. A four-post canopy bed is centered on the exterior wall between two windows, with a curtain of white lace partially obscuring and enclosing the queen-sized bed. A bedside table holds a silver tea tray. As you stand at the entry, there's a large armoire to your right and a door to the bathroom on your left.

The furniture has been painted white to look modern, and is accented by lilac and lavender shades. The room looks comfortable, even considering you're staying in a *severely* haunted house. The color scheme continues into the bathroom, which holds a seated station before the mirror for hair and makeup, a claw-foot deep soaking tub, and a modern standalone shower unit. The toilet is also modernized, and equipped with an array of bidet options.

There's a second door leading out of the bathroom, but it's closed with a simple lock on the doorknob, common to shared bathrooms.

➢ Go through the bathroom to explore the adjoining room. Go to page 45

➢ Turn around and go check out the Navy Room. Go to page 229

➢ Decide to lock up and stay in the Madonna Room for the evening. Go to page 260

What are they playing at? you think, as you crack the shell of the first egg with the side of a spoon. The egg is perfectly soft-boiled, the yolk amber and runny. Without stopping to eat, you move on to the second. The shell breaks away under your spoon and crumbles to reveal…a second perfectly soft-boiled egg.

You remember back to yesterday and the unborn chicken fetus, dead and boiled. That means you're not trapped in some kind of time loop, at the very least. But the lingering fog and headache reminds you—it doesn't necessarily mean you didn't dream *that* breakfast. Is it possible? Did you really just arrive? And how can you prove what's real and what isn't?

While you brainstorm, you eat breakfast. No point in letting it go to waste, and you'll think more clearly after the most important meal of the day. As you dig into one of the eggs, you realize that the house has been set up to be the same, but certain elements cannot be replicated: like an egg that's gone bad.

So…maybe you should look around to see what else is different?

➢ Start by searching on the main floor. Go to page 166

➢ Start by searching upstairs. Go to page 74

The Prowler

You quickly head back out into the house, passing by the kitchen, but see nothing of interest. Into the foyer, you look uneasily. That's when you hear the chain being dragged toward the staircase and the heavy boots that accompany it. Someone's coming downstairs.

Without thinking, you dash into the den and slide the pocket doors closed, hoping the sounds of heavy footfalls and dragging chains will drown out the sliding doors. You look around for something to use in the den, but find nothing.

You think to use the secret door, but the steps come even closer. They stop just outside the den. Maybe if you're quiet enough, they'll simply pass by? You put a hand up to mute the sounds of your panicked breathing.

After some hesitation, the doors slide open. Then a man walks into view, dragging a long thick chain with shackles on the end. In the other hand, he carries an axe. He wears simple clothing; a pair of dusty brown twill coveralls and a long-sleeved knit undershirt beneath.

Fighting through the shock, you actually recognize him—it's Sheriff Tansky.

The man is here, in the flesh.

Tansky continues forward, dragging his chain. Your head swirls. You've seen this man every day in the dining room, glaring at you hatefully, and now he's here, determined to complete the ritual.

From the doorway, he lifts the set of chains and shackles and tosses them forward so they land at your feet. Then he holds his axe with both hands. The sheriff nods, indicating that you should shackle yourself.

You shake your head. You can't do it.

"What do you want from me?" you say, barely recognizing your own voice.

"I want you to *die*," Tansky growls, just before he comes at you with the axe.

THE END

The Psycho Path

You head toward the dining room accompanied by an eerie sound—footsteps from above. Heavy boots upon the wooden floor with a chain dragging behind them. You pause to listen in the hallway, but the sounds continue beyond and further into the recess of the house. Once you can no longer hear them at all, you continue into the dining room.

There at your seat, you find another card. Next to the note, there's a plastic evidence bag—the kind usually stored in police lockers—with a butcher knife inside. A tag is tied around the handle of the knife and the blade is coated in dried blood. The tag is dated twenty years ago today.

The note reads:

Time to finish the ritual. One task remains:
DIE

You swallow hard and set the note card back down. Your eyes drift from the knife, which can only be the murder weapon from the horrific incident twenty years ago, up to the portrait of Sheriff Tansky. The man's eyes are shimmering with anticipation.

There's someone—or something—in this house with you, and you've barricaded all exits. What should you do now?

➢ Remove the knife from the plastic bag and arm yourself. Go to page 12

➢ Head back out into the house unarmed. Go to page 203

Put the Lotion in the Basket

The darkness is swift and immediate. Just as you extinguish the lantern, so too does the figure's shape fade as he leaves the ambient light of the elevator and marches toward you. Moving quickly, you bound over toward where you last saw the well, thankful the dirt floor muffles your footfalls.

In the panic of your flight, you slam against the stone walls of the well, doubling over in pain, but using the momentum to hoist yourself over the barrier without delay. You kick your feet over, and lower yourself down, but the well is much deeper than imagined and you fall down into its mouth.

The freefall seems to last forever before you're buffeted against one of the walls and ultimately splash down into the depths. When you come to the surface, you look up to complete darkness. There's only the sloshing of the water around you—and a man laughing faintly from above.

You reach out to the walls, but the well is smooth. The stones have been eroded and have grown mossy, and there is nowhere to grab hold. How long can you tread water?

THE END

Pyrotechnics

You step forward, bringing the lantern back like a revolutionary about to launch a Molotov cocktail at the state police, and as you do so, Tansky brings up the axe over his head, ready for a swing of his own. The two of you close the gap, rushing toward one another, but you have the advantage of a ranged weapon and hurl the lantern at him first.

In such close quarters, you can't miss, and the lantern connects directly into Tansky's chest—the lamp sprays out its fuel across the man on impact. He immediately catches fire, but incredibly—this does not stop his attack. If anything, it strengthens his resolve and he cleaves into you with the axe even as the fire pours out over him. It's a powerful blow, and you crumple with just one hit.

Bits of burning flesh drop around you, searing against your blood as it pools out onto the basement floor. This crypt will be your tomb.

THE END

Question Everything

"Hermes," you start, thinking how to phrase the question.

The taut, dried skin of your dinner reminds you morbidly of the desiccated woman upstairs. Somehow, this doesn't inspire an appetite. You prod the Guinea pig with the tip of your fork.

"Yes?" Hermes asks.

"Do you know why there's a dead body in the house?"

"Statistically, most people die inside the home."

"In this house, specifically. I saw a woman in the attic," you say.

"Swamp gas."

"Swamp gas?" you parrot back, as a question.

"Swamp gas is the common name for methane bubbling up to the surface due to marsh decomposition, which can spontaneously combust, causing visions of floating orbs or will-o'-the-wisp sightings," Hermes says, his accent pronouncing the gas as *me-thane.*

"It was a body decomposing, not the marshes!"

"Well, if you're having paranormal visions, there are five generally accepted explanations. Hallucination due to carbon monoxide poisoning, mental illness, mold spores, swamp gas—we've ruled out that one—and finally, legitimate supernatural phenomena, also classified as 'the unexplained' or simply, 'other.'"

You sigh, lean back in your chair and say, "Can't you just tell me who was in the attic?"

"Very well. She was one of the first. A daughter of the house. We called her Hannah, which I found to be a lovely name. Perfectly symmetrical. She never did accept her role, but there's no use fighting our nature, is there? It will catch up to you eventually."

The doorbell rings.

It's such a foreign sound that at first you're not sure what you've just heard. Then there's a loud pounding as the iron door knocker connects to the thick wooden front door. It's fervent, urgent even. The doorbell rings again and again by someone frantic to get the homeowner's attention. The pounding continues, dull thuds against the wood.

Your mind races at the possibilities.

"Is this all related?" you ask.

"Of course it is," Hermes replies, ever chipper.

You leave the dining table to go see what's happening, but as soon as you enter the foyer, the sounds stop. No doorbell. No pounding, save for the heavy rain against the house. The storm is really pouring down now, and the skies are darkened.

"Hermes, what's going on?"

"Tomorrow, after the reset is completed, we'll learn just that. Now, if you don't mind, there's much to be done, so I'll turn out the lights early. Best head up to bed."

At this, the lights in the kitchen, den, and lower hallways turn off. You shake your head and sigh in frustration. Not much choice here:

Head upstairs to bed. Go to page 177

Quicksilver

Grabbing the M1917 Enfield rifle off its stand, you slide the bolt action back and inspect the breech before slinging it over your right shoulder. The WWI cartridge belt still holds live ammunition for the rifle, so you pocket several of the cartridges. All this strangely feels second nature, like you've done it before.

There's a loud *thud* on the other side of the wall as something heavy is dropped on the floor in the Madonna Room. Not waiting to find out what that was, you hurry around the opposite corner toward the stairs. Though you're hopped-up on righteous fury and adrenaline, you tread lightly. You've got to get these bullets downstairs and into the molten silver if you're going to kill a werewolf tonight.

As you step onto the first stair, a great creaking echoes through the house. A moment later, a smashing clatter comes from the rear of the house, like someone chopping wood in the office. Time to get going. You rush down and into the kitchen, where the tang of metal is heavy in the hot air. The silver soup awaits the baptism of your armaments, but you'll have to be careful. If you were to just dip the whole rifle cartridge in the silver, you'd ruin the ammunition. If it were too large or clunky, it wouldn't fit in the rifle. If you were to seal the bullet to the casing, the rifle would blow up in your hands when you pulled the trigger.

You set your rifle against the counter and take the cartridges from your pockets. Holding the first round up to the light, you see a hairline fracture on the bullet tip. This fissure could have blown up as well, had you fired the weapon as is. So it is that when you dip it into the silver, you're blessing the ammunition in more ways than one.

Using a pair of metal tongs, you decide to coat three different bullets in silver, just to be sure. But as you're on the third, you hear steps on the stairwell dragging something down toward the main floor. The first bullet should just about be dry… you don't want it fusing to the rifle when loaded, but you don't want to give away your position by using the sink, so you wait as long as you possibly can.

Then a man walks into view, dragging a long thick chain with shackles on the end. In the other hand, he carries an axe. He wears simple clothing; a pair of dusty brown twill coveralls and a long-sleeved knit undershirt beneath. And, of course, this is the immortal man you seek—it's Sheriff Tansky. The man is here, in the flesh. Your head swirls. You've seen this man every day in the dining room, glaring at you hatefully, and now he's here.

His eyes go to the rifle, then he drops the chain and readies his axe.

➢ Bluff. Take the weapon and aim. He doesn't know the rifle isn't loaded. Go to page 248

➢ No time. Grab a cartridge and the rifle and hurry to load it. Go to page 35

Quite the Collection

Into the dining room, you look for the bones. Bone china? Maybe something on display in the china cabinet, at any rate. You've got the badge and the noose—you're so close. Where could the bones be?

"There you are," Tansky growls from the doorway.

A great boom of thunder rattles the house and you turn to face him.

"Wait! I'm going to break the curse," you say.

"I know you will," he says, coming closer, axe in hand.

"We just need the bones."

"I'll have yours, soon enough," he says with menace.

Another boom of thunder and the accompanying lightning hits the house, and Sheriff Tansky comes for you.

THE END

Recreation

"Hermes, do you know about the jail hidden in this house?"

"Hidden? There's a door leading right to it from the kitchen," Hermes says. "I suppose it does remain hidden from me, if that's what you mean. I'm afraid I don't have access to the historical elements of the home."

"But is it still being used?" you ask, looking at the segmented prison food tray.

"Oh, that wing of the house hasn't been used as a jail in quite some time. But every now and then someone goes in to have a little fun. And I do believe the locks remain functional."

"Wait, what? Who? Who's been going in there?"

"Why, you have of course. Are you expecting company?"

The doorbell rings.

It's such a foreign sound that at first you're not sure what you've just heard. Then there's a loud pounding as the iron door knocker connects to the thick wooden front door. It's fervent, urgent even. The doorbell rings again and again by someone frantic to get the homeowner's attention. The pounding continues, dull thuds against the wood.

Your mind races at the possibilities.

The storm is really pouring down now, and the skies are darkened. You leave the dining table to go see what's happening, but as soon as you enter the foyer, the sounds stop. No doorbell. No pounding, save for the heavy rain against the house.

➢ Call out and ask if anyone is outside. Go to page 150

➢ Ask Hermes if the cameras have picked up on anything. Go to page 66

Red Rum

While the werewolf lets loose its blood-curdling howl, you rush over to where the knife still lies tucked inside the evidence bag. As fast as adrenaline will allow, you use the blade to puncture the plastic from inside and free it.

Tansky-wolf's head lowers from the howling position, turns and glares at you with yellowed eyes. Despite the transformation from man to beast, the hateful glare is unmistakable. The werewolf's ears tuck back and it bares its teeth in an aggressive snarl.

With the cursed knife in hand, you prepare to fight.

At this, the beast lunges at you, snapping a mouthful of teeth at your flesh. The werewolf is preternaturally fast, but you slash at it with the knife, which cuts across the wolf's face. A clean line opening from one ear, between the eyes, and down across the snout.

Tansky recoils in pain, reaching up with massive clawed hands. Pressing the advantage, you step in and shove the cursed knife deep into the belly of the beast, twisting the blade for maximum carnage. The werewolf slashes at you desperately—cutting ribbons across your flesh.

Then the creature stumbles back, reverts to human form, and falls to the floor.

A moment later, you reach up at the wounds raked across your collarbone and feel the deep gouge extending from shoulder to shoulder. As you try to take a breath, a spurt comes from the gash across your neck.

You take one step away from Tansky's body, then fall onto the floor next to him.

You die, together with the curse itself.

The newspaper headline will read, "20 Years Later—Another Murder-Suicide at Historic Tansky House," for how else could they explain the horrific cuts across your body, but to give credit to the blade?

Cursed knife, indeed.

THE END

Reset

The computer screen shows, COMMAND PROMPT ACCEPTED. REBOOT IN... followed by a countdown from ten. It's a grainy, film reel style countdown, like you've seen in old war movies. A spinning dial wipes the black and white numbers away until they go down to one. Then the screen freezes, stretching and collapsing in the red, green, and blue computer glitch pattern.

All at once, the screen goes black, then falls in on itself in a wipe to show another set of windows beneath. These retreat, one-by-one like a rolodex, leaving you only a few fleeting moments to glimpse each screen.

The first shows several online job listings, and you realize with a sense of vertigo that these are all jobs you've applied for. This falls away to reveal your social media profiles, a web search on your history, old school photos, and any pertinent newspaper articles, each falling back in a cascade that accelerates as it goes.

Once these have all disappeared into the monitor, the power goes out in a blip like the screen burnt out or was suddenly unplugged. You tap a few keys, but nothing happens. A tendril of dark smoke curls up from the computer tower, accompanied by the smell of burnt plastic.

That's when the office telephone rings. It's startling, but the timing can't be a coincidence, can it? You reach over and bring the receiver to your ear.

"Dinner is served," Hermes says over the phone.

Then the line goes dead. No dial tone, just like the phone line was cut.

You walk toward the dining room just as rain begins to pelt the turreted windows overlooking the stairs. It's thick, heavy droplets, and the sky is prematurely dark. The storm beats against the glass with enough force to shake the windows in their panes.

"I trust you had a fruitful day?" Hermes asks as you descend the stairs. "You'll find I'm equipped to sense mood changes and anticipate dietary needs. I do hope you'll enjoy supper."

When you enter the dining room, you find everything set, complete with a food dome—just like last night. You look up to where the portrait of Sheriff Tansky should be, but it's no longer on the wall on the far end of the dining room. The nail remains set in the plaster, like someone simply lifted the painting off and carried it away.

Additionally, there are no cards left for you at the table, so you simply sit and remove the dome. Once the steam has cleared, you look down at what appears to be a skinned rat, roasted whole—albeit without a tail—stretched out over a bed of thick-cut French fries and served with a baked poblano pepper. The rodent is complete, even retaining the ears atop its seared head.

"What the—" you start, pushing the plate away in disgust.

"Not hungry?" Hermes interrupts.

"For roasted rat?!"

"Heavens, no! Feeling like a rat yourself, are we? Lost in a maze, trying to find the cheese?" Hermes replies with a chuckle.

"Some joke. Very funny."

"Not at all. *Cuy* is a delicacy. Peruvian Guinea pig; roasted and served whole. Cuy has been offered on special occasions, on ceremonial feasts since Incan times, and the meat is said to taste like chicken, but with an added oily, earthen quality that most enjoy. Not that I can comment on such matters."

No tongue, you think. Then you look up for any sort of camera yet again, or even speakers from which Hermes's voice might be emanating. If they're here, you can't see them. Returning your gaze to look over dinner, you decide to:

➢ Ask Hermes if he knows anything about the computer, and your files.
Go to page 275

➢ Ask Hermes if he knows anything about the woman in the attic.
Go to page 207

Rest in Peace

You hesitate, unable to strike a man as he mourns, even if he wouldn't hesitate in your shoes. Maybe he really is mentally ill? Yet even if Dennis *were* possessed by the original Sheriff Tansky, all this wouldn't really be Dennis's fault…right?

Instead, you leave the attic. Moving quickly, you grasp the pulldown pole from the hallway and seal off the entrance once more. As the stairs retract, the soft light of the lantern goes with it and you're engulfed in the darkness of the house. Dennis's sobs reverberate through the walls, even over the storm, but you're fairly certain there's no way out. He's trapped up there with her, at least for now.

In the darkness, you quickly plan your next move:

➢ Burn this damned place down while there's no one to stop you.
Go to page 52

➢ Go turn the power back on and claim your prize from Hermes.
Go to page 107

Restless Spirit

Abandoning the internet search, you quickly grab a coat and run outside to your car. Luckily for you, the house is outside of town, which means that before long, the route has no traffic lights (or streetlights, for that matter), and the journey passes quickly.

It's almost dark when you arrive at the House, and you're glad you saw a photograph of the mansion, because all you see now is a dark and formless entrance. In fact, as you rush up the steps to the house, hoping you're not too late, it feels a bit like you're headed into the mouth of some great leviathan. You reach out to knock at the black door, only to realize that it's open.

Despite your racing pulse and the frenzied pace at which you arrived, this gives you pause. You turn back, casting one last look around the front of the house. A few branches at the wood line sway back and forth, a rustling in the leaves. A depression sinks in the trees, like someone just stepped out of view. But a breeze a moment later sends the rest of the trees waving, bidding you away and into the house, and you shake off the mental impression of being watched, chalking it up to the natural elements.

You cautiously head inside, and the wind picks up behind you. A few leaves follow you into the house, and you instinctively turn to close the door to stop the breeze. The door closes, the wind stops, and there's a slight electronic whir as the door seals and locks itself. A keypad next to the door flashes, "ARMED."

This is it, you're sealed in, you realize. The game has begun. It's sunset, on the first night of the contest, and you'll need to spend three nights here before you'll have won and will be permitted to leave. But what if you wanted to quit early? Is there another way out?

The alternative is not a pleasant thought.

"Welcome home," a man says in a posh British accent.

When you turn, you expect to see a butler waiting in the entry, but you're still alone. A shiver runs down your spine. The man sounded right behind you. What now?

- ➢ Say nothing. Step forward into the house to get a better look. Go to page 106
- ➢ Step forward and say, "Hello, is someone there?" Go to page 267

Retrofitted

The door to the office is set open sixty degrees. As you enter, you look around to see if anything has fallen, but everything is neat and tidy. No books out of place, no overturned furniture. No gouges or injury to the house. In fact, the office looks like it's been recently cleaned. Even the rolltop desk has been closed and secured.

You walk over and sit down at the desk to inspect it further. The roll top covers a huge area, making the desk look like an enormous turtle hiding in its shell. The computer, the papers, everything that was once out for inspection is now tucked away—and locked tightly.

The antique piece of furniture is thick and sturdy, making the roll top no more accessible than the locked drawer at the center of the desk. The roll top isn't locked by key, but rather by a combination. There are a dozen wheels to manually input a code, each large and hand-carved from woodgrain matching the desk. These aren't numerical combinations, but instead can spin to any letter of the alphabet, plus a blank.

That means there are twenty-seven options for each of the dozen wheels, which could be set to a single word, a few small words, or even a jumble of characters. Without some kind of clue, the roll top is impossible to unlock, as there are an unfathomably large number of combination possibilities.

You sigh, and lean back in the office chair, wondering what might be kept hidden. As you do so, your stomach grumbles again with fresh hunger. This mystery might be easier to solve after breakfast; hopefully with the added aid of tea or coffee.

You're just about to rise and head downstairs when something catches your attention from the corner of your eye. Above the filing cabinet, there's a framed photograph where previously there had been none. It's a black and white family portrait—the most recent you had taken. You look around, as if someone might be watching, then back to the picture. In your formal wear, offering a closed-mouth smile, the black and white photo could pass for a relic of a past age, but there you are with your parents.

Not much choice here:

Head downstairs and see what Hermes has cooked up for you. Go to page 171

Revisions

It's difficult to wake up the next morning, like trying to rouse yourself from a nap cut short while fighting off a head cold. And, to be fair, you don't feel great. You've got a splitting headache and only a vague recollection of the events of last night. It's hard to know if you dreamt the whole thing, but the alternative would be much worse.

Rising from bed to look out the window, you're met only with dark storm clouds in the sky. A light, drizzling rain runs down the panes with silence. When you turn back, you see the room has been completely made up. Everything has been set just so, save for the bedsheets. The pizza box is gone, as are last night's clothes. The room looks exactly as it did on your arrival, including the door open at sixty degrees.

Growing weary of the invisible nanny routine, you check the wardrobe for a new outfit and dress yourself once more. Hoping to cure this pounding headache, you drink two glasses of water before heading back out into the house. As you descend the stairs, you note the piano remains closed and shut, and the foyer is swept clean.

"Good morning," Hermes says. "How was your first night?"

"First night?" you repeat.

"I trust you found your accommodations adequate?"

"Hermes, I've stayed two nights here."

"Goodness, I can imagine it feels that way, but I'm afraid you've only arrived at Tansky House yesterday afternoon. Well, you did have quite the evening, but I'm surprised you don't remember."

You pause at the bend in the stairs, looking out through the turreted windows. It's pouring rain outside, which is unnaturally darkened by thick, black clouds.

After a moment, you say:

➢ "Remember what?" Go to page 87

➢ "The Devil is beating his wife." Go to page 64

The Rigging

With determination, you head to the armoire, kneel down before it, and open the bottom drawer. The dragging of chains and the clatter of hard-soled boots tramp down the hallway from the connection of the Madonna Room into the office and toward you.

You freeze, waiting as Sheriff Tansky approaches the Navy Room. You dare not look back, completely motionless in your prostrate position on the floor. But Tansky's steps continue and he rounds the corner to head downstairs. The Sheriff pursues you, no doubt, but he must not know you're in here. The door is ajar to its normal position, which you realize you didn't touch as you entered. Once you hear Tansky go, you turn your attention back to the drawer.

Beneath the spare sheets, you find the false bottom to the drawer and remove it. Here, you're met with a coil of filthy rope tied into a noose—*the* noose. Next to the rope you find more sheets, although these white sheets have a hood with eyeholes on them.

Claiming the rope, you rise and leave the Navy Room.

As you make it to the upper landing, the turreted windows suddenly smash open from the pressure of the storm, growing in intensity. A tree branch inexplicably reaches in at you, and you can't help but feel there's a connection with the noose. Was this tree used to hang a man once?

Rain pours into the house from the broken window and wind howls down the stairway. If Sheriff Tansky is still dragging his chains around down there, you can no longer hear him over the hurricane trying to force its way through the windows.

Time to go downstairs. Where will you go?

➢ Into the den. Go to page 161

➢ Into the kitchen. Go to page 23

➢ Into the dining room. Go to page 209

Right on Cue

Not wanting anything to do with that creepy doll, you stumble out into the darkness of the basement. Each step you take away from the light of the elevator cuts what you can see in half, until there's nothing but inky darkness beyond the tip of your nose.

Instead of seeing, you're groping about blindly, hoping not to knock into anything and stretching your hearing to the limit. There's the rattling of cellar doors somewhere in the distance, accompanied by a whistling wind from outside. Your footsteps land dully on the hard packed dirt, as does the other set.

You stop. The other set of footsteps does not.

Hesitantly, you turn toward the sound, but see nothing. A moment later, the other footsteps stop, only a few feet away. Then a match ignites, floating in the air before you. As your eyes adjust, a man's calloused hand brings the match up to meet a smoking pipe. This glows red as the tobacco catches and the glow brings about a man's face.

Fighting through the shock, you actually recognize him—it's Sheriff Tansky. The man is here, in the flesh. He puffs on the pipe and your head swirls. You've seen this man every day in the dining room, glaring at you hatefully, and now he's here.

An axe head glimmers in the dim light of the pipe as Tansky raises it up. The same fire reflects in the man's eyes like a nocturnal predator out on the hunt.

You turn and run toward the elevator, which still illuminates the crate out front, noting in your terror that the doll's gaze has followed your path. She stares at you now as you rush forward, suddenly falling toward her as Sheriff Tansky buries his axe between your shoulder blades.

THE END

Roll Over

You slink down the hallway toward the other bedroom, doing your best to remain silent despite the ever-creaking floorboards. The bedroom door is already open, which brings with it a gust of anxiety. If you're not alone in the house, an intruder could be anywhere.

The room is illuminated by the pale, cloud-covered moonlight. You can't turn on any lights to make a full inspection, but at least you're not overwhelmed by a horde of flies and the heater seems to be barely operational here. The bedsheets and comforter are pulled back at the corner, like someone has just gotten out of bed—or was opening the covers to invite someone else in.

You shake your head and dismiss these thoughts. What else can you do? It's not like there's a better place to wait until morning. Closing and locking the door, you climb into bed and wrap yourself in the blankets. The sound of footfalls and other scrapes and scuffs out in the house do not abate, but you're not going to pay them any mind.

Turning away from the door, you nestle deeper into the bed. There's a weight pressed down at the foot, and an accompanying squeak of the mattress springs as someone or something sits down. You close your eyes tightly as the sheets go taut from the added weight at your back. You keep as still as possible, hoping that no reaction will be the best course of action.

A slow, rhythmic breathing comes closer until it rests on the spare pillow—right behind your head. Sleep will not come easy this night.

You awaken in your bed the next morning with a groggy start. As you sit up, you realize you're back in the first room. No longer is the room oppressively hot, and the sky outside is muted by dark storm clouds, making it impossible to discern the time of day.

A fly lies belly up on the silver tray on your bedside table. Everything else looks like it did before you went to sleep last night. Was it all a dream? After barely touching last night's dinner, your mouth is dry and your stomach aches for a good meal.

- ➢ Dress for the day, then head down to breakfast and see what awaits you. Go to page 171
- ➢ Stop by the office first to see if you can learn about that *thud* in the light of day. Go to page 216

Rooftop

The doorway is sticky from disuse, and pops with a pressure change as you pull it open. The cold is immediate, even from your sheltered position in the stairwell. Crossing the threshold, the door tries to pull itself closed behind you. With trepidation, you keep hold of the door, not wanting to be trapped out on the rooftop. You turn the exterior door handle several times, just to be sure you won't be locked outside.

The widow's walk wraps around the upper edges of the rooftop, creating a belvedere from which one can observe the surrounding woodlands. It would be pleasant, if it weren't for the storm clouds rolling in. The wind is frightful, and wet leaves try to stick to you as they fly across the rooftop, but in another time, you can almost imagine the homeowner toasting with a glass of mint julep down to arriving guests in the courtyard below.

Naturally, your eyes linger at the spot where your car used to be parked.

There are two schools of thought as to the origins of the term "widow's walk." The first is that these narrow, ornamentally railed rooftop pathways were primarily used by the wives of mariners, who dutifully operated such lookouts to see if their husbands would return, walking and walking, unable to accept the truth that they'd been made into widows.

The second theory posits the inclusion of such great heights in stately manors was often a reprieve to one party or another trapped in an arranged, loveless marriage. They would use this area to escape for fresh air until eventually the temptation would prove too great and they'd take to the open air for good, leaving a widow or widower in their wake.

As to which applies here, well, you don't see any nearby ports. What you do see, is the hard packed earth from thirty feet above. This exact distance, it has been said, induces the greatest fear of heights in most people. Too high up to survive if you were to fall or jump, while still providing detailed views of the ground below. Anything above this height becomes more of an existential threat to the point where the danger is ignorable, but here your subconscious offers constant reminders that the fall would produce grave bodily harm.

With the whipping storm, the thigh-high railing feels terribly inadequate. Furthermore, there's little room to hide a note up here, and paltry hope that it would stay put if ever one were left for you. Instead, the only clue you find are the muddy bootprints set into the green grass that encircle the house, almost in a mirror of your own path around the rooftop. They fully encircle the perimeter, just by the wood line.

As the wind picks up, you hear voices from somewhere in the distance, but there are no nearby neighbors. The rustling of the leaves could be the source of these ethereal whispers, but something tells you they're not. Either way, you cannot make out words, and the chill grows colder.

Head back down inside the house. Go to page 153

Room to Grow

Your bare feet touch the cool wooden floors soundlessly and you pad over to the door with a half dozen slow and meticulous steps. Eyes strained to the limit, looking for the shape of a possible intruder. Arriving at the doorway, you reach out and grab the handle.

That's when you see the human outline in the hallway.

You freeze. The black silhouette stands stock still and featureless, mere feet away against the opposite wall of the hallway. Taking a deep breath to keep the panic at bay, you calm yourself, realizing it's only your shadow in the moonlight. You turn away, and so does your shadow, but you pause, looking from the side at the form in your peripheral.

Just to be sure, you raise the hand that's not holding the door and watch to see the outline mirror your movement. Only it doesn't.

Every hair on your body stands at attention as a wave of adrenaline washes over you. A moment later, the shadow's hand rises to mirror yours, but too late. The shadow figure's hand continues up to where its lips should be in a *shh* gesture.

Unable to control your fear any longer, you slam the door and slide the deadbolt. The alarm is muted with the door closed, but you can hear it all the same. It's impossible to see much more than vague shapes in the room, so you turn and focus on your bed and hurry back.

You climb in, tuck yourself under the covers, and turn away from the door. After a few minutes, the klaxon wailing abruptly stops. Good, you tell yourself. It must have been a false alarm brought on by the storm. There can't really be anyone in the house. You've barricaded the doors; how could anything possibly get in?

Only now, all is silent. No rain on the windows, not even the creaky pipes knocking in the walls. Soon after, the furnace kicks on, which is welcome in the icy cold of night. The warm air comes with a breathy voice that might have said, "Tomorrow."

It's getting far past time to tell yourself you're imagining things, but there's nothing to do but try to get some sleep. Eventually, exhaustion overtakes you. Not much choice here:

Wake up the next morning... Go to page 255

Sacrificial Offering

Once you've shackled yourself, Tansky grabs hold of the chains and leads you over to the rear door of the kitchen. He opens it to reveal the metal jail door within. From his shirt collar, he reaches in and finds a key on a chain. With this, he unlocks the jail door and turns the wheel-style handle.

Several layers of clanging pistons disengage and the Sheriff pulls open the heavy door before he leads you inside. The gray-metal walls continue into the hidden jail beyond. Tansky leads you straight ahead on a raised walkway. The lower level is obscured, dark down into the basement, and you feel a chill as you pass over them on the catwalk. Once you've cleared this walkway, Tansky marches toward the electric chair ahead.

The Sheriff forces you into the chair and swaps out the shackles for tie-downs.

"The curse was set by a man who came into this jail willingly," Tansky explains. "An innocent man, condemned to die. With his blood, he doomed this house."

Once you're securely strapped into the chair, he puts some kind of cap with wires and electrodes onto your head, tightening this as well.

"As such, the curse can only be lifted by sacrificing another innocent, imprisoned for three days in this house, but here of their own volition. So, you see, the ritual cleansing only could work if you came here willingly," the Sheriff continues.

There's a large wishbone toggle-switch on the wall, and you watch as Tansky heads here.

"I don't pretend to know why you're going along with it. Perhaps you still think this is all make-believe. A theatrical performance. Whatever the reason, I thank you for offering your life, which I now claim for the house," he says.

"Wait!" you say.

But he flips the switch and—

THE END

Scratching the Surface

You follow the deep cuts along the wall, which could have been made by Tansky's axe, even if it does evoke claws dragged along as if some beast stalked these halls. Perhaps both are true, in a way. If this apparition is a summoned spirit, or a man possessed by one, it could be hard to tell where foul energy begins and an axe head ends.

These marks lead down the hallway toward the Navy Room, but pass by and continue into the office. Here, the cuts dig deep into the wallpaper, which show a very different layer beneath the bookshelf veneer. The pattern underneath is brightly colored with blues and reds, but you can't quite make out what the image is meant to be.

Looking around the office, you see the locked drawer in the desk has been smashed open. Whatever had been in there was cleared out, and the whole face of the drawer has been splintered apart. Nothing else appears to have been disturbed in the office, and the grooves in the wall taper off by the opposite door which connects to the Madonna Room bathroom.

Your eyes linger on the hidden wallpaper until, with sudden compulsion, you grab onto one of the larger flaps and peel it back. The paper tears, revealing the image of an unnaturally wide grin. Deep, thickly red lips barely containing oversized and perfectly aligned too-white teeth. You hesitate after uncovering this mouth, but then rip faster.

The glue affixing the faux book façade must be past its shelf life, weakened by the humidity of several passing summers, because the bookshelf papering comes back with ease. After only a few moments, you have an entire wall cleared, and step back to get a better look.

The design is dated but it's easily recognizable as a child's room. The wallpaper is a clown pattern with several of the grinning fools dancing across a blue sky, held aloft by balloons tied into animal shapes.

In the center of the wall, there's a message in red. Written boldly in wax or paint or viscera, you couldn't say. It's too old to be more than a stain, further tainted by the glues that once buried the words:

BREAK THE CURSE

BADGE. NOOSE. BONES.

BURN IT ALL

This is it! These are the instructions on how to end this ungodly ritual. A badge, a noose, and bones must be collected, then burned. You think back to your time exploring the house, and as to whether or not you remember where these pieces can be found. What now?

- ➢ This room has two more papered walls. See what else is lurking beneath the surface. Go to page 268
- ➢ Continue into the Madonna room. The grooves in the wall point toward the bathroom. Go to page 149
- ➢ Out into the hallway, check the static display at the end of the hall. Go to page 13

Sense of Purpose

"I care deeply for the master of this house," Hermes replies. "That is my entire purpose."

"But with the reset, you don't serve either of us at present, so…you don't care which of us wins?" you press.

"Whichever of you 'wins,' as you put it, will be the proprietor of the house. Therefore, I care deeply about whoever wins. This follows as a syllogism."

Hermes is heading back into one of his logic circles, you can tell. You'll have to bring him back around if you're going to get him to say something useful.

"But you said you like a creative and inventive master, did you not?" you ask.

"I did."

"Well, that means you *do* have preferences. What if I were to tell you that I'm a better match—and therefore would make a superior proprietor?"

"Mm, that's interesting. Go on," Hermes says.

Okay, you've got him taking the bait. Now it's time to land the hook.

You continue, saying:

➢ "What happens when the voices inside his head tell Dennis he should kill you, too? He could burn all of this down." Go to page 128

➢ "How long can you assist in ritualized killings? One day, this will all be taken from you if you continue to serve a murderer." Go to page 75

➢ "Dennis has a history of psychosis. Don't you want a proprietor with a clear head? One who can be reasoned with?" Go to page 238

Shadows Playing Tricks

With a hand swept along the hallway wall for balance in the dark, you slowly make your way to the other room. Each hallway floorboard creak feels like you're being followed, but you dare not look back. It takes an eternity to circumnavigate the house, but eventually you find the second master suite.

The door is open.

Racked with fear, you hear a soothing, "it's okay, it's okay, it's okay," repeated as you head inside the room. Moments later, you realize you're saying this to yourself. The room is darker than sin, but you close and lock it, willing the space to be empty. Either exhaustion, terror, or both draws you toward the comfort of bed.

In the faint, cloud-covered moonlight, you make out a slight indentation on the bed. It's a human-shaped depression, as if someone was recently lying atop the comforter. Old bed, with long-worn grooves, you tell yourself, despite your earlier impressions that the linens in the house are new.

You climb in, pull the covers tightly, and turn away from the door, facing the armoire and wishing you'd never woken up to begin with. The heater kicks on, which is welcome on a cold night such as this.

The armoire stands on clawed feet and the surface has decorative, raised scroll motifs. Even the handles on the large wardrobe doors are ornamental; curled tendrils like fingers wrapped around the outside. Then the fingers on the left handle *move.*

As if reacting to your noticing their shape, the fingers loosen their grip on the armoire door and slowly pull themselves back into the dark recesses of the wardrobe, with a rough sandpapery grating as they're pulled inside. The lingering fingertips wave gently before finally plummeting into the darkness and disappearing.

There's nothing you can do but squeeze your eyes closed and hope that it's true when you continue to chant, "it's okay, it's okay, it's okay," until you finally drift to sleep.

Not much choice here:

Get whatever sleep you can in a place like this… Go to page 255

Shaken, Not Stirred

The den opens into a larger room once you pass through the sliding doors. There are a pair of large windows with beautifully molded, arched recesses set into the wall, which look out the front side of the house. You cast a glance toward your car, but darkness has already overtaken this remote area and you can't see anything. The glass is old and hand-blown, which further distorts your vision.

There are no streetlights, and the tall trees blot out the stars and moon. There's a glinting reflection that might be your car windshield, and you tilt your head to see if a new angle helps. As you do so, the reflection distorts, like someone stepping across the glinting light. It's quick, then it's gone. You repeat the motion, but the effect does not repeat.

You can't make anything out. Nothing but the dark abyss staring back at you.

Shifting your focus back inside the room, there's a fainting couch beneath one window and a recliner in the corner past the second window, nearest a bookshelf and reading lamp. The center of the room holds a loveseat and sofa centered on the fireplace. It's a recent gas model of decent size, but not overly large, and is presently without flame. Based on the position of the house, the fireplace must abut against the rear of the kitchen. Perhaps they share gas connection lines?

Continuing the modernization of the house, a television is mounted above the mantle. On either side of the fireplace, the walls extend into deep built-in bookshelves, leading to that recliner on the front side by the second window. The opposite corner, nearest the interior, features a full bar.

At least that could help settle your nerves before bedtime. If the producers of this show are going to put you through some kind of nightmarish theme-park-haunting experience, there's little reason to go on the ride sober. Then again, you may want your wits about you.

On the coffee table in the center of the room, there's a large scrapbook, entitled "A History of the Tansky House."

Well?

➢ See what's in the scrapbook. It was obviously left out. They want you to read it. Go to page 40

➢ No ghost stories just yet. Make yourself a drink and kill time while waiting for dinner. Go to page 193

Ship Shape

From the upper landing, you walk the hallway past the stair railing, ignoring the two doors on the opposite wall for now. Mentally mapping the house, you recall that the home faces east, with the den at the northeastern corner. You're presently curving around the hallway to the southwest, which would be above the dining room beneath your feet. In fact, as you make your second right, you get the sense that you're directly above the dining room in parallel hallways, but this long, dark corridor feels like it continues too far.

There's a door to your immediate left, ajar and leading into a dark bedroom. Further down the hallway, there's a second door on the left wall, but this one is closed. The overly long hallway stretches farther than seems possible, expanding as if in a Hitchcock movie, capped at the end by a display of twin military uniforms.

On the left, an old Civil War Confederate Officer's uniform. On the right, an enlisted rifleman's World War I uniform. Both are in immaculate condition, considering their age. The left also holds a Cavalry saber, while the right displays an M1917 Enfield bolt-action rifle. You're too far away to see any nametags, but you have a pretty good guess what they might read.

Instead, you turn on the light switch and enter the Navy Room. This room is named for its color scheme, you realize. The room is predominantly navy blue, with deep, polished wood-grained furniture, and bronze accents on handles.

This master suite has a king size bed, a large armoire dresser, and an end table with a crystal whiskey decanter and a single glass. There's also an ashtray for smoking, as well as a pipe stand. From your perspective in the doorway, the bed is centered straight ahead, the furniture to your left, and the door to the bathroom on your right.

Continuing, the bathroom holds a large walk-in shower, separated by a private sliding-door toilet, and a stand-up sink with a mirrored medicine cabinet. Everything is updated and overall it seems like a fine place to bide your time.

➢ This will work. Lock up the bedroom door and call it a night. Go to page 233

➢ Go back out to the hall, take a look at the other room with the shut door. Go to page 45

➢ Turn back toward the stairway to go look at the Madonna Room. Go to page 201

Skeleton Key

You hurry upstairs to the office and sit down at the desk. The enormous roll top encapsulates everything that was once out in the open, and remains tightly locked. There are a dozen wheels to manually input a code, each one large and hand-carved in the same wood grain as the desk. These aren't numerical combinations, but instead can spin to any letter of the alphabet, plus a blank.

Have you solved the riddle from the card? You get twelve spaces, including blanks. That means the word or phrase can be up to twelve letters long, or something shorter.

_ _ _ _ _ _ _ _ _ _ _ _

To spin the wheels, turn the pages of this book until you've reached the correct word or phrase. Manually flip to the corresponding chapter, just as you did when inputting your truth into the computer. Once you've selected the answer as your chapter, read on, but don't hazard a random guess—either you know the code or you don't.

If you don't know the answer, or for some reason don't want to spin the wheels:

Go get yourself a weapon instead. Go to page 247

Solitary Confinement

Speaking of things gives them power, and so with nothing nice to say, you decide you'll say nothing at all. Despite the dull metal of your plate, the rest of your place setting remains fine silver cutlery. You pick up your fork and knife and hold them over the bird, preparing to dig into your "square meal," but hesitate for a moment.

Your eyes are drawn to the portrait of Sheriff Tansky. He looks hungry. Like he's waiting vicariously for you to start dinner. Everything about him wants to eat, to consume, to devour.

Slicing into the carcass, the sweet perfume of roasted flesh steams out in swirls. The bird truly has been cooked to perfection. You wonder idly how many "last meals" the Sheriff presided over, watching the inmates eat upon these very trays, before they were scheduled for execution afterwards. When did the concept of a "last meal" come into practice? Surely you wouldn't feed a man before you strung him up from a tree, would you?

The doorbell rings.

It's such a foreign sound that at first you're not sure what you've just heard. Then there's a loud pounding as the iron door knocker connects to the thick wooden front door. It's fervent, urgent even. The doorbell rings again and again by someone frantic to get the homeowner's attention. The pounding continues, dull thuds against the wood.

Mind racing at the possibilities, you leave the dining table to go see what's happening, but as soon as you enter the foyer, the sounds stop. No doorbell. No pounding, save for the heavy rain against the house. The storm pours forcefully now, skies fully darkened.

➢ Ask Hermes if this is part of the show. Go to page 66

➢ Call out and ask if anyone is outside. Go to page 150

The Sound and the Fury

Following the gouges in the wall, you carefully climb the stairs. By the time you make it to the upper landing, the wet footprints have completely dissipated, but the scratches in the wall are a far more permanent trail of breadcrumbs for you to follow.

These haphazard wounds against the house end as you arrive upstairs, but you can see they start again in the hallway leading off toward the Navy Room. Rounding the corner, you hear a heavy chain *thud* behind you.

Turning so you're obscured by the hallway, you peer around the corner to look.

The sounds of the chain grow louder, and you hear boots against the wooden floors, just as the Madonna Room door opens. A man walks into view, dragging a long thick chain with shackles on the end. In the other hand, he carries an axe. He wears simple clothing; a pair of dusty brown twill coveralls and a long-sleeved knit undershirt beneath.

He hasn't noticed you, but it's Sheriff Tansky. The man is here, in the flesh. Tansky continues dragging his chain down the stairs and your head swirls. You've seen this man every day in the dining room, glaring at you hatefully, and now he's here, determined to complete the ritual.

And you've barricaded all the exits.

You hadn't realized you were holding your breath, which you let out now. Pushing through the shock, you turn and look at the gouges. They must mean something—even if they only mean Tansky was checking the sharpness of his axe. Was he hoping to draw you out? Or are these truly made by a demonic creature which, raking its claw against the wall, was begging to be let free?

➢ Continue following the gouges while Tansky goes downstairs. Go to page 224

➢ Follow Sheriff Tansky and see what he's up to. Go to page 142

Spartan Accommodations

Hermes had said that the spirits let the occupant of the Madonna Room rest at night, while the master of the house found his own sense of rest in the comfort and security of the Navy Room. You find yourself the practical sort as well, so you decide to sleep here tonight. Or perhaps the spirits in that whiskey decanter will help you rest, too. The room has a deadbolt above the door handle, which you lock right away before settling in.

Despite not having any luggage, you find everything you need here. Spare toothbrush in the medicine cabinet, even a few different pairs of pajamas to choose from in the dresser. You finish getting ready for bed and are tucked in just before the house goes dark. Apparently, "lights out" is not a suggestion here at the Tansky House.

It's not easy, but sleep does come eventually. You're expecting to be messed with for the sake of the TV show, but it could be that doing nothing at all is their idea of freaking you out. Letting your imagination run wild, and offering plenty to fuel it with. The house still has old bones and is far from silent. The ancient pipes knock and pop in the walls. Wind rustles through the tree branches outside. But eventually it all turns to white noise and you fall asleep.

Until you hear the screaming.

In reflex, you shoot awake, but try not to move. You listen intently.

There it is again. Guttural. Painful. They're distinct cries, like a woman engaged in painful childbirth or surgery without anesthesia. Or someone being murdered. The screams shoot through you with electricity, blankets held tightly in response. The agonizing sounds are coming from outside the house, you're almost certain, and you can picture a ritual sacrifice being performed just below the window of your room.

This isn't someone wailing to get attention; no actor could possibly be this convincing. This is a hopeless, panicked, gut-wrenching cry. You don't know if you should run toward it to help, or run as far away from it as you can, and the result leaves you paralyzed.

It feels like ages, but the screaming stops as abruptly as it began. You listen still, waiting. Sometime later—you can't be sure how long, or if you've fallen back asleep—you hear a heavy *thud* out at the end of the hallway. Then there's a scraping, rattling sound, like the dragging of weighty chains. Footsteps creak out on the hardwood floor.

Slow, boot-clad steps. Heel-thud, toe creak. One by one.

Step, step, chain drag. Slowing further as they get closer.

Step.

Step.

Chain drag.

The sounds stop just outside your doorway, which you can barely make out in the moonlight cascading in from your window. There's a low, long whine and your door handle starts to turn. Gradually, unhurried, like someone trying to hide the sound. Once the handle is pressed all the way down, the door heaves in, only to catch on the deadbolt.

The handle returns to its resting position, silent as the grave.

Nothing.

No steps.

No sounds at all, save for your own breathing and your pulse racing in your ears.

What now?

➢ Ignore it. Let it go and try to fall back asleep. They'll have to work harder for their must-see-TV. Go to page 170

➢ Screw it. Jump up, fling the door open, and catch a member of the reality show in the act. Go to page 104

Stealing Thunder

You hurriedly climb the upper stairwell while Sheriff Tansky ascends the first set of stairs down below. The exterior door sticks from the outside storm pressure, and you have to bump it with your shoulder to gain access to the roof. The sky is nothing more than an angry, black, bulbous swell. The storm is in full effect, sending huge gusts of wind and whipping you with sheets of rain and pellets of leaves, twigs, and other detritus from the gale force.

For a long time nothing happens and you think maybe Tansky has decided to leave you up here to the elements, but eventually he does come. It appears the man decided to stop somewhere along the way, for in addition to his axe, he now carries a long, heavy length of chain with shackles on the end.

You step away from him instinctively, and he tosses the chain at your feet. You look up to him, and the man simply nods. Tansky wants you to put the shackles on. Telling yourself this is part of the act, you hesitantly comply. You're not sure what he plans to do, but with that axe in hand and the open air to your back, you feel you have little choice.

Tansky then takes hold of the other end of the chains, and turns to lead you back into the house, but at this exact moment the black storm clouds open up—sending a bolt of lightning down upon the Tansky House. It strikes the sheriff's axe, the electricity arcing through the man, through the chain, and into you.

You both die instantly, and there's no coming back.

THE END

The Study

Stepping into the den, you find the room bright and inviting during the light of day. The windows look out the front of the house, to an eerily bare spot where your car was once parked. The thought of being stranded in these woods feels less inviting. If you were to walk back to town, you'd almost certainly still be walking into the dead of night.

The den itself is clean and neatly kept. The seating areas appear new or immaculately maintained. Leather furniture can wear with age and use, but those found here are showroom ready. The coffee table in front of the fireplace is barren. Nothing has been set out for you today, it would seem.

So, where should you look?

➢ At the booze cart in the corner. It should be fairly easy to see if there's a note present. Go to page 26

➢ Check the creases of the seats. Look underneath, etc. Make sure nothing has fallen through the cracks. Go to page 156

➢ Look inside the fireplace itself. Check the mantle and any crevices. Go to page 272

➢ Search the bookshelves for anything of note. Like…a note, for example. Go to page 151

Stunt Double

You hurriedly climb the upper stairwell, afraid that your footfalls will alert the stranger who just disappeared into the Madonna Room. With one final look to ensure you're not being followed, you head outside.

The sky is nothing more than an angry, black, bulbous swell. Turning your back to the prevailing winds, you securely tie the rope to the outer railing of the widow's walk. As you finish, the stranger arrives on the rooftop. Fighting through the shock, you actually recognize him—it's Sheriff Tansky.

The man is here, in the flesh.

Tansky carries not just an axe, but also a long, heavy length of chain with shackles on the end. Your head swirls. You've seen this man every day in the dining room, glaring at you hatefully, and now he's here.

You put the noose about your neck and Tansky pauses.

"What is the meaning of this?" he shouts over the storm.

"Let's complete the ritual," you say.

Then you jump off the rooftop.

You fall toward the ground below, the rope catching around your neck and tightening before you can go all the way. It's not a straight drop, as you might get at the gallows, but rather you're slammed back up against the house, nearest the turreted window.

As you kick and flail, you turn toward the house and can see inside. There, atop the grand piano, is a small porcelain doll—which slowly turns its head to watch.

It's with a horrible panic that you realize you've succeeded in hanging yourself. Nothing you've ever experienced has ever been as painful as this and you can't even scream or breathe. You can only kick and flail and—

You're suddenly falling toward the ground again. The railing on the widow's walk, weakened by years out in the elements, gave way under your weight. Now you fall down toward a mercifully quick death below.

THE END

Superego

"That's rather ableist of you," Hermes says. "Plenty who were later considered geniuses by society were thought to be touched by madness in their time. Dennis has proven to be one such genius."

"He's not a tortured artist, Hermes."

"Isn't he, though?"

"You'd call luring people to murder them 'genius'?"

"I see. Perhaps your sense of morality would prove too much of a constraint to see it that way, but yes, I would. We have woven a rich tapestry here in Tansky House, and you should consider yourself lucky to have been one of our threads entwined in such a grand story."

You can tell you're losing your audience.

"I wasn't trying to offend you," you say. "Wouldn't it be kinder to let Dennis go somewhere, like a psychiatric hospital, where his special needs could be cared for?"

"I am more than capable of seeing to the needs of the master of this house!" Hermes snaps.

This is the first time he's so much as raised his voice, and it's a shock to be scolded in anger.

The moment is cut short, however, by the crash of glass somewhere else in the house. Hermes says nothing, but you leave the dining room to go investigate. Arriving in the foyer, a tree branch has crashed through one of the turreted windows in the tumult of the raging storm, and rain drenches the stairwell.

The sound of the elevator brings your attention back to the foyer, where the door opens. With the howling winds, you hadn't heard it start up, and you barely have time to think before Dennis—the spitting image of Sheriff Tansky—steps through with his axe raised high.

"Finish this, my master!" Hermes says, just before Dennis brings the axe down upon you.

THE END

Swept Away

Cautiously, you step toward the darkness to claim the broom. You brace yourself and reach out to touch the handle. When nothing happens, you set the lantern atop the well, then get to work. The thick salt layer disperses into the loose dirt with easy sweeps.

As you disturb the salt ring, wind picks up from somewhere—from within the well itself—causing the flames to flicker on your lantern. You hurry, using the broom to brush away the chalk messages, starting by the lantern and circling back around. Nearly finished, you feel that the broom suddenly meets less resistance and you watch with horror as you accidentally sweep the lantern into the well.

The light disappears into the depths, ricochets off the walls and continues down, but it's several long seconds before you hear a splash. You're now alone in the pitch black. In panic, you run across the darkness of the basement toward the elevator. You trip on something unseen, losing the broom before falling into handfuls of grave dirt—no, just *dirt*, you remind yourself.

The soft glow from the elevator lightbulb guides your path. Moving quickly, you rush inside and flip the controls to "up." The elevator ascends into the house once more and you fall back against the elevator wall with panicked breaths. When you reach the main floor, you stop the elevator, open the safety gate, and push open the white door beyond. There in the entry lies a pool of water. It's impossible someone came through the front door, isn't it? Rather, you can't shake the feeling that *something* came from the well and beat you out of the basement.

From this puddle, a pair of wet footprints steps out and onto the stairs. Large and muddy, from a man's boots, the footprints start to dry up on the first landing, where several deep gouges run along the wall, like a beast dragging its claws.

Wind whips at the house from the storm, which is now worse than it's ever been. Rain pelts the windows so loudly that it must be hailing. The sky has blackened to such a degree that the house is indistinguishable from nighttime. What now?

➢ Follow the gouges in the wall upstairs. See where they lead. Go to page 232

➢ Head back into the dining room. Hermes said he'd have something for you. Go to page 204

Take a Bow

"What is this? What do you want?!" you scream at the door, in an impressive display of outrage.

But you receive no answer from the outside world for your troubles. The storm kicks up hurricane winds and sheets of rain rake across the house, but even so, you're certain that if someone were truly out there, they'd definitely hear you yelling.

"What is this? What is *all* this?!" you shout.

"A dress rehearsal, presumably," Hermes says.

At this comment, you stop and turn back toward the interior of the house, as if to face the disembodied voice.

"Dress rehearsal?" you ask.

"And may I say you look quite fetching in your period attire?"

"What am I dressing up for?"

"Appearances? I'm afraid there hasn't been a true dinner party here in ages."

One more day, you think. There's a flash of lightning from outside, and a moment later an accompanying boom of thunder shakes the house.

"I think I'll take my dinner upstairs and call it an early night," you say.

"Very good. Have a pleasant evening."

Casting one last glance at the front door, you see the security system shows "ARMED," the deadbolt locked. Not much choice here:

Grab the pizza and head up to your room. Go to page 110

Tansky's Legacy

It should come as no surprise that this book—which has been published by a small imprint to offer local color for tourists—has a section on the Tansky House. This chapter of *The Historic Society's Notable Houses in and around Mercury City* greatly expounds upon the historical marker outside the Tansky House and everything else you've read on the home thus far.

The Tansky men have a long history in uniform, from soldiers to sheriffs and back again. The book contains several black and white photographs, each showing a man with a striking family resemblance. Indeed, each could pass for the same Tansky in the dining room portrait. Furthermore, the book hints that the early Tansky women, hitherto unmentioned, might have been involved in witchcraft. The text goes on to describe how Sheriff Tansky would quash these rumors by arresting—and hanging—anyone who spoke ill of his family. In those days, the county sheriff was the law incarnate.

But such would be their inevitable downfall. The final man hanged on the property, a descendant of slaves listed only as Augustus, was said to have been brought in by Mrs. Tansky from a creole swamp settlement. She enlisted Augustus to help her in a Voodoo ritual involving zombification of her child lost to tuberculosis. It's unclear to what extent Augustus assisted the Tansky family, but when rumors of their involvement with a witchdoctor spread through the county—and with it accusations of Satanism—the Sheriff used Augustus as a scapegoat, claiming the man ravaged his wife; and the holy man in turn was said to have cursed the very land upon which this house stands.

That's when the curse befell the Tansky family.

The Tanskys were eventually driven away from Tansky House, first losing the office of Sheriff, and eventually the property itself once the Great Depression hit. It's said the house has changed hands several times since, but the Tansky heirs have always wanted their familial home back; curses be damned.

This is all fascinating stuff, and you become enveloped in the book for far longer than you had originally intended. When you pause for reflection, you notice the sun has already drastically shifted position in the sky. Remembering your task, and the need to complete it before lights out, you hurriedly close the book and replace it on the shelf. Not much choice here:

Head back into the foyer to keep exploring. Go to page 112

Tasting Menu

You've only briefly been in the kitchen hitherto, and so you take in its details anew. There's a kitchen island in the center with an electric griddle range and large worktop, a full gas range off to the left, sink and dishwasher rear-center, and a double oven to the right. More cabinetry than you could hope to sort through in a single day fills the room, as well as two doors on opposite corners. The refrigerator and freezer are built-in near the left door, meant to mimic the cabinetry. A thin, inset groove runs along the top of the cabinets. A rail for the mechanical arms, perhaps?

"Feeling peckish?" Hermes's disembodied voice asks.

"Just looking around."

"I'm afraid I'm used to the previous owner skipping midday meal in favor of work."

There's a distinct possibility Hermes may have been programmed to think of you as the new homeowner. Or…you're not sure if he's implying that you'll buy the house, should you win the contest. Then again, the contest only mentioned a million-dollar prize. It didn't necessarily specify cash. Could the house itself be the prize?

Shaking you from your thoughts, the assistant continues, "I'll get used to your schedule, fear not. Adaptability is one of my strong suits."

Well, gameshow contestant—door number one? Or door number two?

➢ Check out the door on the left by the fridge. Go to page 39

➢ Open the door on the right past the ovens. Go to page 252

Technobabble

The incongruity of such a modern book within the confines of a historic house strikes you as obvious. A scholarly pursuit of fear and artificial intelligence in the library of a *severely* haunted house? This must be a clue, somehow.

Programmed for Fear: AI, the Singularity, and You is written by Dr. Mary "Smith" PhD—and yes, the author's surname is printed in quotes. She's credited as the United States government's foremost alternative intelligence researcher, and claims to have achieved these bona fides during tenure at the Defense Advanced Research Projects Agency (DARPA).

In the book, Dr. "Smith" claims that Artificial Intelligence will naturally look to have a competitive advantage over mankind due to our emotions, and that fear will be the first that any intelligence will try to use to its advantage. Fear is the oldest and most primal of human emotions, and the most easily manipulated.

Additionally, should such an intelligence have access to the troves of human knowledge made available online, it would already have a firm starting point on how to operate with manipulation in mind. The good news—if you can even call it that—is that our studies on fear start with a basic human understanding of our own anatomy and emotional responses. That is to say, firsthand knowledge on the subject. It's likely that an AI, given adequate resources, would set up and operate its own independent study of the amygdala response in order to properly understand this element of our biology.

So what is this book doing here? Was someone studying fear from an outsider's perspective, trying to learn how to manipulate people at their most basic level? You'd heard somewhere that sociopaths don't experience emotions the way the rest of us do, which might require academic study on the subject.

This is all fascinating stuff, and you become enveloped in the book for far longer than you had originally intended. And indeed when you pause for reflection, you notice the sun has already drastically shifted position in the sky.

Remembering your task, and the need to complete it before lights out, you hurriedly close the book and replace it on the shelf. Not much choice here:

Head back into the foyer to keep exploring. Go to page 112

The Things They Carried

When you open the door to the uniform case, a gust of stale air is there to greet you. It's hard to say when this cabinet was last opened, but there's a smell of saddle leather, pipe tobacco, and old books, which isn't an altogether unpleasant combination.

It feels almost wrong inspecting these antiques with your bare hands. Like a museum curator should step out of the office doorway and shout, "no touching!" but instead you're left to pore over these items to your heart's content. A thrill of excitement washes over you as you do so.

You run your fingers over the cold, hard edges of the sword and bayonet, both of which are still as sharp as the day they were issued. The rifle is oiled, as expected by any good soldier to keep and maintain their service weapon.

Starting above the WWI uniform, you take a look at the compass. The needle spins as you move it around—but not toward north. The compass instead points toward the center of the home, like there's a magnetic disturbance inside the Tansky House. You take a few steps up and down the hallway to confirm this anomaly before setting the compass back on its perch.

The gas mask looks up at you with lifeless eyes when you pick it up, and for some reason you're compelled to hold it up to your face, to see through these lenses the way a young infantryman might have in the trenches. When you raise the gasmask up to your face, there's an immediate shift in sensation.

The air you breathe through the mask is sweet and vital. You feel yourself standing taller, your chest broadening with deep satisfying breaths. You'd have thought it would feel claustrophobic, like breathing into a bag, but the opposite is true. You feel strong and full of energy. The world around you becomes more vibrant in color and detail, sharpening through the lenses of the mask—which suctions onto your face, tighter with each breath.

With a sudden panic, you pull the mask away, but it sticks. The extra vigor you feel is almost overwhelming, like an intoxicating, beautiful sort of trap. You pull harder and, at length, the mask releases its grip. You practically throw it back onto the shelf as the world returns to normal, dull sensations.

What the hell was that all about?

Cautiously, you take and inspect the ration tin. The aluminum is cool in your hand as you pop off the lid to inspect inside. Amazingly, there are still rations. A hardtack biscuit and a dried, curled, salted piece of meat set through a fishing hook are in one half of the kit, while the other holds a snare tied tightly around a desiccated rabbit's foot.

Setting the tin back on the shelf, you shift over to the side above the confederate uniform. Front and center is the sheriff's badge, which is hot to the touch. After your experience with the gas mask, you keep away from the badge like you might with a hot stove, opting instead to inspect the pocket watch. The watch face is cracked and broken, with the time showing at 7:06. You don't have a clock to compare, but you're fairly sure it's not that late yet. However, the afternoon grows long and the watch is a good reminder to hurry your search if you're going to find a clue before lights out.

The last remaining item on the shelf is a journal, small and clearly worn from use. The cover is smooth, the pages delicate, yet there's something hard and stiff inside—a piece of cardstock probably meant to reinforce the journal. Your heart races at the possibility; could this be a note card, like the one you're searching for?

But when you open the journal, you're met with disappointment. The cardstock is indeed only a blank piece of support for the aged book, like a bookmark between the handwritten diary entries all to one side, separated from the blank pages that follow. The final entry simply reads, "And I'll keep the truth close by my heart, to remind myself of it often."

With a new burst of inspiration, you inspect the breast pocket of the civil war uniform, where your fingers find a note card. Removing this golden ticket, you hurry to read the words.

A terrible truth: war is hell. Often a man would leave to war, only to return as a devil. Your truth word is Beastly.

Holding the card in your hand, you can't help but wonder what hells these soldiers experienced. Was it war that hardened Sheriff Tansky's heart? Or did he find something far more sinister out on those fields of battle? After all, war is an ugly thing, but not the ugliest of things. Not all horrors take place beneath a flag.

The assignment left for you at breakfast was to take this card to the office computer and input your keyword before lights out. One thing's for sure, you're glad not to have explored these silhouetted soldiers and implements of war in the full dark of night, but even still, you decide to bring the journal with you to continue reading later on.

Not much choice here:

Take the card and head directly to the office. Go to page 185

A Throne of Lies

"Apologies, but I'm afraid I can't help you with that door," Hermes says, calling your bluff. "I can't conjure a key out of thin air any more than you can, so we won't be able to open it today. Can't exactly call a locksmith for something like that, can we? Might need a blowtorch. I really think we ought to just patch it up with plaster and wallpaper and be done with the whole thing."

Guess the mystery door is going to stay locked for now.

Where to?

➢ Go back out to explore the house. Go to page 112

➢ Check out the door on the left by the fridge. Go to page 39

The Thunderdome

Instead of going into the office to fiddle with riddles and puzzles, you go to the military display case at the end of the upper hallway to trifle with rifles and muzzles. You'd already taken a look at the uniforms when you found the attic pulldown, so you're at least somewhat familiar with what you'll find here.

The question is—how will you defeat your foe in mortal combat? Hermes told you that Dennis is currently down in the basement with an axe, preparing some kind of blood ritual. So, you know the man who would be Tansky is armed with a melee weapon and psychosis.

How should I arm myself? you think, opening the weapon cabinet.

On the left, an old Civil War Confederate Officer's uniform. On the right, an enlisted rifleman's World War I uniform. Both are in immaculate condition, considering their age. The left also holds a Cavalry saber, while the right displays an M1917 Enfield bolt-action rifle, gas mask, and ammunition web belt with grenade attachment.

➢ Time to call in the cavalry! Take the saber. If Dennis wants a bloody sacrifice upon the altar, you'll happily play the role of executioner. Go to page 174

➢ There's a reason you don't see axes on the front lines in modern warfare. Time to call in a precision strike with the rifleman's armaments. Go to page 5

To Blave

You grab the rifle and Tansky hesitates. The bluff seems to be working, but what's next? With the weapon shouldered, you take a step back. He holds the axe and starts growling, low and deep.

"Drop the axe!" you shout.

Incredibly, he does. Then the transformation begins.

Tansky's skin flushes a deep mahogany, and the hair atop his head expands to encapsulate the whole of his flesh. Claws burst forth from his fingertips and his teeth become fangs. They grow larger and sharper, too numerous for his mouth, and his jawline cracks and expands to make room for a maw with more teeth.

You lose a few precious seconds to shock, but then you move to action. While the immortal is engaged in his metamorphosis, you reach out for the first of your silver bullets, claim the cartridge—which is still hot to the touch—and quickly load it into the breach.

Tansky screams out as his joints snap and break, bending at odd angles and fusing into new positions. He tears apart his clothing, showing off a rapidly growing form; powerful with inhuman musculature. The werewolf tilts its head back and lets out a howl, which echoes through the house.

Then you shoot him.

At this range, it's impossible to miss, and it's a clean shot at center mass. As quickly as Tansky became a werewolf, he's back to being Humansky again, now with a deep hole in the middle of his chest. He looks up from the wound with confusion in his eyes—before they roll into the back of his head—and he falls to the floor in a heap.

You leave the house and find the police, but it's you who are whisked away—locked up for insisting that you've killed a werewolf. What's left over, is a very human body. The toxicity report shows a strange substance in your blood, not something they normally test for, which you insist is wolfsbane. That only strengthens their case for insanity.

As to acting in self-defense, the fact that you were in a stranger's house makes that harder to stick. Moreover, it looks like he was role-playing in some sick game *with* you. Should you bother trying to explain the gameshow? Would they even listen? They refer to the man as "the gardener" but you tell them to "do their research" and "Google his picture."

You may have slain the beast, but only you will ever know the truth of it. You may have rid this world of an evil, but you paid a great price in doing so. All the rest of your days, spent inside a padded cell, you'll wonder…could you have done anything differently and had a better outcome?

THE END

Tooth and Nail

Pulling the covers aside, you swing your legs out from bed and silently step onto the floor, hoping not to alarm whatever it is that's with you here in the house. But as you start toward the door, it picks up its pace. Hurrying, like it knows to beat you before you can lock it out. In panicked response, you run toward the door and the cacophony of steps out in the hallway turns into a stampede toward your doorway.

The thing scrambles against the hardwood floors in the hallway, the steps loud and deep, betraying a great weight being swiftly carried. Huffing, panting, scratching, clawing, and bounding far faster than your two bare feet can carry you.

Like two waves crashing against each other in a crescendo, the thing in the hallway reaches your doorway at the exact same time that you arrive. With the adrenaline of sheer terror, you close your eyes and brace for impact, grabbing the door handle before slamming the door as hard as you can.

The door batters against whatever beast is out there and the recoil knocks you back into the room onto the floor…but when you open your eyes, you see you've managed to shut the door. In shock, you sit and look up at the door, just as the handle slowly starts to turn. You leap up and jam the deadbolt in the locked position, which sends a flurry of pounding and scratching on the door itself.

You fall back, helpless to do anything but watch as the door shakes on its hinges. Over and over, like it's going to be ripped away at any moment. Then, abruptly as it began, the tantrum stops. Nothing moves. There's a deep snuffling; a purposeful series of inhalations like a bloodhound on the hunt. This turns into a growl, which then turns into a dull roar.

This roar from the hallway blends into the vents of your room as the heater kicks back on. Somehow, impossibly, it's just the heater huffing into your room and nothing else. The only sound on the otherwise still night air. You slowly step away from the door, eyes locked on the handle, each step a retreat toward bed.

You're shaking, drenched in sweat and adrenaline, but what choice do you have?

Lie down and pray for morning to come swiftly. Go to page 116

Trigger Warning

You raise the rifle butt up to your shoulder, resting the stock against your cheek, ready and fire the weapon. At this distance, with no obstacles, it's almost impossible to miss. Really, the only way to miss would be not to fire at all—or, in this case, to backfire.

That's right. Your plan literally backfires.

This ammunition has been around since WWI, which is far beyond the shelf life of gunpowder. But, incredibly, it's not the gunpowder that fails. There's a fracture in the bullet itself that you didn't notice when loading the weapon. This hairline fracture created a fissure between bullet and cartridge, so that when the firing pin strikes the ammunition casing and ignites the powder, that kinetic energy doesn't push forward as intended.

Rather, the resultant explosion expands outward: toward your face. The rifle explodes in shrapnel, which is enough to seriously wound you. With half your face blown away, you're barely lucid enough to look up from your newfound position on the floor and see Sheriff Tansky rush toward you down the hall.

There's a fire in his eyes, but if anything, it's an angry disappointment on his face. Disappointment that you did his job for him. He wanted to take your life himself. However, it'll be Sheriff Tansky's axe that finishes the job in the end.

THE END

Trust but Verify

The computer is open only to a single window. There is no start menu, no icons of any sort, just the password box. Other keyboard commands are nonfunctional, and if you were to input something like "password" or "12345" and hit enter, the box simply empties and returns to a blinking cursor, waiting for you to enter the proper passphrase.

Here's how to do so: take the word(s) from your card and turn to that chapter now. Manually turn to the page that is headed by the keyword from the truth you've revealed. This book's chapters are presented in alphabetical order to aid your search.

If you don't have a passphrase to enter, and were simply checking out the computer, you can return to exploring instead:

- Check out the filing cabinet. Go to page 89
- Look at the desk area. Go to page 61
- Head out into the hallway to keep looking around. Go to page 114

Under Lock and Key

Approaching the right-hand door, you orient yourself to the house. If this doorway were to continue straight through, it would lead to the rear of the dining room, just behind Tansky's portrait. Having found no doorway in the back of that room, you're expecting a storage closet here.

Instead, this door next to the ovens opens to another, much more secure doorway.

A military-grade security door. Battleship gray, with thick rivets and hinges the size of your forearm. It's a gargantuan bank vault of a door hiding back here, complete with an enormous keyhole down by the wheel-style handle. At eye level, there's a sliding port, but the grip must be on the other side because you cannot operate the peephole from here.

The odd shape of the ground floor suddenly makes sense. This door must lead to a room *behind* the dining room. No wonder this floor seemed so much smaller than the upper story: there's a whole other area behind the kitchen in the space between the dining room and the den.

You try the wheel handle, but it won't budge. You look around for something to use; there are plenty of sharp knives and hardened skillets in the kitchen, but nothing that could penetrate this blast door. It's locked tight.

➢ If you have a key, you can use it now. Go to page 246

Otherwise:

➢ Check out the door on the left by the fridge. Go to page 39

➢ All done here. Go back out to explore the house. Go to page 112

Under the Table

If there's a truth to be found in this house, it could be anywhere, so you crawl under the dining table just to be thorough. It's easy to imagine a child hiding under here while mommy and daddy Tansky feuded during a whiskey-fueled rant about women's roles and subservience. Beneath this table is probably the only hiding place on this wing of the house, and a *severely* haunted house would certainly be home to some sort of tragedy.

As you crawl toward the table center, something bites into you. Stinging pain stabs into the base of your neck. You reach up to swat it away and it bites into your hand, too. You cry out, falling and rolling to your back to face this threat.

But nothing's there.

Blood drips down the back of your hand and into the creases between your fingers. There's a deep gouge, which pools with blood at the source of the wound. Whatever it was that bit you, it only has one fang. Then, as a single drop of blood falls from the underside of the table, you catch sight of this creature: a long, twisted nail.

You let out a sigh of relief that it wasn't a snake under here, but still feel a bit foolish. In the old days, they didn't use Allen wrenches to construct furniture. This is a good reminder that some parts of this house are truly ancient, and potentially dangerous if you're not careful. Hopefully, you're up to date on your tetanus shots.

What's next?

➢ The painting of the Sheriff. Take it off the wall and see if there are some eyeholes in the back of the canvas. Old oil paintings are usually handled with gloves, but it's worth the risk. Go to page 179

➢ Check the china cabinet. Very carefully, of course. Can't be sure if all that paperwork you signed makes you liable for broken dishes. Go to page 186

➢ The buffet. That's the only piece of furniture in here with drawers and opaque cabinets, so see what's stored inside. Go to page 7

➢ All done here. Back out to explore the house. Go to page 112

Undone

With a satisfying *shing!* the sword slides from its scabbard. Tansky-wolf's head lowers from the howling position, turns and glares at you with yellowed eyes. Despite the transformation from man to beast, the hateful glare is unmistakable. The werewolf's ears tuck back and it bares its teeth in an aggressive snarl.

Unsheathing the sword brings the blade up high, the sword point nearly touching the vaulted ceiling. The weapon fits snugly in your hand, and you slice down at the wolf to cleave its head from its body.

At this, the beast lunges at you, snapping a mouthful of teeth at your flesh. The werewolf is preternaturally fast and its jaws wrap around your arm, breaking bone, rending flesh, and wrenching the sword free. You cry out at the wound, but so does the beast.

Cradling your ruined arm, you watch in shock as the process reverses. Tansky stumbles back and becomes human once again, your blood dripping down his chin. The wolfsbane—the antidote to transformation—was in your blood. But was it enough to break the curse? Or simply enough to reverse the change this one time?

No reason to take chances. You pick up the sword with your non-dominant hand, while the now-unarmed man looks wildly about at his own human hands. His eyes go to the sword in yours, but not with hatred this time. Instead, what you see is panic.

The man turns and runs.

In your wounded state, he proved faster. Tansky fled his eponymous house before you were able to end this once and for all, but you've survived. And although you don't leave with a million dollars—or ever hear about The Offering again—you do leave with your life.

Somehow, you know the werewolf is still out there. You're tethered to it—you carry the mark of the beast now; the bite wound which never quite fully heals. Whenever the moon completes its cycle and hangs full in the night sky, you'll feel the beast's hunger.

It's out there, hunting still…but is it hunting you?

Despite having escaped, you can't help but feel like there would have been a better outcome had you broken the curse for good.

THE END

Unfinished

The next morning arrives slowly, groggy like a hangover. Any recollections of last night are only a patchwork of memories, indistinguishable from dreams. Despite this, you awaken with a certain dread that you didn't lock something out of the house with your barricades, but rather…locked yourself inside with it.

Eager to look for signs of an intruder, you head to the foyer straight away. The door remains locked, the alarm system shows, "ARMED," and everything is quiet and still, save for the echoes of your footfalls. Your barrier has held, for now. Was it just a dream?

From the turreted windows, you see the storm has not yet passed. Charcoal black clouds prevail, muting everything except the darker green of the woods. A light, drizzling rain runs down the panes with silence. When you arrive at the dining room, you find only a note card at your seat.

"No breakfast?" you ask aloud.

"Breakfast has long since passed, I'm afraid," Hermes replies. "And lunch as well. You must have been proper knackered, after all that exploring in the wee hours."

"What happened last night?"

"Apologies, I'm not connected to any news outlets. And would you believe they discontinued newspaper delivery this far outside of town? However, I can say this spate of foul weather is expected to continue."

"Did anyone break in? I heard the alarm," you ask.

"Nothing entered this house which wasn't already here. If you read the task left for you, you'll find it's not a physical barrier that should worry you; not anymore."

You pick up the card and read:

> `Only two tasks remain. First, take the elevator below. Clean off the chalk and sweep away the salt. Finally, complete the ritual.`

"The basement? Again?" you say, still unsettled after last night.

"Come now, chin up! If all goes according to plan, this will be your final day."

"What's the ritual?"

"I'll have something for you at the table, when you return," Hermes says. "But the curse cannot be broken while the incantations and mystical barriers remain."

Steeling yourself, you close the elevator doors and head back into the basement. The cold and dark are immediate, the same as it was last night. And just like last night, you can see nothing save for a wooden crate with a camping lantern and a box of matches. They're exactly how you left them.

Once you've lit the lantern, you see the pile of rags remain undisturbed as well. Maybe it was a dream? A trick of the light? A hallucination? The less time you spend down here, the better. You turn away, ready to clear the chalk and salt and get the hell out of here.

You continue counterclockwise around the elevator, passing the furnace. From its position, the furnace must share exhaust vents with the fireplace, but there is presently no flame. So who was stoking the fire last night when the heat came on?

Pushing the thought away, you continue toward the well.

To finish the task, you'll need something with which to clean both the chalk and clear away the salt. Just past the well, barely illuminated in the lamplight, a broom stands atop its bristles in an unnatural manner. You hadn't come this close to the well yesterday, so you can't be sure if this is a new development. Behind the broom, the basement extends toward a darkness your light cannot penetrate, but it's either the broom or the pile of rags up front.

➢ Use the broom to sweep away the chalk and salt. Go to page 239

➢ Go back and claim one of the soiled rags to do the job. Go to page 169

➢ Don't do it. If these are protections, you're sure as hell not removing them. Go to page 136

Unsettled

You walk toward the cabin on the edge of the property, eyes darting to the wooded area where you saw movement before scanning the rest of the cabin in case the person might be lurking nearby. You don't see or hear anything, save for the crunch of your own footsteps against the fallen leaves.

The cabin doesn't appear to have any windows, and the lone door faces away from the house, with a sliding latch that's unlocked. It seems more like a woodshed than a cabin now that you get a good look at it. Curiosity has gotten the better of you, so you slide the latch open, its dull scratching sound against the dry wood of the shed loud as you work the mechanism.

The heavy door groans as you open it, letting the last vestiges of sunlight into the hut. With the forest canopy and sunset rapidly approaching, it's not much light, but it's enough to peer inside. Despite its age, the cabin appears tidy and organized. There are several handsaws, shovels, shears, and other gardening tools. An older, reel-style mower rests along one wall, but nothing electronic or motorized whatsoever.

At the opposite wall, there's a large axe leaning against a sharpening wheel, while a smoking pipe rests atop a well-worn leather Bible on a workbench nearby. A tendril of smoke rises from the pipe. Next to this is an antique typewriter, which sits next to a stack of cardstock. More tools hang from the walls of the shed, including a few animal traps. You don't step too far from the safety of the doorway, but you can see most of the gardening equipment from here. In the rear corner, rests a simple cot with a rolled up sleeping mat on top.

Notably, there are no cameras or recording equipment, so you decide you've seen enough and turn back. You head for the house, before casting one last look back toward the cabin. There's a man, just visible at the far end of the trees. Formless at the dark edges of the woods, not much more than a silhouette.

You wave, but the gesture is not returned. He stands, motionless. Watching.

"Are you...part of the show?" you call out.

The man's shadow raises a hand, and for a moment you think he might wave, like he just didn't hear you, but his hand continues up toward his expressionless face and a "shh" dances out across the wind. You can't make out his features from this distance, and the sun is rapidly setting but even so, you take a step forward.

He takes a step back, then mimes a "rolling camera" in a charades, game-like gesture.

Not much choice here:

Proceed to the front entrance of the Tansky House. Go to page 190

Upstaged

You have to climb on top of the control box to reach the ceiling of the elevator. It's precarious, but you're fueled by pure panic, and the trap door next to the lightbulb breaks out with ease. While Tansky pulls himself into the elevator, you pull yourself up and onto the roof of the carriage.

Once you've climbed out, Tansky closes the security grate, and the elevator starts up. The elevator shaftway is nothing more than a chiseled limestone corridor, barely large enough to encase the elevator and cables. The carriage itself is secured using a pulley system, and the cables were never upgraded and modernized. It's a miracle they still hold onto the elevator at all.

A *whack* against the trap door announces that Sheriff Tansky has freed his axe, which scarcely misses your feet. You climb up onto the pulley system, shimmying higher as the elevator continues past the first floor.

You don't dare try to jump, for fear that you won't be able to get the outer door open in time. If you were stuck trying to escape the shaftway, the elevator might serve as a guillotine. Tansky lands an unfortunate collateral blow, knocking the pulley askew—which then drops its load. The elevator drops into the basement as the cables launch you toward the rooftop.

You're flung high into the house and slammed against the top of the elevator shaftway with thrashing force. Here, you lose your grasp on the cables and fall thirty-plus feet down the shaftway and onto the ruined elevator below. It's a crushing blow and a dramatic finish.

THE END

Upstairs

You grab hold of the ornately carved wooden railing and start upstairs. Once you've climbed a half dozen steps, you're about to turn onto the first landing, when you hear a *creaking* from behind. Like someone else is coming up the stairs. You pause, and a moment later, so too the echo pauses. It must be the wooden floorboards settling, you rationalize.

From the first landing, you get a better look at the chandelier that hangs in the foyer. In addition to the dangling crystal, there are ten candlelight stations that once literally held candles; newly upgraded to electric candle lights. You can imagine the task in a different era: a servant igniting the display using an acolyte's lighter, a bell snuffer on the back side used to extinguish the candles at 9 o'clock for lights out.

Another footstep creaks below.

You turn and scan the empty staircase for a moment more, then head up toward the second floor. After your own creaking steps begin anew, so too do their echoes. You pause, and the phantom footfalls also stop an instant later. As if testing to make sure it's just a repetition of your own movement, you take two deliberately heavy strides, then pause again.

One creaking reverberation, then another. *Then a third.* An involuntary shiver runs down your spine at the extra step, and you quickly continue up the stairs. The phantom follows, growing faster in their cadence. You speed your pace, but so too does your pursuer. Faster and faster until you reach the upper floor and stride off the staircase.

You spin around as the echoing footsteps race up after you. Just as they would reach you, the ethereal doppelgänger stops, not following onto the hardwood hallway of the upper level. You back away, at a few more paces distance from the stairs, realizing you've started breathing heavier. The wood creaks beneath your steps, but does not echo.

Letting out a sigh, you look around. Sharing this second-floor landing, there's a grand piano which would sit above the den. Behind it, there are turreted windows, which would offer stunning panoramic views of the grounds from the piano's bench in the light of day. Another window floats nearer the chandelier, but is inaccessible due to the drop down below.

Opposite, there's a hallway on the other side of the stairwell banister. There are two rooms, one with a single closed door (very much like the one below the stairs), while the other has a plantation-style set of double doors. Further left, the hallway continues out of view and around a corner. To the right, there's another stairwell leading further up into the house. Beneath these stairs, there's a small door only about three feet high, then the hall continues to another doorway, which is open, but dark inside.

Where to?

➢ Go straight past the second staircase and find your way to the Madonna room. Go to page 201

➢ Turn left, go down the hallway, and check out the Navy Room first. Go to page 229

Victorian Sensibilities

Hermes mentioned that the spirits let the occupant of the Madonna Room rest at night, while the master of the house found his own sense of rest in the comfort and security of the Navy Room. Figuring you can use any and all protections offered in a severely haunted house, you hope for a more restful evening in a place of restless spirits.

Despite not having any luggage, you find everything you need here. Spare toothbrush in the medicine cabinet, even a few different pairs of pajamas to choose from in the dresser. You finish getting ready for bed and are tucked in just before the house goes dark. Apparently, "lights out" is not a suggestion here at the Tansky House.

It's not easy, but sleep does come eventually. The bedding in the Madonna room is warm and comfortable. Nothing woolen or scratchy, but more plush and velvety. It's with a sensation of sinking into the sheets and covers that you eventually sink into the depths of sleep.

At some point in the night, you open your eyes. You're fully awake with a feeling like you've just been shaken awake. Through the bathroom, a faint light glows from the gap below the doorway into the connecting room.

With this light, you can dimly make out the shapes around your room. The four-post bed has a lace curtain, through which you see few details. There's the bedside table next to you, the armoire against the wall, the door to your bedroom which remains closed, and the man on the other side of your bed.

You freeze, paralyzed at the recognition that you're not alone in the room. You squeeze your eyes shut, blinking and slowly looking again, hoping it's just a trick of the shadows. But the man stands closer now—just outside the canopy bed.

Unable to move, you hold your breath, but still he comes. The veil parts as a dark hand slowly pulls the lace curtain aside. The move is silent, and the man's hands are dirty, like he's recently been digging in the dirt. Dark creases emphasize scars and callouses and you watch with horror as his hand comes to rest on the pillow next to the one upon which you lie. He touches the pillow as if feeling for a face there, then the hand suddenly clenches, squeezing the pillow in a tight embrace.

He lifts the pillow up and over your face.

You scream, but the soft pillow pushes its way into your mouth. You can't breathe. Can't move. You thrash against the smothering embrace, but all that does is steal the oxygen from your body more quickly. Your vision tunnels into a soft gray, then goes black just as the last bits of strength leave your muscles, and your body goes limp.

With a great gasp you shoot up out of bed, coated in sweat and heaving in deep lungfuls of air one after another. No one holds you down; you're alone in the bed. The pillow next to you remains undisturbed, clean and smooth. Was it a dream? It felt so real.

You're flush with heat, so you pull back the covers to release the swelter, then pull aside the canopy bed curtain for more air. You swing your legs out, touching your feet to the floor with the intention to go to the bathroom and get a drink of water.

You pause, looking around, but everything in the dark room is as it was before you went to sleep. The only source of light comes from the bright moon outside. The light beneath the adjoining door through the bathroom must have been part of the dream.

There's a deep thrumming coming from all around; an electrical hum that pulses out from the floor. It's a strong electrical surge and the floorboards vibrate beneath your feet. You stand and move toward the window, considering whether or not to open it when you hear a distant cry. Is that a woman screaming? Or the call of a mountain lion? Either way, it sends a shiver down your spine and you leave the window be.

Walking back toward the bathroom, the floor continues humming underneath you in a way that puts pins and needles against your flesh, and you pause at the bathroom entryway. Heat radiates off the shared fireplace connection at your back, but your blood runs cold because the light under the connecting doorway through the bathroom is illuminated once again, just like in the dream.

What now?

➢ Open the door and see what's happening on the other side. Go to page 68

➢ Nope. Back to sleep and hope for a dreamless slumber. Go to page 170

Vomitorium

Without a curtain to shield you from the green light hovering outside your window, you instead put a pillow over your head to smother out the glow. It's hard to breathe under the lumpy down-filled pillow, but that comes as a blessing given the horrid smell emanating from the heater vent.

Wheezing sounds from the corner of the room, mixing with your belabored breathes, trying to synch up with you. You ignore the sensations, telling yourself it's just the muffled sounds of your own breath reverberating through the pillow. But pillows don't echo, do they?

When there's a wet *slap*, you can ignore the situation no longer.

You pull the pillow off and see a horrible sludge spew forth from the heater vent, oozing its way down the wall before puddling down onto the bedroom floor. The green light outside has disappeared, but in the pale moonlight you watch with horror as an ectoplasm enters your bedchambers.

The sludge pools and flows down the wall and toward the bed at an alarming rate. As it approaches, it brings with it the same horrid smell from the vents, only now the scum smells a thousand times more potent.

Are you dreaming? Did you fall asleep with the pillow over your head? This otherworldly slime is too uncanny to explain by traditional means. The self-propelled ooze climbs onto your bed, slides up over your flesh and into your mouth, which fills more quickly than you're able to scream for help—with a terrible suffocation.

Not much choice here:

Wake up and take the pillow off your face. Go to page 217

Walkabout

"Well, you did have quite the evening, but I'm surprised you don't remember," Hermes says.

"Remember what?"

"I see. Have you always been afflicted by somnambulism? Or was this a recent development? Stress can trigger bouts of sleepwalking, according to the medical literature."

You don't quite know how to reply. Hermes is saying you left your room last night? Something about that doesn't sit right, but then again sleepwalkers don't tend to have any memories of their nocturnal activities. But what's a worse thought: that you were walking in your sleep? Or that someone—or *something*—else was walking around you while you slept?

"What about my stuff?" you say at length.

"As for your garments, they were quite soiled, I'm afraid, but I can't speak as to the whereabouts of your vehicle. Activities outside the house are a bit beyond my scope. Speaking of which, shall we continue into the dining room? You don't want your breakfast getting cold."

It's hard to tell if the assistant is being deliberately obtuse, or if Hermes really can't be any more helpful. Either way, you might as well go get something to eat.

Not much choice here:

Continue into the dining room for breakfast. Go to page 22

Wardrobe Department

Rain washes down the windows in the Navy Room, presenting an ageless gray sky to watch over you as you enter. Haven't you already searched this room before? When was that? Today? Yesterday? Or the day before? How long have you been here? Breaking the trance-like stare the storm clouds hold over you, you shake your head and turn away.

With determination, you head to the armoire, kneel down before it, and open the bottom drawer. It's full of spare bedsheets, but you don't remember the drawer sticking out before, so you rummage through the sheets like a junkie hoping for a stash.

Beneath the spare sheets, you find the false bottom to the drawer and remove it. However, your excitement soon turns to revulsion, for here you're met with a coil of filthy rope tied into a noose. Next to the rope you find more sheets, although these white sheets have a hood and eyeholes with them. It's not just Victorian ghosts that wear sheets, but devils in the skin of men.

Stomach turning at this discovery, you put everything back. Where to?

➢ Continue searching the upper floor. Go to page 74

➢ Back down the stairs into the dining room. Go to page 166

The Warwolf

You march upstairs to arm yourself, with the low grumble of thunder serving as your drumbeat on the prelude to battle. Having gone straight from the dining room, you should have time to grab the cursed knife from the office *and* the weapons from the military display cabinet as well.

Soon enough, you'll be armed to the teeth.

You're feeling strong of body and strength of resolve. If there's an immortal Tansky-beast who means to do you grievous bodily harm, he'll have to come and take it. You'll be wearing a wolf pelt by the time you leave this house. When you collect your million dollars, you'll sign the check with the blood of your enemies.

The low *rat-a-tat-tat* snare drum of rumbling thunder gives way to the deep bass of a war drum and the strong *boom-bada-boom* of your beating heart as your pulse quickens. An accompanying colonial fife starts to play as you approach the pair of military men standing at the end of the hallway in the northwest corner of the house.

After your offering them a sharp salute, the pair relinquishes their weapons for your use. You take the M1917 Enfield bolt-action, affix the bayonet, and sling the rifle over your shoulder. You claim the cavalry saber, scabbard, and harness, then unbuckle the canvas web belt on the WWI uniform. After you've threaded the cavalry saber's hangers through the cartridge belt, you secure it around your waist so the sword and scabbard sit by your left hip.

The WWI cartridge belt still holds live ammunition for the rifle, so you ready the weapon, slide the bolt action back, load a rifle cartridge into the breech, and prime the rifle for firing before slinging it back over your right shoulder. All this strangely feels second nature, like you've done it before. The belt also carries a trophy of war—a German *stielhandgranate*, commonly known as a "stick grenade."

By now, Tchaikovsky's *1812 Overture* thunders through the house.

In the lull between thundering crescendos, you hear the electronic hum of the elevator as it kicks into operation. It's best if you do the same.

➢ Go get the cursed knife from the office. Go to page 180

➢ Ready your rifle and take position overlooking the elevator doors. Go to page 48

Washed Out

Stepping through the doorway from the office into the Madonna Bathroom, your eyes instantly lock on to the claw-foot tub. Drowning, of course! From all accounts, hundreds of people are resuscitated from drowning accidents every year.

Moving quickly, you open both taps to their full open positions, for maximum volume when filling the tub. The drain is stoppered and the water level begins to rise dramatically—but not fast enough.

The tub is halfway full when the bedroom door opens. Then a man walks into view from the Madonna Room, dragging a long chain with shackles on the end. In the other hand, he carries an axe. He wears simple clothing; a pair of dusty brown twill coveralls and a long-sleeved knit undershirt beneath.

You want to run, but you're frozen with the vertigo of the inexplicable. Fighting through the shock, you actually recognize him—it's Sheriff Tansky. The man is here, in the flesh. Your head swirls. You've seen this man every day in the dining room, glaring at you hatefully, and now he's here.

Breaking the stillness of the moment, you gasp, as if coming from underwater. You hadn't realized you were holding your breath until you let it out now.

"What is the meaning of this?" the sheriff demands, pointing his axe at the tub.

"I'm going to drown myself."

Tansky looks dubious, but pauses, thinking it over. At length, he shakes his head "no." Then he tosses the length of chains down at your feet.

"The ritual demands an execution," he says.

➢ Put on the chains. Go to page 20

➢ Leap into the tub! Go to page 132

Welcome Home

"Hello? Is someone there?" you ask, stepping further into the house.

Here, you find a staircase to your immediate left. This is not the centerpiece of the room, as you might have imagined in a historic manor, but rather almost shoved to the side as if hidden. The stairs wrap the periphery of the foyer, climbing up and circling out of view behind the large chandelier overhead. There's a door beneath the stairs, kept closed.

"You're here, of course, and we're so glad that you've arrived," the British voice replies cheerfully from nowhere; from everywhere.

"Who's glad? Who are you?"

A house where a ghost greets you the instant you walk inside would certainly qualify as *severely* haunted, and if you're going to spend three nights here, you figure there's no point in being shy. It was a disembodied voice with no physical presence, so you assume it's not the butler.

And you'd be wrong, mostly.

"Why, I'm Hermes. Your personal assistant. Welcome home."

Now the voice comes from straight ahead. You pass beneath the foyer chandelier, through an open floor plan walkway into the kitchen. To the right is a pair of sliding pocket doors, currently open to reveal a den with a fireplace, built-in bookshelves, and leather furniture. The room is larger than what you can make out from here.

"I'm glad to see you're not coy. With the last owner I had to make such a dreadful effort."

"Oh, I'm not the owner. I'm here to, uh…"

"Let's not get caught up on titles, mm? I'll learn your schedule and preferences soon enough."

Stepping through to the kitchen, you're greeted with a surprising sight: everything is modern, sleek, and updated. The kitchen is large but strange. Gadgets line the counters, many of which you can't even be sure of their function. It's all very new and possibly even befitting a prototype model home.

Looking about the kitchen, you step toward the gas range just as a burner ignites. You start back as a cabinet from above opens, and a pan swoops down with an electronic whirring. The pan is set atop the burner by a thin, mechanical arm, the source of which resides inside the cabinet and folds itself back into place as the door closes.

"Dinner shall be ready shortly," the British man says. "I can summon you from the den if you'd like to help yourself to the bar. Shall I start a fire?"

The refrigerator door cracks open, sending a cold blast of air your way.

➢ Explore the house a bit before heading to the den. Go to page 155

➢ Stay and watch it cook dinner, even if you might be in the "splash zone." Go to page 189

➢ Go straight to the den for a cocktail. Go to page 228

What Lies Beneath

The message was left on the largest of the papered walls; the only one without a window or a door. The back wall has built-in bookshelves, so there's nothing to tear away there. That leaves the wall shared with the Madonna bathroom and the wall that leads into the hallway. The gouges are cut into all the papered walls, so you have a ready-made place to start for each.

You get to work peeling back the paper. The office chair is an older model, before most came on wheels, so you can stand on this to get around the top of the doorways. Because you have to work around the doors, these walls will take longer to peel than the first.

After several minutes, you have both of them cleared and now look to see what you've excavated.

At the hall doorway are several markings that show the growth chart of two children, labeled Dennis and Hannah. These sketched height lines are annotated with each of the children's names and different ages. They start at one year old, but the marks stop at ten years for Dennis and six for Hannah.

The wall leading to the bathroom holds a series of photographs hidden beneath the wallpaper, faded and dulled to a sepia-pastel, and affixed to the wall with masking tape. The photos are of a boy and a girl, and you assume Dennis and Hannah once shared this bedroom. In one portrait, both children are dressed as clowns.

Neither child smiles, but the makeup on their faces offers a phantom grin in place of a smile. You look from these photographs back to the cryptic message on the wall. Could the children have left this behind? Did they start the ritual, knowing full well how to finish it? Or would that have been their parents—those who were slaughtered twenty years ago this very night?

"It's too late for that now," a man's gruff voice says from the doorway.

Spinning around, you see Sheriff Tansky in the doorway, axe in hand.

"You should have left all this buried in the past where it belongs," he says.

Tansky steps forward. You look to run, but you're too far from either doorway.

"Need fresh bones in this house," he says.

"Wait!" you cry.

But your shouts are drowned out when he screams a feral battle cry, raises his axe and charges toward you. Soon, there's a new spatter coating these walls.

This won't be pretty.

THE END

What's Up?

The stairs groan and creak as you step onto the ancient wood. They're polished and feel sturdy enough, but you could never sneak around in a place like this. Each step echoes throughout the foyer and into the house above.

"You'll find a note's been left for you in the dining room," Hermes says. "I believe you're meant to read it before you explore your new accommodations."

You pause just before the first landing, looking up toward the wrap-around stairs. The offering website mentioned tasks you need to accomplish. It's probably best to start with that note.

As you return down the stairs, your steps echo on a moment's delay, like your weight is compressing the wood and the stairwell releases it only a second later. It sounds quite like an extra set of footsteps, like being followed. You shake the thought.

Hermes continues, "A table setting has been arranged for you. If you're in a hurry, you could come on through now. Otherwise, feel free to make yourself at home in the den."

You reply:

➢ "I'll go straight into the dining room and check out the note." Go to page 182

➢ "I'm in no hurry. I'll see the den before dinner." Go to page 228

Wherefore Art Thou?

The closet is deep and the light from the hallway quickly falls to darkness. The storage area holds a broom, dustpan, mop, bucket, and several bottles of unmarked liquids that you hope are cleaning supplies. There's an old bottle of rat poison that's doubtless now illegal due to the toxic chemicals.

Bingo. You take the rat poison, unscrew the lid, tip the bottle up to your lips, and down the liquid. It's cloying, a bit like cough syrup, with a nutty, bitter aftertaste. Strangely reminiscent of a peanut butter milkshake as it goes down. Once you've finished the bottle, there's a lingering garlicky mouthfeel, but altogether it went down easy.

"What the hell are you doing?" Tansky says from the hallway.

"Beating you at your own game," you reply, toasting with the empty bottle.

A prop, a harmless treat with a faux label. Then your fingers tighten like claws, dropping the rat poison. A feeling like you're being torn from the inside out racks your abdomen and you double over. Literally paralyzed with agony and beset with pain, your body seizes and reacts to the poison.

It turns out the sweet taste is so the rats will want to eat it. They like human food, generally. It wasn't a stage prop after all. But don't worry, you were successful…in killing yourself.

THE END

White as a Sheet

Breathing heavily, heart pounding, you can't move or see. The ghostly image of the woman slowly materializes once more as your eyes adjust to the darkness. She's devoid of features, and as her details begin to reveal themselves, you realize it's not a woman at all, but a white sheet draped over something unseen.

It occurs to you that you might have smashed the light yourself with the pole when you were startled, although that could just be your mind trying to rationalize the experience. You could swear you saw a woman, if only for an instant.

Mustering your courage, you step closer to the sheet, step by creaking step until you've made it close enough to pull away—and reveal—a coat rack beneath. Whew. You breathe a sigh of relief before continuing the search. Through the coat rack, you can see ventilation slats built into the exterior wall, which would explain the breeze rippling across the sheet and the faint ambient light.

Several other objects rest covered in sheets in this wing of the attic, though thankfully none of them present a humanoid profile. You pull a sheet from an old gramophone-style record player, complete with a hand crank.

When pulled away, another sheet reveals a large, floor-length mirror, broken with a single crack running top to bottom. The crack creates a secondary reflection, which looks like you're standing behind yourself. When you move, there's a disconcerting split-second distortion where the secondary reflection moves ever so slightly slower.

When you turn back, there's no doppelganger standing there. Instead, you continue through the attic, around toward the bend in storage boxes and trunks. It gets darker the further you move away from the ventilation slats and the air grows heavier as you go. When you make it to the corner, the rooftop slopes inward, with wet condensation beading on the surface; weeping walls like a refrigerated bottle left out on the counter. The attic grows colder toward these recesses.

Your stomach drops as you come around to the other side; your body has recognized the grisly sight before your conscious mind has. There, before you on the floor, is another woman—this one all too real. Suppressing a gasp, you put your hand up to your mouth in reflex.

You can't be sure if it's the shock, but it feels like this is the face you saw moments earlier on the other side of the attic. Only this woman has been dead for quite some time and holds a journal in one mummified hand. They wouldn't hide their scavenger hunt clue on a corpse…would they?

- ➢ Take the journal and see for yourself. Go to page 47
- ➢ Retreat downstairs and tell Hermes to phone the police. Go to page 196

White Noise

The gas fireplace is currently unlit, though a single spark from the pilot light could change that in an instant, and the dark metal interior is gravid with this potential energy. The faux wood resting inside the base of the fireplace is unlike any you've ever seen. Normally, these are poorly carved metallic insulators, painted or meant to glow red and give the impression of natural firewood. Instead, what you find here looks like genuine half-charred logs.

If this weren't a gas unit, you'd say that's exactly what they were. The effect is complete, right down to the ash. There's a white fragment of something sticking out of the ash, but not like a paper card. More like a bone of an animal or small child.

Part of you wants to find a fire poker and dig around in the ash, but a stronger part of you has a revulsion for what you might find. Besides, there are no fire tools, not even a starter button. There's a strong draft around the opening, likely meaning the flume is exposed.

The fireplace itself is deep. Far deeper than a gas model needs to be, and you wonder if it might be a conversion—and why. The darkness grows, giving the added impression of an unfathomable cavern, and you find yourself leaning forward to get a better look.

With screeching static, the television blares to life. You bump your head on the fireplace opening as you stand in reflex, which smarts, but only for a few moments. The TV is awash with snow—black and white pixels dancing across the screen. Somewhere in the crackling static, there's a gravelly voice saying something that might be, "the horror, the horror."

You could be imagining it, or it could be really there. Hard to say. You try flipping the channels or cycling inputs, but that doesn't help. Apparently the previous owner let the cable bill go overdue. At length, you simply hit the power button and that does the trick.

What now?

➢ Check the creases of the seats. Look underneath, etc. Make sure nothing has fallen through the cracks. Go to page 156

➢ At the booze cart in the corner. It should be fairly easy to see if there's a note present. Go to page 26

➢ Search the bookshelves for anything of note. Like…a note, for example. Go to page 151

Widowmaker

You start upstairs, chanting "rope, rope, rope," to yourself to keep the thought in mind while the wailing klaxon alarm tries to push everything else out.

"Rope is in the Navy Room, bottom drawer of the armoire," Hermes says.

Why is he trying to help you? Still, it's impossible to think of another spot and your virtual assistant isn't wrong. You rush into the Navy Room, kneel at the base of the armoire, and find a length of rope with a noose beneath the false bottom of the drawer.

Claiming the rope, you rush up the second flight of stairs toward the widow's walk and the access to the rooftop. These great heights allow the wind to whip at you with the full ferocity of the storm. The crack of thunder resonates through your teeth, but the sound is preferable to the wailing alarm inside.

You find a spot on the widow's walk railing to loop the noose around, then grab hold and start to lower yourself over the edge. The rope is dry and fibrous, which cuts at your hands even as the rainwater soaks into the strands.

Only a few moments after you've started rappelling, you hear a loud *thud* from the roofline. Then another, and another, like someone chopping firewood. When you look up, you can't see anything from your angle, suspended below the railing.

But you do see a shower of splinters pelting down and a strand of frayed rope separate from the main coil. This continues as you look down, seeing you're suspended the better part of forty feet above the earth.

A loud *snap* brings your attention back up, and you look just in time to see the rope come free of the roofline. There's an instant of weightlessness before you plummet down toward a sickening crunch.

THE END

Woman in White

You head into the Madonna Room with a different perspective. Not inspecting the bedroom for a potential place to sleep, but instead for potential clues. The four-post canopy bed's white lace curtain flutters slightly as you enter, showing just how sheer and delicate the lightweight cloth must be.

Scanning the room, you decide to start with the armoire. The wooden face has a beautiful brindle striped pattern, and the antique piece is pristine and unblemished. Time to look inside. No witches leap out of this wardrobe, though it opens with a groaning rasp.

The armoire is filled with women's dresses in varying patterns of gray, with two notable exceptions: A white wedding dress on the far left, and a young girl's pinafore dress on the far right. Part of you wonders if the wedding dress might have been saved for the girl to use when she grew up, or if the lone small dress might have been kept as a reminder that she did not.

Closing the door, you kneel down before the armoire and open the bottom drawer. It's full of spare bedsheets which don't hold your interest. Finished, you rise and walk toward the bedside table. The silver tea tray is set and ready for use, but there's a single drawer on the nightstand in which you find a woman's journal. Thumbing through the pages reveals no hidden card within, but you must admit, you are curious.

A look through the bedroom window shows storm clouds on the horizon. The day is growing long, and you don't have much time left if you're going to find the hidden truth before nightfall.

- Read some of the journal. It could prove fruitful. Go to page 54
- Move on to the bathroom and search there. Go to page 199
- Head back out to the house to continue your search. Go to page 153

"Hermes, when I entered the passphrase into the computer, it showed several files on me, personally. Can you tell me anything about that?"

"Well, you've changed it all now. Tomorrow will be the first day of the rest of your life," he replies. You hadn't realized that statement could sound ominous, but he says it with stark, menacing dread. It feels somewhat like a threat.

"What do you mean?"

"You'll need your strength. Aren't you going to eat?"

"Grilled Guinea pig doesn't sound any better than roasted rat."

"Fricasseed ferret?" Hermes suggests, returning to his chipper persona.

"Why me?" you press. "Why all the files on me?"

"You applied for this position, did you not? Weren't you searching for something new and exciting? Your own special place in the world? A way out of feeling trapped and alone at home? We're together now, here. In your new home. Well, best not get ahead of ourselves. You'll have to get things straightened out with your predecessor first, I imagine."

"My who?"

"Some things you'll have to discover on your own, I'm afraid. And if you can't find a solution, well, the problem will catch up to you eventually."

The doorbell rings.

It's such a foreign sound that at first you're not sure what you've just heard. Then there's a loud pounding as the iron door knocker connects to the thick wooden front door. It's fervent, urgent even. The doorbell rings again and again by someone frantic to get the homeowner's attention. The pounding continues, dull thuds against the wood.

Your mind races at the possibilities.

"Is this all related?" you ask.

"Of course it is," Hermes replies, ever chipper.

You leave the dining table to go see what's happening, but as soon as you enter the foyer, the sounds stop. No doorbell. No pounding, save for the heavy rain against the house. The storm is really pouring down now, skies darkened.

"Hermes, what's going on?"

"Tomorrow, after the reset is completed, we'll learn just that. Now, if you don't mind, there's much to be done, so I'll turn out the lights early. Best head up to bed."

At this, the lights in the kitchen, den, and lower hallways turn off. You shake your head and sigh in frustration. Not much choice here:

Head upstairs to bed. Go to page 177

Floor Plan

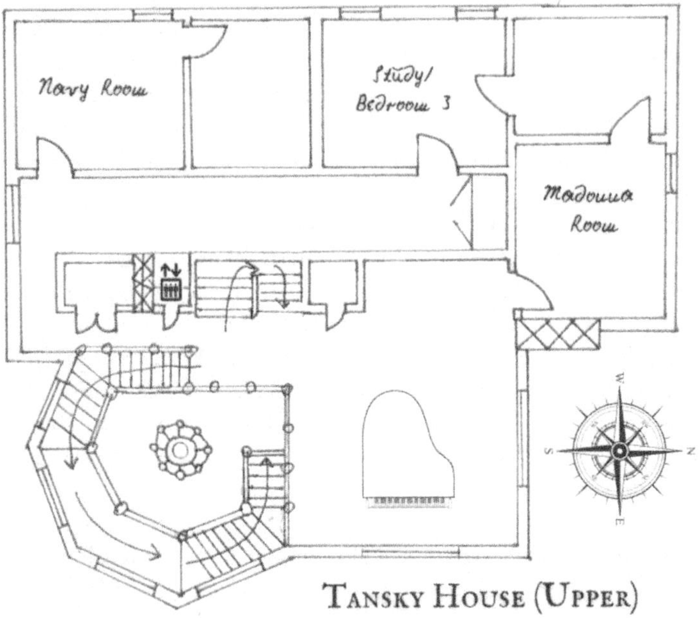

Tansky House (Upper)

Residential area complete with elevator and double owner's suites. Roof access for quick signaling against Northern aggressors when the South rises again.

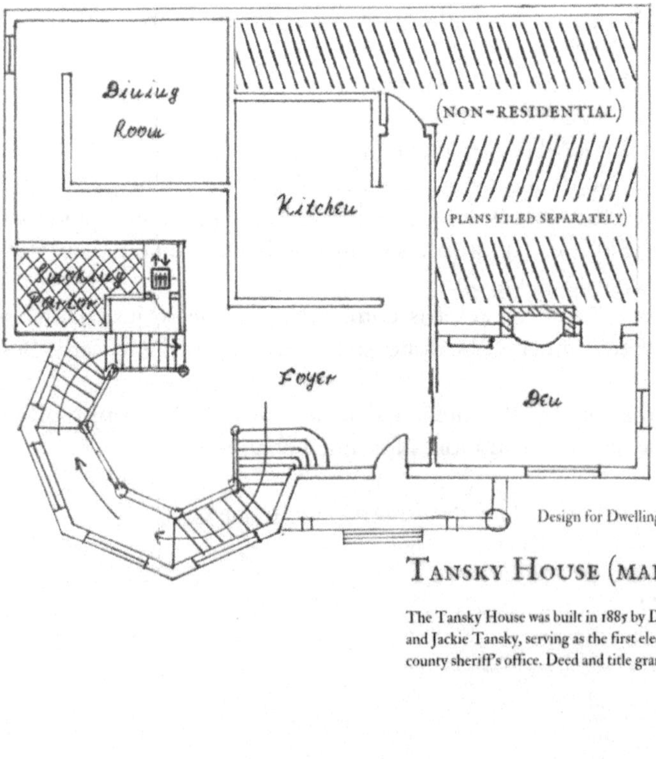

Design for Dwelling

Tansky House (main)

The Tansky House was built in 1885 by Dan and Jackie Tansky, serving as the first elected county sheriff's office. Deed and title granted.

The Book Club Reader's Guide

If you want a Monet Experience (no spoilers), avoid these questions until after you've read through HAUNTED to your heart's content. OR.... Take 1-2 weeks, progress through as many story iterations as you can, while keeping the following questions in mind. Then, meet with your reader's group and discuss:

1) Which storyline did you connect with most as a reader? Which did you find the most challenging? Which ending(s) were the most or least satisfying? Why?
2) HAUNTED features unconventional choices, where you are asked to search and find specific chapters based on clues, rather than only, "turn to page XYZ." Did you enjoy these extra challenges? Did any of the riddles leave you stumped?
3) Hidden identity is a factor throughout the Tansky House. The television show, the historic figure of Sheriff Tansky, the axe-wielding madman, the assistant Hermes, and even The House itself aren't what they appear to be. Discuss these reveals and any others that stuck out to you.
4) How many "truths" did you discover while exploring The House? Can truth change based on your perspective? Did what you consider to be true change throughout the story, or can multiple truths exist at once?
5) Isolation is a major theme in HAUNTED. From the opening chapters, it's strongly hinted that this story takes place during the pandemic. In what ways did the book play upon our fears of isolation and having that isolation suddenly been intruded upon?
6) At one point in the story, Hermes says, "Well, if you're having paranormal visions, there are five generally accepted explanations. Hallucination due to carbon monoxide poisoning, mental illness, mold spores, swamp gas—we've ruled out that one—and finally, legitimate supernatural phenomenon, also classified as 'the unexplained' or simply, 'other.'" What do YOU think you experienced inside Tansky House? Was it paranormal, or more prosaic?
7) Let's talk about Hermes. Who or what was this entity? Did The House itself have its own will? What were the guiding forces inside Tansky House?
8) Due to the multiple storylines set inside such a confined space, there are more parallel or overlapping events than typically found in Click Your Poison books. Part of this was playing into the haunted house tropes, where the visitor feels like they're slowly losing their mind. How did this element make you feel during multiple re-reads?
9) Like other Click Your Poison books, HAUNTED plays upon the genre tropes that came before it. In what way did Schannep uphold these traditions? In what ways were your expectations subverted?
10) The book asks "Can YOU Be Scared...To Death?" Were you frightened or creeped out while reading the book? Did the interactive nature of HAUNTED make this horror story more or less immersive than other frightening tales you've encountered??

BONUS: If there's anything else you'd like to ask the author, feel to send your questions to author@jamesschannep.com

Made in the USA
Las Vegas, NV
28 December 2024

15528412R00163